More titles from Kristopher Rufty

Hell Departed: Pillowface Vs. The Lurkers
Anathema
Master of Pain
(written with Wrath James White)
Something Violent
Seven Buried Hill
The Vampire of Plainfield
Desolation
Bigfoot Beach
The Lurking Season
Jagger
Prank Night
The Skin Show
Oak Hollow
Pillowface
The Lurkers
Angel Board

Jackpot
(written with Shane McKenzie, Adam Cesare, & David Bernstein)
Last One Alive
A Dark Autumn

Collections:
Bone Chimes

PROUD PARENTS

Kristopher Rufty

Proud Parents
2nd Paperback Edition

Editing for 2013 Edition by Don D'Auria
Cover Art by Stephen Carpenter
Paperback wrap by Lynne Hansen www.LynneHansenArt.com

ISBN: 9798743454525

DEDICATION

For Logan.

PROLOGUE

Three minutes had passed since Sgt. Macowee last knocked. He'd been tolerant, but with this being his third attempt his patience was pretty much gone.

Tanner, his much younger partner, stood with him, eager to kick in the door. Macowee knew better. He'd been a cop way longer than Tanner. Although Tanner was a damn good cop, he lacked common sense in situations like this.

"It seems awfully quiet," said Tanner, smacking his gum hastily.

"Good observation there, Tanner," replied Macowee, not taking his eyes off the door.

"*Too* quiet."

Macowee crossed in front of Tanner, stepping over to the picture window. The blinds were drawn tight. Smashing his face against the glass, he couldn't see past the shield of the blinds.

"I already checked. You can't see shit," Tanner said. Macowee sighed at his partner's colorful vocabulary. "What do you think happened?"

"I don't rightfully know. But it seems kind of odd to me that two social service workers would come out here and just up and vanish."

At first, Macowee had suspected the social workers had gotten lost on their way back. He could understand it; this house wasn't an easy one to find. They'd had quite a time themselves, even though Tanner had sworn he used to date a girl that lived nearby. The car could have broken down; a flat tire was also a possibility. He'd half-expected to find them sitting in their car on the side of the road on their way in. He hadn't. Suspicion had nudged at him, skittering up his spine, but he didn't allow it to consume him just yet.

Play it by ear. No jumping to conclusions.

The house was located on the outskirts of the county, almost outside their jurisdiction, in the thick forests of Clintonville, Wisconsin. The appearance of the house gave Macowee the creeps, but he refused to admit it, even to himself. It stood alone, surrounded by woods; old, but not dilapidated, though it could use some repairs to the exterior. The white paint had faded and peeled in places, pock-marking the house with the bad complexion of neglect. A Victorian-style house, it stood two stories tall, coming to a point on the top floor.

The report Sandy had read to them said that a call came in around 5:00 p.m. from Earl, the supervisor at the Department of Social Services. It stated:

Two of my girls, Glenda Holt and Terri Blanchard, went to the home of Paul and Sara Gordon to investigate a tip from the local mailman. From what the mailman states, the Gordons must have a kid, though he'd never laid eyes on one. He has delivered many packages from Internet pharmaceutical distributers to this address, not thinking much of it. Then, following several occurrences of screams, almost guttural roars that put him in mind of some form of inhuman pain, he became suspicious and began looking into the contents of the packages. What he discovered was that the prescriptions were for a child, as well as many extremely strong medications, like tranquilizers and such. He felt guilty for snooping in their mail, but he was very concerned about what was going on in that house and if anyone was being harmed. He felt it may be best to have someone check it out. So, I sent Mrs. Holt and Ms. Blanchard to the home shortly before 11:00 a.m. this morning and I haven't heard anything from them since. They had another appointment at 1:30 p.m. that they did not return to the office for.

Sally went on to add that Earl was worried and he'd tried phoning them both for a few hours before finally putting the call in to the police. Macowee wished he had called sooner. Maybe they would have found something.

All we have now is a deserted house and an empty driveway, with the exception of our cruiser.

Tanner spoke, startling Macowee from his thoughts. "Yeah, you're right, it doesn't sound right." Tanner sighed. "Think maybe they tried to take the kid and something happened?"

"That's what we're here to find out. I'll knock one more time and then call it. We can give Sandy a buzz and see if we have grounds to enter on probable cause."

Tanner turned around and leaned against the rail, crossing his arms. "I say we call her now. No one's here."

Macowee ignored him and pounded on the door with the bottom of his fist. Hearing a clicking noise, he stopped. The door slowly swayed inward with groan.

Tanner joined Macowee at the door. They shared a look of concern and then looked back to the partially open door.

"Well?" said Tanner, his hand moving to his gun.

"You know what to do," Macowee answered.

They drew their guns.

Macowee leaned his head into the gap between the door and the frame. "Hello? Is anyone home? It's the Clintonville Sheriff's Department!" He waited for an answer but received none. Macowee took a deep breath. "One more time, Clintonville deputies here, and we're at the front door! We're coming in if you do not respond!" Tanner went to rush past him, but Macowee held his left arm out, blocking his way. Macowee continued to wait, but still got no reply.

"Are we going in?" Tanner asked, impatiently.

"Yeah."

Macowee stepped inside. Tanner followed. Pointing their guns this way and that, they skulked into what was most likely the living room. They walked to the center of the room and pressed their backs together, each keeping an eye on the way in. Tanner faced the entrance they'd used while Macowee focused on the rear, the direction they would be heading.

Macowee cast his gaze over the room, scanning each shadowy crevice that could possibly hide someone. No one was there.

The room itself had been demolished: the coffee table turned over, magazines strewn across the floor, an end table lay on its side. The TV was on, but the image flickered with static and there was no sound. A couple blankets were strewn about a pile of children's coloring books that were on the floor. Broken crayons littered the top.

"Jesus Christ, what happened here?" asked Tanner, his voice shaky. He kept one eye squinted, looking down the barrel of his gun.

"Looks like we have a positive on a kid," said Macowee, thrusting his chin toward the coloring books.

"Yeah..."

"Let's split up, check the place out. You take the left, I'll take the right."

"Got it," said Tanner. He darted across the room, disappearing on the other side of the doorway that led into a hall. His footsteps echoed in the hallway on the other side of the wall.

After giving Tanner time to move on, Macowee whipped his gun around and slipped through the same doorway Tanner had just gone through moments ago. He could see his partner investigating the kitchen to the left. Tanner glanced back, making eye contact with Macowee. They both nodded. Macowee pointed in front of him, indicating to his partner that he was heading forward.

Then he was moving again.

Macowee searched the rooms that occupied the narrow hallway. Other than mess and discarded debris, he found nothing out of the ordinary.

He searched a spare room that was mostly empty and a bedroom he assumed belonged to the parent or parents, due the size of the bed. The bathroom had also been pillaged, but it was empty.

He made his way down the hall, to the last bedroom on the left. The door was slightly ajar. He paused, taking a deep breath and slowly releasing it.

Entering, Macowee found the room was pitch black. He could almost make out two sets of windows on the far side of the room, but they had been blacked out with either a dark tarp or plastic, which took away all hope of any light from outside getting in.

He switched the gun from his right hand to his left and fumbled his fingers across the wall in a mad quest for the light-switch. Arching his fingers like a spider, they crawled along the wall. The tips tinkered over a hard plastic cover. He stopped.

"Let there be light," he mumbled, flipping the switch. The room filled with a dark blue light, the kind you would normally see at the zoo while exploring the reptile exhibit; certainly not what Macowee had expected.

He took a couple steps forward, entering the shadowy bedroom. It was as dark as moonlight. Stopping a few feet inside, he took the gun and placed it back in his trigger hand. He pointed it forward, preparing himself for anything.

He scanned the room. He checked the dressers to the left. The drawers had been pulled open and left that way. Empty. A few articles of clothing had been left behind, draping over the gaping drawers. A shirt sat crumpled in a wad at the foot of the dresser. Tanner knelt down and snatched it with his free hand. Holding it by the collar he flung it wide. The shirt opened up. It was small, big enough for a child around the age of six or so. The design on the front was a Tyrannosaurus Rex towering over a quivering Stegosaurus.

A kid definitely has been here. Where are you now, little guy?

He dropped the shirt on the floor, stood. Adjusting his belt, he moved on.

The closet was just a few feet from the dresser. The door stood open. He stepped to the opened frame and removed his flashlight from his belt. The closet's interior was even darker than the room. Holding the flashlight by his head, he clicked it on. A small beam of light cut through the black. He shined it here and there, only discovering vacated thin-wired clothes hangers inside.

Sighing, Macowee turned his back to the closet. He scanned the room with his flashlight as he walked toward the bed. Shining the light to his left, the round disc skimmed across crayon drawings taped to the wall. From the skill with which they had been created, he figured the artist was a child. The drawings varied. Some were just shapes or scribbled lines, but the ones scattered on the floor were what intrigued him the most.

He made his way to the scattered stack and crouched. He set the flashlight on the floor, keeping the beam pointed at the drawings. Flipping through the sketches he found crayon creations of madness, as if a six year old child had been drawing a horror comic, telling tales on the gore-drenched pages.

A lady, scribbled in blue and red lay on her back while a small, fuzzy creature tore into her stomach, pulling out her intestines. The intestines were drawn with red in curved lines. The guts wrapped around a greenish-colored ball for a hand. The fingers were a row of small lines.

The creature was apparently feasting on the red lines.

Feasting on the guts...

Macowee tossed the picture aside, disgusted. Underneath was a sloppily drawn man on white construction paper in black crayon. The featureless man held a shovel over a patch of scribbled green lines that Macowee guessed was grass. Stick arms and legs protruded from the green patch. While this man was apparently burying bodies, the creature sat on a rock and watched. Both figures in the drawing had curved lines for mouths. Smiles. Either happy from the grave digging, or just enjoying the time together.

The last drawing was somewhat a pleasant one: a family of three holding hands. The man with the shovel was on the right, a woman with black hair was on the left, and in the middle was the creature. This drawing depicted him with light brown hair on top of his head, a light green body the color of plastic Easter grass, and little brown lines waving across its body which Macowee assumed were tiny hairs.

"The whole family," he muttered.

Nauseated, Macowee stood up and turned around. His eyes landed on the bed. He paused. He hadn't checked there yet, but he really didn't want to, either. Although he hadn't found much of anything useful, he felt as if he had found a hidden cemetery in this room.

Still might, he realized.

Aiming the flashlight to the top of the mattress, he saw blankets piled and bundled into a massive ball. They'd been folded and wrapped around one another. It wasn't a gigantic mound, but definitely one that was large enough to conceal a kid.

He slid his thumb over the safety lock on his gun and flipped it the left. The gun was ready to fire. He stepped over to the bed, his tread soundless on the padded carpet. At the bed, he slouched over, using the barrel of his gun to sort through the blankets. He pulled sheet after sheet away on his way to the bottom.

Sticking his barrel deep into the mound, it smacked something solid with a thump.

He'd gone too deep for someone of any size to be hiding under the blankets, but he'd definitely found something that wasn't the mattress.

With the help of his left hand, he jerked the blankets out of the way, unveiling the solid object his gun had poked.

He jumped back, screaming once he saw the surprise waiting for him below the sheets. "Tanner? Shit, get in here! Now!" He pressed the side of his gun against his thudding heart.

The sound of Tanner's frantic approaching footsteps came from the hallway. Tanner appeared at the doorway, panting. "What'd you find?"

"This," said Macowee, pointing to the severed female hand. Blood had dried and stained her fingertips. One of her nails had been ripped from the cuticle and dangled at the tip. Pieces of bone jutted out from the wrist stump like a stem.

Tanner grimaced at the gruesome amputation. "Shit." His breathing rate intensified. "Now what do we do?" His voice was nearly a whine.

"You saw the outside of the house just as I did, there's an upstairs, and most definitely a basement. We've got more ground to cover."

"But..." He shook his head. "Shouldn't we call...?"

"Not yet. Let's cover the rest of the house first. This time, we *don't* split up."

Tanner's face looked even paler than normal. His face was covered in sweat, the bangs of his hair glued to his forehead.

They searched the upstairs first, which was nothing more than a large, walk-in attic. Like the rest of the house, it had been ransacked. Some things had been left behind, but nothing that would tell them much about who'd lived here. There was a drawing table against the window overlooking a nice view of the woods behind it. Macowee wondered if one of the adults was an artist. They found no artwork that could quench his curiosity.

Macowee led Tanner through the house and down a flight of wooden stairs that creaked under their shoes. Reaching the bottom, they stepped into a gloomy basement. They stood in an island of light shining down from the opened door, the darkness surrounding them like inky-black water.

There were little bricks of diffused light along the tops of the walls from tiny windows caked in dust.

Observing the dense darkness, Tanner asked, "Where's the light?"

"Right here," Macowee said, holding up his flashlight. Clicking it on, he turned to his partner with confidence.

Smirking, Tanner then got his flashlight out as well.

"Let's move," said Macowee.

He searched the basement with Tanner at his backside, never letting down his guard. They explored a work bench, checked behind the stairs, near and around the washer and dryer, making their way to a large, metal two-door locker against the far wall.

The two cops shared a look.

As if reading Macowee's mind, Tanner said, "Let's check it out."

"Yep." Macowee's voice wasn't so assertive anymore. He dreaded looking inside the locker. He swallowed the dread down with a gulp, deep into his gut. He gripped the handle.

Tanner aimed his gun at the locker, waiting.

After another deep breath, Macowee turned the latch to the left and jerked the door open wide.

Expecting a sight of unreal horrors hidden inside, they found nothing but empty space. They had prepared for a corpse, or weapons, possibly the killers themselves to be hidden inside. Instead, they found a big slab of zilch.

Tanner lowered his weapon, confused. "What the hell?"

"I don't know, this doesn't make much sense," said Macowee, returning his gun to its holster.

"Do we call it in? Or do you want to look through the house one more time?"

"I really don't see the point," admitted Macowee. "I guess let's put a call in to Sandy and let her know what we *did* find."

The image of the severed hand reappeared vividly in his mind.

"All right," said Tanner.

Macowee stared into the left side of the locker, aggravation building. Out of frustration, he revved his left foot back and kicked the other door with all his might. The locker shook immensely, rattling as it banged against the brick wall behind it.

A clunking came from inside, followed by a thump, and roll.

The brunt of his kick forced two bodies, wrapped from head to toe in black plastic, to fall from the other end and smack against this side of the locker's wall.

Tanner and Macowee screamed in unison as the bodies collapsed onto the cemented floor.

Clutching his chest, Macowee stepped forward, beads of sweat dangling from his chin. "Oh my God…"

"You okay?" Tanner asked, more than a little concerned.

"Yeah, I'm fine, just caught me by surprise is all."

"You and me both," admitted Tanner. His weakened legs could no longer hold him up. He dropped to his knees and held his stomach.

Macowee kneeled down to the bodies, patting his partner on the back as if to ask, *Are* you *all right?*

Understanding Macowee's gesture, he nodded.

Macowee reached behind his own back and opened a pocket on his belt. Inside the small compartment was a knife.

Setting his flashlight on the floor, he unfolded the blade and began to tear into the plastic.

Tanner retrieved his own knife, joining him as they cut away sheet after sheet of plastic. They sliced for several minutes until there was nothing left.

Mummified under the plastic, they unveiled the corpse of a woman. Possibly in her forties, but too gnarled-up to tell for sure. The cadaver's face looked as if a beast had gotten it: rips, tears and serrated slashes, eyes completely removed with only hollowed sockets and ragged eyelids drooping like perished curtains.

"Fuck me running," said Tanner. Revolted, he wrinkled his nose.

"I'm willing to bet a month's salary that these are our social workers." On the outside, Macowee managed to keep his composure while staring at the grisly view ahead of him. Underneath, he was petrified like a little boy scared of something lurking in his closet.

"So, they come out here to check on a kid that was allegedly being neglected, but get mangled instead?" Tanner's wrinkled look crumpled into a frown of confusion. He scratched his head like a dumb ape.

"Looks that way," said Macowee.

"Why?"

Macowee let his hands droop limply in front of him without offering an answer.

"If this is the social workers, then where are the parents...and the kid?"

"God only knows," said Macowee. "One thing's for certain... They're not here."

CHAPTER 1

Todd Parker stood outside his lovely home on Sunwalk Drive in Lamberson, North Carolina. It was seven in the morning and the birds were already singing, delightful chirps that were both relaxing and settling. Standing on his porch dressed in his robe and pajamas, he stretched, taking a deep whiff of the crisp air.

Someone had mowed their lawn recently. He could smell the watermelon-like scent of freshly cut grass. Ever since he was ten years old, Todd had loved the smell of fresh-cut grass. It reminded him of playing baseball as kid on Saturday mornings during summer vacation. He'd go to the ball field for an all-day challenge with the other neighborhood kids. The grass on the field would always be just mowed, thanks to Spanky the yardman. Being the nice man that he was, Spanky would also lay a fresh coat of white chalk around the diamond for them. By the end of the day, they'd be wearing it on their clothes from sliding into the bases and running along those powdered lines.

Stepping into the yard, he felt the springy tickle of damp grass under his feet. He thought maybe his yard could use its first mowing of the season. Maybe he'd take care of that on Saturday morning. He'd have to do some spring maintenance on the mower: change the oil, sharpen the blades, new spark plug.

The newspaper waited for him at the edge of the lawn. He trotted across the grass, and fetched it off the ground. Thankfully, the paper guy had thought of the dew and slipped the paper into a plastic sleeve so it wouldn't get soaked. Todd hated a wet newspaper. He'd have to let it dry before he could read it if it was wet, and then the paper would be all wrinkly and the ink smeared.

He tilted the sleeve, dropping the paper into his hand. Then he removed the rubber band and unfurled the paper. As Todd skimmed the front page, he caught the faint sound of a door closing off to his side.

At first, he thought it had been his own front door, but when he turned and looked he found it to be still closed. He shrugged his shoulders, assuming one of his neighbors was fetching their own paper. He went back to scanning the paper but was soon bothered by the soft sound of footsteps whispering through grass.

The footsteps were nearby, so they weren't coming from the house across the street, and the house to the right was too far away to be able to hear much of what went on over there. So, it must have been coming from the house on the left. It had been vacant until a few weeks ago when the *For Rent* sign had been taken down. Todd had yet to see anyone next door. No moving van, no people. Nothing at all to indicate someone had really moved in or was planning to.

Until now.

Peering through the corner of his eye into the yard beside him, Todd discovered a young man, probably in his early thirties, slinking down the steps of the rental's front porch. He kept looking around himself guardedly, as if ensuring no one was watching. He hadn't yet spotted Todd on account of the bushes that separated their properties.

The man quietly scampered through his yard, and knelt down, reaching into the weeds that choked his lawn to retrieve his newspaper. As he stood up, placing the newspaper under his armpit and turning to head back inside, he spotted Todd. Like a deer in headlights, the new neighbor froze in place.

Todd felt like a ghoul. To the new guy on the block, Todd Parker must look like a nosey asshole. Todd had been busted snooping, something he rarely did, partly because he was no good at it, and mostly because it was rude. Wanting to show the fellow next door that he wasn't really a jerk, he politely raised his hand and offered a wave.

As if the sudden movement from Todd had startled him, the man turned and darted back inside his house like a frightened animal. The bang of a slamming door followed. Todd could hear the subsequent faint sounds of many locks engaging.

Todd dropped his head low and rolled the newspaper, returning the rubber band to its center to bind it.

"Great job, asshole." He sighed.

Lisa Parker had been in the kitchen all morning preparing breakfast for three. Usually, she was the first one up, but surprisingly Todd had beaten her out of bed today. She was fine with that. It gave them more time together after Jenny left for school, and before he barricaded himself in the office to write for nine hours.

Lisa was a couple years younger than Todd, and if you

asked him she was always a sight for his sore eyes. She wondered what he would call her appearance this morning, dressed in a silk robe that ended centimeters below her firm bottom. Her wavy brown hair hung in tousled disarray about her shoulders, framing a smile that hadn't left her face since their amazing performance of the night before.

Todd entered the kitchen wearing a confused mask over his handsome face. He tossed the paper on the table and walked to the window over the kitchen sink, looking out. If you were to stare through it like he was, you got a good shot of their side yard and the neighbor's house.

She wondered what he saw out there.

Lisa left the bacon sizzling on the stove and went over to where Todd was standing. She snuggled up to him and looked out the window. She didn't see anything that should have captivated his attention as much as it had. She gave him a kiss on the neck.

"Good morning," she said.

"Huh? Oh, hey babe. Good morning to you too." He gave her a quick glance and then gaped out the window again.

"Is that all I get after last night?" She laughed playfully, catching her lip between her teeth.

A child-like bashful smile curved Todd's lips. His face flushed. "Oh, of course not. My apologies to the lady." He wrapped his left arm around her, and pulled her tightly to him. He kissed her.

Lisa's legs felt weak. He had always had that effect on her and after all these years together, it hadn't faltered.

Pulling his lips away he said, "Good morning."

"That's better." Lisa gave him another kiss then walked over to the stove. She took the last strip of bacon out of the pan, dropped it on the stack with the others, and moved on to the eggs. Snatching an egg out of the carton, she cracked it open on the pan. It sizzled as it started to cook.

Todd walked over to the plate of cooked bacon. He snatched the one she'd just put on there, and took a bite.

Lisa saw the thievery over her shoulder and laughed. "Can't you wait?"

"I'm hungry," said Todd, making gasping sounds as he tried to chew the hot bacon.

"I bet. You were out of bed before the sun came up."

"I had to get back to writing, you know the drill. The readers crave more blood and guts, so the publishers are on my back to deliver it to them. I get to be the lucky guy who delivers them their literary mayhem."

"You make it sound so patriotic," said Lisa.

Todd smiled at her then returned his gaze to the window above the sink.

Lisa stepped away from the stove. "What's so special out there that it deserves your attention more than I do?" She joined him, hugging him from behind.

"Have you seen the new neighbors yet?"

"No, I haven't. I feel bad about it too. They've been there for a few weeks now and I haven't even as much as said hello to them. Why do you ask?"

"I saw a man come out of there when I was getting the paper. I waved at him, but he hauled ass back inside and slammed the door." Todd shook his head. "Made me feel like an asshole for trying to be nice." Todd leaned against the counter, his back to the window, and crossed his arms.

"You worry too much. Maybe he's just shy."

"Maybe. We should probably go over there soon. Take them a welcome gift or something."

"And give you a chance to show you're a nice guy?"

"Exactly."

Lisa tried not laugh, but she couldn't help it.

Todd looked at her, frowning. "What's so funny?"

"I'm sorry. I'm not laughing..." She snorted, trying to hold her laughter back.

"Are you sure? Sounds almost like a witch's cackle you've got going on over there."

She took a deep breath and shook her head like a mother seeing her child try to shove a square block in a round hole. "You always get like this."

He sighed, knowing what she was about to say. "I do not."

"Yes, you do. It's cute, really."

"What's so cute about it?" His voice was low and pouty.

"You worry so much about people thinking negatively of you because of what you write."

"I do not..." He stopped, shrugged.

"Do you think they might drag you to the town square and burn you at the stake?"

"No, it's not that..."

"It's okay, honey. You write horror novels and have fun doing it. That's fine."

"Some don't think so."

"No, some don't, you're right. And some also don't enjoy drinking Pepsi. But you know what?"

"Some do?"

"That's right."

"I know what you're saying, Lisa, really. And I get it. Hell, I even agree with it. But..."

Lisa understood the true reasoning behind that *but*. He'd lost a really good friend, James Duggan, after he'd read one of Todd's novels. James had not only told Todd he didn't like the book, he'd also chastised him for being so proud of writing the kind of filth that littered those pages. She'd read Todd's books herself; not all of them, but more than a couple. Sometimes they got a little intense for her tastes, so she could understand, to a point, why someone like James would think of it as pointless immorality. On the other hand, she didn't agree with his statement and she knew a lot of other people didn't either. But that didn't matter to Todd.

James's opinion had hurt him more than any review ever could. He had stopped talking to Todd and a friendship of ten years was over in the course of one day. He'd never told Todd which book it was he'd read, and that had also haunted Todd. Some days she would catch Todd standing in front of the bookcase in his office, staring at the shelves that lodged his novels. She knew what he was doing: trying to pick which book it had been that had cost him such a good friend.

"But," she continued, "going over there is a great idea. I'll take them one of my flower baskets."

Lisa owned Lisa's Purdy Flowers, a flower shop that covered weddings, funerals, special deliveries, and so much more. Thanks to the amount of success she'd had over the last decade of owning it, she'd been able to hire someone on full-time to manage the shop for her, which freed her up to spend days at home and evenings with her family.

Gladys handled all the orders and arrangements that came in and was very good at her job. A retired elementary school math teacher, she'd been working for Lisa for three years now and showed no signs of stopping anytime soon.

"Yeah," agreed Todd. He added, "Then maybe I won't feel like such a dickhead."

Laughing, Lisa began to set the table. Todd finished off the bacon and crossed the kitchen. He stopped in the doorway and turned to his wife.

"Where's the kid?" he asked.

"She better be upstairs, getting ready for school. She has to leave in twenty minutes and she hasn't eaten yet."

"On another diet, you think?"

Lisa shrugged. "Possibly. With graduation coming up, summer vacation, then her beach trip, she just might be."

"Getting her bikini body ready?"

Lisa laughed. "Most likely."

"Not if I can help it. What time did she finally get in last night?"

"Late."

"Later than curfew?" asked Todd.

"Not too bad, but yeah, a little later."

Todd sighed. "Great. Should I punish her?"

"You never have before," said Lisa, setting a plate of scrambled eggs on the table.

Speaking in a Spanish accent, he said, "Saying I don't gots the cojones?"

Smiling, Lisa said, "I'm not *saying* anything, though maybe you give in to her too much? She has you wrapped around her finger. She has since birth."

"Well, she's my baby girl. Of course she does."

"At least you admit it." Lisa crossed the kitchen, taking the bacon from the counter.

"Well, I guess I better go give her one of my lectures."

"They do *so* much good," she said with a wink.

"Ouch. Below the belt." He held his hand in front of his crotch, as if protecting it.

Todd turned from the doorway, chuckling as he started up the stairs.

CHAPTER 2

Jenny sat in front of the vanity mirror, applying the final touches to her make-up. She had never worn an abundance of it like other girls did, just enough to highlight her features and look as if she weren't wearing any at all. Staring at her reflection, she smiled, approving of her appearance. She put the cap back on the lip gloss and opened the drawer beside her, dropping the tube inside. She returned her gaze to the mirror. Plastered on the glass were pictures of Jenny with her friends, though a majority of the pictures were of her with Doug. She kissed the tip of her finger and placed it on Doug's lips in a picture taken while they were at the park one day after school at the beginning of the year.

It was one of the fondest memories Jenny had of Doug. And it might be the last legitimately good time they'd had together. He'd been so wonderful to her that day, charming. Always a handsome guy, it seemed that he was even more gorgeous than usual that day. His hair was styled just right, and he'd worn a tight T-shirt that showed just how much muscle he'd accumulated the previous summer due to his excessive weight lifting. Those hadn't been the *only* reasons she'd given her virginity to him that day, but they had sure helped. He had been the perfect boyfriend, especially that day, so she'd caved and let him have what he wanted.

Since then, he'd become obsessed with it. She wasn't a prude, she enjoyed sex a lot, but his need for it far outweighed her sensuality.

Jenny grabbed her wallet, checking that her license was inside and there was some cash in the slit. Seeing everything was where it should be, she snapped it shut and walked to the bed. She dropped it into the front pocket of her book bag, zipping it up tight.

On the window sill was her ash tray, a burning cigarette resting in a groove. The window was raised just enough to filter the smoke out. To her, it was chilly outside, so she couldn't stand opening it any higher. It left her room smelling smokier than usual.

She grabbed the cigarette and took a drag. Exhaling the smoke she thought, *I look good, I feel good, it's all good.* It was an arrogant chant she told herself every morning, but it was also a confidence booster that she desperately needed. It wasn't always easily remembered, even on days like today when she couldn't deny she was a pretty girl. Actually, these days were the hardest to be convinced she was anything more than something nice to look at. It was hard for her to believe otherwise. Today, though, might be different; when she'd soundlessly recited her little maxim, she'd actually believed it.

Then someone knocked on the door and her cheerful vibes retreated. It was her dad's knock. She knew it from anywhere.

"Shit," she gasped. Her stomach felt like someone was squeezing it with icy hands. Panic seeped in as she stabbed the cigarette out in the ash tray. To buy herself a bit more time, she lied and said, "Hold on a sec, I'm not decent."

Jenny took the ash tray and slid it under her bed. She dashed over to her dresser and pulled out the top drawer. Buried underneath an abundance of panties was where she kept a hidden can of air freshener. It would have to do since she didn't have enough time to burn some incense.

She ran through the room spraying the can high above her head, crop dusting the smell of stale smoke with the misty aroma of flowers and fruits. When she finished, she tossed the can under the bed also. Using her opened hand, she fanned the fumes through the room.

Taking a whiff, all she could smell has the heavy scent of freshness and wondered if anyone else would buy it as legit.

She doubted it.

Dammit! Why didn't I just wait until I got in Doug's car?

Opening her pocket book, she dug around inside for some gum. At the bottom of the clutter she found a pack of Orbit. On her way to the door, she crammed two sticks in her mouth. She pulled the door open. Her father was waiting on the other side.

Putting on the innocent routine, she smiled and said, "Hi, Dad."

"You're running late, Jen."

"I know. I'm running a little behind. Is breakfast waiting?"

"Yes. It's been waiting for a few minutes." Dad examined her, looking her up and down. "Care if I come in?"

Shit!

Holding in a scream she replied, "Um sure…of course." She stepped back to ration room for Dad to enter.

He stepped inside. Then, as if catching a whiff of a bad fart, he grimaced. His nose wrinkled. "Jesus kiddo, you went a little nuts with the air freshener."

Nervously gnawing at her bottom lip, she prayed he couldn't detect the smoke smell. She stole a quick glance of the foot of her bed, making sure all the evidence was safely hidden. It was.

"Your mother said you came home a little late last night."

"I did. I'm sorry. It was my fault. We were eating at George's Diner and I lost track of the time." She studied her Dad, looking for any hint that he may know more than he was letting on.

"You lost track of time, or did you just ignore what time it actually was?"

She shrugged. "A little from column A, a little column B?"

Air hissed out from his nostrils. Jenny lowered her head, abandoning the attempt to charm him with humor.

"Your curfew is midnight. I think that's pretty reasonable, especially on a school night."

"You're right. It's very reasonable. Most of my friends have to be home by ten."

And she meant it. Her dad was very evenhanded, much more so than a lot of the dads she'd heard about.

"Coming home after midnight doesn't give you much time for sleep. And, you're coming up on finals *real* soon. You need all the rest you can get."

She'd already felt guilty for coming home late; now she felt lousy for upsetting her dad. On rare occasions she entertained the idea of letting out a wild streak, but deep down she was really just a normal girl, and she enjoyed being one. She also appreciated her parents being proud of her.

"You're right," she said. "I won't do it again."

His stern expression relaxed some. "All right, you better not. Your mother thinks I'm way too easy on you, and I don't want to have to start being a hard-ass like my dad was to me."

"You *are* too easy on me. And, I really don't mean to take advantage of it, but sometimes I do. I'm sorry." She felt her throat tighten.

Don't cry, he'll think it's a charade.

"It's all right, kiddo. I just want you to be happy and successful."

"Thank you, Daddy."

Raising his finger, he said, "But mark my words, if you do badly on one of those finals, just *one*, you're going to be grounded for the entire summer. No Doug, no April, and no beach trip. *Nothing*. Understood?"

She believed he really would take the trip away if she messed up. "Understood."

Dad nodded, then walked back to the door. On his way out, he stopped and turned around. "One more thing."

"Yeah?"

"Air freshener never covers the smell of cigarette smoke. It just sort of makes the room smell like cigarette smoke *and* air freshener."

Shit! He knew this whole time.

Jenny's muscles constricted, her face flushing red. "What do you mean?" She hoped she'd sounded confused.

"When I smoked, I tried the same thing one time I had attempted to quit. Your Mom caught me every time. The smell is really noticeable, even with an overkill of air freshener."

"Ah..." Wanting to say something to convince him she hadn't been smoking, she balked, unable to come up with a convincing lie.

Dad continued, "Let's just hope I never catch you with a cigarette in your hand. Got me?"

Jenny nodded. She couldn't bring herself to look at him.

"All right, good deal. Be downstairs in three minutes so you can get some food before Doug gets here to pick you."

"But, Dad, I'm on a diet..."

"You aren't dieting this morning. Two minutes. Downstairs. Food. Got it?"

She nodded.

Walking backwards, he stepped out of the room, and pulled the door closed.

Jenny flopped down on her rump at the edge of the bed. "Fuck me running." Collapsing backward on the bed, she stared at the ceiling.

And groaned.

Not wanting to come inside to let Jenny know he was here, Doug lightly honked the horn from the road. He sat inside his '89 mustang and waited. Other than Jenny, his car Bernadette was his most cherished possession. Since Jenny could put out, that granted her a couple of points over the car. Like Jenny, he loved to show Bernadette off to all the guys, letting them drool over what he had and they didn't.

He'd think to himself, *Take a good look fellas, you'll never have it this good. I've got the car, I've got the girl, and you don't have anything. You wish you were as cool as me.*

He looked at the Parker's house. Jenny wasn't on her way yet. What was taking her so long? If she kept him waiting much longer, her Dad might come outside and try to talk to him. He hated that. Jenny's Dad seemed nice enough, but he could tell that Mr. Parker wasn't one for bullshit. If Doug looked at Jenny wrong, Mr. Parker would probably give him a stiff punch to the lip. Doug liked his lips the way they were just fine, and the last thing he wanted was for his face to be used as a punching bag.

Doug had a reputation for being a pretty boy. Although he didn't mind the label, he would rather be associated with the jock crowd, but that title was only held by football players, not basketball guys like him. It wasn't that he was too small to play football, because he stood over six feet in height and was thick enough to handle the hits. He just wasn't very good at it. He was clumsy and a bit timid, even if he would never admit it. He had tried out for football the summer of his sophomore year, but was cut from the roster early on. Luckily he had made the basketball team, or else he would've been heckled for the rest of high school for being dropped from that roster as well. He thanked God that he was able to dribble a ball!

The faint bump of a door shutting pulled him from his thoughts to find Jenny trotting to the car. The straps of her book bag pulled her shirt taught against her, giving him a great view of her large twin peaks. It was one of the many things Doug enjoyed about her. Just having turned eighteen, she was stacked like the girls on porno sites. He felt a slight thrill watching them bounce as she scampered to the car.

She opened the door and sat inside, then slammed the door after pulling her skirt in. Doug hated the way she shut the door to his car, always slamming it. He cringed every time. She leaned across the seat. They kissed. Doug tried to slip his tongue in her mouth, but she pulled away before he could get it in there.

"We've got to get going. My Dad's on my back, so I can't be late for school." She tossed her book bag in the backseat then adjusted her shirt so it wasn't so tight.

"Well good morning to you too, dear," said Doug, sarcastically.

Jenny made a face. "I'm sorry, that sounded terrible, didn't it?"

"Only a little."

"I'm sorry. Good morning, baby." She leaned in and kissed him again, this time she allowed a little bit of tongue in before pulling away. "*Now* let's go."

He groaned. "All right."

Doug sat back in his seat and cranked the car. As he gave the engine a few good revs, he looked over at Jenny sitting beside him. He scanned her perfect body, his eyes focusing on her smooth, already slightly tanned legs. The hem of her short skirt hung far back on her legs, showing him the curve of her thigh.

Groaning again, he said, "Babe, it's too early in the morning for you to be doing this to me."

Jenny followed his gaze to her legs. She tugged at the skirt, as if wanting to lower it some. "Doug, we don't have time for games and I'm not in the mood. Let's go, okay?"

"All right, if you insist, but I'm gonna have to take an extra cold shower in gym today." He smiled his precious smile at her, knowing she adored it so much.

Smiling back, she said, "Whatever it takes." Then she patted his leg and gave it a gentle squeeze.

Doug sighed. "Yeah…" He put the car in drive, and took off.

CHAPTER 3

"Are you spying?" asked Sheila from behind.

Greg pulled his fingers out of the blinds, letting them snap shut.

Sneaking up behind Greg, she hugged him from behind, wrapping her arms around his chest and resting her chin on his shoulder.

He leaned his head against hers. He could smell the sweet scent of her shampoo. "Spying? Nah, more like observing."

"Now you've advanced to observing the neighbors through the window? Well, that's a start."

"Sheila…give me a break."

"You should've said hello to the man this morning."

"Well…I didn't know what to do. He looked *right* at me."

Sheila turned him around to face her. "It's going to happen from time-to-time. People *will* look at you. And you know what? Some of them might actually speak to you." She smiled at him.

"That guy next door *waved*." Greg spoke as if the man had violated him in some unspeakable way.

"And how did you respond to such, such *madness?*"

Great. She was teasing him. He half expected her to take it so far as pulling out a teddy bear and demanding he show her on the bear where he'd been touched.

"You *know* what I did," he said, finally.

Laughing, she said, "Ran."

"You make it sound so...childish."

"Well, it is...kind of."

"How is it childish?" Placing his hands on his hips, he shifted his weight to one side.

Sheila sighed, then turned away from him and headed for the kitchen. While Greg watched her walk away, he couldn't help taking a moment to observe her beauty. Even when she teased him, like she had been all morning, he still found her incredibly gorgeous. She was just as beautiful now as she had been the day they'd met.

A blind date organized by another couple, Steve and Donna, who were their mutual friends. Greg had worked with Steve at Hellstorm Comics, and Sheila had roomed with Donna in college. Steve and Donna had decided they needed a couple to hang out with, and since they didn't know any couples they figured they'd create one.

Enter Greg and Sheila—two single people, one male and one female. Neither of them had known they were being set up on a blind date until they'd arrived. Greg had been five minutes early and Sheila had been five minutes late. He'd ordered a greasy hamburger and she'd gotten a salad with grilled chicken strips on top. For dessert, they'd decided to tag team a giant piece of red velvet cake.

They'd stayed at the restaurant two hours longer than Steve and Donna.

And they'd rarely missed a meal together since.

Greg stared at Sheila as she made her way to the kitchen.

Before entering, she stole a fleeting glance of him from over her shoulder. The slight smirk of her lips, the narrowing of her eyes, sent a tingling shockwave through him, much as it did every time.

If someone were to ask him to put her beauty into words he'd fail. She was exotic, no doubt about that. Her skin was caramel-colored and soft; the softest skin he'd ever felt. Her curvy eyes suggested a hint of Asian and Hispanic heritage. A jet black mane hung partway down her back, and swayed when she walked. She had an enormous, warm and caring smile that dimpled her cheeks and made her eyes squint. The laughter that accompanied that smile was a deep booming chortle. When she unleashed it, Greg would laugh too. Her presence alone could stimulate him, recharge his batteries and get his creative juices flowing.

He'd drawn several portraits of her throughout the years. Each one he'd hated because he felt his skills never captured just how gorgeous she really was. He'd never shown her any of them, then one day she found them while cleaning one of his old offices. Since they'd moved around a lot it was hard for Greg to remember which office, but he'd found her sitting at his drawing table, thumbing through sketches, paintings, and charcoals.

In a cold sweat, he'd watched her, his gut twisting and turning while waiting for her reaction.

After she'd gone through them all, some more than once, she'd cried. He'd wanted to get rid of the artwork, but she wouldn't let him; she'd taken them and put them in a trunk. It had gone with them from house to house.

It was impossible to fathom how he'd nabbed someone like her. And he wasn't too shy to ask her on occasion why she had settled for a freelance comic book artist. She was a woman more beautiful than any model who'd ever graced a cover.

Her response was always the same: "Who else are you going to find to take care of you?"

He'd retort: "Who else would *want* to take care of me?"

When they used to go out—it had been years since they had, six to be exact—he imagined that the guys eyeing her must have thought he was rich.

Sheila liked to remind him of how persistently hard he was on himself. She'd point out he was a great looking guy. Through the years he'd managed to keep in shape, and being thirty-four he still had a full head of hair. Perfect hair that behaved and did whatever he wanted. The one thing Sheila constantly nagged him about was his smoking. He'd never been able to quit, even though he'd tried often enough.

Greg realized he was still standing by the window. He could hear Sheila scuttling inside the kitchen—the sounds of dishes clanging, the clinking of silverware.

He walked into the kitchen.

Sheila stood at the table gathering up the three empty plates from breakfast. Greg joined her, collecting the glasses. Holding them between his fingers he said, "The reason I didn't say hello was because it would have brought him into the yard. Casual chit-chat would have followed. Then do you know what would have happened?"

Sheila was at the dishwasher now, loading in the dishes. "You might have had a good conversation?"

Greg took the glasses to her. As he handed them over, he said, "The chit-chat would have escalated to him asking questions. And I didn't want to try and explain the newest version of our situation, not yet. I'm a terrible liar, Sheila. Come on, you know this. You guess your Christmas presents every year."

"That doesn't make you a terrible liar."

"I'm awful at it, and you know it."

"Well…that makes you a good person."

"Oh please." He sighed.

"If you were a master liar, I'd be worried. And, I wouldn't trust you." Sheila put the last glass on one of the skinny pegs, rolled the rack into the washer, and raised the lid. "But if we're here to be a family, a *real* family, then we have to try and live." She typed in a combination of buttons. The washer came to life, sloshing water on the dishes inside.

Standing up straight, she folded her arms over her large breasts tucked behind a sun dress. "Your words, not mine."

Greg leaned against the counter. Raking his hands through his hair, he groaned. "You're right. I should've just…said hello. I panicked."

"It's okay. I probably would've done the same thing in your situation." She patted him on the butt then walked back to the table, snatching the wet rag slung over the conduit separating their double-sink on her way.

"Then why are you giving me such a hard time about it?"

She glanced back at him, a silly smile on her face. "You're cute when you're flustered." She laughed. "You're the husband. You're supposed to do all the talking and handle all the business. Isn't that how marriages work?"

"Yeah, maybe in the fifties."

Laughing, she started walking toward him. He met her halfway and they embraced, holding each other tightly.

With her face buried against his chest, she said, "Let's do it right this time. From the beginning."

"You talk about it like…like the problem doesn't exist."

"I'm trying not to look at it like a problem. You told me to do that, and I'm doing it."

Greg squeezed her tighter, agreeing. "You're right." He said, leaning his head back and not letting her go. She met his stare with her gorgeous smile. "But, first things first."

"Don't..."

"We have to pay our old friend, Dr. Conner, a visit."

Her enthusiasm faded with her smile and worry took its place. "I know. How do you think he'll react to seeing us after so long? It's been six years..."

"I honestly don't know..."

Greg wasn't expecting Conner to pop a bottle of champagne and celebrate their reunion, but he also hoped he didn't shut them out. Dr. Conner had been an element to the start of this. He *had* to be the one who could help them.

Sheila must have been thinking the same thing. "What if this doesn't work? What's plan B?"

"We'll have to come up with a plan B." Gently, he placed his hand on the back of her head, easing her back against him. His fingers became entwined in her soft hair.

They stayed in the kitchen for a very long time, hugging. Neither of them mentioned a possibility for plan B.

CHAPTER 4

Dr. Henry Conner had been blessed with the nicest lawn in the community. It was a title he held with utmost pride. His grass always seemed to be just a shade greener than the neighbors, and was as soft as carpet under his feet. The flowers and plants that lined the front of his house were ultramarine, their colors extravagant against his white vinyl siding.

Henry stood in the front yard, a water hose pointing ahead of him, spraying the garden with its regular dose of water. He made sure each plant got its own period of special attention. With one hand in his pocket, he walked alongside the plants, spraying. He wore a smile that could barely fit on his face.

He loved days like this. Summer was just around the corner and the humidity hadn't kicked in. The warm air was pleasant and light on his skin. Not heavy and thick like it got in June and lasted throughout the rest of the summer. It was the first weekend of May, and so far it had been perfect. But even if the weather was atrociously hot, he'd still be out here, hose in hand and drenching his babies. He didn't mind working up a sweat in the lawn, he rather enjoyed it.

The extra work he put into his lawn care was worth it when he got results like this. And knowing his neighbors were constantly envious didn't hurt either. While taking his evening strolls through the neighborhood, he often passed other neighbors on their own walks. He'd stop to watch them pass by his house, observing it with shaking heads. He got a slight thrill from it. Being in his early fifties and single, it was one of the few times he could enjoy any type of thrill.

He was almost done with the front. Before he moved on to the backyard, he decided he'd go inside and get his outdoor safari hat. It was an exaggerated head garment for the amount of outdoor labor he actually did, but he liked wearing it. It looked good on him.

Being so captivated with his lawn he hadn't noticed the man who'd wandered into his yard.

"Dr. Conner?"

"Jesus!" His arm jerked up, shooting water into the sky. Some of it rained back down on him, dousing his shirt while the rest splashed the siding on his house. Holding his hand over his chest, he turned around, laughing at himself. "You startled me."

A young man stood a few feet away. Right away Dr. Conner saw something about him that was familiar. He'd seen him before but couldn't recall where. Something told him he should know.

The man spoke. "Sorry I snuck up on you. I thought for sure you'd heard me."

"It's okay, no harm done. Sometimes I get so carried away while I'm out here that I tend to shut off the outside world." Henry laughed again. "So, can I help you with anything?"

"Wanted to say hello. My family and I are the new neighbors, just moved in down the street a couple weeks ago."

Something about the look in the man's eyes made Henry think he was waiting on him to say something particular. It made Henry uncomfortable. Ignoring the vibe it gave him, he said, "Oh that's wonderful! How are the people of Sunwalk treating you so far?"

"We haven't been out and about enough to be social," the man said.

"That's too bad. The people here are very nice." He forced a smile. It felt awkward on his face. He was already trying to think of lies to tell this man so he'd leave, though he wasn't sure why.

"Is that why you're here, Dr. Conner? To start fresh?"

That was the second time he'd referred to him by his professional name.

Did I tell him my name?

"Um...sure," said Henry. "I suppose everyone likes a fresh start."

The man erupted with such ferocious laughter that Henry recoiled back. As sudden as the mad laughter had started, it stopped.

The man stared at him in unnerving silence.

Henry cleared his throat. He tried to speak, but there was still some unnatural phlegm in his throat. He cleared his throat harder and tried again. "Is there anything I can help you with? If not, I must be getting back to work here and..."

"You asked if you can help me with anything?"

"Um..."

"That's such an open-ended question. First of all, you'd have to actually remember who the hell I am before you could possibly help with anything."

"Uh..." Henry backhanded sweat off his brow. He'd been working outside for over an hour and had hardly shed a bead of sweat, and now since this stranger had shown up, he couldn't stop. It was as if his head was a faucet, showering his face with a never-ending supply of perspiration. And yet, he still shivered.

The man continued. "You have no *clue* who I am, do you?"

Henry absently scratched his chest. "We've met before?"

Of course we have. You know this man. Who is he? Who?

"Oh, yes. We've met. I'm Greg Heyman. My wife's name is Sheila. You might remember us as John and Ashley Spacey."

It all clicked.

Henry's eyes widened, mouth rounded. The hose dropped from his hand. It landed on the trigger, shooting another spray of water across the house before turning onto its spout. He took an involuntary step back. "Oh...my God. How did you find me?" His legs felt wobbly, too weak to support his upper body.

"It wasn't easy," Greg said. "You're very smart. You covered your tracks well. It cost us a lot of money over the course of the six years you've been incognito. We thought *we* were keeping a low profile...but *you?* It was as if you'd completely vanished."

"I *had* to. I was ruined. I had to leave the university, erase everything about who I was, and there was always the possibility I could be arrested. And...I was lucky that I even survived the...assault. How did you...get away?"

"We ran. It was all we could do. Ran and haven't stopped."

Henry nodded. "I had to get away so I could rebuild my life."

"Rebuild *your* life? That's a funny thing for you to say.

That's why we're here. That's why we've spent the last six years searching for you. It's like you said, 'Everyone deserves a fresh start'."

CHAPTER 5

Henry had followed Greg Heyman or John Spacey, whatever he was calling himself, back to his house, but not before grabbing his medical bag at Greg's request, and making a quick stop at his liquor cabinet for a bottle of bourbon.

With his bourbon in hand and his medical bag on the floor, he now sat in a chair across from Greg and his strikingly gorgeous wife, Sheila. If it had been her who'd come wandering up on his front lawn, he'd have recognized her right away. Someone that lovely wasn't easy to forget.

He poured bourbon in a glass with shaking hands, and was very generous with the volume. Still in a state of shock from the sudden arrival of his hosts, he raised the glass to his mouth and drank. The bourbon tasted good but burned his throat and chest on its way down. It heated his stomach with a calming warmth.

He regretted coming here, fearing what they might say or *do* next.

Greg and Sheila were seated on the couch, watching him as he chugged all the bourbon in three long swallows. Henry set the glass down and quickly poured some more as he began to tell his side of the last six years.

"It wasn't supposed to happen the way it did. Those were um…unusual side effects." He chugged two big gulps and lowered the glass, gasping. Now his throat was really on fire. He didn't care. It was helping him relax, loosening his lips so he could say all that he needed to.

"Unusual? You call what happened unusual?" Greg's voice was gaining an edge. He was on the verge of shouting.

"It wasn't just *your* son that suffered from the…illness." He set his glass on a coaster on the coffee table. "The entire project was a disaster. Babies were being stillborn or born as mutated freaks. When word got out about what we were doing, the project had to be destroyed. I had no idea our investor would go to the extreme lengths he did to assure the truth wouldn't get out."

"Like killing everyone?" asked Greg.

Henry nodded.

"How did the media find out what was going on? All I knew is one day we were in our bunk at the compound and we saw this woman sneaking around with a cameraman. She was narrating what they found for the camera as they went."

"Did she try to talk to you?"

"Oh yeah. She talked to everyone. Asking us questions about the project and about some man named Hawthorne."

Henry felt a cold tweak between his shoulder blades at the mention of the name.

Greg's eyes narrowed. "Do you know who he is?"

"No," said Henry, his voice a whisper.

"But, how did the reporter find out *any*thing? I thought the compound was sealed up tight. It wasn't like we were allowed to leave."

"I'm guessing one of the families or staff reached out to

the reporter. Maybe it was a joint effort? She had to have been let into the compound by someone on our staff. Without those access cards, you couldn't get around anywhere. *And* we were heavily guarded."

"Did you know?" asked Sheila. "Did you know what was going to happen?"

Henry had known, and he was sure the look on his face told them that he had.

"Why didn't you warn us? Or the others?"

"I couldn't. By the time I found out what the investor was going to do, it had already been arranged. I was advised to vanish, so that was what I did." He had to sell his various properties, the house at the beach, his cabin in the mountains. He said good-bye to all his stocks and dipped into his confidential bank accounts that he had always kept hidden from the IRS. That, and the money he brought in from working at a small family practice in town, was what he lived on now. He did all right, but wasn't the medical pioneer he'd been built up to be. He'd moved halfway across the country to escape the madness that project had garnered. Obviously, he hadn't gone far enough.

"And what about Dr. Vanhoy?" asked Greg. "Wasn't he the brains behind this?"

"I *was* the brains, me, he just had the seniority I didn't, so he got to lead the project. They were my theories and *my* calculations…"

Greg held out his hands as if saying to calm down. "Okay…but is he…alive? We could probably use his help. If you know where to reach him…"

Henry took a heavy slug from his glass. "He's dead. Suicide."

Greg put his hand on Sheila's knee. She laid her hand on

top of his, then turned to Henry. "How many were part of the project?" she asked.

"Participants?" She nodded. "Six, out of the countless numbers that volunteered. They came in droves, all willing to be subjected to the experiment. Once we had our families narrowed down, we got right to work."

"So all this time," she said, "we thought we were the only ones involved, but you're telling us there were six families total?"

"Yes," answered Henry.

"Why weren't we notified there were other families?"

"It was all top-secret. They didn't know about you, either. The compound was *huge*, to say the least. And you were all kept in different sections so you wouldn't know about each other. But, the reporter who triggered this backlash seemed to know all of this. And she didn't show up until after the offspring started being born..."

"Offspring?" said Greg, disgusted. "You talk like they're lab animals."

"Well...if the shoe fits..." Henry immediately regretted saying that. Especially when Greg started to stand up, a look on his face that showed Henry was about to get his face smashed in.

Sheila put her hand on Greg's knee and that seemed to take the hardness out of him. He settled back on the couch.

She looked at Henry. "Tell us everything."

"That will take months."

"Give us the simple version."

Henry laughed. "There isn't one. But, I'll tell you what I think you'd want to hear the most, and probably a lot of what you don't want to hear at all."

"Whatever it takes," said Greg. "We want to know."

Henry nodded. And, he began to tell them. He admitted the experiment hadn't been approved through the proper channels and it was a make-or-break project. Dr. Alex Vanhoy, himself, his colleagues, his staff, all the lab assistants were confident the experiment would be successful. They'd created their own embryos in the labs, mutated the structures by taking what they needed from the hosts—mothers—and various other animals, such as primates. Reptilian DNA was used for its dramatic capabilities to reproduce. In theory, the human cells should have dominated the others, taking what they needed from the others. That was not the case. After the male's seed was implanted, and the created egg was inserted into the mother, they merged together into a separate form of DNA entirely: a new species, a hybrid.

Then he confessed to staging the ultrasound photos and videos. Once they'd taken the first blood samples after the test subjects had become pregnant, he'd known. All of them had known the kind of offspring that was developing inside the wombs of six unsuspecting mothers, and they'd continued, wanting to know what kind of species had been produced. Two mothers died during the term, their bodies unable to host the egg. Four mothers carried full term.

"And *their* babies?" Greg asked.

Henry refilled his glass, then continued his story.

He told them the entire procedure was viewed by their investor through hidden windows, like watching fish swim in an aquarium. The investor had witnessed the horror of the surviving mothers giving birth: three creatures born two hours apart. Two lab assistants had been killed when one of the offspring had suddenly turned hostile and attacked them while they'd checked the little girl's vitals.

Their only success had been the Spaceys and their

offspring: a normal-looking baby boy. The project had been funded with heavy hearts and good intentions of giving women with the inability to conceive and carry children the ability to reproduce as many offspring as they wanted. It would have been an amazing scientific break-through, had they succeeded.

Instead, they'd failed. And lied about it.

"I was ruined," Dr. Conner added.

"*You* were ruined?" said Greg. "What about us? What do you think this kind of nightmare brought us?"

"I'm sure it hasn't been easy...you're fortunate you survived at all. How...did you?"

Greg suddenly looked haunted, the memory taking hold. He stared off to the side as if watching it replay in front of him. "They were everywhere. Men with guns, wearing these nylon masks."

"Secret soldiers," said Henry.

"They started shooting everyone," said Sheila.

"Bonnie, our nurse, came rushing into the room with Gabe. She handed him to us, and said she would show us the way out. She took us down this tunnel that went underneath the compound, dark and dingy, pipes running along both walls. She led us to a secret stairway and told us where to go once we were above ground."

"Bonnie?" said Henry. "Did she make it out with you?"

Greg shook his head. "She went back for the others. But, the building exploded a few minutes later."

"Then she didn't make it," said Henry. "No one survived the blast."

"We didn't think so, either."

Henry sighed. "I'm afraid if anyone knew you did...or knew where to find you..."

"Yeah," said Greg. "That's why we haven't exactly made it easy to be discovered."

"*I* know you're alive," said Henry.

"Are you going to tell anyone?" Sheila asked.

Henry frowned. "Who could I tell?" He stared into his empty glass, contemplating pouring another. His lips were already numb and his vision a little blurry. If he drank any more, he might just pass out right in this chair. "Do you have any photos of your son that I can look at?"

"Photos?"

"Yes. Before he passed away."

"Passed away?" Sheila made a face. "Dr. Conner, he's not dead."

Henry shivered so uncontrollably he dropped his glass in his lap. A few droplets spattered his thigh. "What?"

"He's a healthy, growing boy," said Greg.

"How? There's no way that could be possible." He leaned forward, returning his empty glass to the coaster. Collapsing back into the chair, Dr. Conner pushed his forehead into the crease of his hand, rubbing his eyes with a thumb and forefinger. This was incredible. "Even if the other offspring hadn't been terminated, there was no chance they could have survived. We thought the same about your son."

Sheila took a deep breath. "We want you to see Gabe."

"I'd like that," said Henry. "How is he?"

Sheila leaned her head back, her eyes aimed at the ceiling. "When Gabe turned two he started to change..."

"Define change."

"We were living in Oregon then. We'd already been moving around so much that we felt like we were on tour. Visiting a city for a short time, then packing up and heading out of there quickly. We never stayed in one spot for too long. But, we liked it there, and things with the project had seemed to calm down. So, we thought it was safe to make Oregon our home."

"What happened?" he asked.

"So we're living in Oregon, and all these reports start circulating about some kind of beast ripping dogs apart and eating them."

Greg took over. "It didn't happen every night, just now and then. Something was getting in their backyards and devouring the dogs. A few months later a baby was found ripped apart in a swing on the back deck of Marlene Albright, one of our neighbors. She'd left the baby there, swinging, while she'd gone back into the house to make him a bottle. She said she heard a vicious growling sound and then her infant son shrieking in pain. As she ran outside to find out what was going on, a sound like raw meat being ripped apart overwhelmed the crying and growls. She opened the door, and must have startled the creature, because it took off running."

"What did this creature look like?" asked Henry.

"She said it was small, a pale green color but hairy. We'd hired a private investigator to look into Project: Newborn, hoping to track down survivors. Before he disappeared, he was able to dig up some files that hadn't been destroyed in the fire. There were reports of other families, and how their kids had...mutated."

It was Sheila's turn. "But we didn't understand because Gabe looked normal. Just like any regular boy. He was a little big for his age...but we just thought he was healthy."

"Until we *saw* him change."

Sheila started to cry. Greg put his arm around her.

"Explain this change," said Henry, horrifyingly fascinated.

Greg looked at him. "Like in some kind of damn movie, he just changed into this *creature* right in front of us. He was sitting in his plastic chair, the kind with the attached tray? He was just sitting there, eating some Cheesy Puffs and then out of nowhere his skin started to bubble. We heard popping sounds. And he started turning green and growing scales... These damn spikes sprouted up on the back of his neck..." Greg shook his head. "And hair just sort of, I don't know, sprouted up. You know how it looks when there hasn't been rain in a long time? The ground gets hard, but you see these weeds poking up from the dried up dirt?"

"Yes," said Henry.

"It was like that."

Sheila took over. "He grew fangs. His nails turned into points."

"My God," said Henry. "And he can just oscillate appearances like this? Change at will?"

"For a few months. At first the changes only lasted a couple hours, then it was a day or so. A few months later there would be three-to-four days in a row where he'd stay like that. And last year, shortly after he turned five, he changed again..."

"And hasn't changed back to normal," completed Greg. "We're afraid he's stuck this way."

"Such an extraordinary account," said Henry. "And did his appetite strengthen with his mutation?"

Sheila nodded. "You have no idea how much."

"I see. And did anyone ever catch on? I mean judging by what you're telling me, I assume it was Gabe who attacked the canines and the infant?"

Sheila's lips quivered. She nodded.

"There have been some that began to put some of the

pieces together," said Greg.

"And what happened to them?" asked Henry.

"We had to make sure they never told anyone, by any means necessary. Then we'd move. We've seen a lot of our fabulous country in the last few years, Dr. Conner. Not quite the kind of family road trips we wanted to take, but it is what it is. We have a guy that creates bogus identities for us. We're his most valued customers. Becoming the Heymans was a discounted price."

Henry understood Greg's meaning behind making sure people never told anyone. He'd been involved with similar actions himself over the last few years, mostly in playing cover-up to the scandal that was Project: Newborn. He wasn't proud for having participated in it; sometimes he even had nightmares the victims had come back from the dead as revenge-seeking zombies, but the necessity for it to be done had outweighed the guilt. "And this is your life now?"

"Yeah…since Gabe was two. Something always happens, so we try not to get too comfortable. Last time it was an unexpected visit and home search from social workers. With the fear of being taken away, Gabe retaliated. That was one of the worst. We'd had to be out of our home and well on our way out of the state within a couple hours."

"How do you survive?" he asked. "I don't mean to be nosey…"

"We survive by the seat of our pants," Greg answered coldly.

"That's why we're here, Dr. Conner. It took us a long time to make it this far."

"What is it you think I can do?"

"We need you to help Gabe. We need a cure."

Henry laughed like a loon, though he hadn't meant for it

to sound so shrill. Greg and Sheila watched him cackle, stone-faced, not seeing the humor.

Wiping the tears away from his eyes, Henry said, "I wouldn't even know where to begin."

Greg stood up. "Meeting Gabe is a great place to start."

Henry stopped laughing. He grabbed the bourbon, poured another generous glass, and drank. If the kid looked anything like what they described, he might need the rest of the bottle to handle seeing him.

CHAPTER 6

Other than the blue-tinted UVB lighting and obvious warmer temperature than the rest of the house, Gabe's room was how Henry imagined any average six-year-old's room would be. A SpongeBob poster was tacked to the wall, toys littered the floor. A fifteen-inch LCD TV sat on a nightstand and some PBS cartoon was teaching the importance of sharing.

Henry was understandably chary of meeting this kid. The brief amount of history explained to him was unnerving. It made him queasy thinking about the people Gabe had killed, and the others the parents had doubtless killed to keep matters quiet. He wasn't any more honorable than the Heymans, but he was worried what would happen to him if he had to tell them there was nothing he could do to help.

Don't tell them that. No matter what, don't let them think you can't help.

But he'd only be able to keep up the charade for so long before they realized he had no clue what to do.

Henry looked around the room. The leather medical bag was slippery in his sweaty grip. Although he didn't see the little boy, he could have been hiding anywhere. With the room cast in faint blue light, there were plenty of shadows for him to lurk in.

The light reminded him of the reptile exhibit at the zoo he visited when he was a kid. It had been his favorite place back then, but now, standing in the same kind of clammy climate in a child's room, he was terrified.

Trying to keep quiet, Henry slunk behind Greg, walking deeper into the room. He stepped on something hard. It crunched under his feet.

Oh God! Was it him?

Dr. Conner lifted his foot and examined the broken remains of a toy tractor.

What a relief. At least it hadn't been the kid's arm. God only knew what the evil monster would have done to his leg had he stepped on him.

Greg stood in the center of the room, his fists on his hips. "Gabe?"

From under the bed, Henry heard some faint skittering, the sound of scratching carpet. The bed skirt flickered.

A green arm coated with indurate scales and frilly strands of hair reached out from under the bed. The hand had two fingers and a thumb with sharp talons at the tips.

A cold sting traveled through Henry. He could feel those claws slashing into his skin. His stomach cramped. Invisible pain shot through him.

Gabe emerged from under the bed. With his scaled arms held out wide, he ran over to Greg and hugged him. He moved so fast Henry barely caught a glimpse of the kid. He saw a dash of brown hair, bright pajamas and slippers.

He watched the father and son embrace, and he couldn't help his chill from seeing a normal-looking guy hugging such an appalling monster. Gabe excitedly grunted a few times as he squirmed against his father. Henry hoped he wasn't grimacing. He attempted a bogus smile that seemed flat on his face.

Even with his palpable ugliness, the Heymans treated Gabe like a normal kid. And other than the obvious mutation, he could have been. His hair was the typical little boy haircut: long bangs over beady yellow slits that were eyes, and a little shabby over his pointed ears.

"How long have you been awake, booger?" asked Greg.

A couple sustained grunts. Henry could make out distinctive speech patterns, although no real words were being said.

Greg nodded, apparently understanding what his son was telling him. "Not much of a nap, then, huh?"

Sheila sighed. "We may have to start giving him something stronger."

"I don't feel comfortable giving him anything else. I hate it now as it is."

"I don't like it either, Greg, but it's not keeping him asleep like it used to. It's the only thing that keeps his...*excitement* tamed down."

"I can help there," said Henry. "I have a thick pad for writing prescriptions in my desk drawer at home. I can think of three off the top of my head that will slow down his metabolism."

Greg frowned. The husband and wife continued their little tiff, but Henry heard none of it. He'd become transfixed with Gabe. His initial reaction had been one of shock and appalled horror. Now his fascination with the creature overpowered his stress.

Gabe glanced at him, caught him watching, then began moving to his right which forced Greg to turn as well. Now

Greg's back was to him, blocking Gabe from Dr. Conner's sight. *Smart little shit...* He'd deliberately made his dad move without Greg even realizing it, so Henry couldn't see him.

Greg rubbed his hand through Gabe's hair. "Booger, this room is a mess."

Sheila added, "I hope it gets clean before supper." Standing with her weight on one foot, a hip jutted out, she tapped her foot on the carpet. "Will it?"

Two enthusiastic grunts, which Henry interpreted as a yes.

"That's Mommy's good boy."

Like a puppy wanting a treat, Gabe whined, nodding his head slowly.

"Yes, you are my good boy. You always will be."

Greg glanced at Henry, then turned his attention back to Gabe. He crouched down in front of his son. "Listen, Booger. There's someone here who wants to see you, okay? He's an old friend of ours from a long time ago. Do you understand?"

Grunting, Gabe nodded his head. Henry watched them communicate in amazement.

Greg looked at Henry. "All right. Come on."

His stomach tightened. His heart hammered in his chest so hard it felt as if it might burst through. He had to force himself not to sprint over there and keep his pace casual.

Greg stood up, stepping back with his wife to clear some space for him. "Gabe, this is Dr. Conner."

The boy turned. Seeing him in full made Henry want to flee the house, go back home, and lock his door to the Heymans forever. Standing before him, Gabe looked a solid foot taller than the average kid his age. His upper body was heavier than his back could support, forcing him to slouch. His arms dangled just above his knees. His legs, though they looked to be a good length, were bent at the knees as if he was premeditating a leap and had assumed the position.

Stepping closer, the blue shadows pulled away from Gabe's face. He could see Gabe's eyes, yellow marbles with a line of black straight down the middle. When Gabe blinked, a whitish-callow film flickered across the yellow from one corner to the next.

Gabe's wide mouth curved at the sides, as if nervously smiling. Behind the slimy, scaled lips were queues of needle-pointed teeth. Henry counted two rows on top and two on bottom.

Forcing a smile in return, Henry spoke, "Hi there, Gabe. It's been a long time since we've seen each other."

Gabe tilted his head, studying him. Then he suddenly dashed away, hiding behind an inflatable Elmo chair.

Henry looked at the Heymans, holding his hands out. "I..."

"Sorry," said Sheila. "He's shy."

She followed Greg behind the chair. They both crouched down. Henry could see their hands rubbing across the pale shape of Gabe's back. Henry took this moment to backhand the sweat off his forehead. More instantly replenished what he'd wiped off. What was he doing here? He should get the hell out of this house as soon as possible. But he couldn't. He had to find out more. He needed some time with Gabe. And he couldn't get that time if the little shit didn't come out from behind the chair.

As much as the Heymans wanted help for their son, they weren't the kind of parents to force it. So if they couldn't will the kid out peacefully, he wouldn't be coming out.

He started to join them, but a low, throaty growl froze him in his place. "What was that?"

"It's Gabe," said Sheila.

"Wha-what's wrong with him?"

"He's getting mad."

"Gabe," began Greg. "It's okay. He's not going to hurt you..."

Like I could.

Another growl. Suddenly Henry had to pee.

"Is he okay," he asked Greg.

"He doesn't like you," he replied firmly.

Well, what the hell?

"He'll warm up to you," said Sheila. "Don't worry."

"How do you know what he's saying? Does he actually speak?"

Greg sighed. "No, he doesn't talk. We've tried to teach him, but he just can't do it. He communicates with us just fine, though without talking."

"Think I could come over there and examine him?"

What are you doing? Just go home. Now's the perfect time. The kid doesn't want you near him. Tell them you have to go.

Motioning him over, Sheila said, "Sure." She turned to Gabe, hugging him. "Now, honey. I want you to be nice for Dr. Conner. Do you hear me?"

Gabe's sunken eyes and straight-lined pupils glared at Henry. A warning growl droned from his chest. As scary as it sounded, and its point being clear as freshly polished glass, it still wasn't as threatening as the first.

"Gabe," warned Greg.

The growl petered off to a whine, then stopped.

"It's all right, you can come over here."

Against his better judgment, he walked over to the chair. Greg slid it out of the way and Henry sat cross-legged on the floor. He put the bag in his lap. He unsnapped the latch around the handles, and pulled it open. Then he removed a stethoscope. Blowing some hot air on the diaphragm, he smiled at the Heymans.

"Can get a little cold," he said.

They nodded.

To Gabe, he said, "I'm going to put this on your chest, okay?"

Gabe took a tentative step back.

"It's okay, sweetie," assured Sheila. "He just wants to hear your bump-bump."

Gabe looked at his mother, then stole another uncertain glance at Henry.

"That's right," he said. "Just a quick listen to your bump-bump."

"Do I need to unbutton his shirt?" she asked.

Henry shook his head. "No. He's having a hard time trusting me as it is. Doing that might really frighten him."

"Right," she said, nodding.

"Here we go." He cautiously lowered the diaphragm, hesitating just a moment before placing it against the boy's chest. The moment the round amplifier touched the kid, Henry's ears were invaded by savage thumps. He flinched at the loud beats. "Whoa…such a strong heartbeat!"

"Yeah…it really goes when he's nervous."

"This hard?"

Sheila nodded.

"Amazing."

"Is it…you know…okay?"

"What? Oh yes, absolutely. *Very* healthy." Adjusting the diaphragm, he positioned it at the center of his chest to listen to his lungs. "Just want to hear him breathe for a minute."

Henry detected a waning growl under Gabe's fast

breathing. He assumed the kid was doing it just for him, knowing his parents couldn't hear it.

Little asshole. Still letting me know he doesn't like me.

The feeling was mutual. Henry didn't like this kid, or any kids for that matter. But he was definitely intrigued by this one. He'd outlived all the other subjects, his advancement was incredibly remarkable. Why this one's mutation had been delayed when the others were born with it confused Henry. He would have to find out. With Gabe being the last remaining specimen, he needed to study him as much as possible.

Maybe I can get it right…if I…

He made those thoughts stop but the idea had already taken root in his mind.

What if…?

"Mind if I take a blood sample?" he asked.

Both parents shared a tentative look, and he couldn't blame them. He wasn't even sure why he'd asked them. Especially with Gabe being so suspicious of him.

He rushed to explain.

"Just a small amount. I have a basic setup at my house, so I should be able to analyze it there. I have a friend at the hospital and he might be able to bring me some other equipment and I could examine him further later. But, we'd need to get Gabe to my house for that."

"That will be hard," said Sheila.

"We'll worry about all that later, after I get the equipment."

The friend at the hospital was a lie but getting the equipment wasn't. He still had a way he could reach the funder, Hawthorne, if the man hadn't completely vanished from the radar. And if Henry was to tell him he had a living and healthy specimen at his disposal, he would supply him with what he needed to monitor its development.

Or he just might try to take him from me.

That seemed the most likely scenario, and Henry would try his best to hold off contacting Hawthorne. But, Henry didn't have many options, particularly if any real amount of effort was going to be attempted.

"Does this mean you'll help us?"

"It means I'm going to try. But I'd need that sample…"

He stuck his hand in his bag, retrieving the syringe. When he showed it to Gabe, he was surprised to find the kid wasn't frightened of it. And why would he be? This needle wouldn't be menacing to anyone of his stature. Henry attempted his best soothing voice which sounded strange even to him. "I'm going to stick this in your arm for just a couple seconds. There will be a quick sting and then it'll go away. Can you count, Gabe?"

Gabe nodded.

"I bet you can count real high, can't you?"

Gabe nodded again, a little more enthusiastically this time.

"Tell you what, I'll do what I have to do and you count for me, okay? When we're done, I'll even give you a *Scooby-Doo* Band-Aid and lollipop. How's that sound?"

This time Gabe didn't respond, just watched him from his spot on the floor. Sheila hugged the boy, patting his arm.

"Here we go," he informed everyone. He removed the plastic cap from the point. Lowering the needle down to Gabe's arm, he pressed the tip against the kid's skin. Instead of penetrating the green plates, the needle snapped off like the lead on a mechanical pencil.

Henry raised the broken needle, observing it in wonder. "I might need a thicker needle."

"I think you just might," agreed Greg.

CHAPTER 7

Greg and Sheila walked Dr. Conner to the door. He had his bag, the bourbon tucked away inside, but no lollipop. He'd left that with Gabe. But Gabe wouldn't eat it. Unlike other kids, Gabe didn't have that addiction to sweets. Greg wished he did. At this age, most parents were trying to wean their kids to healthier snacks while he and Sheila would have been thrilled to see him choose a Snickers bar over raw chicken meat.

"I'll see what I can do about getting a stronger needle. Then I'll analyze the blood, do some tests, but…I can't make any promises…you know that."

"We know," said Sheila.

"But I'm going to do what I can."

As much as Greg wanted to wholeheartedly believe the scientist, he just couldn't do it. He smiled though, hopefully coming across as pleased as Sheila appeared to be. "Thank you for helping us. Even if nothing comes from it. At least we know we tried everything to get Gabe back to his old self."

Were they making the right choice? He wanted to think they were. They'd fantasized about this moment for so long and now that they'd located Dr. Conner, gotten him and Gabe together, and even managed to get him involved, Greg felt emptier than he had while they'd been searching—a bit disappointed, but mostly guilty.

He wondered what Gabe was thinking about all this.

"Thank you for being so understanding. Remember, I'm just coming back into this. So it will take some time before I can even determine if I have a snowball's chance in Hell at being able to do something, but when I get back to the house—"

Dr. Conner stopped talking at the sudden bong that filled the house. Greg recoiled as if a bullet had whizzed past his head. Sheila hugged his arm.

It took Greg a moment to realize the sudden bell-like clamor had been only that: a doorbell. This was the first time he'd heard it.

The three of them stood together like a trio of statues. Another earsplitting din brought a quick gasp from Sheila.

"Who is it?" she hissed.

Befuddled, Greg snuck over to the peephole. He pressed his eye to it and wasn't surprised by who he found. "The neighbors," he whispered.

"The Parkers?" asked Dr. Conner in the same hushed tone.

Greg shrugged. "I guess. I don't know their names."

Sheila whispered, "Is that the guy you saw earlier?"

"Yeah, plus one." Greg turned around. "I'm guessing his wife."

"Taller guy with dark hair. The wife, curly blonde?"

"Exactly."

"That would be Todd and Lisa Parker. Very nice people."

"With shitty timing," said Greg.

"Most shitty," agreed Dr. Conner.

"What should I do?" asked Greg.

"Well…they know we're here," said Sheila.

"How?"

"Our car is parked in the driveway."

"Dammit. I told you we should've cleaned the garage out last weekend."

"Greg."

"Huh?"

She crossed her arms. "Answer the damn door."

Greg groaned. "Shit. All right. Shit. I guess… I guess I better." Taking a deep breath, he took a moment to keep out the tremble that wanted to get at him. He turned around, put his hand on the knob, and slowly opened the door.

He put on the best polite face he could muster.

Standing on the other side of the door was the man from earlier and a lovely woman. They also wore polite faces that probably matched Greg's. The woman had a wicker basket of beautiful flowers in the sling of her arm.

"Yes?" he said.

The woman's smile stretched. "Hello! I'm Lisa Parker and this is my husband Todd. We're your neighbors."

Greg nodded. "Oh, hello there." He glanced back at Sheila. She nodded. Turning back to the Parkers, he said, "Please come in."

Lisa's smile grew even bigger. If it kept going like this Greg wondered if it would cover her whole face.

"Thank you," she said with the fervor of a cheerleader.

Greg let them enter, and shut the door behind them. The Parkers noticed Sheila and Dr. Conner. They swapped smiles.

Lisa placed a hand on his arm. "Well, Dr. Conner, it's always nice to see you."

"And, you too, but I'm afraid I was on my way out."

Todd Parker nodded at the medical bag. "Making a house call, Doc?"

Greg almost cringed. "Yes," he said a little too quickly. "It's just allergies, though." He laughed, a much-too-loud bullshit laugh that seemed to reverberate off the walls around them. He wouldn't have been surprised if the others inserted their fingers in their ears.

"Right," agreed Dr. Conner. "Greg here got a fit of the sneezes, but all is fine now."

Lisa put a hand to her chest. "That's good to hear."

"Well, I really must be going," said Dr. Conner. "It was good seeing everyone."

"Swing by the shop soon," said Lisa. "I was told your seeds came in."

Dr. Conner gasped. "Really? Much sooner than I'd expected."

"I told you I'd put a rush on it."

"And did you ever deliver," he said, shaking his head. Dr. Conner glanced at Greg and almost gasped. It was as if he'd forgotten where he was. "Lisa owns a flower shop in town and that's where I get all my lovely flowers and plants from."

"He's my best customer!"

Greg gave them another bullshit laugh and this time, Sheila joined him.

Dr. Conner smiled. "Well, I will let the four of you get acquainted. I must be on my way."

Greg opened the door for him. "Please be in touch soon."

"I most certainly will."

He left. Greg shut the door. When he turned around he

saw three sets of eyes peering at him. He stepped back, pressing himself against the door. He wished he could turn into mist and drift out through the keyhole.

Sheila took the initiative. "Hi there. I'm Sheila Heyman and that's my husband, Greg."

Greg almost slapped his hand on his forehead. He hadn't even introduced himself or Sheila to these people. "Yes. Sorry... I don't know where my brain is."

"Must've *sneezed* it all out," said Sheila.

At first, Greg had no idea what she meant by that. Then he remembered the ridiculous lie he'd whipped up on a whim. "Right. It's probably around here somewhere." He looked around at the floor, pretending it might be down there.

This time it was the Parkers showing their skill at bullshit laughter. To Greg, it sounded much more developed, as if they'd been in this game a lot longer than he and Sheila. He wondered what kind of situations they'd found themselves in where that laughter was all that kept them sane.

Some of his uneasiness went away.

Todd looked at him. "Sorry about earlier. Didn't mean to...you know..."

Greg held up his hands. "Don't even worry about it. That was my fault, completely. I'm a bit shy when it comes to new neighbors. I forget my manners. I hope you understand."

"Of course," he said.

Lisa turned to Sheila. "These are for you."

Taking the proffered basket, Sheila said, "Oh, thank you very much. They're beautiful."

"If you put them in water, they should last you a good two weeks. Just keep the water fresh."

"Listen to her," Todd said. "She's an expert."

"I bet she is!" said Sheila.

The Heymans erupted once again with bullshit laughter.

The Parkers joined them.

When neither couple could keep up the charade any longer, Lisa said, "We just feel like such jerks. You've been living here for a few weeks and we haven't been over to introduce ourselves."

"Oh, that's okay," said Sheila. "The road goes both ways. We could've just as easily come over to your house and said hello. But we didn't."

"We'll accept your apology if you accept ours," said Lisa.

"Deal," said Sheila.

Look at them. Practically girlfriends already.

Greg was already trying to come up with reasons to send the neighbors away.

"Why don't you come in the living room and sit?" said Sheila.

Obviously, she had different ideas.

They followed Sheila into the living room, Greg taking the rear. When Todd asked if it was just the two of them living here, he wanted to shout *I told you so!* at Sheila. This was how it always began. A simple, harmless question in normal circumstances, but theirs was hardly normal.

Sheila must have sensed his thoughts. She gave him a quick apologetic look that the Parkers missed. "No. We have a son, Gabe. He's six."

Todd smiled. "Wow, such a great age."

Sheila smiled back, polite, but Greg recognized the sorrow behind it. "Yeah. He's a handful but always keeps us entertained."

"Where is the little guy? I'd love to say hello."

Greg quickly intervened. "You can't!"

He could tell his sudden outburst caught the Parkers by surprise from the matching looks of concern on their faces.

Greg was quick to attempt putting them at ease. "What I mean is…he's sick."

Lisa frowned. "That's too bad. Is it a cold? Those summer colds are the worst."

Sheila joined in on Greg's fib just as she normally would. Greg and Sheila each played a part in reciting Gabe's story, a watered down version they'd created together years ago. This was her line. "We wish. He has a rare skin disorder. It keeps him from being able to go outside like other kids. The sun and any bright lights are too harsh for him to handle, so he stays in his room mostly."

And like everyone else usually did, the Parkers looked like they'd just accidentally killed their favorite pet: a blend of embarrassment and pity.

As expected, Todd was the first to speak. "God…we're so sorry."

"It's okay," said Greg, taking his cue. "He's also very self-conscious about it, so we let him keep to himself."

"Again…I'm sorry."

Greg smiled an appreciative smile. "It's okay. Other than that, he's a normal boy."

"That's good to hear," said Lisa.

An uncomfortable haze clouded the room. Greg realized no one had sat down yet. He looked at Todd who quickly looked away. He turned to Lisa. She smiled, albeit awkwardly, like she might be constipated. Then he looked at Sheila. She gave him that look she normally would whenever she recognized that he was on the verge of going ape.

So, she quickly turned the conversation to the Parkers. "Do you have any kids?"

Todd cleared his throat. Greg heard the relief in it.

"Yes," Todd answered. "A daughter in high school, Jenny."

Greg was impressed. These two looked remarkably good to have a teenage daughter and he told them so.

Todd nodded. "That's because we aren't old enough. We started young, way young. By mistake."

That would about do it, Greg figured. If anyone was wondering how this moment could have gotten even *more* uncomfortable, he found a way. "Oh jeez…I'm sorry. I didn't mean anything by that."

"It's okay. I didn't take it in a negative way." He laughed.

Greg and Sheila didn't bother with another bullshit laugh.

Lisa clapped her hands together. "Well…we should probably go. We didn't mean to just drop in on you like that. But we wanted to say hello and introduce ourselves."

"You don't have to leave," said Sheila.

"You all were busy with Dr. Conner and probably have a list of other things you need to get to today. We don't want to impose any longer than we already have."

Sheila lowered her head. Greg figured she knew it wasn't worth trying to convince the Parkers otherwise. They already assumed they'd been more of a nuisance than a blessing.

Greg quickly spoke up. "It was our pleasure." Going against his usual practices, he added, "Please, come back again. We'd love to get to know you."

Lisa smiled a genuine smile at the suggestion. "That would be wonderful. We're right next door, so just stop by anytime."

Todd added, "Maybe the four of us can go out one night for dinner or something."

"Eh…we'll see," said Greg. "It'll be tough but we can

work out something, I'm sure."

Sheila looked at him, puzzled. Probably wondering why he was going out of his way to be extra nice to these people. He was wondering the same thing.

"Fair enough," said Todd.

They kept up minimal conversation on their way to the door. There, they said their byes, and Greg let them out. Then he shut the door, and turned around with his hands pressed against his temples and pretending to scream.

Sheila gasped. "I know! That was so awkward."

"I know, God. First this morning I run away like Todd was Godzilla or something when he looked at me, and then this..." He waved his hand around, making a face like he'd bitten into a lemon. "Whatever the hell *this* was."

"I feel awful. I need to do something in return for Lisa. She was so nice, making me that basket of gorgeous flowers and I'm sure I came off as a bitch."

"How do you think I feel? Todd is obviously looking for a pal and I keep throwing a middle finger in his face."

"First chance we get, we'll make it up to them."

Greg hoped so. Usually, this was the kind of reaction he liked to get from their neighbors because it meant they would be left alone afterward. But for whatever stupid reason that Greg couldn't figure out, he didn't want the Parkers thinking of them in that way. He wished he knew why.

CHAPTER 8

Jenny, as always, sat up front with Doug. They were parked outside her house by the front lawn, and she was trying to squeeze out another minute or so with him before having to go in. It was nearly impossible to enjoy it though, thanks to the disgusting smacking sounds of April and Phil making out in the backseat.

Going at it like they're at a Drive-in.

She looked at Doug and caught him watching the show in the rearview mirror.

Okay. You can stop gawking at them.

Glancing at her, he quickly chuckled like it was something silly. "Real subtle, aren't they?"

"Who, them or me?" She leaned over and pressed her lips to his. Her mouth moved over his hungrily, as if she couldn't get enough of his kisses. After a couple minutes she pulled away with a loud smack.

Doug sat behind the wheel, panting, a surprised smile on his face.

That should show them that I can play that game too.

Turning around and ready to gloat, her pride slipped away when she saw April and Phil hadn't even noticed. They were still at it. Jenny wouldn't have been surprised if they started doing it right in the backseat. Jenny turned back and faced the front again. "Doug, don't let Phil get you into any trouble tonight."

Phil pulled away from April. She lunged at him for more, but he dodged her attack. "Why else would we be going out except to get into trouble?"

April smirked. "I don't think so. You boys better behave yourselves."

Doug turned in the seat, putting his back against his door. "You two could come with us. Going to the Atomic Drive-Thru without you two is just gonna make us look like a couple fags anyway."

April laughed. "Well good. Maybe it'll keep all those horny bitches away from you."

"Yep," agreed Jenny. "So go be gay, boys."

Phil leaned closer to April, pouting his lips. "Just come with us."

"Not tonight," she told him. "Unlike the two of you, we're going to try and get some studying done. Jenny's helping me out some. If I fail the exams I'm gonna have to repeat Trig in summer school, and I definitely don't want to do that."

"You'll do fine," said Jenny.

April sat up, pulling her face away from Phil. "And it's girl's night. We've got movies to watch, hair to do…"

"And nails," added Jenny.

Doug snickered. "Maybe you two are the gay ones."

Jenny slugged his arm. "Can a gay girl hit like that?"

Wincing, Doug rubbed the hurt spot. "No, but a dyke can."

Phil cackled a hysterical, hyena-like laugh.

Sitting in the recliner, Todd had a perfect view of the road through the window. He'd been reading an Alan Spencer book when he heard the rumble of Doug's Mustang nearing the house. It had been a poor day for writing, so he'd retreated to his favorite chair, ready to read a bit from a friend's book in hopes of gaining some inspiration to type up his own horrific fiction. It seemed to be working at first, but now that Jenny had been sitting in Doug's car for nearly ten minutes, his anger was starting to smother his creativity.

"You know that makes you look crazy."

Todd jumped at the voice, dropping the book in his lap. It closed. Now he'd lost his place. Looking at his wife's amused reaction calmed him.

"What does? Obsessively spying on my daughter?"

"That. Yes."

"She's been dating Doug for over a year now, and I bet I've only spoken to him half a dozen times."

"That's odd. I've had many conversations with him."

"He won't even look me in the eye."

"And whose fault is that?"

"Not mine. He only comes inside when I'm not home."

"Well...that's because you intimidate him."

Todd raised an eyebrow. "I do?"

Lisa nodded.

It was hard for him not to gloat.

"I recognize that look, Mr. Smug."

Laughing, Todd held his hands out as if confused by what she meant. "Who? Me?"

"Yes, you. That makes you feel good, doesn't it?"

"Eh...maybe a little."

"And you wonder why he doesn't talk to you."

"Maybe I'll flex my muscles next time he's around." He

demonstrated for Lisa, bending his arms in front of his chest and growling.

"Whoa. That's *really* intimidating."

"Think so?"

"Has me shaking in my boots." He enjoyed this about Lisa. How he could just have fun with her. They both knew he lacked in the muscle department. But it was fun to kid around about it.

He looked at her bare feet. "You're not wearing any boots."

"See? Shook so hard they flew off."

Todd laughed. It stopped when he heard two quick thumps of car doors. He returned his gaze to the window and saw Jenny and April with their backs to him. Waving as the car pulled away from the curb.

He liked April but he could tell she'd been having sex with her boyfriend. It was in their body language, how they weren't too shy in expressing their attraction for each other. Didn't matter who might be watching, they occupied themselves with each other as if no one else was around.

He hoped Jenny never got like that.

When the car had gotten far enough away, Jenny stopped waving. April kept at it as if Phil was sitting on his knees, gazing out the rear windshield and waving like a kid being taken away by Grandma.

Finally, she let her arm drop. Her hand smacked a thigh. They started walking toward the front door.

"How could you even breathe with Phil's tongue crammed down your throat like that?"

Laughing, April hitched her shoulders up high, grinning. "Sorry. Was it gross?"

"Disgusting."

"I bet it was. I just can't control myself when I'm around him."

"Obviously."

"He's so dominating. I love it."

"Love what? Being dominated by him?"

"Yeah... I honestly don't think it'd matter who was the dominator."

"Shut up."

"I'm serious. I think I might have a problem."

Though her tone tried to come across as joking, Jenny recognized the sincerity in her voice. She *did* have a problem. Jenny had witnessed examples of his dominating behavior herself. And it had worried her how quickly April had submitted to him. Just like in the car. Had he tried to tug down April's panties out from under her plaid skirt, she would have let him. No question. Also, if he had pursued the act any further...well...Doug definitely wouldn't have been able to pry his eyes away from that rearview mirror.

Jenny sighed. Doug. What was she going to do about him?

"What's wrong?" asked April.

She shrugged a shoulder. "Doug tries to be dominating. It's a little uncomfortable when he does it. But he's quick to back down, which is good."

"Just let him get it out of his system. He'd be a great aggressor."

"I don't *want* an aggressor. What kind of relationship would that be?"

"A *fun* one."

"You're so weird."

"Yeah," said April. "I guess I am."

They mounted the porch. Jenny was about to go in but

April started talking again. She figured it might be best to wait. She didn't want to continue this conversation within earshot of her parents.

"So, you and Doug must be really serious, though. I mean, you've been together for a year. And you've...you know, done stuff."

"I wish it was the kind of serious I'd like it to be."

April looked confused. "What would you call it then?"

What *would* she call it? The word that she thought of wouldn't go away no matter how mean it sounded. Knowing she wouldn't be able to think of anything else, she decided just to say it. "I don't know. It's convenient."

"What?"

"It is what it is."

"What does that even mean?"

Jenny put her hand on the doorknob. "We'll talk about it later. Let's go find something to eat."

Her comment already forgotten, April beamed at the idea of food. She seemed to always want to eat. "Yes. Food is a great idea."

They went inside.

CHAPTER 9

Dinner was done, the afternoon had departed and evening had debarked. And like many other times, Greg was in Gabe's room. He sat on the floor with his son, playing with toys. He enjoyed it, maybe even a smidgeon more than Gabe did. It was a reminder to him that Gabe wasn't entirely different than most kids. Sure, he had his obvious handicaps, but underneath was the heart of an everyday kid.

Gabe couldn't possibly understand how much it hurt Greg knowing that the only friend his son could ever have was him. He was terrified of what might happen if he were to die. Who would play with Gabe then?

Sheila could try but it wouldn't be the same. Gabe had more fun with Greg. Not that he despised playtime with his mother, but she never got into like Greg did. Like now. Flying a toy jet through the air, making the air-splitting sounds and all.

Gabe laughed and clapped as he watched his daddy make the plane twirl, go one way and suddenly turn back and flip some more. Greg loved Gabe's laugh. Even though he could unleash a bone-jarring growl now and then, his laugh was so innocent and sweet. Hearing it, he couldn't help but laugh as well.

"Gabe, come on man. Are you going to play too? You know this jet needs a comrade in the sky."

Gabe held up a boat, letting it hover around the jet. Greg observed this, tilting his head.

"That's a boat, son. Is the boat flying with the jet?"

Gabe confirmed that it was with a grunt and head nod.

"But it's a *boat*."

Gabe didn't seem to mind that, realistically, this could never be a possibility.

Shrugging, Greg decided to go with it. "All right, Gabe. It's your rules. Whatever floats your boat." He laughed. "Get it? Whatever…floats…?"

His son only stared at him. The joke had gone over his head.

"In a couple more years you'll find that hilarious."

Lying on the couch, Sheila struggled to read a ponderous book on parenting. Her eyes skimmed the words, but didn't read any of them. She adjusted her reading glasses, squinted her eyes. She was going to do this. She didn't care how much she disagreed with the points the author tried to make, she was going to read the whole thing.

Sighing, she closed the book.

Who was she trying to kid? She had yet to make her way through an entire book on how to be a better parent. It made her feel awful when she stopped reading them, but even worse while reading. She wanted to read these books, had a tote full of them in the basement, but they made her so *mad*. She wondered if any of these writers even had kids of their own.

The sound of Greg impersonating explosions filtered

down from upstairs. She smiled. Hearing him play with Gabe was better than reading this stupid book anyway. She could lay here and listen for hours. It was more relaxing than listening to music.

Sheila had attempted joining them a few times before, but she could never get into it like Greg. He was like a big kid, so she let him handle all the toy time. She did the cuddling and the reading, and they teamed up on everything else. They each had their areas of expertise when it came to Gabe and stuck with it.

The doorbell startled her.

She sat up with a gasp. The book tumbled off her lap and slapped the floor, cover down.

Now who?

They'd gone from having zero visitors to having three in one day. Confused as to who it could be, she stood up and headed to the door. She checked the peephole and was surprised to see Lisa Parker condensed and flattened inside the lens. Sheila opened the door and was greeted with such a friendly smile that it brought dots of tears to her eyes.

"Hi, Sheila."

"Lisa? Hi. This is a surprise."

"Bad time?"

Sheila did a quick glance over her shoulder for Gabe. Knowing he wasn't back there, she turned back to Lisa and smiled back. "Not at all. Come in?"

"Oh, that's okay. I didn't want to impose, but I did want to see if I could borrow you for a few minutes."

"Borrow me?"

"Yes. For a walk? Every day I walk around the neighborhood. Just a way to get some kind of exercise. Todd usually comes with me, but he's skipping today. Care to join me?"

Lisa hardly looked like someone who required exercise of any kind. She was tight and fit, slim in the right places and curvy in the better ones. But if she wanted some company on a walk, Sheila would love to oblige.

A walk? I can't believe it. Such a sweet gesture.

Then she realized how unfair it would be to leave Greg and Gabe cooped up in here while she went out and had fun. Even though it was just a walk that would probably only last half an hour, she felt guilty her family couldn't be a part of it.

"Sounds like fun, honey."

Sheila looked behind her and saw Greg standing at the foot of the stairs. He was smiling.

"What?" she said.

"If you want, take a walk with Lisa. Have fun."

Sheila felt like she was going to cry. Greg had given her his blessing to go and have fun. *Fun.* With someone who she might be able to be friends with. She loved her husband even more at this moment.

"You're sure you don't mind hanging back with Gabe?"

"Yes, I'm sure. I bet you'd like to get out of the house without the boys, so go on. We'll be fine."

"All right, I will."

Lisa clapped. "Great!"

Sheila walked over to the floor mat where they left their shoes and slid her feet into her sandals. Then she returned to the front door. "Okay, let's go."

"Let the walk begin!" declared Lisa.

Before closing the door, Sheila looked back at Greg. She mouthed him a thank you. Kissing the tip of his finger, he waved it at her. She kissed at him, then shut the door.

It felt great outside. Warm, but with a thin, mild sheet

draped over. The sun was setting, flooding the sky in bright pinks and lavish reds. Frogs and crickets filled the dusk with their steady current of sounds as birds chirped sparsely, settling down for the night.

A wonderful evening.

Sheila even went so far as taking a whiff of the evening air. She sighed at its pleasantness. Not once had she taken a moment to relish the country air. But she would now. She'd make sure of it.

Together, she and Lisa embarked on their walk. Sheila refrained from clicking her heels.

For the first time in years, Greg was alone in the house with Gabe. Usually, it was Sheila who stayed behind while he went out doing the grocery shopping, getting new clothes, whatever needed to be done. He handled it to save Sheila from having to. Sometimes she would have these...episodes. Part panic attack, part something else entirely, that came on at random times. Greg doubted she'd have one while walking with Lisa. She was doing something she was actually excited about.

But still...he worried.

She'll be fine.

But what about Greg? How will he be?

Lonely. He sighed. Seemed really quiet in here.

Walking to the stairs, he put his hand on the bannister. "Gabe?"

He heard the faint grunt of a response.

"I'm gonna step out for a second. Stay in your room, okay?"

An understanding grunt. Even he probably knew it was Daddy's cigarette time.

"I'll be on the back porch. You behave, okay?" Greg stared up the stairs to the shadowy upper floor. He saw a brush of movement. Then two glowing eyes appeared in the darkness. Greg restrained a shudder. After all this time, it still got to him. He doubted he could ever get used to the way Gabe's eyes mirrored light like the reflectors on bicycle tires. This was his son, for better or worse, and he felt guilty for his initial startled reaction.

He liked to pretend Gabe was too young and naïve to sense what his parents thought about. But no matter how much he told himself differently, he knew Gabe was smart enough to identify his parents' reservations. And that hurt him even more.

Gabe waved a slow roll of the fingers.

Greg smiled at his son. "Stay in your room."

A nod, then Gabe backed into the shadows. His eyes had dimmed, but he could still see them.

The *glowing* eyes.

Greg turned and headed into the kitchen. He opened their junk drawer on his way through. His cigarettes sat on top of the clutter. He took the pack, and went out the back door.

Outside, the sweet smell of cut grass and honeysuckle tickled his nose. He liked it. Reminded him of summers as a kid in Tennessee, evenings spent catching fireflies in jars, and playing flashlight tag. He smiled at the memory. One day Gabe would be able to do that with other kids. One day they wouldn't have to find a house lost in the middle of nowhere just so Gabe *could* play outside. And, one day, they'd be able to trust that Gabe's instincts wouldn't take over, so he *could* play outside. As it stood now, they worried too much about Gabe running off to do God only knew what.

The house here in Sunwalk was more communal than they

were used to. They'd lived in dilapidating, singlewide trailers if it had meant seclusion. But, Sheila had liked this house. So had Greg. Betraying their agreement of absolute privacy, they'd moved into a neighborhood. A small one, but it was the most populated area they'd inhabited since before Gabe changed.

Greg fished a cigarette from the pack, rolled it around his fingers, then slipped it between his lips. He put the lighter to it and inhaled a welcomed drag. The smoke rushed into his throat, swirled around his lungs, and came out in a heavy plume when he exhaled. He quickly took another drag. The nicotine went to work on his nerves, trying to settle them.

There was a table with a rotted umbrella bulging up the middle. Ringing the table were a few rusted chairs with flat, and probably uncomfortable, padding. He'd yet to try them out and figured now was a good time to see just how badly worn they actually were.

Pulling one out from under the table, the cushion dipped forward. He pulled it back, then sat. It felt like there was nothing separating his ass from the metal bars of the seat. He didn't care. Leaning back, he propped his feet on the table, and took another drag.

"What brand do you smoke?"

Greg looked toward the fence that divided his property from the Parker's. Todd stood where the fence ended and the woods began. He wasn't alone, either. He'd brought two bottles of beer with him.

Wanted to borrow Sheila for a walk my ass.

They were victims of an intentional effort of the Parkers attempting to bond. Greg wasn't mad, but he should have predicted it.

Greg smiled. "American Spirits. You smoke?"

"On occasion."

"Is this one of those occasions?"

"I'm thinking it just might be. How about I trade you one of these beers for a smoke?"

"That is one hell of a trade. You've just made yourself a deal."

"Glad to hear it."

Todd walked over to the porch and up the rear steps. He set the beer on the table. Greg tossed him the pack, then the lighter. After Todd had one lit, he held the cigarette out, admiring it.

"Wow," he said. "These are good. Smooth."

"No additives. Pure tobacco. And I think they mean it."

Todd laughed. "They've convinced me."

"Not that they won't kill you…"

"Just not as quickly."

"That's one way of putting it." Greg nodded at the chair across from him. "Sit? Plenty of table space for some extra foot proppin'."

"I'd be a fool to pass on that."

"You would."

Todd walked to the available chair and sat. He made a face like he'd sat on something sharp. Greg supposed he wasn't too impressed with the cushion on his chair either. He readjusted himself a couple times, gave up, then leaned back, propping his feet on the table.

Greg exhaled a long drag on his cigarette. "Not the best seating accommodations, I know."

"I've sat in worse."

"That's a damn lie."

Todd laughed. "So what if it is?"

Now Greg laughed. "Won't hurt my feelings. These chairs

were here when we got here."

"I can tell." Todd dragged on the cigarette. "Look..."

"I know what you're about to do and it's not necessary."

"Maybe not, but I've been working myself up to say it since before dinner, and I'm going to say it."

Greg smiled, nodded. "Fair enough. Go for it."

"I want to apologize about earlier. The way Lisa and I just dropped in unexpectedly and threw ourselves at you. I know it was probably a little uncomfortable..."

A little?

"...but we had good intentions, really."

"It's all right," said Greg, and meant it. "I made that comment about you guys not looking old enough to be parents of a teenager, so I guess we're even, right?"

Smiling, Todd nodded once. "All right. We're even."

"You know, the fault was mostly mine anyway. I'll be honest. I'm not used to neighbors welcoming us like this. We're accustomed to having to seclude ourselves away from other people, and I really don't know how to react to it."

"I'm sure you and your family have been through a lot..."

If only he knew.

"...and Gabe can't come outside at all?"

"No...he can't handle the sunlight. And he just really doesn't like going outdoors."

A lie and you know it.

Greg took a deep breath, signaling the real pitiful voice he'd gotten so good at performing. "I guess he's just built himself up such self-consciousness about it all."

"That's sad. I bet the little guy just wants to be a part of the world so bad."

Greg was having a hard time lying to Todd. He found himself wanting to speak truthfully to him, even if it was a tweaked version of it. "He does. We do too. It breaks our hearts. But, you know, we just try really hard to give him a normal life. We play GI Joe, we watch SpongeBob, so it's not all bad."

"Hey, I watch SpongeBob."

"You're good people, Todd."

They each grabbed a bottle and held them up.

"To SpongeBob," said Todd.

"And the Krusty Krab."

They clanged the necks together, then drank.

"So after Todd's third book was optioned for a movie fifteen years ago, we were able to buy our house and have lived here ever since."

"That's so cool," said Sheila.

Lisa smiled. "It was at first. Now it's his job, you know? If you asked Todd, he'd say it's cooler for me than it is for him. I mean, he definitely wouldn't be able to survive without writing, but I think he keeps his fingers assaulting that keyboard these days because it's his nine-to-five. He has deadlines, schedules he keeps to, and always makes sure he turns out a certain daily quota."

"Like a real job."

"Yeah...but that's if you asked *Todd.* But I know he loves every second of it." She laughed. "So what's Greg do?"

"Right now he's trying to find someone hiring."

"Oh, I'm sorry."

"No...don't be. It's fine. We're okay for now. He'll nab a work-for-hire spot soon enough."

"What is he, a hitman?"

Sheila laughed. "Close. He's a freelance artist. He's drawn comics for a lot of the major comic companies and that's his passion. But mostly he draws satirical cartoons for magazines and newspapers."

"Oh wow, that's excellent! Anything I might have seen?"

"Probably, but he's done so many, I can't even think of any right now."

"That's good work. Is he a good artist?"

"He is," said Sheila, thinking of all those portraits he'd done of her. He was *better* than good. "It pays the bills, big time. And he can work from home. These days it's even easier. All he has to do is scan his artwork into our computer and upload it to the company's server. A paycheck is direct-deposited into the bank and he doesn't have to leave the house."

"I bet that helps a lot with Gabe."

Sheila nodded. "Yeah, it keeps us together. And with me selling jewelry on eBay, I never really have to leave the house either."

"What kind of jewelry?"

"*My* kind! It started off as a hobby and somewhat became a career...a very, very part-time career."

"You make it yourself?"

Sheila nodded. "I do. But sometimes I find some ratty old jewelry at a pawn shop or something and fix it up, then sell it for a ridiculously high price."

Lisa laughed.

"It's true. I'm not proud of it, but people usually buy it."

Lisa continued to laugh.

"Lisa Parker! Oh, thank *goodness!*"

Both Sheila and Lisa gasped at the sudden shrill exclamation. A portly lady stood on the far side of the street, waving a stack of papers above her head like a white flag of surrender. She was probably over fifty, and was dressed in a well-worn pink robe with her hair pulled up tightly behind her head.

"Shit!" hissed Lisa, pasting a tight smile on her lips.

Sheila laughed. She was surprised to hear a curse word come from Lisa. She seemed too sweet of a person to cuss.

"Who is that?" asked Sheila.

"Betty Andrews. You know how every neighborhood has at least one older neighbor that sits by her window with binoculars and spies on everyone?"

"Yeah..."

"That's her."

Sheila frowned. The last thing she wanted was to have someone ogling her and Greg's every action. She should have known this little speck of a community wouldn't be spared of someone like Betty Andrews. Lisa was exactly right; *Every* neighborhood had at least one. Why should here be any different?

Betty Andrews hurried across the street, constantly looking from left to right as if a car would suddenly bull down on her. As she got closer, Sheila could make out that the stack of papers in her hand were posters. She glimpsed the dark font of the *Missing* caption at the top of the page, one that she had seen so many times over the last four years. A picture was printed underneath but she couldn't tell what it was of.

By the time Betty Andrews reached them, she was so winded that her face matched the pink hue of her robe. "Lisa...have you seen my Posey?"

"Oh! No...sorry Ms. Andrews, I haven't."

"Oh pooh...he ran off sometime last night and hasn't come back."

Sheila didn't know who Posey was, but she thought he was probably very smart. "Who's Posey?"

"My *baby,*" said Ms. Andrews.

She held up one of the fliers so Sheila could see the picture. She supposed it was a dog, but it looked more like a rat that had been eaten at least once already and puked up. Sheila fought the grimace trying to wrinkle her face.

That is the ugliest damn thing...

"He's very sensitive," added Ms. Andrews. "And I'm sure he misses his Mommy."

"I haven't seen him," said Lisa.

"Neither have I," said Sheila.

Ms. Andrews pouted, her bottom lip poking out and quivering. "Oh...okay..."

"But if I do," said Lisa, "I'll be sure to let you know."

"Oh, that's wonderful, thank you! He's been humping just about every damn-thing he comes in contact with lately. He probably ran off looking for a bitch in heat. He'll come back when he's gotten all his ruffles out."

Sheila and Lisa shared a look. Both held in their laughter.

"So Lisa, introduce me to your friend."

Lisa nodded. "Right. This is Sheila Heyman. She just moved in next door to us with her husband and son."

"They finally rented that place out, huh?"

"Yep," said Sheila. "To us."

"About damn time we get another family in the neighborhood. I thought that place would never get filled. Just renting, I assume?" She cocked an eyebrow as if the idea of renting a house was as accepted as breaking wind in church.

"Sorry to say," said Sheila, nodding. She felt Lisa's elbow prod her. Looking at Lisa, she saw the amusement on her face and nearly laughed herself.

"How do you like it?" asked Ms. Andrews.

"The neighborhood or the house?"

Lisa made a snorting sound as she struggled valiantly not to laugh.

If Ms. Andrews heard her, she gave no indication. "Well...both, I guess."

"They're both great. Everyone has treated us so nicely."

Ms. Andrews nodded, a satisfied expression on her face that showed that was the answer she wanted to hear. "That's just what I like about it too. Everyone *is* nice. You seem nice also, so you'll fit in fine. How old's your boy?"

"Six."

"Oh, such a wonderful age! I have a granddaughter that age. She comes and visits all the time. You should bring your son by!"

Dammit.

Sheila felt a slight tremor of panic. She was thankful Greg hadn't been here to hear Ms. Andrews. Invites like that always got him riled up, usually sputtering through words while trying to concoct some bogus explanation as to why Gabe couldn't possibly "come by".

The skin disease usually did the trick.

To save herself from the routine this time, she said, "We'll see what we can do."

Ms. Andrews seemed delighted with the answer. A smile stretched across her pudgy face. "That would be just swell. Maybe I'll have my daughter bring her by sometime this week!"

Sheila wondered if her face displayed the dread she felt.

Ms. Andrews whistled like someone who'd just heard a price way too high. "Guess I better get back on the hunt." Squinting, she checked the sky. "Getting dark. When I find that mutt, I'm going to give him a swift kick to the hindquarters, I swear to you. If you see him anywhere, let me know."

"We will," said Lisa.

Ms. Andrews nodded, then squeezed between them. She continued on her journey, leaving them on their own.

After she was out of hearing range, Lisa turned to Sheila. "Like a bitch in heat?"

Sheila laughed. "I nearly peed myself when she said that."

Laughing, they headed back toward home.

Our home.

The thought brought a smile to Sheila's face. A nice warm feeling, and the first time she'd felt like they actually had a home since Gabe was two years old.

But, lying dormant underneath those pleasant sensations was that persistent wedge of dismay. And like always, it reminded her that her good mood wouldn't last.

CHAPTER 10

Mommy and Daddy were asleep. They'd done the thing where they took off their clothes and rolled around the bed while Mommy made those noises. It sounded like she was laughing and being hurt all at once. He didn't like her making those noises, but she didn't seem to mind and Daddy liked it too.

After his parents had finished, lying in bed hugging, Gabe waited a little longer before sneaking out of his room. He could see in the dark like it was the day, so he didn't have to turn on any lights. He never needed to. He liked the night, liked how he could go wherever he wanted and be hidden at the same time.

They hadn't tied his hands to the bed tonight. He'd pretended the medicine made him go to sleep like it used to. It still made him a little drowsy, but that was about it. He snuck downstairs, hooked a left and hurried into the kitchen. He'd watched Daddy go out this way earlier to smoke a cigarette and sit out there talking to someone. He recognized the scent as being from the man that had visited them earlier today. Not the doctor; this man had a pleasant smell, a *nice* smell. Gabe could always tell the nice ones from the mean ones.

The doctor was hard to figure out. He seemed like a nice one, but also had qualities of the mean ones. He didn't think he liked the doctor. But Mommy and Daddy did, and that made Gabe scared.

And, being scared made him hungry, the kind of hungry he didn't like. It made him do things, like disobeying his parents' rule of not going outside. But he *had* to. It was the only way he could get what would stop the sharp, jabbing pains in his stomach. He felt awful he had to do it, but he'd learned it was best not to fight the hunger. If he didn't eat, the pain would get worse and make him cranky.

He had trouble getting his fingers around the doorknob. They were too long and sharp which made it hard to grab anything without corners. Finally, he got just enough of a grip to make the knob turn. The door popped open, the hinges groaning. Gabe spun around, staring at the pale shape of the kitchen doorway.

Listening.

He focused his ears, angling them toward the stairs. Tuning out everything around him, he could hear the subtle snoring of his mommy, and the slow, dragging breaths of his daddy from all the way upstairs. Both still slept. Neither had heard the sound of the door.

Gabe went outside, leaving the door slightly agape so he wouldn't have to risk making more racket on his way in. The cool night air floated over him. He loved being outside. He just stood there, letting the breeze stir his hair, feeling it on his skin.

After a while, his hunger urged him to move. He scampered alongside the house, moving in silence. As he was about to enter the woods, he caught a scent. He stopped. Raising his nose into the air, he sniffed.

Smelled like Daddy's cigarettes. But there was something else mixed with it. Something sweet. Fruity. Sometimes Mommy smelled like that when she rubbed her smell-good cream on her skin.

Then he heard laughter. It was a girl.

Crouching, he moved to the fence. The smell was stronger here, but trailed away from him, coming from somewhere else. He could see the neighbor's gigantic house. To Gabe, it could have been a castle, as amazed as he was by its large size and fascinating design. It was dark over there except for a square of light shining down from a window on the top floor. More laughter and Gabe ducked down, squatting. He hunkered down on all fours and scurried across the grass to a large tree that supplied him plenty of shadow to hide in. He stayed there, squatting, his arms held tightly together between his legs with his hands flat on the ground. If he heard anything that he didn't trust, he could spring up and run. He could sprint very fast and would be long gone before anyone even realized he'd been there at all.

A brush of movement at the window pulled his gaze up. His breath snagged in his throat.

A girl—older than him, but still younger than Mommy was the one making the smell like Daddy's cigarettes because she was putting one in her mouth like Daddy did. That faint fruity smell returned. He sniffed at the air again, taking longer and longer whiffs and holding them in for a while. It made his chest feel funny, his stomach tingly. The girl was the source of that smell too. He couldn't tell what she looked like since all he could see was her back and long dark hair. He wanted to see her better, but to do that he'd have to be closer.

In the open.

Before he could decide the best way to see her better, he heard something rustling in the yard, followed by the scuttle of little feet moving through the grass. He looked to the back of the yard, where the light couldn't reach.

And there it was.

A tiny critter.

He licked his lips. It hadn't taken him anywhere near as long to find food as he had thought it would.

The little creature yelped, panting. Gabe prepared to lunge.

Jenny hung her arm out the open window and flicked the ashes off her cigarette. She sat on the sill as if it were a bench, slightly bent forward with her back brushing the bottom of the window. It was uncomfortable sitting like this, but it was worth it so the smoke could go out.

A cool breeze drifted against her back, giving her a small chill. She might have to put on a long-sleeved shirt. Wearing only shorts and a tank top, her skin was pebbled with goose flesh. She looked like a damn raw chicken.

Gross.

"I can't believe you're smoking," said April from the floor. She'd been flipping through a magazine before pausing to offer this unsolicited advice. "When did you pick *that* up?"

Jenny took another drag. The smoke hit her throat like foggy spikes. Thankfully, she held in the cough the smoke nearly triggered. That would have been great to do in front of April. "Well…when my dad used to smoke all the time, he was incredibly happy. But when he quit he became really moody, until he relapses. Then he's happy again. So, I figure if I smoke, not only will I always be happy but I'll never be moody."

"How's that working for you?"

"Not one bit. I'm the same moody bitch I've always been."

"Then why do you still do it?"

"I'm hooked."

Laughing, April tossed the magazine aside. "You don't have anything to be *not* happy about."

"I keep telling myself the same thing…"

"So, what's up with you lately?"

"What do you mean?"

"You've been…I don't know…weird."

"Weird?"

"Yeah…weird. That's the only way I can think to describe it. Off? Not yourself? Is that better?"

"I'm not meaning to be."

"Well, you are. Moping around like someone strangled your kitten or something. What's your deal?"

"I've had a lot on my mind."

"You're seventeen. What the hell could possibly be on your mind? I'll be eighteen next month and I can honestly say that *nothing* is on my mind."

Jenny laughed. "I believe it."

"So, why are you stressing yourself out so much?"

"I'm at a point in my life where I'm trying to decide what I want to do with it."

"Again, you're seventeen! We graduate in a couple weeks, we have the summer, and our beach trip…"

"So?"

"So…you have time to think about it."

"Not hardly."

"I'm saying, you've got plenty of things ahead of you, and there's no need to weigh yourself down with anything else.

You don't need to figure it all out in a couple weeks."

"You're right. But what do I do after summer when I've started at the community college? Where do I go from there?"

"How the hell should I know? You shouldn't even be letting this stuff bother you until this time next year. Let's just focus on our summer. Graduation, and then our trip, followed by the rest of the summer. Just you, me, Doug, and Phil, partying at the lake, the mountains, or wherever the hell else we feel like. Okay?"

Laughing, Jenny raised the cigarette to her lips. She noticed it had stopped burning and the ashes were a hardened point. It looked like a cigarette bullet.

"It's Doug, isn't it?"

Jenny nearly fell backwards out the window. She slapped her hands on the sill to stop the plunge. The cigarette, broken, fell to the floor. "What?" Kneeling down on the carpet, she began picking up the shards of paper and tobacco and the charred tip.

"You don't want to be with Doug anymore."

It wasn't a question, but a statement spoken as a fact.

"I do..."

April looked at her as if waiting for her to continue. She slightly shook her head. "But...?" She reached forward and grabbed the bottle of water she'd been drinking. Twisting off the cap, she raised it to her lips.

"But I think he might have cheated on me."

April choked on the water. "Why...do...?" She coughed, making a sound that someone drowning might make, and tried again. "Why do you think that?"

Wondering if she should even tell April, she sighed. "He doesn't...kiss the same." She looked at her friend and saw a brief flicker of something on her face. It was subtle, but she'd known April long enough to have learned her markers. The slight arch of an eyebrow, the quick deflection of her glance.

Maybe April had the same suspicions.

"What do you mean by that?" she asked.

Jenny stood up, the ruined cigarette in the cup of her hand. "There's not that same kind of feeling behind it anymore. Before we got all physical, he acted like he wanted me for *me*, but now the only thing he seems to want me for is sex."

April's expression slowly changed, from engrossed to confused. Her mouth went slack as her eyes started to cross. "You lost me."

Of course I did! My paranoid head is always looking for something that isn't there. Maybe I'm just getting used to Doug's kisses.

Or he might be getting bored.

She hoped he wasn't bored. If he wasn't cheating on her now, boredom just might be what led him to it.

Maybe I can shake things up. Do something to catch him off guard.

Like what?

She wondered about that. She had no clue. She thought about asking April for some suggestions, but decided not to. For some reason, she suddenly didn't want to talk about her sex life anymore. And that was strange, since April was her best friend, and had been since the eighth grade.

"Are you *happy* with Doug?" asked April.

Groaning, Jenny walked over to her desk and tore a piece of paper out of her notebook. She dropped the cigarette's remains onto its sleek white surface, then wadded the page into a ball. She dropped it in the trash on the way back to the window. Before answering April, she snatched another cigarette from the pack and quickly lit it, inhaling deeply.

"That's a loaded question," she said, finally.

"Well, unload it."

Jenny laughed softly. "Well." Where to begin? Another groan, then she said, "I've been beating myself up a lot here lately, thinking about the future."

"I can tell. And, I've told you to knock it off. You can think about the future *in* the future."

"But what if I've been trying to build my future around a guy who doesn't even want to be with me like that? I'm planning college, a job and my life for the next year with Doug. What if I've been doing all this planning for nothing?"

"I doubt it's for nothing..."

"What if he's planning on breaking up with me this summer?"

"You think he will?"

Jenny pointed at April. "Why? Did you hear something? Did Phil tell you Doug was thinking about it?"

April closed her eyes, shook her head. "No. Phil hasn't said anything like that."

"The way you said that..."

"No, I didn't mean anything by it. I was shocked you said it."

"Oh."

"You worry too much. You didn't used to be like this."

"Great. Now you're saying I've changed."

"No... I'm saying you're stressed and it needs to stop. I'm sure Phil would tell me if Doug was going to break up with you, just like he'd tell me if he was cheating on you."

"No he wouldn't. That's a guy thing."

"I'd tell Doug if you were cheating on him."

"That's good. I'd tell Phil if you were cheating on him.

See? *That's* a girl thing."

April was about to say something else when a tumult of agonizing shrieks and yelps interrupted her. They sounded as if they were coming from right below her window.

Jenny's muscles went taut and cold. "What the hell was that?"

"I don't know. It sounded terrible!"

Frightened, April got up and ran over to the window. Jenny stood up and turned around. Both girls planted their hands on the sill and leaned out, scanning the yard.

"It sounded like a dog," said Jenny.

"How could you tell?"

"We've got to go see."

"No. We should wake your dad up and tell him."

"The hell we will. I've been smoking. He'll smell it all over me."

"That's fine. I'll shut the window, you go take a shower and we'll forget we even heard it."

"What if it's hurt?"

"I'm sure it is."

"It might need our help."

"You'll have to wake up your dad for that too. We can't help anything, so forget it."

April made sense. A lot of it. "Okay," Jenny said. "Let me change my clothes and brush my teeth real fast. Then we can go wake him up."

"Shit...okay."

"Keep an eye on things," she said as she rushed to her dresser. She pulled open a drawer, found a pair of lounge pants, and grabbed them. She quickly pulled off her shorts. She checked to make sure April wasn't watching her; thankfully she wasn't or else she'd probably tease her for not wearing any panties. Probably say something like,

"Wearing that for me?"

April didn't swing like that, but she'd surely give her a hard time.

Jenny crammed her legs into the pants and hiked them up to her hips. She opened another drawer, found a long T-shirt that used to be her dad's and swapped it for her tank-top. It hung down to the middle of her thighs. She loved sleeping in his shirts. They were like night gowns on her.

Wearing this made her feel better, warmer and more decently clad.

April turned to her, grimacing.

Jenny rubbed a hand across the shirt. "Yeah...it's a little big. It's one of my dad's."

"Not that..." April looked outside again. "I *hear* something out there."

"What?"

When April faced her again, she was pale. "Sounds like something's being eaten."

"Eaten?"

"Yeah...and there's grunting."

That was all Jenny needed to hear to send her marching out of her room. She went straight to the bathroom, dabbed her toothbrush in toothpaste, and quickly scrubbed her teeth. When she had a mouthful of foam, she leaned over and spat in the sink. While she was down there, she sucked in water, swished, then spat that out as well. Blowing on her hand, she took a few whiffs of her breath. She couldn't smell any smoke. Hopefully, neither would her dad.

And hopefully he wouldn't be pissed at her for waking him up.

CHAPTER 11

Todd heard footsteps behind him and turned to find both Jenny and April following him through the yard. He aimed the flashlight at them. They raised their arms to shield their eyes from its glare.

"I told you to stay on the porch with your mom," he said.

Lisa stood on the porch, slightly bent over, her arms hugging her stomach. "It's okay."

He looked at her, then turned and scowled at his daughter. "I'd rather you stay up there."

"I want to stay with you," said Jenny.

"Me too," said April.

The girls stood together, their arms lightly touching. His daughter had on an old shirt of his. He'd been wondering for weeks where that shirt had gotten to. Jenny had always been like that, though. Taking shirts from his dresser to either sleep in or lounge around in, ever since she was a little girl. He was glad she'd never outgrown doing it. But he would have to take this shirt back from her. It was one of his favorites. A few years ago a retro horror T-shirt company had created an entire series of apparel based off his books. Not using the original covers, they'd taken liberties and created their own designs. This one was from *Flesh Flood*, the shirt depicting a scene where a flooding river of flesh was devouring an entire city like *The Blob*.

Not one of his favorite books after all these years, but he did love the shirt.

"Fine," he said. "Just stay real close. There's no telling what you heard. I don't want to risk anything."

"Okay," said Jenny.

She and April hustled to him, bumping against his side.

"Not *that* close," he said.

"Sorry," said Jenny.

She scooted over, granting him a hair's width of space. Facing forward, he shined the light this way and that. A tunnel of light cut into the blackness. Lit in its dim glow, he saw tops of bushes, the wooden fence and...

Movement at the back of the fence.

"There," he said.

He jogged toward the fence. On his way, he stepped in something wet and his feet slipped, nearly making him fall. He held his arms out to balance. As he was about to warn the girls to mind the wet spot he heard them shriek, followed by two wet thuds of them hitting the ground.

Todd stopped running. He looked back and saw they had both landed on their rumps. They were leaned back with their legs raised up, bent at the knees, wincing and groaning. Their feet must have slipped right out from under them, dropping them straight down.

Before checking on them, he waved the light at the woods where the fence ended. The branches were swaying, but no wind blew. Whatever he'd seen had run through there.

"What is this shit all over me?" That was April.

"Gross, it's slimy..." Jenny.

Todd walked over to them, training the light on their legs. Jenny's pants were sodden around the ankles, her slippers soaked and dirty. At first glance, Todd thought it was mud, but as he got closer, he realized the color wasn't brown.

It was red.

Blood?

Looking down at his feet, he saw his white Nikes were spattered with it and there were streaks across the cuffs of his pants. He turned the light on April. She was holding her hands in front of her, aghast and grimacing. Her fingers were slick and dripping as if she'd dipped them into crimson-colored honey.

"Dad, what *is* this stuff?" Jenny asked.

"Get up, Jenny. Slowly, so you don't fall again."

"Something's under me..."

"What is it?"

"I don't know," she said, angling up to her knees. "It's lumpy." She reached behind her, patting at the ground. She paused, her face scrunching up, then giving way to a frown. "Oh God..."

"What?"

"It's furry..."

Todd reached down, offering her his free hand. "Here." She took it, and he hoisted her to her feet in one quick pull. Now *his* hand felt sticky and cold. Checking the seat of her pants, he saw they were drenched in red, adhering to her buttocks and the backs of her thighs.

April screamed.

Todd whipped around. April was trying to squirm away,

but kept slipping in the mess as she tried to crab-walk away. He realized the hand holding the flashlight had been wavering back and forth as he'd tended to Jenny and April had gotten a good look at what Jenny had been sitting on.

By this time, Lisa had run over from the porch. She was helping April get up, having trouble getting her to stand on her kicking feet.

As April's shrieks reverberated through the night, Todd stared in sickened shock at the mangled remains of a dog. It looked like an animal slipper filled with raw meat to the point it had burst: clumps of fur and bone, protruding dagger points of a broken ribcage. A hollowed out stomach and skinny ropes of entrails lay flattened on the ground between its tiny legs. Although the poor guy had been torn apart, he still recognized what was left of its face.

It was Ms. Andrews' dog, Posey.

"Shit," he muttered.

CHAPTER 12

"We're going crazy over there," said Greg.

Henry filled his glass to the rim with bourbon, his shaking hand causing some to spill.

"This is exactly how it started last time." Greg puffed on a cigarette. Although he hadn't asked for permission to smoke in his home, Henry was allowing it. "It was cats, then. Somehow, he kept sneaking out and snatching up cats from the neighborhood. He's not an evil kid, Dr. Conner, he just gets this hunger..."

"It's an instinct, a need."

"Whatever it is, he's not a bad person. He just wants to eat."

"How did you get him to stop with the cats?"

"We started locking him up. Strapping him down and giving him drugs to help him sleep, tranquilizers. We also worked out a deal with the local butcher and he would...order us a pig."

"Like a shoulder?"

"No, like a whole damn pig. Not dead, a live one. He would deliver it to the house in a small cage. We'd pay him handsomely, and he'd be on his way. When it got dark, we'd let the pig run loose in the backyard so Gabe could stalk and kill it."

"Gabe has to kill?"

"I don't know... I don't like to think that he does."

Henry shrugged. "Maybe he does, maybe he doesn't."

"Like what we were telling you about our last house, with the two Social Workers? Someone thought we were abusing Gabe. Apparently they'd seen the toys in the yard and had heard Gabe's growls and screeches. Hell, maybe we *were* abusing him, keeping him shackled up like a damn prisoner."

"Chains?"

"Not really...restraints...but not chains...not yet, anyway."

"Ah. I see."

Henry poured another glass just as full as the last. He couldn't believe he'd already finished the first one. His lips tingled as the bourbon flowed between them.

"When they showed up at the house, there wasn't much that we could do *but* let them in. By law, they could be there."

"What'd you do?"

"We let them see Gabe like they wanted. We knew how he'd react."

"And?"

"He felt threatened."

"And retaliated?"

"He killed them."

"Of course he did. A stranger comes into his habitat, threatening to remove him from it, naturally he will strike back."

"We couldn't stop him, Doc. He was out of control. He didn't let up until he was full."

An uncontrollable killing machine. At six years old. Fantastic.

Henry was partly fearful but mostly intrigued. This little kid was fascinating him more and more. To single-handedly dispatch two adults was very impressive for anyone, especially someone Gabe's size.

He's big for his age, though.

Not *that* big.

"What the *hell* are we going to do?" said Greg.

"Nothing for now. Calm down."

"How can I? Ms. Andrews is on an insane search to find out what could've killed her damn dog. We've seen her walking through the woods, and the Parkers have heard that some of the other neighbors have found her in their backyards, snooping around. She's been at it for two days!"

"Police said it was coyote that did it. Wandered down from the hills looking for food. We don't have anything to worry about. Not yet, anyway."

"Level with me right now," said Greg, jabbing his cigarette in the air with each enunciation. "Why is he like this? Why must he kill? And don't give me that bullshit story about unexpected side-effects, either. I want to know *all* about it."

Henry sighed. What was the point in keeping quiet at this stage? Just like him, Greg and Sheila were crucial parts of this too. In fact, if he really wanted to, he might even say the three of them were the last of the project. They were certainly the only remaining proof it had ever existed.

And Gabe, of course...they couldn't forget Gabe.

Henry downed what was left of his drink. His brain felt like it was resting on a pillow of cotton. "Dr. Vanhoy and I had been working on the formulas for close to a decade. He always did his work more by the book than me. I was the one who took chances, ignored policies and safety measures. Did everything the wrong way, I guess, but I always got results. Needless to say, he wasn't too eager to tolerate my methods, but he permitted them. The formulas I came up with were so farfetched that there was no way they could work, and for the longest time they didn't. Then one day, by accident, we created a life form."

"What do you mean by *that?*" The color drained from Greg's face.

"It was an organism that needed a host but could also reproduce on its own. It was Dr. Vanhoy's idea to implant it into a monkey. We removed one of the primate's internal eggs, implanted some DNA we spliced from the organism, and returned it to the mother's womb. And we monitored its process. It died. They always died, for the longest time."

"Did *any* survive?"

"Oh yes...two of them. We named one Barney and kept him locked in a cage until he became too hostile and we had to put him down."

An image of Barney emerged in his head, no matter how much he tried to fight it. He had an elongated snout, four sets of fangs, and talons on his hands and feet. There were beady yellow eyes the color of urine, and it had a ravenous hunger that could never be satiated.

"You said there were two?" asked Greg.

Henry was thankful Greg started talking again, effectively distracting him from his memories of Barney. "Yes...there have been only two that have survived long enough to document."

"Who was the other one?"

"Gabe."

Greg walked over to the bar and dropped his cigarette into the glass Conner had been drinking out of. "If I didn't think you could actually help us, I would kill you now for all the pain you've caused my son. Hell, for all the pain you've caused my *family*."

Henry picked up the glass, swirling it around as he stared at the dampened cigarette filter. The ash had turned clumpy in the small dabs of bourbon left in the glass. He slammed it down so hard it cracked. "Don't you dare make me out to be the villain here! You put your name—your *real* name—on that goddamn dotted line at the bottom of that contract of your own free will. I didn't put a gun to your head and force you to do it. You threw yourself at my feet, subjecting yourself to whatever I chose to attempt as long as it gave you a child."

"We wanted to be parents, not ghouls having to live in the dark, housing a monster!"

"And you did what had to be done, just like me, just like my team. You sold your soul. I did too. Now we're all in this hell together!"

Greg's arm shot across the countertop, smacked Henry's chest, and gripped a handful of his shirt. He jerked him forward. "We signed up for a baby…*not* for this. Did you know this would happen? All the time, *did you know?*"

"There were possibilities and risks, of course. That's why it's called an experiment. We would have kept going until we got it right…but you know what happened. It was a chance I was willing to take, and so were you."

Greg fumed, his nostrils hissing. His eyes were narrowed to slits and his mouth had crunched up into a smirk of pure rage. At this very moment, Henry was more frightened of him than he had been of Gabe during their introduction.

Henry continued, "We're all in this together, knee deep in science fiction bullshit."

Greg huffed.

"We've got to figure out where we go from here. What's next?"

Greg released Henry's shirt, shoving him away. "That's your call. You're the reason we're here, in this town, in this neighborhood."

"You'll work with me no matter what on this, correct?"

"We've come this far..."

"Good. That's good to hear."

Very good to hear, indeed.

Henry needed their trust. He didn't quite know what he had planned just yet, but he could feel the inklings of an idea starting to sprout somewhere inside his head.

He was becoming convinced that a phone call to Hawthorne was definitely in order.

CHAPTER 13

Betty Andrews skulked through the woods. She'd brought a walking stick with her, and not for aid. Instead, she'd been poking bushes and shrubs with its narrow tip, pushing back twigs and leaves to see the other side. She wasn't looking for any one particular thing, just a clue of some kind or other. And any clue would do.

If she had to, she'd use this godly stick as a weapon. Hopefully on whoever had murdered her poor Posey. She did not agree the culprit was a coyote like the police had insisted it was. They'd never had any problems with those mutts before, so why now, and with her poor Posey having to suffer for it?

I'll find ya, wherever you are. I'll find ya and stomp your bastard ass good.

The tragedy had occurred in the Parkers' backyard, but she didn't suspect them of any involvement. She'd known that family long enough to know they were incapable of such grisly violence. Actually, they were about the only neighbors she did trust. Funny how a man who wrote such bloody books could be the nicest man she'd ever met, with a peach of a wife and a gorgeously sweet daughter, to boot. She liked the Parkers and was glad to call them her neighbors.

But, these new people, the Heymans, she didn't like them, didn't trust them, and she didn't want to get to know them. Lisa Parker had taken a shine to the Heyman woman, but Betty had detected something just beneath the surface of that attractive smile of hers.

She was hiding something.

And not just any little something, it was huge. Betty recognized it in the woman's posture, in her eyes and facial expressions.

Hiding something big!

That was why she'd steered her search here, behind the Heymans' house.

A new family shows up and soon afterward my Posey is murdered?

Too convenient to be a coincidence, if you asked her.

Betty had spent the last two days investigating, however she wasn't ready to make a citizen's arrest on the Heymans just yet. She needed more proof. She'd ascertained the blood trail had led away from the Parkers and into the woods. A few feet beyond the treeline, it suddenly stopped.

Why?

The police weren't concerned enough to figure out why, but she certainly planned to. It was as if whatever had been soaked in Posey's blood had suddenly taken flight. The one detective, Garner she thought his name was, had suggested an owl might have attacked Posey, mistaking it for a mouse.

Please.

Shaking her head, she thought that had been about the dumbest thing she'd ever heard. Posey was a small dog, but he wasn't *that* small. Even a blind-as-shit bat could tell the difference.

Stupid detectives. Only out here to waste my time and theirs; whatever it takes to get that paycheck.

Betty wished she'd had her wits about her that day. But with Posey's slaying and subsequent burial and funeral, she'd been a wreck. Since her husband Tom had died four years ago from the cancer, all she'd had to keep her company was Posey. She'd needed valium to sleep that night. But the minute her eyes had opened yesterday morning, she'd had a plan: to start her own investigation.

And the theory she'd come up with this morning, while drinking her coffee, had nearly knocked her right out of her recliner. The reason why the blood trail had suddenly vanished was because the culprit was no longer on the ground. But it hadn't flown away like Garner had suggested.

It'd been picked up.

Yes. Lifted off the ground and carried away.

I have a granddaughter his age, Betty remembered saying to Sheila Heyman.

The little boy. She was so convinced he'd slaughtered Posey that it would take a miracle to dissuade her. She hadn't bothered phoning Detective Garner to tell him her idea. He'd have laughed at her. She would need substantial proof to make him believe.

So, Betty planned to get something substantial for him.

And here she was, in the woods behind the Heymans' house, a tree shielding her from anyone seeing her. Despite the overgrowth of the tree, she could see just fine. Everything seemed quiet, almost desolate. Their grass was a little high and could use a good trimming. She saw the well-house, a shed and a side door at the rear corner that must open to the basement.

The house itself looked similar to most others in Sunwalk, with the exception of the Parkers' home, of course. It was a two-story structure, with a huge picture window in the front and a narrow wraparound porch that led around to the back. The back porch had a table and some chairs on it, and at the bottom of the steps were two tin trash cans.

Nothing about it suggested a killer lurked inside.

She frowned.

Maybe she was wrong in her suspicions. Just because they were new to the neighborhood, that didn't automatically make them evil.

What am I doing here?

Sighing, Betty Andrews admitted defeat. She jabbed the walking stick against the ground, heaved another sigh, then turned to leave.

And noticed the dots of blood on the ground.

She froze.

Droplets of all sizes started just an inch from the stick's point, scattering across the brown leaves. A dripped trail led to the border of the Heymans' backyard. She could even see a small dab on a blade of grass whenever it waved in the breeze. The sun would catch the grass just right and there it was.

She raised her head. The Heymans' house was straight ahead.

Bastard asses. Got you now, don't I?

Slowly, she crept into the yard, leafy branches sliding across her arms as she exited the woods. Wearing a pair of bright green capris, she could feel the grass tickling her calves. It made her skin feel itchy. She wished she would have worn something less eye-catchingly vivid. Her white shirt and bright pants reflected the sunlight like cotton mirrors.

Too late to go back and change now. She was here and she wanted to keep going.

More drips of blood farther ahead. Hardly noticeable to most, but Betty spotted them right away. If she hadn't been so intently looking, she'd have probably passed right by.

She approached the trash cans. If she could do it without making a lot of racket, she wanted to go through them. Never know what she might find. People don't just put their skeletons in the closet; they also stuff them in bags and add it to the garbage. Out of sight, out of mind. But, if there was something in there, she wanted to find it.

If she could wait until they wheeled the can to the street, she could legally snoop through it. Wouldn't be a thing the Heymans could do about it, either.

She noticed another tiny splat on the bottom step. She bent over to study it. Sure enough. Blood.

Posey's blood.

Her jaw tightened as her teeth ground together. She felt a dull throb in her gums.

Her foot landed on the step. Another one. She kept going until she was on the porch, putting each foot down softly. Heel first, she rolled her foot forward to the toes. It kept her tread light and silent.

There were plenty of windows on this side of the house. None of them were open, the blinds down. The door had many tiny panes of glass, all blocked by a curtain. Nearly groaning her annoyance, Betty looked up. The upper story was closed up too!

How was she supposed to peer through a window if all of them were covered?

She couldn't. But, she could listen. There was an idea. Slightly crouching, her shoulders hiked up high, she tiptoed to the door. She leaned to the side, bending at the waist.

As her ear neared the door, it opened.

Betty loosed a startled gasp. Sheila did the same on her way out. Both women jumped back a couple steps.

Water plopped on the porch. Betty saw suds, bubbles popping across the slippery spots. When she looked at Sheila, she saw she was hugging a plastic bucket, a sponge caught between two yellow-gloved fingers.

Sheila rushed forward, coming outside and snatching the door shut. "Ms. Andrews? What are you doing here?"

A hand to her chest, Betty tried to catch her breath. "I could ask you the same question."

"What are you talking about?"

"Going to wash up something, I see."

Sheila glanced around, as if looking for others. "That's my business."

"It's my business now."

"I beg your pardon?"

"I followed my poor Posey's bloodstains all the way over here. I see there's even some on your porch."

"This is private property, Ms. Andrews. I would like to think you'd be mindful of that. What gives you the right to sneak around my home?"

"Private property my fanny. I have plenty of right. Tell me why you have a blood trail in your yard. Why is there blood on your porch and the steps? And what are you doing with that bucket? Were you about to clean it up? Who are you covering for?"

"My son was outside playing and cut himself, that's all. It's my business, not yours."

"Cut himself, huh? The blood's too dry for it to have happened recently. So, are you sure he just didn't get my Posey's blood everywhere after he killed him?"

"Ms. Andrews, my son is six years old..."

"Show me this cut. I want to see it. If it's there like you say, I'll leave you alone and apologize. If it's not, I'm calling the police and showing them the blood before you get it all cleaned up."

Sheila's face went dark, a dirty look wrinkling her forehead and tapering her eyes. "You are *not* getting near my son. I suggest you leave right now, before something happens."

"Did you threaten me?" Betty raised a finger to her chin.

"Take it how you want, but if you try to get near my son, you'll find out for sure."

"You *did* threaten me." Betty was aghast by Sheila's nerve. "All right, fine. You think you're scaring me with all that talk? Think again! I'm going to see if the little shit really does have a cut. Out of my way!" She started for the door, ready to shove Sheila aside if she needed to.

Hot, soapy water splashed Betty in the face. It doused her hair, flooding down the collar of her shirt. The water streamed over her gigantic breasts and seeped through her shirt. It stung her eyes like accidentally getting some shampoo in them while washing her hair. She could still see, but her vision was blurry. Sheila looked smeared and streaky.

"I can't believe...you..." Betty tried wiping her eyes with the backs of her hands. But since those were wet as well, she only accomplished rubbing more soapy water into them. "I thought you were *nice* people!"

Betty turned around, clawing for something stable to grab. Her hand hit the porch railing and she gripped on. Using it as a guide, she staggered to the steps. She could see them descending away from her as if they were under water. It took some effort but she made it, somewhat safely, to the ground. One foot twisted, but she caught herself before putting all her weight down on her ankle. Had she done that, it would have snapped for sure.

Both feet down and flat, she started to run. Her large breasts bounced in front of her, tearing free of the bra that had struggled to hold them up when she hadn't been running. She felt them knocking against her pumping arms.

Her eyesight was clearing but it was still difficult to see much at all. She saw solid green ahead of her and knew it was the woods. That was where she would go.

Skin hot and tight from the scalding water, it felt like it was being stretched as she ran. She bet she had second degree burns on her face and arms. The police would definitely hear about this. Betty didn't care if she was trying to barge into her house or not, Sheila shouldn't have done *this.*

They might try to say Shelia was only defending herself.

Betty didn't care. The police were getting a call as soon as she got home.

Tree limbs slapped her arms, bringing about a fresh series of stings. The burns really hurt. She might need to go to the hospital.

Good. They'll ask what happened too. I'll tell them. I'll tell everyone!

An exposed root snagged her foot and she went down. She landed on her chest, breasts smashing against her. It felt as if they might have burst through her back. Air blasted out of her lungs just before her jaw hit the ground, clacking her teeth together and dislodging the dentures. They flew out of her mouth and bounced across the ground.

"Shit!" she gasped.

Pushing herself up to her knees, she planted a hand on the ground to hold herself steady. She took a few deep breaths.

A crunching sound came from behind her. Another followed on its way toward her. Footsteps. The soft tread of someone stalking closer.

A foot came into Betty's view. A foot covered in sandals. She looked up, seeing two dark, smooth legs, shorts, tank-top, upper slants of lovely breasts, long dark hair and a pretty face. One arm hung by her side, the other was behind her back.

Sheila...

Betty began to quiver.

"You've got us all wrong, Ms. Andrews. We *are* nice people, very nice. But we're stuck in this...situation. And we're trying to get out of it. Our little boy tries so hard to be normal. He *wants* to be good. He just can't. It's not his fault, though. He can't help doing what he does..."

"Sheila...just let me get up. Let me get my teeth and go. Let's forget this even happened."

"And you'll go get the police."

"I won't!"

"You said you would! If only I would have cleaned up the damn blood sooner...this wouldn't be happening!"

"I won't tell, I swear!"

"You will. Maybe not today, but in a couple days, after you've thought about it, you'll call them. You'll send them to our house."

"Sheila...?"

Tears leaked from her eyes. "We just want to be a normal family, like everyone else." She brandished the large chef's knife from behind her back. Its silver blade threw a gleaming bar across the shaded trees. "We'd kill for it, don't you understand? We'd kill anyone who might hurt our family.

Even you, Ms. Andrews..."

Shaking her head, Betty leaned back on her legs, holding up pleading hands. "No, Sheila...don't do this"

The knife hit Betty's palm, and stabbed through the top. Betty saw it twist a moment before being yanked back out. Before she could scream, the blade slammed into her opened mouth. Its sharp point wedged into the back of her throat.

Sheila pounced on her. Raising the knife and bringing it back down in a series of wet punches.

Blood sprayed all over.

CHAPTER 14

Greg walked along the verge of the road, hands stuffed in his pockets, head down, staring at his shadowy form stretched ahead of him on the asphalt. The sun was hot on the back of his neck, sweat beading on his brow. He felt a drop trickle down his side.

This wasn't shaping out how he'd hoped. And he felt disappointed in the lack of progress, even a little guilty.

We've only talked with Dr. Conner a handful of times in three days. What kind of progress was I expecting?

Deep down, he'd envisioned Dr. Conner had a cure just lying around, ready to be administered. Maybe locked away in a secret safe behind a painting. He should have known better than to think such nonsense.

So that meant they'd be putting Gabe through more tests, probably painful ones. Could he live with that? Was it worth it, really?

He wanted to think so. But, he also wanted to keep Gabe's

welfare in mind, above his own. His son seemed content with how he was. So, who was this really about?

That's not fair.

But they just could not keep living like this. Could they? There was no way the rest of their lives could be spent moving from town to town, state to state, just to keep Gabe hidden. The older he got, the more intense his hunger would probably become. Before too long, they wouldn't be able to contain him at all. And, what would happen after he and Sheila died? Who would look after Gabe then?

No one.

It was the three of them, from here on out, unless they could cure Gabe and introduce him into regular society. Gabe deserved a normal life. All of them did.

But can *he be cured?*

What if no matter what they did, nothing fixed Gabe?

At least we'd know we tried.

That didn't make him feel any better, in fact, he felt worse.

He continued to walk, following the bend around to the other side of the road. He could see the Parker house up ahead on the right, and his house beyond, peeking up from behind the fence. Nothing looked to be going on at either house. He was grateful for that but it did nothing to deter the dreadful anticipation he felt stirring in his bowels. The calm before the storm. Whatever gale was on the horizon would be here soon. It always came, so Greg shouldn't be surprised.

He wondered where Ms. Andrews was. Could she be out in the woods right now, on her mad hunt for the beast responsible for her Posey's death?

He stopped walking and scanned the woods that encircled the tiny community. Tops of trees seemed to stretch endlessly onward, green and bushy, vibrant with the life of the looming summer. His favorite time of the year was the span of weeks as spring neared its conclusion and summer was anxious to launch. There would be about three, sometimes four, weeks of absolutely comfortable weather, crisp evenings with a mild chill and days full of warmth that wasn't overbearing. It was perfect weather, if you asked him.

A fantasy of Gabe playing in the backyard manifested. It made him smile.

Someday, booger. I promise.

He started walking again. Sheila was probably wondering what had taken him so long.

At the end of the driveway, he checked the mail. Bills and sales flyers, as he'd expected. Usually it was all he ever expected unless a paycheck was coming. Soon he would have to put together another portfolio and start submitting his artwork under the new name to get some penciling jobs. They weren't in any danger of going broke, but he wanted to get money coming in before they were.

He remembered the days of finding birthday or holiday cards in the mail. Back then, he'd read them, smiled at their sweet messages, and had thrown them away afterward. Now he wished he hadn't. Just to be able to see his mother's handwriting again would be delightful.

Stopping himself before his thoughts depressed him, he pulled down the metal door to his memories. The last image of his mother entombed in his mind was of her headstone. He'd missed the funeral. He hadn't even known about it until three months later. Searching online for updates on his family members from an open Internet line in a library, he'd found the obituary. The next day, he and Sheila began their two day travel back to see her.

Authorities had been searching for him and Sheila for a year by that point. They were the only ones unaccounted for that had participated in Project: Newborn. Greg had severed all ties with his relatives and friends, to do what was right for his immediate family.

All right, that's enough. Don't go inside with that glum look on your face. Sheila will see it and she'll start feeling bad too.

He took some deep breaths. When his exhales were no longer trembling, he opened the door and went inside with the mail tucked under his arm.

From the brightness outside, it felt like he was stepping into a movie theater.

"Sheila? I'm home. I had a not so great chat with Dr. Conner. Overall, he seems to want to help, but I'm guessing he's just as clueless as we are."

Entering the living room, he tossed the mail on the coffee table.

And heard the soft sobs.

Turning around, he saw his wife sitting on the couch. She was leaning forward, elbows propped on her knees, face buried in her hands.

Something's happened.

Rushing over to her, he crouched at her legs. He flinched at the streaks of blood on her bare legs and arms, the yellow cleaning gloves on her hands. There were splashes clumping in her hair.

"What happened?" he asked. She shook her head. Greg struggled to keep his voice calm. "Tell me. Is Gabe all right? Did he do something?"

She shook her head, then slowly tilted it up. More dried blood was on her face, smeared around her eyes like runny makeup from her tears.

"My God. What happened? Are you all right?"

"I'm fine. And Gabe is fine. He had his medicine and is upstairs sleeping. He didn't do anything this time." She paused. "I did."

"*You* did?"

What has she done?

Sheila nodded. Sniffled. "I'll show you."

Any moment now, Sheila expected Greg to lose his control. He stood over Ms. Andrews' corpse, rubbing his mouth with the back of his hand. His eyes were wide, shock-filled orbs. While he stood there, gaping at the displayed carnage, she'd narrated what all had transpired during his visit with Dr. Conner.

Finally, Greg let his hand drop. There was a smacking sound when it hit his leg. "So…she just tried to come inside?"

Sheila nodded. "Yes. Wanting to see the cut on Gabe's arm that wasn't there. She wouldn't stop, and there was no persuading her otherwise. I know I said I'd clean up the blood, but I forgot. I was on my way out to do it, and she was standing right there." Sheila gnawed at her bottom lip. "Are you mad at me?"

Greg's appalled expression softened. He walked around the bloody, stab-filled remains and hugged her. "Why would I be *mad* at you? You did what needed to be done to protect Gabe."

Her face was pressed against his chest. He was wearing the cologne she liked. He smelled wonderful. "I didn't *want* her to die. But I didn't know what else to do. She was going to tell."

"Your motherly instincts took over. It's okay."

"Are we going to have to run again?"

"I can fix this, I think. Only a small setback."

"What are you going to do?"

Letting Sheila go, Greg turned around and scoped out the woods. He looked from one side to the other. "Why don't you run up to the house and get some trash bags while I go to the shed."

"Trash bags?"

"Yeah. Make it quick, but don't wake up Gabe. If he catches the smell of this blood..."

"I know. He'll be out here in a flash."

Greg nodded.

"Okay. I'll run get them." She started for the house, but stopped and looked back at her husband. Such a wonderful man. So good to her. "I love you."

He looked at her, his piercing eyes reaching her soul. "I love you too."

Sheila got moving again, now with a smile on her face. Greg would fix this. He usually could whenever she screwed up. She ran through the back yard, slowing her speed once she got to the porch. She didn't want Gabe hearing the stomp of her footsteps. Still moving quickly, she kept the weight off her feet, her movements nearly silent.

In the kitchen, she turned on the sink, sticking her arms under the running water. She winced at the shock of cold as the water streamed over her skin. The scabby blood stains thinned, then she squirted them with dish soap and scrubbed. The water draining down the hole went from clear to pink. Small flakes of crusty blood were sucked down as well.

After a little bit of work, her arms and hands were clean and soft. They felt much better. The itchy feeling was gone. She wanted to wash her face, but that would have to wait until she could take a shower.

Sheila opened the cabinet under the sink, grabbed the box of trash bags, and quietly shut the cabinet back. Moving as quickly and quietly as before, she left the house silently. Once her feet hit the grass, she bolted for the woods.

When she got back to the scene and saw Greg standing over Ms. Andrews with an ax, her blood went cold. He nudged her legs with the toe of his shoe, parting them. Her arms had already been outstretched. After he finished, she was a human-shaped X. Sheila's stomach felt hot and mushy. She noticed a shovel leaning against a tree off to his right.

Greg, a morose look on his face, walked over to her and took the trash bags. "Thanks honey."

Sheila vacuously nodded. "You're going to chop…her up?"

"Well…yeah. Maybe this is a blessing in disguise."

"How can it possibly be?"

"Maybe her meat will be enough for Gabe, to keep his urges from taking over again."

Hearing the words made Sheila feel sick inside. "We're going to *feed* her to Gabe?"

"Yeah…one died, and others will live." A lunatic's smile parted his lips. "You think?"

"You really think it'll work?"

"I don't know. But she's here, so we might as well give it a shot."

It was insane, what Greg was suggesting. But she also agreed with what he was saying. She wondered why they'd never thought of it before. Ms. Andrews was a big woman, and she had plenty of *meat* they could store up for Gabe. Maybe she could vacuum-seal them, make it keep for a very long time.

Her husband was brilliant. She loved him even more now

than she had the other day, when he'd encouraged her to go walking with Lisa.

"Honey?"

Sheila looked at Greg, dreamily.

"Why don't you head back to the house? Maybe take a shower? I don't think you'll want to see this."

"I'm sorry..."

"Don't be. It is what it is, and we'll make the best of it."

She smiled. "Okay. I'm going to take a shower and wash this gunk off me. Might need to burn these clothes, which really stinks because I like this shirt."

"It does look good on you."

Blushing, she said, "Thank you."

"Maybe you can find another like it online."

"Maybe. I'm going to go and leave you to...this." She pointed at Ms. Andrews' body. There were thirty or more narrow slits in her chest, shoulders and neck. Even an eye had been stabbed. Her already pale skin had turned insipid and tacky.

"All right," said Greg. "I'll be up in a little while."

"Okay." She leaned forward and kissed Greg softly on the lips. It sent a faint tingle through her. "Be careful."

"I will."

They kissed again, this one lasting longer. It was hard for Sheila to pull away. Finally she did, and started walking away. As she approached the edge of the woods, she stopped, and gave fleeting look back.

Greg stood next to Ms. Andrew' shoulder, raising the ax above his head. He brought it down. Sheila quickly turned away, putting her back to the soggy thud of an arm being severed.

CHAPTER 15

Greg put the last of Ms. Andrews in the freezer. He'd wrapped the meat in wax paper, then bundled it in black plastic, as if they'd picked it up at a butcher's shop. "We might need to get some of that white paper, you know, the kind meat comes in from the market?"

"Okay." Sheila was watching him, her rump against the counter and arms crossed. Her hair was still a little damp from the shower. She'd thrown on a long shirt, bare legs tapering out from underneath the hem.

I wonder if she has any panties on under there.

With the meat tucked inside the freezer, he shut the door, glad to be done with it. He'd wrapped what was left of the body in the same trash bags and buried it deep in the ground.

"That's the last of it," he said.

"And if he runs out?"

Greg shrugged. "We'll worry about that when it happens."

"Okay."

"But, we're out of trash bags."

Sheila nodded. "I'll put it on the list."

"I need to make a store run?"

"Later. Not right now, okay?"

She gave him a pleading face that told him plenty. She didn't want to be left alone right now. He wasn't planning on leaving her by herself anytime soon, but he could definitely use a break to himself, a stint of time where he wasn't disposing of a dead body his wife had slaughtered.

Sheila continued to stare at him. Then she started to smile. Checking behind him, Greg wanted to make sure it was directed at him. He didn't see anyone else back there. "Are you smiling at *me?*"

"Yep." She bit down on her bottom lip, bashfully.

"Why?"

"Because! You're amazing!"

"Are you *sure* you're smiling at me?" He looked behind him, expecting to find someone from the front of a romance novel standing in the doorway. There was no one there.

"Oh, I'm *very* sure."

She pushed off the counter with her rump and crossed the kitchen. Standing in front of him, she hugged her arms around his neck, staring into his eyes. She smelled wonderful, fresh and clean like fruity soap.

"How am I amazing?" he asked.

"The way you just took charge out there. You already had a plan to fix everything. I was so scared."

"I was scared too, Sheila."

"Yeah, but you didn't let it defeat you. You're strong." She kissed him on the lips. "Smart." She kissed him again. "And you take care of us better than anyone else ever could." She kissed yet again.

"Well...I try." The back of his neck had gone hot. His cheeks flushed. "You're not so bad yourself—"

Her lips, mashing against his, cut off his words. They felt soft and cool, her tongue warm and plush when it pushed its way into his mouth. Her affectionate assault caught him off guard, but he was quick to match Sheila's pace.

Their hands rubbed each other's backs, massaging and clutching. She touched the waist of his pants, slipped a hand in, and squeezed his buttocks. He groaned as they stumbled sideways, brushing against the fridge in a full circle, and when her back was to the cabinets again, Greg reached his hands behind her. He grabbed her naked rump and lifted her onto the counter. He was right, she hadn't worn any panties.

They continued to kiss. Her hands groped at his belt, caught it, and struggled to unbuckle the clasp. He helped her, then unhooked the button on his pants. She shoved at his pants, getting them down his hips.

"Is this shirt expensive?" he asked.

"Hmm? No." She shook her head between kisses. "I actually don't remember where it came from..."

"Good."

He gripped the collar with both hands. She gasped as he ripped it down the middle. Pushing the now partitioned shirt out of his way, he grabbed her breasts. She sighed into his mouth. He fondled their smoothness, filled his hands with their springy softness. His thumbs pressed against her stilted nipples.

"Come on," she said, trying to grab his boxers. "I need..."

She didn't have to finish the testimonial. He knew what she needed because he needed it too. His hardened penis felt trapped and restrained inside his boxers. He freed it, pulling it through the small gap in the front.

How she was positioned on the counter, slightly leaned back, her crotch angled toward him, was just the right elevation for a comfortable entrance. He pushed into her. She sheathed him, tight and wet and slippery. Her breaths turned ragged and trembling, her head leaned back. He put his lips to her exposed neck, teeth nibbling.

She was so drenched that when he pulled his hips back to thrust, he fell out.

"Oh," she gasped. "Put him back, put him back..."

He did, ramming deep and hard. Sheila's legs constricted, squeezing his hips with her thighs. Her legs climbed him, higher they went, and deeper he plunged. She took a handful of his hair and pulled. Her body shuddered as he slammed into her, rocking her against the cabinets. She let go of his hair, digging her fingers into his buttocks as his thrusts became powerful drives.

After several intense minutes of lunging, Greg burst, filling her with his spurting warmth. She quaked against him, pulling him tighter against her chest. Together, their bodies were hot and slick, their skin slippery with sweat.

They held each other, breathless and tired, for several minutes.

Henry was a bit tipsy. He'd had way too much to drink already this evening and it was barely past dinnertime. He leaned over his dining room table, his forehead resting in the bridge of his fingers as the tips massaged his temples. Papers were spread all over the table's surface, his laptop sat tilted on top. The folder that contained the paper was opened underneath the clutter, Project: Newborn written in a black sharpie somewhere on its cover.

All he'd managed to save. Before the lab was raided, and

the fire started, he'd scrambled to take with him as much data as possible. And this was all of it. To most it would look like plenty, but to Henry, who'd personally researched each bit of information for a decade, it was hardly a dribble of the meticulous work he'd put in.

He looked back at the laptop. An article he'd found from the Doverton Post was opened on the screen. It was about several animal mutilations and killings in the area. Wisconsin authorities were quick to suggest either a wolf or coyote as the culprit, the townies blamed some local legend called Haunchies, but Henry knew without a doubt it had been Gabe. The Heymans, going by the name Strand during this time, had lived in a doublewide for a span of seven months. Out of all the towns he'd linked them to, the stay in Doverton had been their shortest.

He wasn't sure why he'd felt so inclined to research their past, but he'd been scouring the internet for links to articles that could have been about Gabe.

Amazing. I created that kid.

Mostly. The parents' DNA had helped, but the majority of it had come from his relentless work. But the other children born mutated and hostile had suffered agonizingly after birth before being mercifully terminated. Somehow Gabe had nearly been spared. His mutation had been delayed. Why? What made him so special?

Does the secret lie in the Heymans themselves?

Somewhere in their DNA could be the answer he needed. Gabe, all things considered, was a success. His *only* success.

Progress. Great progress.

Gabe was *all* the progress he had. All these papers were total shit and wastes of his time compared to the kid. And he wouldn't let the kid get away. Judging by the articles, and what he'd gathered from their past experiences, the Heymans never stayed in one place very long. And as rapidly as Gabe had begun sampling the local cuisine, this stint in Sunwalk might be their shortest yet.

Sighing, Henry grabbed his cell phone and set it beside the laptop. It slid down the paper mound, so he resituated it. This time it stayed where he put it. He flexed his fingers a few times, working up the courage to make them dial the number.

Just do it already.

He knew he had to make the phone call. Suck in his pride and worries and just dial the damn number. Hawthorne was the only person who could help him.

But would he?

There was only one way to know for sure. Call.

"Damn," he muttered. Henry wiped his sweaty hands on his pants.

Hawthorne still worked at the university in Virginia. He'd been smart to participate in the project as a silent partner, so he was the only one unscathed by the scandal. Hopefully he'd be willing to take on that role of silent partner one more time.

Dialing the number, he was surprised at how naturally it flowed from his fingertip. After all this time, he hadn't forgotten it. This wasn't Hawthorne's office line, his cell phone, or even his home number. This was the secret line that only a handful of people had access to.

Henry almost hoped it had been changed.

There was a click of the call connecting.

Please be out of service!

If it was, that would put him right back to where he was. Clueless. Whether he liked it or not, Hawthorne was his only option.

It hadn't finished its first ring before it was answered.

"Who is this?" said the annoyed and mistrusting voice from the other side.

Hawthorne. He sounded a little older and raspier from the two-pack-a-day cigarette habit.

"It's me," was all Henry said back. It was all he would have to say.

"I told you to never call this number. That was our deal. I *let* you walk away, you're supposed to *stay* away."

"One of them lived." A pause. Henry's lungs began to burn, making him realize he'd been holding his breath.

"You're lying," said Hawthorne.

"I'm not. I've seen him, interacted with him."

"Him?"

"Yes. A boy. He's six."

Another pause. "The Spacey offspring?"

"Yes."

"I'd given up the hunt for them. I figured they were dead, like the others. But, the offspring lives?"

"Alive and well."

"And?"

"Mutated."

A sigh. "Then why should I care? Why should you? He should be terminated like the rest."

"Because he lived for over two years before the mutation took hold. The parents said before then, he would mutate randomly for certain periods of time before transforming back to normal."

"A constant metamorphism?"

"Yes. Frequently. Then he changed, and never changed back."

Hawthorne's raspy breath sped up. "My god, Henry. Have

you imagined the possibilities of something that changes on its own will? Not just the possibilities of curing infertility…"

"It's crossed my mind more than once."

"How is he? How does he look?"

"Not like the infants. He's different. He has the normal structure of any kid, just enlarged, but his skin is hardened, claws, four rows of sharp teeth, spikes in various places."

"A hybrid of sorts?"

"Absolutely."

"Where are you? I see you're calling from a blocked line."

Henry was hesitant of telling him just yet. "In due time, Hawthorne. Let me handle some things on this end."

"You won't even tell me where you are? How you came across this living specimen?"

"They found me actually. The parents showed up at my doorstep, begging me to help them cure their son."

"Cure him? Are they mad? As if we could if we wanted to."

"I'm not so sure. Maybe it *can* be done. Like I said, this kid's different than the rest. If he was able to mutate and alter back to normal before, maybe he still can. Perhaps there's something in his cell structure that's causing this. He might even change back to what he used to be and never mutate again. I don't know. It will take time, studies, research…"

"Have you told the parents this?"

"Of course not. I don't want to get their hopes up. If they do, they might be crushed later if I can't do anything and run away. In the meantime, I plan to work on it."

"You plan on working on a cure, do you?"

Henry wasn't sure what he planned on doing, but he would do whatever possible to keep Gabe close. "I'm working an angle. I *can't* let the kid get away. They never stay in the same town long, constantly shuffling locations to keep under the radar. Every new town, new state, they have a new identity and a lie to live as."

"I see. This would explain why I never found them. I was able to recognize the forgery in their death certificates, so I knew they'd gone into hiding. I had no idea they were this smart. How long before the parents realize you're bluffing them?"

"I'm not bluffing them, not really."

"Tell me where you are. I can be there with a team in a flash."

"Not yet. Let me do some things on my own for a bit."

"Afraid I'll rush in and take it away from you?"

That was exactly what he was afraid of, but he wouldn't tell Hawthorne that. "If you come in with a team, it will probably scare them away. Right now they trust me, and I'd like to keep it that way."

"I understand. I always liked you, Conner, which is why we're able to have this conversation now. You were much more of a team player than your colleagues. But how much work can you do there by yourself? You'll need instruments, the specific software and programs, our computers, access to laboratory equipment that you can't get there."

"When I get to that point, I will reach out to you again. I just wanted to make sure you were still interested in the project."

Another long pause. "I've never stopped being interested."

"Good. I think we might be in good shape after all."

Hawthorne's laugh sent a river of chills through Henry. It made him think of speaking to the devil himself.

"Agreed," Hawthorne said. "Our military clients will also be *very* interested in your discovery. You may have just made us all extremely wealthy."

Before Henry could say anything else, the call was severed. On the screen in big white letters was: Call Ended.

Henry wiped his forehead. When he brought his hand back, his fingers were dripping in sweat. His hands trembled. He wished he could advance without Hawthorne's involvement, but he knew there wouldn't be much he could do without it. Hawthorne had the money, the means and access to everything they would need to start again.

He'd made the right decision calling him.

Right?

As he refilled his glass, he couldn't help feeling he'd just made the biggest mistake of his life.

CHAPTER 16

"Think you might be going a little overboard?"

No answer. The kitchen appeared empty except for a scrumptious blend of aromas. The bubbling of boiling water made it sound as if Todd had entered a scientist's laboratory.

He stood in the doorway, gawking at all the trouble his wife had put into the preparation of tonight's meal. Each burner was covered with a different pot or pan: corn on the cob, green beans and tiny elbow-shaped noodles that were probably going to be Lisa's special recipe of macaroni.

He looked at the oven and could see in the dim orange light inside the shape of the main course: prime rib, wrapped in aluminum foil. He'd purchased it this morning just for tonight.

As he was starting to wonder where Lisa was, she appeared from the pantry. Her arms were pressed together in front of her stomach. Nestled in the basket of her arms were more vegetables.

For a salad, most likely.

"I can cut that up for you," he said.

Lisa gave him a quick smile. "I got it. Did you get finished up?"

For a moment, he wasn't sure what she was referring to. Then he understood. Writing. He'd been unable to write this morning, since he'd volunteered to do the shopping for the feast so Lisa wouldn't have to. He'd wanted to get out of the house anyway, a chance to clear his mind before going back to this stubborn chapter he was dealing with on the new book. Shortly before Jenny came home from school, he'd locked himself up in his office and gotten to work. And, he'd barely been able to write five hundred words, way below his daily quota of two thousand.

Lying, he said, "Close enough."

"Then you should get back to it, for another hour."

"Nah, I'm good."

"But, the deadline?"

"It'll still be there. Maybe after everyone leaves tonight, I'll get a little more done."

He doubted it. Truth was, this book hadn't been as much fun as most of his others. Not all of them ever were. The last three he'd written had been agonizingly painful to complete. In the older days, he could crank out fiction in a series of chaotic sessions, and never stopped smiling while doing it. But lately it took him longer, sessions ranging from four hours to nine that left him drained and glad to be done. Then he dreaded getting started the next day.

Maybe he was getting burned out. He'd built up a prolific library throughout his career, and could probably slow down, not work as hard. Maybe instead of putting out three novels a year, he could drop down to two, releasing a book every six months.

He knew all too well that doing that would only make him feel worse. He had to work like this; there was no way he couldn't.

When I'm cold and dead I'll slow down.

He looked at Lisa and found her staring at him with a worried frown. "Everything okay?" she asked.

"Hmm?"

"You're acting...strange."

"I'm fine. Just got lost in thought." He walked into the kitchen, joining her at the island. She already had the cutting board out, a large bowl beside it. "Grab the lettuce?"

"Sure." She went to the fridge, opened it, and leaned in. Her rump was stuck in the air, slightly arched higher on the left. Todd got a great look at it flexing as she dug out the lettuce from the produce drawer. She stood up, turned around, and caught him looking. She smiled. "Enjoy the show?"

"I did. It was too short."

"Hmm...maybe I'll do an encore."

"After I cut the salad?"

"Yes. A girl needs a little break in-between shows."

"Maybe a nice massage will work out any kinks in those muscles."

Laughing, Lisa set the lettuce in front of him. "Listen at you. Just looking for any reason to grab my butt."

"Can you blame me? It's a nice one."

"I'm glad you think so."

Todd started to tear the plastic sheathing the lettuce.

"Eh!" said Lisa, swatting his hand gently. "Wash your hands first!"

"Oh, right." He walked to the sink, lifting the tap on the faucet. He grabbed the dish soap, squirted a dab of blue fluid in his palm, and rubbed his hands together under the water. His hands became engulfed in bubbly lather, then he rinsed. When he turned around, Lisa was waiting with a dish towel. He dried his hands. "Thank you, dear."

"Sure. *Now* you may chop the salad."

"Looking forward to it."

He returned to the counter, unwrapped the lettuce. After a quick rinse in the sink, he set it on the cutting board. Putting the knife in the center of the leafy ball, he pushed the blade down. It went through without much effort, separating the lettuce into halves in a crunchy slice. He began to cut each section into smaller, green shards.

Lisa went to the stove, stirring all the pots.

Todd looked over at her. "You're doing a lot of work, you know."

Back to him, she shrugged a shoulder. "I guess so. I just want it to be perfect for them. It's been a long time since they've gotten to do something like this."

"I know. That's what makes you awesome."

"Please. It's overkill. No one can eat this much food."

"It'll be fine."

Lisa turned around. "That was pretty slick, you know. Getting Dr. Conner to babysit."

Todd smiled. "Well. I just wanted to make sure they could come. I'm glad they weren't offended by it. They might have looked at it like I was going behind their backs or something."

"It was a good idea. Smart move." She took three cucumbers to the trash can and began to peel off their green skin.

"Unless they didn't want to come, and now we've made it impossible for them to say no."

Lisa laughed. "Don't worry." With the three naked cucumbers in her hand, she walked over to Todd. She set the cucumbers on the board, laying them abreast. "If you would have heard Sheila on the phone last night, you wouldn't even be *thinking* that. She was super-excited. That's why I want the food to be perfect."

"Smells like it will be."

He lifted the cutting board. Using the knife, he scraped the chopped lettuce into the bowl. Then he started on the cucumbers, cutting them into tiny wedges.

"You don't think prime rib is too much?" she said.

"Absolutely. The damn thing was a small fortune."

Laughing, Lisa poked him with her finger. "You know what I mean."

"Afraid our choice of cuisine is a tad on the snobby side?"

"Think so?"

Shaking his head, Todd said, "Not at all." He paused. "Hopefully not, anyway."

Lisa sighed. "Great."

Jenny ambled by them as if they weren't there, on her way to the fridge. Todd glanced toward the doorway and saw April standing there, a shoulder against the frame.

The fridge door popped as Jenny opened it. She snatched two sodas, turned around, and bumped the door shut with her hip.

"Hello girls," he said. "How's the studying coming along?"

Both of them looked disgusted by the question.

"That good, huh?"

Jenny came toward him. "You'd think after a year of hearing this sh..." She stopped, her eyes widening. "This *stuff*...that some of it would've sunk in."

"Not to us," said April.

"I think you're stressing yourself too much."

Lisa snorted. "Wonder where she gets that from?"

Todd gave her a look. *Thanks, Lisa. Throw me under the bus.*

His wife shrugged, giving him a look right back.

Jenny handed April a soda and the fizzy snaps of cans being opened reverberated through the kitchen.

"Refueling our batteries," he heard Jenny say.

"Too bad you don't have any energy drinks," said April.

"Dad doesn't believe in that stuff. It's outlawed here."

Todd laughed. "That's right."

Jenny turned around. "Can April stay for dinner?"

Lisa winced. "Oh, I don't know if tonight would be a good night."

"Why not?"

"We're having the neighbors over for dinner."

"So. Can't she meet the neighbors?"

Todd said, "I don't see why not."

April held up a hand. "If it's any trouble, I understand."

Lisa laughed. "It's not like we're ashamed of you or anything. Of course it's not any trouble."

Jenny turned to her friend. "Want to meet the Heymans?"

The look on April's face showed she wasn't exactly thrilled with the notion. "How about this? Why don't you just give me a call after you're finished with dinner and we can go hang out?"

"You sure you don't want to stay?"

"It's cool. We'll hang out later."

"Whoa now," said Todd. "Not on a school night."

Both girls looked at him as if he'd cocked his leg and

farted.

"It's Friday, Dad."

"No, it's not."

Lisa put her hand on his shoulder. "Honey, it is."

He thought about it. There was no way it had been almost a week since they'd found Ms. Andrews' dog torn to furry shreds in the backyard.

"Wow," he said. "Time flies when you're having fun, I guess."

April laughed. "Sounds like you're having the kind of fun I want to have. I'd love to forget about this past week."

"Staying and eating some prime rib will help with that," said Todd.

"Did you cook it in wine?" she asked. A moment passed then she slapped a hand to her mouth.

Jenny shook her head. "Maybe you *should* go on home."

April nodded, then turned away, walking in the direction of the front door.

Laughing, Todd said, "Tell your dad hi for me, April."

"I will," came her hand-muffled reply.

"Do you think I embarrassed her?" asked Lisa.

"How?"

"By saying no about her staying for dinner right off the bat like that."

"Nah, I doubt she really wanted to stay anyway. I think Jenny put all of us on the spot by asking."

"Yes, she did. Remind me to beat her later."

Todd laughed. "I'll break out the gloves and we'll make a day out of it." He put his arm around his wife and pulled her against him. She laid her head in the crook between his shoulder and chest.

The sounds of bubbling water and meat sizzling drifted

through the room.

CHAPTER 17

Greg wanted a cigarette but didn't want to be rude by asking if he could smoke. Dinner was delicious and everything seemed to be going well. He didn't want the mood to shift to awkward by either asking if he could smoke or excusing himself to go outside. Sheila hadn't stopped laughing since shortly after they'd started eating. Her food was still on the plate, hardly touched, but she was on her third glass of wine.

That was probably a good source of her sniggers.

But Lisa seemed equally giddy, laughing so hard she was snorting while sharing stories about her and Todd. Even some about their daughter, Jenny, who only rolled her eyes as her face turned scarlet. She was a good sport about it, though, even if Greg could sense how embarrassed she was to hear them.

Greg was never much of a drinker, and on the rare occasions he did, it was usually beer. Rarely ever more than two or three. Just like tonight, he was only on his second, and there was still half the bottle left to go.

But the food was fantastic, delicious. He'd had to restrain from overeating, although Todd had encouraged him to eat more and more.

"We'll never be able to finish this stuff, keep eating."

So he did, shoveling in two full plates and two pieces of pumpkin pie—heavy on the whipped cream—Lisa had made, which tasted divine.

Sheila's explosive laughter pulled his attention to her. She had both arms flat and rigid on the table, head leaned back and mouth wide open as a floor-shaking guffaw tore through her. Her breasts shook behind her blouse, and he could see a thin layer of perspiration on her forehead.

It felt good seeing Sheila having such a good time. This was the first time they'd been away from Gabe together. Either he'd left the house, or she had, but never once had they left together in six years. He didn't count every instance where they'd fled or the rare occasions they sat outside, drinking coffee and talking after they'd put Gabe to bed.

"I'm sure Greg can relate to that," said Sheila.

He hadn't heard what they were talking about, but nodded as if he had. For all he knew he'd just admitted to suffering from erectile dysfunction.

"How do *you* handle it?" asked Todd.

Have *I just admitted to not being able to get it up?*

"Um..." he shrugged. "Well...depends on the situation."

"I hear you on that. It's hard to cut things out of my books, especially when I know it needs to be there, although no one else agrees with me."

Oh, okay. We're talking about creative control. But why was that so funny to Lisa and Sheila? I really need to pay attention...

Todd continued. "But then there are those instances when I wrote it and loved it, but then it was pointed out to me why it doesn't work, and I'm thankful that it was."

"The only problem I ever have is when an editor wants me to change the angle of a panel. Let's say I draw superhero-man throwing his elaborate fist right at the reader, and the editor says 'No, that's too much fist in our face, make his arm carrying the punch over and turn him slightly...'"

"And that pisses him off," said Sheila.

"Yeah, it does. Because I believe that the flashier the page, the more the reader will remember the artwork. It's not often that someone closes a comic and focuses on the art, usually it's the story that they come back for. I mean, sure, there are those comic fans that only look at the pictures, but this isn't Playboy, they're mostly there for the words."

"Todd," gasped Sheila. She nodded toward the teenage girl sitting across from Greg.

Whoops.

"Wow," said Todd. "You're right about that."

Greg shrugged. "I want them to take as much from the drawing as they do from the story, you know? Not take away anything from either."

"Naturally, you would. You're the artist and it's *your* art assisting the storytelling. It should be as vital to the reader."

"It's good hearing someone agree with me," said Greg, laughing.

Todd raised his beer. "It's called stubbornness. I'm full of it, so I know where you're coming from."

"You're full of something," said Lisa.

They all laughed at that.

Jenny looked at Greg, surprised. "You draw comics?"

"Yeah," he said, suddenly becoming bashful.

"How long?"

"Since I was your age. I got my first gig for an independent studio when I was seventeen, about to graduate high school."

"That's so cool!"

"Thanks. I like to think so."

"My boyfriend would *die* if he knew that."

"He reads comics?"

"Yeah. He tries to keep it a secret because he wants to come off as this big jock guy, but he loves them. Every week we drive an hour away to visit the only comic shop around. Plus, no one from our school is ever there, so he can be at peace."

Greg laughed. "He's an in-the-closet comic reader?"

"Big time."

"What does he like to read?"

"Oh wow, all the popular ones, you know. But there's this one I had never heard of until we started dating. Dark Salem, I think?"

Greg nodded. "He's got good taste. I drew on that book for the first twelve issues."

He noticed Sheila tense up. She looked at him, her eyes wide. It didn't take him long to realize why. He'd just admitted to being the artist on Dark Salem. All someone had to do was check the credit block in an earlier issue and see his name didn't match the one on there. Questions might get asked, people might start to snoop...

Great job, asshole. Way to go.

"You drew that? Doug is always saying how the artwork went downhill at issue thirteen. Holy sh...crap!" She looked at Todd. "Sorry, Dad."

"It was deserved, I'm sure."

She turned back to Greg. "You'll have to autograph something for him sometime."

Shit on me, he thought, but said, "I'd be honored."

Sheila cleared her throat. "Oh Jenny, you better stop. Greg will talk your ear off about comics until the sun comes up."

Yeah and get us in even more trouble. Shit, I hope I didn't screw up.

"Yeah, she's right. I do get a little *passionate* about that stuff."

Jenny waved a hand as if it was no big deal. "I'll have to introduce you to Doug one day. You two can talk and talk..."

"Sounds good," he said, already going through the laundry list of reasons to back out.

Stop it. You might have a good time talking comics to a fan.

But he shouldn't talk to *anyone* about his old work. He couldn't risk someone figuring things out.

He's just a kid. What harm would it be?

He realized Gabe was just a kid, and his son could be very harmful.

Lisa poured herself another glass of wine. "I'm very happy Dr. Conner agreed to watch Gabe so you could come over. I'm having such a good time."

Sheila angled her empty glass toward Lisa. "Me too. It's been awhile."

Lisa hesitated. Then she poured more wine into the glass. Not nearly as much as she had been, but Sheila didn't seem to notice.

Cutting her off.

Even Lisa noticed Sheila had reached her limit.

Todd set his beer on the table. "Greg, care to join me for a cigarette?"

Yes!

"Absolutely. Where's the smoking section at?"

"My office. Head upstairs with me."

"Dad!" Jenny frowned. "You're smoking again?"

"Rarely." She shook her head as Todd turned to Greg. "Ready?"

"Sure."

Greg pushed the chair back, setting his beer on the table. He noticed Sheila ogling him with a gigantic smile stretched across her face.

"Have fun, honey." Her shoulders scrunched up to her ears. She looked like a proud mother who'd just seen her son get his first kiss.

Greg stared at her moment. "No more wine for you."

"Okay, honey."

Lisa held up a hand. "I'm locking up the bottle."

"Thanks," said Greg.

He followed Todd to the stairs and up them.

Sitting on the floor in Gabe's room, Henry was surrounded by toys. A lollipop sat next to him, tightly shrink-wrapped. This one was even bigger than the last one he'd given Gabe. He'd made a special trip into town, stopping by the bakery just to buy one.

He'd also made a visit to the meat market.

The UVB lights hummed like a nest of flies, throwing black rags of shadow all over. Reaching into his medical bag, he grabbed his personal voice recorder. He'd erased the memory card so he would have plenty of space to record his studies of Gabe.

Too bad the little brat wouldn't come near him.

Gabe had been sitting on the other side of the room, his back to him, humming. His hums sounded normal, like a regular kid his age, nothing at all like the inhuman growls he could produce.

So, to show the kid he could make a point as well, Henry turned away, putting his back to Gabe's back. Pretending he wasn't interested in what the kid was doing, he raised the tape recorder to his mouth, clicking record with his thumb.

"Dr. Henry Conner, recording from the bedroom of Gabe Heyman. As we can hear, the subject is humming. And, I will note that it is amazing how he can snarl with such ferocious growls and yet his voice can be so angelic. I'm willing to theorize that he has at least two sets of lungs, and maybe an enlarged vocal sack."

He snuck a peek over his shoulder and saw Gabe had finally acknowledged he was in the room. The kid glanced over the arm of his inflatable chair, saw Henry watching, then ducked back down. Maybe this bout of reverse psychology was going to work. He'd had reservations about being alone with the kid, but the parents had made Gabe promise to behave. Now he was thankful he'd agreed to babysit the brat.

If only he could get close enough...

"Gabe was the first born and only known survivor of Project: Newborn. And he is exceptional."

His gaze landed on his bag again. Then it flicked toward the lollipop. Plan B was about to be initiated.

"Gabe, want this sucker?"

He held up the giant multicolored disc on a stick. Gabe hardly gave it a glance.

"Didn't think so." He dropped it on the floor. He set the voice recorder next to him. "It's probably too sweet for you.

You might need something a little more...juicy."

Then he removed a two pack of steaks from the bag. It was cold and damp through the plastic. Blood had puddled in the Styrofoam tray.

A grunt.

Now he had Gabe's attention. Henry scooted around, using the heels of shoes to dig into the carpet. Facing Gabe, he held the steaks up, where he knew the kid could see them clearly. "Want these?"

Gabe was a dark shape against the dim light. He nodded eagerly.

"All right, then you have to come here and get it."

The kid came out from behind the chair without uncertainty. He didn't walk over, though, stopping halfway. Raising his arms up to his face, his hands dangled limply at the wrists. Piercing claws caught the light like icicles reflecting the moon.

A cold pain scraped at Henry's spine. Just seeing those claws reminded him of the danger just being in this room. He was alone with a monster, a *real* monster. One that he'd created.

What the hell am I doing here?

Gabe seemed to detect Henry's shift in mood. The kid's willingness to communicate dropped to wariness. Head tilting, a soft growl vibrated in his chest.

Henry snapped out of it. "It's okay, Gabe. I'm not going to hurt you. I couldn't if I wanted to. I mean, look at me. You're *much* stronger than I could ever be."

They were close to the same height, with Henry a little taller, but he outweighed Gabe. Not muscle. He'd been thin and gangly all his life, no matter how much he ate or how intensely he exercised.

"Want these steaks?"

The growl cut off. Gabe leaned forward, sniffing. Henry detected an odor emanating from the kid. Slightly stale, like a dog that needed a bath.

"Gabe, want to come here for a second? Let me examine you like your mommy and daddy said, okay?"

Hesitant, Gabe slowly made his way to Henry.

"Have a seat," he said, patting the floor in front of him.

This much closer, Henry could really smell him. Definitely a stench of wet fur.

Henry reached for Gabe. The kid flinched, causing Henry to snatch his hands back with a gusting gasp. And this caused Gabe to leap to his feet and sprint back to the darkened area behind the inflatable chair.

Heart pounding, Henry's lips felt dry and flaky. He licked them, and then situated himself onto his knees. Holding up the steaks, he waved them. "Let's try this again."

Gabe shook his head.

Henry sighed. This was going nowhere.

CHAPTER 18

Greg admired Todd's office in understanding awe. It was the kind of office he used to have, with framed covers, cartoon strips, and various other artwork he'd drawn hanging on the walls. But Todd had signature sheets, cover reprints and several photographs of himself from magazines adorning his. A shelf had been mounted to the wall and on top were a line of awards. One that stood out from the others was an old creepy mansion with *Stoker* on the front.

There were bookcases lining the room, and nearly every shelf was occupied by books: hardcovers, paperbacks, trades, chaps, comics and magazines. There was a bookcase devoted just to Todd's books, and that was where Greg stood now, smoking a cigarette.

Todd was sitting behind his desk, an ashtray on the corner, and also smoking.

Greg bent at the waist so he could read the titles on the

third shelf. "You've written a lot of books."

"Yeah...not all of them are that great, though."

"I'm sure they are to your readers."

"Nah, they're harder on them than I am sometimes."

"I've learned that sometimes people just *have* to criticize. It's what makes them who they are. Don't let it bother you."

"Oh believe me, I know. I've met several. They work in the publishing business."

Greg laughed. "And the comic industry."

"A lot of the books you're looking at there are reprints in different formats. It helps pay the bills when you have a paperback, eBook, limited hardcover and audiobook for people to choose from."

"What happened to the days of just buying a *book?*"

Todd sighed. "Those days are *gone*, my friend. Too many markets to cater to."

"When I heard that comics were going digital as well, I nearly died. There's nothing that can replace the smell of a recently printed comic book. The ink on the page, the paper, it's a perfect blend. If they bottled that scent, I'd beg Sheila to wear it."

Todd exploded with laughter. "I feel the same way. Years ago, paperbacks smelled different than they do now. I call the old smell the Dean Koontz scent because his books always had that great smell, they still do actually. Mine never smell like that. Just reminds me of me being in high school, reading in the cafeteria, completely out of touch with what was going on around me. Which was usually food fights, fist fights, or boyfriends fighting with girlfriends..."

"Damn, did you go to the school of hard knocks or something?"

Todd laughed. "Please. Out here? I wish."

Nodding, Greg read the titles on the spines facing out: *Georgia Ripper, Flesh Flood, Carnival of Skin, Vampire Outing.*

Then one stood out from the rest. It had a yellow cover and the title stamped in silver, with the tips of the letters swirling and touching. Greg had to strain his eyes to read it.

"Love Slap?"

Todd choked on the smoke he was inhaling. "Shit..."

"By Sophia Ginger?"

Todd hacked up something and spat it into the tiny trash can by his desk.

Greg stood up straight, looked at Todd. "You all right?"

Holding up a finger, Todd nodded. He coughed a few more times. "I forgot that was up there..."

Taking it down from the shelf, Greg looked it over. It was an aged paperback, with creases in the cover and a wrinkled spine. The edges of the pages were yellow as if they'd been colored with a marker. The front cover was an old painting depicting a man on a horse, his thin white top draped burly abs and a strong chest. His arm was out to the side, hand extended and swinging at a redhead with large breasts packed into a purple negligee.

Love Slap.

"One of my early books...the first thing of mine that was ever published, and the *only* book I ever wrote as Sophia Ginger."

"A romance novel?"

"Sort of. More like a porno novel."

Greg raised an eyebrow. "Did it sell?"

"You better believe it did. It got me an agent, a home in a publishing house, but I didn't want a career writing that stuff. I was twenty and in college, and wrote that over summer break. By the time spring rolled around, I was walking around on campus and seeing all these girls reading it…I thought it was cool, but when it came time to write another one…" He shook his head. "I didn't want to. Horror and thrillers was my genre. I knew if I wrote another Sophia book, I'd be writing them for life."

"I bet that was tough. Your art or your career."

"Yeah… I made the right call, though. Todd Parker's books didn't start off with nearly as big of a bang as Sophia's did, but eventually I got there."

"That's what counts."

"Pick one," said Todd nodding toward the books.

"Pick one for what?"

"To take. I'm offering any of them to you."

"To have?"

"You bet."

"Nah, I couldn't *take* one. I can buy one, though."

"I absolutely would not take any money from you."

Greg sighed. "So this is what we're doing? The old cliché where two proud guys argue over one not wanting to get something for free and the other being too humble to accept a payment?"

Laughing, Todd reached over, stamping out his cigarette in the ash tray. "Call it what you will."

"How about we settle? I'll *borrow* one."

"Fair enough. Which one do you want to read?"

"This one." He held up *Love Slap,* waving it.

"Damn. I knew that was coming." Todd held up his hands. "Tell me what you think of it."

"Nah. I'll keep that to myself."

They both laughed. As they settled down, Todd took in a deep breath. Greg knew he was about to either state or ask something that he'd been working his way up to.

"Ever heard of the Terrorbot Fright Con?"

Greg stared at him blankly. At first he thought Todd was joking and had made up that ridiculous name, then he realized he was being serious. "No…what is that?"

"A convention for horror folks. Film-makers, actors, authors and comic books."

"Ah. Okay. No, I've never heard of it, but it sounds fun."

"It is. It's in Charlotte next month. I'm going to be a guest there."

"Cool. Congratulations."

Todd waved a hand. "No, I'm not trying to brag. I've done a few of these in the past. It's my first in a really long time, though. Like you said, they're fun. I bring it up because there are going to be a few comic book guys there, and I wanted to see if you wanted to come along, maybe attend the big dinner for the guests, mingle a bit."

"It's been so long since I've mingled, I wouldn't know how."

"Bring Sheila with you. She can do the mingling for you."

"Yes, she's much better at talking in large groups than I am. But I think Jenny's boyfriend might be a good candidate at talking to the comic book guys, more so than me."

Todd smiled. "Possibly. I was thinking if you just happened to have a portfolio with you, we could show it to some of these people and you never know where it might lead."

What Todd was suggesting was a sincere, kind gesture. But Greg didn't want to go. In an environment like that, someone was bound to recognize his work from past comics. Sure, he tried to alter his drawing style from project to project, but people that worshiped the stuff always saw the similarities.

He would have said no, but Todd was a hard guy to let down. So he nodded. "I can't believe you'd do that..."

"I don't do it for everyone."

Greg believed him, and still couldn't figure why he would for him.

"You're good people, Greg. You and Sheila, both. I'm sure when I get to meet Gabe, I'll think the same about him."

"Maybe. You've only known us for about two weeks, though."

"Nah. I can read people really well. You're on the level." Todd smiled, again. "Let's smoke one more before heading back down."

Todd was lighting up as Greg digested what he'd just agreed to. Yet, he didn't feel scared about it. These were the kind of opportunities he wanted and needed, but whenever they came up he usually turned them away. *Not this time.* He was going to go for it. Sheila would be happy to hear about this.

What about Gabe?

He'd worry when it got closer. They could probably get Dr. Conner to sit with him, as long as Gabe hadn't run him off by then.

Or worse.

Greg realized he was sweating. He quickly lit a cigarette of his own.

Todd sat back down behind his desk. "Want to make a bet that our wives are completely shitfaced by the time we get back down there?"

"I'm not a gambling guy, Todd, and even I know not to bet with those odds."

They both laughed, enjoying their cigarettes.

Henry ripped the cellophane off the meat, raised it to his nose and sniffed. It smelled raw and bloody. There was a tang to it that suggested it would spoil soon.

"Yummy," he said. "Doesn't that smell good?"

Gabe's head poked up from behind the chair. His eyes started to glow.

Henry stifled the scream that tickled the back of his throat.

Shit, oh shit! His goddamn eyes glow!

He couldn't even theorize how such a trait was possible. But it was. He was witnessing it right now. Choosing not to question it, he made a mental note to add it to the digital recorder later for documentation.

Next time bring a video camera.

He didn't have one, but he was going to purchase one tomorrow for sure. He needed proof of the kid's abilities.

"Want to eat?" He could hear the hissing breaths of Gabe sniffing. "Smells good, doesn't it?"

Gabe slunk out from behind the chair, his nostrils flaring as he continued to sniff. He moved closer, and then even closer. Finally he was just a few inches away from Henry again.

Setting the tray on the floor, Henry leaned back to observe.

A scaly hand with tiny fibers sprouting from the dimples removed one of the steaks. Henry studied those fibers, determining they were downy new hairs. He wondered if the kid would lose the scales eventually, or just gain additional hair in various spots on his body.

The slurping sound of the first steak being devoured was like music to Henry's ears and he smiled, absorbing the sounds of the wet tears of meat being ripped up. Pulling the tray out of Gabe's reach, he put it behind him. Then he took the needle out of his bag. With Gabe distracted, he removed the plastic cap from the thick point. He'd had to special order a needle of this size. To his aggravation, the warehouse had been out of stock with the item on backorder. It'd taken longer than he'd have liked for the syringe to arrive.

But, with any luck, it would penetrate the kid's skin.

Gabe finished the meat, sneaking a little closer to Henry as he licked his fingers. Henry noted the snake-like tongue, its forked tip. Streaks of blood cascaded down from his black lips. More dribbled down from his claws and onto the back of his hand. Gabe licked that area as well.

"All right, Gabe. Now that I gave you a present, you have to give me one, okay?"

Gabe nodded, agreeing.

"Good boy." Henry raised the needle so Gabe could see it. "Remember a little while back when I tried to get a little of your blood? Well, I'm going to try again, okay?"

Gabe studied him cautiously. He looked as if he *wanted* to trust Henry, but knew that he *shouldn't*. The kid was very smart, could probably detect all of the hidden motivations Henry hadn't thought of yet.

"I need to see your arm," he said.

Tentatively, Gabe held it out, slightly trembling. Henry reached out, moving slow and careful. His fingers brushed Gabe's arm. It felt spiky and a little fuzzy, like rubbing the skin on an alligator with a five o'clock shadow.

"Look at me, Gabe."

The kid did. Henry found himself becoming mesmerized by his stare, a deep focus that he felt zing all through him. Such gentleness and yet a confused and frightened frenzy surged throughout the kid. Henry detected all of this in just an instant. He almost felt bad for the little guy.

"All right now, to most kids this would probably hurt, but it's not going to hurt you. You're powerful, like a superhero."

Gabe raised his head.

"You like superheroes?"

The kid's oddly shaped head nodded, brown hair flopping all over.

"Let's do this. Are you ready?"

Another nod just as anxious as the first.

"Great! Now, let's show the world that a quick stick of a needle is nothing to a superhero like you."

The kid started to grunt. There was nothing threatening about it. The sounds reminded Henry of gorillas at the zoo when they were playing.

Saying nothing else, he jabbed the needle into Gabe's forearm. He felt it tense in his hand as he withdrew the blood. He filled the tube about halfway, making sure he got plenty so he wouldn't have to take more anytime soon.

He extracted the needle, holding it close to his face. The blood was murkier than most. Thick and dark. Gabe whined, squeaking like a puppy begging for affection.

Henry smiled. "Yes, Gabe. You can have the rest." He slid the remaining steak to the kid.

Although he'd just eaten, Gabe tore into the meat as if he hadn't tasted food in weeks. And Henry Conner smiled.

CHAPTER 19

Sheila was starting to show, a tiny jut through her shirt. Greg, lying in bed and watching her sleep, put his hand on her stomach. He rubbed slow, small circles. He could feel the reassuring warmth of her skin through the thin T-shirt. Even in her sleep, Sheila smiled, writhing slightly under his touch.

He loved watching her sleep. She made cute faces and the peaceful scent of her breaths relaxed him. She could always just drift right off. The moment she stopped moving in bed next to him, he knew she was asleep. He'd lie in bed for an hour or more before sleep finally took him, but in moments like this, he was thankful.

Greg left his hand on her stomach. His head on the pillow, he started to drift off to sleep. Then he felt a bump.

He lifted his head, gazing down at his hand.

What was that?

Too soon to be feeling the kid, wasn't it?

He wasn't sure. Sheila would know. He thought about waking her to ask, but didn't want her getting her hopes up that the baby was moving if it actually wasn't.

But...

He felt it again, a soft thump under his hand. A tad harder than the first, but still barely noticeable.

"Hey there..." he whispered.

He should wake Sheila up so she could experience this, but he wanted to feel it one more time to be sure.

It came again, harder still. This time like someone had actually flicked him. A solid tap.

Strong.

A little unnerving, actually. He needed to wake Sheila up. Something wasn't right about this.

As he started to lift his hand, her stomach shot out and gripped his wrist. Through the glove of flesh and fabric of her T-shirt, he saw the unmistakable impression of a baby's hand. But this one looked...different. Larger, and there seemed to be something extending from its fingertips.

Claws?

Then they pierced through the shirt, dripping blood, and Greg knew that was *exactly* what it was.

Greg started to scream, tugging his arm with all his might. He couldn't get it loose. He briefly wondered how Sheila was sleeping through all this. Why she wasn't helping...

When he looked at her, he saw she was a corpse. Her skin was brown and leathery, sunken cheeks, hollowed eyes. His screams turned to shrieks. He finally tore his hand free and tumbled off the bed. On the floor, he held his sprained wrist. A dull throb pumped pain up to his elbow.

"Sheila!"

As he started to get to his knees, the bedroom door was

kicked in. Three men dressed all in black rushed in, their faces blocked by dark nylon stocking masks. Clutched in their hands were automatic weapons.

"Found you," said the one in the middle, the biggest of the three. "Thought you could stay hidden forever?"

Greg froze. His bowels turned to liquid, shivering. "Where's Gabe?"

"We've got him. He's coming with us." The gun pointed at Greg. He felt a cramp at his heart. "You won't be needed."

The last thought Greg had before the gun fired was he'd failed his family.

Then he felt more hands on him, shaking him. He opened his eyes. The room was dim, and he was staring at the ceiling. Sheila's hair fell on his face, her face smudged in shadows and blocking out the rest of the light.

"Greg? Wake up!"

He stopped screaming. Looking around, he realized he was in their current bedroom and that earlier he'd been in their first home, their *real* home. The house they'd gotten a loan for and bought. It had a fenced in backyard, sat on two acres and was as close to perfect as Greg could imagine.

Now he was back in Sunwalk. Drenched in sweat, naked except for a pair of shorts, the sheets clinging uncomfortably to his sticky skin.

Sheila ran a hand through his damp hair. "Are you okay? You were having a nightmare."

An awful nightmare…

"Yuh-yeah…I'm fine." He sat up, panting. He combed his hand through his hair, flinging the sweat off his fingers. "I'm fine."

"Want to talk about it?" She stood up, walking to the door and closing it. She wore a T-shirt that hung low enough to barely cover her buttocks. He saw a hint of black panties on top of her muscular thighs.

They'd had sex tonight. Seemed to be happening a lot lately, and he certainly wasn't complaining, but he did wonder what was behind their current teenager-like attraction to each other.

"It was before Gabe was born...and we were in the house..."

Sheila's worry dissolved into sympathy. She knew how much he'd loved that house. Although Greg hoped Sheila didn't know how much he missed that time of their life, he knew she did. It was moments like these, when she looked at him like he'd just lost a close family member, that made him realize he wasn't as good at hiding his emotions as he thought he was.

"Another dream about our old house?"

He shrugged. "This one was different..."

"How?"

He heaved a sigh. "Let's not talk about it."

"You sure?"

Nodding, he said, "Very sure."

She looked at him a moment longer before nodding. "Okay. If that's what you want."

"It is. I don't want you having bad dreams, too, so I'll keep it to myself."

Sheila walked back to the bed. At the foot of the mattress, she dropped forward, catching herself with her hands. She crawled back to her pillow. Greg liked how her rump arched on one side, then the other, and how her breasts swung freely behind the drooping T-shirt.

He felt himself starting to stir in his boxers.

Easy fella...not right now.

Sheila dropped onto her stomach, her face pushing into her pillow. She rolled onto her side, facing him. Her leg was bent, a knee on the mattress, with her foot draped over the ankle of her other leg. A perfect magazine pose.

"Think you can fall back asleep?" she asked.

"I doubt it. Not for a little bit."

"Want me to stay up with you?"

He reached out, setting his hand on her velvety thigh. He rubbed it. Tiny little goose bumps prickled up on her skin. She extended her leg so it reached across his knees. "Mmmm..." she hummed.

He was about to slide his hand under her panties when the dream suddenly came back to him. He saw an arm snatching hold of his hand with Sheila's skin stretched over it like a flesh condom. Quickly jerking back his hand, Greg got out of bed.

Sheila sat up in a hurry. "What's wrong?"

"Nothing... I'm going to go smoke a cigarette..."

"Right now?" Her posture slackened.

"Yeah...sorry..."

"What was the dream about? It must have been bad if you're this freaked out."

"I'll be fine. Go back to sleep."

"I won't be able to knowing you're so upset."

Greg knew that her intentions were good but he was certain he'd find her snoozing deeply when he returned. "Don't wait up. Just go back to sleep." He reached behind him, groping for the doorknob. He found it and twisted.

Sheila frowned. "Okay. Be careful."

"I will."

"Love you."

"Love you too."

He hurried into the darkened hallway, skittering toward the stairs. His hand touched the post and he stopped. Turning back, he stared toward Gabe's room. There were no sounds coming from down there, which was odd because the kid snored like a sleeping lion.

Something wasn't right.

With his stomach buzzing, he hurried down the hall. Instead of barging in, he stopped outside Gabe's door, putting his ear to it. The surface was cold against his skin. He listened. No snores. Either his son wasn't asleep or...

Shit!

He opened the door.

"Ga...?"

He hadn't even finished saying his son's name before noticing the bed was empty.

Gabe stood beside the bed, staring at the girl who smelled so good. Since the night he first got her scent, he hadn't stopped thinking about her. He'd seen her that night, coming outside with those other people to check on the dog. She was so...pretty.

Pretty, like Mommy but different.

Gabe didn't understand why being around her made his chest feel fuzzy, his stomach cramp. It wasn't like the hurt he got with his hunger. This felt so strange to him, and it was hard to breathe being this close to her.

Her smell radiated from the bed like an invisible cloud of sweetness. She was sleeping on the bed, the sheets crumpled together below her feet. It looked as if she'd gotten hot during the night and kicked them down.

She wasn't wearing pants, only girl underwear. Laying on her back, with her hips turned so her knees pointed at Gabe, her shirt twisted high up on her body. Her midriff bare, Gabe could see her belly button, a small wink on the smooth surface of her skin. Little dots of sweat were spread across her stomach and side. He wanted to poke her belly button, wanted to touch her flat belly. He examined her, looking her up and down. Her skin looked so soft, like it would feel slippery if he touched it.

Her chest rose and dropped back down with the even sounds of her breathing. Her slightly parted lips moved whenever she took a breath in.

Gabe was disappointed that the shirt covered her chest but didn't know why he wanted to see underneath it, either. These feelings were new to him, confusing and exciting all at once. They made him shake, his knees trembling, his hands twitching.

He climbed up on the bed.

Remembering what his parents do in their bed, he suddenly realized he wanted to do that with her. Rolling around without clothes so they could feel their skin touching together as it made soft squeaking sounds from their sweat.

And that smell…that smell that only came whenever they did that.

Gabe didn't like knowing his parents were doing those things, but the smell was something that he understood meant joy. Even when his parents tied each other up and seemed to be hurting each other, the smell still demonstrated pleasure. Somehow, deep inside him, he understood this was something they were *supposed* to do.

And he *wanted* to do that with the girl…

Now.

He just didn't know how.

Crawling between her parted legs, he put his hands beside

each of her hips. The mattress dipped under his knuckles. Leaning over her, he opened his mouth and let his tongue slither out. It dabbed at the air, twirling as it examined the girl.

It detected the salty flavor of her sweat, the fruity trace of the smell-good lotion on her skin. He lowered himself, putting his face close to her and letting his tongue delicately lay on her skin. Her taste shocked him, like the time he'd stuck his finger into the toaster. He felt it all through his body. The girl moved a little, but quickly went still. Gabe's exploration had barely roused her.

Then something happened between his legs. His pee-pee started to grow. It stretched, jutting against his pajama pants. The fabric sustained its development momentarily before his pee-pee ripped through the front. A downy shell distended in front of him, then opened up and his swollen, fleshy member came out. He'd never seen his pee-pee this big before. It was achy but also felt good.

He felt himself becoming frustrated because he didn't know what to do from this point. She wasn't naked…that was one thing that was wrong. But he didn't want to wake her up. She would scream and the others would come and see why.

Gabe trembled all over, the pressure building in his pee-pee. Something was happening down there. He could feel it building up…

Thick stuff shot out of him, spattering across the girl's thighs and stomach in gloppy streaks. It was a body-shuddering sensation that brought tears to Gabe's eyes. But with it, the feelings of wanting to roll around with her quickly went away and were replaced by shame. He felt awful for wanting to do that with her. And, even worse, he'd gone into the girl's room!

What if she wakes up?

He looked down at her. She hadn't moved.

Gabe needed to leave, go back through the window he'd come in from. Trying to get off the bed slowly, he couldn't control how much it shook. He stopped trying to be gentle, scurrying off backward.

The girl started to move. He saw her hand mindlessly reach up and touch her stomach. Her fingers jabbed into one of the gloppy mounds. Gabe started to cry when her faced crinkled up.

"Wha…?" came a groggy response.

Gabe ran. Leaped for the window. He landed on the sill, then gave one last look back. She was sitting up, her sleepy voice turning to a groan. He quickly turned away and jumped. He soared in the air a moment before his hands found purchase on the tree limb several feet from the window. He swung forward and let go. His feet slapped the wet ground, but he didn't slip. They latched onto the earth, helping him catch his balance. He took a moment to let the jar of his landing fade, and then he was off.

Sprinting for the woods.

Greg and Sheila searched the woods behind their house. They'd thrown on clothes, not caring if anything matched, or even what they were. Together, they walked through the trees, their tread crunching leaves under their feet, Greg pointing a flashlight ahead of them. Its funnel of light stabbed into the darkness, and Greg waved it around, shining it all over.

This was their second time searching this area, and still no Gabe.

"Gabe!" called Sheila, keeping her voice to a shouting whisper.

"We should go get the car," said Greg. "Drive through the neighborhood."

"What do you think he's gotten into now?"

"I don't know..."

Greg hoped it was nothing. With any luck they would catch him *before* he got into trouble. There weren't any distant wales of sirens, any screams or rattled calls of distress, so that was a good sign nothing had happened yet.

Yet was the word that kept swirling in Greg's mind.

They walked a ways longer, approaching the Parkers' property line. Gabe had trespassed out here before and killed a dog, but he'd promised to never do so again. Greg wished he could trust his son to keep his promise, but he just couldn't. It was hard to contain even an average six-year-old, let alone one with the urges that Gabe had. But, he also understood it was out of Gabe's control.

"Where are you going?" whispered Sheila.

"Thinking we should check out the Parkers'..."

"What if someone hears you, or *sees* you?"

"I'll risk it."

Sheila huffed. "I'll go with you."

Nodding, Greg moved as quietly as possible, but to him he felt as if he might as well be banging cymbals together. Every step crunched or crackled like gunshots in the quiet night. They approached the verge of the woods.

He was starting to see the safety light atop the power pole casting a dome of blue hues over the back yard. The house was a pale giant sinking in shadows. Taking a deep breath, Greg started to enter the yard.

"Wait," snapped Sheila.

Greg's shoulders sagged. He lowered his head. "Sheila, we have…"

"Listen!"

Greg halted, tilting his ear to the air. At first, he didn't hear anything other than crickets and frogs, but after a few moments his ears detected the faint sounds of sobbing. And he recognized immediately who they belonged to.

"Oh shit…"

"That's him, isn't it?" said Sheila, her voice already suggesting she knew.

"Yes!"

Sheila started to move, but Greg grabbed hold of her arm. "Hold on." Sheila stopped, turned back to him. He listened again. The sobbing was coming from the right. They would have to go back the way they were heading. "Let's go."

By the hand, he led her away from the Parker place and back into the woods. They took the direction Greg thought would get them to their son. It did. They stepped around a small cluster of pines and found him sitting on the ground, hugging his knees to his chest. His face was buried in the groove between his thighs. His broad shoulders bounced as he cried.

"Gabe?" said Greg.

Gabe didn't acknowledge his father had spoken, only cried.

"Gabe?" Still nothing. "Booger?" His shoulders froze. Finally, a reaction. "Hey, Booger, it's me."

Gabe slowly raised his head. Yellow, pussy streaks ran down his cheeks from his eyes. He sniffled, the slashes of his nostrils shrinking then expanding.

Greg's heart sank into his stomach. Tears welled in his own eyes. He ran over to his son, crouching next to him. He slung his arm around his back. "What happened? Are you okay?"

Gabe flung his head from side to side.

"No? You're *not* okay?"

Again, the same hysterical reaction.

Sheila squatted on the other side of him. She put her hand to Gabe's chest, but he flinched at her touch. Sheila gasped as he pushed himself closer to Greg. She looked at Greg, her mouth hanging open in surprise. Tears leaked out from the corners of her eyes. He could tell she was just as confused as she was hurt by Gabe's withdrawal.

"Gabe..." was all she managed to say before she started crying.

"Let's get you home," said Greg. He leaned up, keeping his hand behind Gabe's back. Passing the flashlight to Sheila, he slid his other arm under Gabe's legs. As he stood up, he hoisted his son up with him. It felt like holding a man from his heavy weight.

"I'll go first," said Sheila, her voice quivery.

"Okay."

Sheila led the way, and Greg followed with Gabe in tow. She must not have noticed Gabe's pants, but Greg surely had. They were torn at the crotch. Once they got him home and bathed, he was going to ask his son what he'd been doing out here.

And he would conjure up a way to secure their house so he couldn't do it again.

CHAPTER 20

Usually on Sundays Jenny joined her parents at Johnny Slim's for breakfast. They had the best sausage patties she'd ever tasted, even better than her mom's and that was a praise she didn't give often. But after waking up to find what she could only guess was vomit, all over her, she figured it was best she stay home.

She'd snuck into the bathroom and took a quick shower to wash off the greenish-white fluid from her body. There were slimy little trails on her stomach that had reminded her of a snail's trail. It had nearly caused her to vomit again just looking at the gunk that was on her. Plus, she'd just felt filthy, and gross, like waking up at a party, naked and fondled.

When her dad had come to her room to find out why she wasn't out of bed yet, she'd told him she didn't feel well and was going to skip breakfast. He asked her if she wanted him to bring her a to-go box.

That was an obvious answer. *Yes.*

Now she was perched on her window sill, smoking her third cigarette of the morning while April was in the bathroom, monitoring the pregnancy test Jenny had just taken. April had picked one up from the drug store on her way over. And since Jenny wasn't brave enough to endure that torture herself, April was going to break the news to her whether it was good or bad.

Jenny doubted it was pregnancy that had caused her to throw up, but she wasn't feeling sick, and there hadn't been a nasty taste in her mouth when she'd awakened in the middle of the night.

Unless it wasn't puke...

What else could it have been? It looked a lot like...sperm, but it absolutely couldn't have been. So, she was settled on the notion she'd gotten sick in her sleep.

Please God...don't let me be pregnant.

She'd be just like Tracey Parks, that girl from Brickston. They'd gone to school together until last year. She'd gotten pregnant and dropped out. Jenny didn't want that happening to her.

What the hell is taking so long?

She checked the alarm clock on her nightstand, seeing three minutes had passed since she'd come back to her room. These tests were only supposed to take two minutes to accurately give a result.

Unless...April doesn't want to tell me...

"Oh shit," she muttered.

Her mouth went dry, feeling like she was swishing with a wool sock. The back of her neck felt as if a cold hand had gripped it. Her vision went a little fuzzy, her head feeling light on her shoulders.

April is trying to figure out a way to break the news to me. The test was positive. I'm pregnant! I'm going to be a mother!

The door swung open and April entered, eating an apple. Jenny recoiled at the crunching sound of her taking a bite. She walked across the room, flopping onto the bed. She put her head on Jenny's pillow and stared at the ceiling.

Jenny gaped at her for what felt like months before finally saying, "Well?"

"Well what?"

Jenny heaved a sigh. "The test…?"

"Oh, that. You're good. It was negative."

Jenny's body relaxed as if she'd just leaned back into the bubbling-warm water of a hot tub. Then her relief turned to anger. "Why didn't you tell me that when you walked in, bitch?"

April shook her head. "You didn't ask."

So instead of divulging information that Jenny had been worrying over, she'd gone downstairs and taken an apple from their fruit basket before coming and telling her she wasn't pregnant?

Typical April…

Jenny dragged on her cigarette. "This is funny to you, isn't it?"

"What is?"

"Seeing me in pain, seeing me worry. It was just a damn joke to you, wasn't it?"

April took a bite of her apple. "Not really. I came over to help you…"

"You came over to make fun of me. I was really scared and you think it's damn funny."

"Jeez…we should have known you weren't pregnant because you're being moody and bitchy like you're about to go on the rag." April sat up. "I came over because I'm your friend and you asked me to."

"Yeah…came over to rub it in my face. Damn, I'd hate to see what the hell you would have done if I *was* pregnant."

"I'd have *really* given you hell, then."

"Shut up."

April shrugged. "It's my niche. I don't know how to express myself any other way."

"I'm the only person you treat like this."

"Treat…?"

"Yeah. Everyone else you're not so dry with. But when it comes to me you just go overboard with the sarcasm, the jokes, and there's times I can't tell if you're being serious or just kidding around."

April looked down at the apple, rolling it around in her hands. "Well…" She paused as if trying to figure out what she was going to say. "I spent ten dollars on that test, you got the results you wanted, so I guess I'm done here."

"I'll pay you back. I have cash in my jewelry box." She nodded toward the dresser where the box was sitting. "Just take what you need."

"Forget it. Keep your money."

"Great. Now you're pissed at me."

"Who, me?" She looked at the apple again. "How much do I owe you for this? Wouldn't want you to think I don't appreciate that you let me eat your food."

"It's my parents' food."

"Oh, what-the-hell-ever." She shook her head, then scooted toward the edge of the bed. "You're a piece, you know that?"

"You like it," said Jenny.

April reached the edge of the mattress, swinging her legs

over. She turned to Jenny and was probably about to reply but Jenny noticed her neck. April's hair was down and had been covering the bruises. The momentum of her movements had caused her hair to fall back off her shoulders, exposing them.

Dark purple, villi-shaped blemishes led to a round blot near the center of her neck. A small plump bruise ran under her chin like she'd been wearing a cap with the strap too tight.

Obviously a handprint.

Jenny felt sick. "What happened to you?"

Quickly pulling her hair back down, April looked abashed. "Talking about my love marks?"

"Did someone…do that…?"

"Yes, but I know what you're thinking and no I wasn't attacked. I allowed it."

"You let Phil…*choke*…you?"

"It's cool. I kinda liked it, but I had no idea I would bruise so easily. It's been a bitch trying to keep them hidden. As you can tell, I'm not very good at it."

"When did this happen?"

"While you were enjoying dinner with your neighbors, I was enjoying this." She pointed at her neck, smiling timidly. "Parents weren't home, so I took advantage of it."

That was why April hadn't been eager to stay for dinner; she'd already made plans. But Jenny remembered Phil was working at Crispy Crust Pizza Friday night and that was why she'd asked April to stay over to begin with.

"Wait," said Jenny. "Phil was working Friday night."

April's eyebrows arched then narrowed. "Shit…"

"You *cheated* on him?"

"Jenny, keep quiet about it…"

"You cheated on Phil and let whoever it was do...*that* to you?"

"Don't make a big thing out of it."

"Who was it?"

"You don't know him. He's older."

"I don't care if I know him or not. Tell me who he is."

"Just a guy that comes into the restaurant from time to time, don't worry about it."

Jenny should have known. She'd seen how April treated the customers at the steakhouse, especially the good-looking male variety. Jenny had suspected she'd mess around with one of them eventually, but not while she was still dating Phil. "How long has *this* been going on?"

"A few weeks..."

Jenny groaned. "That long?"

"But you can't say *anything*!"

"We made an agreement, not too long ago actually, that we wouldn't make each other keep this kind of secret."

"I know. But you won't have to keep it for long, because I'm going to make a decision soon. And I'll tell Phil myself."

"Breaking up with him?"

April shrugged. "Probably so. Either way, the guilt has been killing me. It needs to come out."

"When you say older..."

"Don't ask anything else, okay? I don't like lying to you, and I'm not ready to give you all the details either."

Jenny stared at April. The hurt, shame and even humiliation were apparent. Her posture was weak, shoulders slumped. Her eyes seemed to look everywhere except at Jenny. There was more to what her friend was hiding than she was letting on.

Much more.

And Jenny was positive her opinion of her best friend was going to seriously change once she learned what it was.

CHAPTER 21

Greg was drilling a hole in the back door to install the lock. It was one of those bolt and catch designs with an additional eye for a padlock, which he'd also picked up at the hardware store. This one was made of high-quality metal and came with two keys that Greg was going to keep locked up in the safe he'd also bought. Only he and Sheila would ever know the combination and they'd decided to change it once a month.

Keeping all ends covered.

He knew no matter how much effort he put into this, it would only help a little, not solve the problem. Gabe would find other ways out, not at first, but eventually.

He thought back to the rip in Gabe's pants. He'd tried to get Gabe to talk about it, but his son had acted too uncomfortable, ashamed. So, for the time being, Greg had decided to drop it. A little later, he'd bring it up again.

Wood dust flew into his face, catching his lips. He stopped

drilling and set the drill on the counter. Walking over to the sink to rinse his mouth off, he could hear the TV blaring from living room.

Why does she have it cranked so loud?

He turned on the faucet, leaned down to the tap, and let the water rinse the wood flakes off his lips. Straightening up, he shut off the water. He tore a paper towel off the roll and was wiping his mouth when something on the TV caught his attention.

Betty Andrews...Sunwalk...

His heart seemed to lock up, sending a tight clutch of pain through his chest.

"Greg!" called Sheila.

He ran into the living room. Sheila was on the couch, bent forward with her fingers pressed so hard to her lips they were squished. Her eyes were fixed on the TV.

Greg watched. A young reporter stood at the end of a familiar road, staring concernedly into the camera. She seemed to be speaking directly to Greg.

"...authorities are checking with neighbors to see if they can offer any kind of assistance as to the whereabouts of Ms. Andrews, a resident of the quiet drive of Sunwalk..."

"This is bad," said Sheila. "So bad."

"Come on," he said. "We knew this was coming. It always does."

"I know...but I thought that maybe..."

"What? That everyone would just forget about her?"

Sheila didn't answer but Greg assumed that was exactly what she'd hoped for. He had too, for that matter.

Walking across the room to the window, he pulled down a slat of the blinds and peered out. A squad car was parked on the street as another drove slowly by. He saw a man wearing a much-too-warm-for-the-day suit, chatting with a uniform cop. The suit looked basic and plain on an even plainer guy: short hair, feathered to the side, a young face, but the posture and gray slivers of hair suggested otherwise.

The detective most likely…

Greg sighed. Looked like their house was next.

Might as well get it over with.

"Are they out there?" asked Sheila from behind him.

"Yeah," he answered. "I can see a guy, dressed down, bet he's the detective. He'll probably be heading our way in a minute."

"Oh," she whined.

He stepped away from the blinds, and they snapped shut. "Calm down, it'll be okay."

"Will it?" She stood up, her arms crossing over her chest. "Are you sure?"

"Of course I'm not sure."

She closed her eyes, leaning back her head. "I was hoping you'd say you were sure."

"And lie to you?"

Groaning, Sheila looked at him again. "I'm scared, Greg. This time feels worse. I'm so worried they'll catch on…and I don't want to have to run again."

"I don't either…" And that was true. He liked it here. He never thought he could enjoy living somewhere as much as he had their first house. This one couldn't replace that feeling but it definitely came close. "But we should be in the clear, for now at least. I don't think they've found anything that would suggest anything."

"How do you know?"

"We would've heard by now."

Sheila's lip quivered, she nodded. "Okay."

"Where's Gabe?"

"In his room. He's not sleeping, though."

"Okay, maybe we should go tell him not to come out—"

The ding of the doorbell made them both jump. Greg's words jumbled into a gasp.

"He's here," said Sheila.

"Yep."

They went to each other, Greg putting a hand on each of her shoulders as she gripped his hips. Staring into each other's eyes, they took several deep breaths. This was their way of composing themselves, absorbing their fears and trepidations so they could give an impression of normalcy whenever the situation called for it, despite the fact they were feeling anything but normal. Usually it worked, but not always.

"Ready?" he asked.

"As ready as I can be."

"Let's do this."

Greg strolled to the door at a casual pace. He'd learned from past experiences, if you opened the door too soon, it would seem like you were waiting for them to arrive. But, if you waited too long, you made them think you were trying to hide something.

Putting his hand to the doorknob, he glanced back over his shoulder. He saw Sheila flipping the TV away from the news, and settling for a game show he didn't recognize. Then she sat down, propping her bare feet on the table, the hem of her sundress grazing the floor.

She was ready, assuming the role of clueless housewife.

Greg turned away from her and opened the door to the man he'd spied at the end of his driveway, stomping out a cigarette at their doorstep. His face stretched in embarrassment for being caught in the act. Clearing his throat, he bent down and picked up the crinkled butt. "Um, hello there. Sorry about that. I wasn't planning on leaving it here."

"It's okay," said Greg. "I'm a smoker, too, so it's no big deal."

The detective was putting the quenched butt back in the pack with the rest. "Thank God. I didn't want to come across as inconsiderate, but I'm sure it's too late for that." He offered his hand. "I'm Detective Frank Garner."

Greg shook it. "Nice to meet you, I'm Greg Heyman."

"It's a pleasure. But, unfortunately, we have to meet under these circumstances. I'm sure you've heard about your missing neighbor."

"Yes. It was on the news earlier. Is it really serious?"

"Well… Can I come in, so we can talk about it?"

Greg's defense radar clicked on. Something was already off about Frank Garner. He could tell when someone didn't trust him or like him, and he could tell that the faux-bumbling detective did not.

Why did I tell him I smoke?

Because, he reasoned, Garner had seemed so flustered when Greg noticed him putting it out on the doorstep. It must've been a ruse, something to test Greg with. He wondered if he'd passed.

"Sure, come on in." Greg waved him inside.

"Thanks."

Frank Garner entered the house and Greg closed the door.

"Come on in the living room, I'll introduce you to my wife."

"Sounds great. This is a nice a place."

"Thanks. We like it."

"Just you and your wife?"

No point in lying.

"No. We have a special needs son."

"Oh..."

Sheila was standing up, smiling, as they approached. "Hello there."

Like most everyone else, Detective Garner seemed caught unprepared by Sheila's beauty. He stopped walking, doing a little jump back as if he'd stumbled upon a hornet's nest. "Well...hi..."

"I'm Sheila Heyman, and did I hear correctly that you're a detective?"

"Yes ma'am."

"Stop with that right now. Call me Sheila."

"You bet. Sheila."

She smiled. Seeing it caused Garner's cheeks to flush. Reaching into his jacket pocket, he removed a travel-sized bottle of hand sanitizer. He squirted some in his palm, returned the bottle to his pocket, and rubbed his hands together.

Befuddled, Greg and Sheila observed this.

Noticing, Detective Garner smiled. "It uh...helps get rid of the cigarette smell."

"Ah," said Greg.

Sheila nudged him. "Maybe you should try that, sweetie."

"Maybe I should."

They erupt in one of their renowned bullshit laughs.

"I'm a smoker," started Garner, "but I hate smelling like one."

"Would you like something to drink?" offered Sheila.

"Oh, ma'am—I mean Sheila—I'd love that. It might not be summer yet, but it definitely feels like it is today."

"Hot out there?"

"Very."

"Be right back," said Sheila. She hurried to the kitchen.

"Sit?" offered Greg.

"Sure," said Garner.

He took the chair and Greg sat on the couch. Greg grabbed the remote from the coffee table and turned off the TV. Silence blanketed the room.

"So," said Greg. "What's all this about Ms. Andrews?"

"Just a minute," said Garner. "We'll wait for your wife to get back. That way we can *all* talk."

Greg nodded. A few uncomfortable moments later, Sheila returned from the kitchen with a glass of iced tea. She handed it to Garner, then joined Greg on the couch.

Holding the glass, Garner smiled. "Sheila, you are just a dear."

"Well," she shrugged. "I try my best."

"You succeed." He took a hefty swallow, smacking his lips when he was done. "That's some good sweet tea."

"I'm glad you like it."

"I'm from the Midwest, so I was a bit of a late bloomer on this stuff."

"So were we," said Sheila. "My mom was from the south, and I got Greg hooked on the stuff."

"Boy did she ever," said Greg.

Another bullshit laugh from the Heymans.

Garner chugged the rest of the tea. The ice clinked when it dropped back to the bottom of the glass. "That's good."

"Want another?"

"No thank you. Not right now. I might take one in a little bit."

"Okay. Just let me know."

He smiled his appreciation, then let it fall away to a more

somber expression. "I guess we'd better get down to business. I don't want to hold you up too long." Reaching inside his jacket, he removed a notepad and pen. He flipped past a couple pages, found the one he was looking for, and folded the cover back. He clicked the pen. "Since you saw it on the news, I don't need to inform of you of Betty Andrews' situation."

Greg felt Sheila tense beside him. He reached his hand over, putting it delicately on her knee. She sat both hands on top of his.

"It's awful," said Sheila. Her voice sounded thick and quivery.

"Yes," said Garner. "It sure is. Now, we've been able to pinpoint her disappearance somewhere around the end of last week. The facts on which day are a little hazy because different neighbors are naturally reporting different stories and accounts. But from what I've gathered in my preliminary investigation so far is that she vanished somewhere between five in the afternoon on Friday and lunchtime on Saturday. Again, this is just an estimate."

"Sounds about right," said Greg.

Sheila squeezed his hand.

"Excuse me?" said Garner.

"I saw her Friday," said Greg.

"Oh, did you?" Garner leaned forward a bit. "What was she doing?"

"Looking for whatever killed her dog."

"Ah," said Garner. "Okay. That's the one thing the neighbors agree on. Some even said they'd found her in their backyards going through their garbage cans and sifting through the woods around their houses. She was definitely...determined...in her quest, wasn't she?"

"Yes," said Greg. "You could say that."

"I've also gathered she wasn't very popular in the neighborhood."

Greg wasn't surprised to learn that, but said, "I wouldn't know. We're new here, so we haven't had the time to form an opinion about that."

"Not many people seem to have liked her."

"Liked?" said Sheila.

"You're talking about her in the past tense," said Greg. "Do you think…?"

Garner held out his hand. "No, not at all. Just a poor choice of grammar. My apologies."

"It's fine," said Sheila.

Garner looked at Greg. "Now, you said you saw her on Friday?"

"Yes."

"What time?"

Greg puckered out his lips, rolling his eyes upward. "Not sure, really. Late afternoon sometime."

"Would you be comfortable saying between four and six?"

"Make it three and six."

Nodding, Garner jotted it down. "Okay. Great. That helps me some." He looked back up. "But other than that, neither of you have seen her?"

They told him no.

"How about *heard* anything strange?"

"Such as?" asked Greg.

"Anything you're not used to hearing."

They told him they hadn't.

"Have you seen anyone that doesn't belong in the neighborhood? Strangers? A Mexican or Colored perhaps?"

Greg's eyes widened. He was positive his shock was vivid

on his face. "A...colored?"

Garner nodded as if he hadn't said anything out of line.

"No. How about you honey? Any Mexicans or Coloreds?"

Garner turned to her, ready to write it down if she had.

"Can't say that I have," she said.

Greg and Sheila share a puzzled look.

Garner wrote something down, then said, "Neighbors have stated coyotes roam these woods. Apparently there are a lot of them. Have you seen or heard any of those? Maybe caught them rummaging around your trash or anything."

"I've heard them," said Greg. "Yipping at night, sometimes."

"But you haven't seen them around."

"Nope, just like the Coloreds." He felt Sheila's fingernail jab him in the soft fleshy section between his thumb and forefinger. It was her way of telling him to stop being an asshole.

"That's a crazy howl they have, isn't it?" asked Garner.

Greg thought about asking if he was referencing the *Coloreds* but decided not to push his luck with either the detective *or* Sheila. "Yes, it's very disturbing. Sounds like they're in pain sometimes."

"So you venture outside at night a lot?"

Greg smirked. "I didn't say that. And no, I don't, except to sit on the back deck and smoke a cigarette."

"And that's when you've heard the coyotes?"

"Right," said Greg, short.

Garner made a face as if he'd learned something of great value. "Okay." He wrote it down with his other notes, then flipped the notepad shut. "Let me give you my card." He put the notepad back inside his jacket and when his hand reemerged, the pad and pen were gone and in their place was a business card. Slipping it between his first two fingers, he leaned forward, giving it to Greg. "If you see or hear anything strange, call me right away. My cell number is on there too."

"Right. Will do."

Garner started to stand, so Greg and Sheila did the same.

"Want one for the road?" asked Sheila.

"No thanks, I better not. Drinking lots of tea makes you have to pee. Something my grandmother always said and it's true. With all the walking around out there I have to do today, I better pass."

Sheila looked perplexed, as if she didn't know how to respond to that.

Greg started to lead Garner to the door. "Let us know if you need anything else."

"I sure will. And don't worry about a thing."

"After meeting you, I sure won't."

Garner smiled. "Thank you for your kindness."

Greg opened the door for the detective. "Have a nice day."

Garner said good-bye, then Greg closed the door. He turned to his wife. "What the hell...?"

Sheila shook her head, arms held out. "I have no idea..."

"Coloreds? Mexicans?"

"This *is* the south."

"Still...I don't like how he seemed to be trying to set me up for something, like saying Ms. Andrews wasn't liked. He wanted me to say something negative about her. I could tell he thought something was off about us."

"Think so?"

"Yeah. He'll be back, I'm sure."

"Great."

"We'll handle it. Don't worry."

"I'll try my best..."

They hugged.

CHAPTER 22

Doug fought to get his hand under Jenny's bra. She was wearing her pink one, and it was a little tighter than the others, so he was having some trouble. That was fine. She wasn't sure she wanted sex tonight, anyways.

It had been a weird day. Started with finding her bedroom window open, although she was certain she'd closed it before bed. And lying on her window sill had been a dead bird with its head twisted around on its body. She'd called her dad in there and shown him. Although it had clearly bothered him as well, he'd downplayed it. He said an animal had probably killed it in the tree outside her window and the bird had *fallen* onto her sill.

She'd wanted to tell him he was full of shit but didn't dare to. Plus, she'd rather believe it, and she continued to tell herself it *was* what happened.

Even in the car with the windows up, and a muggy night

outside, Jenny shivered. Doug moaned, obviously thinking he'd caused a reaction from her. All she'd wanted right now was to be held. But that wasn't happening unless she let him have sex with her.

Let *him?*

If this was the only kind of affection she was going to get, she might as well take it.

School today was no better than her creepy-strange morning. Being Wednesday and with finals starting on Friday, they'd taken a practice exam in Literature Arts. She'd failed. The daughter of a best-selling horror author failing Literature Arts. Irony was a word that came to mind, stupidity was another.

Doug's hand finally succeeded, cupping her breast eagerly. His thumb pressed against her nipple. It hardened under the pressure. As much as she wanted to convince herself she wasn't enthralled by his touch, she couldn't deny her body's reaction. She felt heat rush through her, killing the chill that had shivered her. She felt a swelling burden between her legs.

Finally, she kissed him back, trying to match his pace. She couldn't do it. Pulling it away, her lips made loud smacking pops. "Why do you kiss like that now?"

Huffing, he said, "Kiss like what?"

He came in for more, but she leaned back. "I don't know. Just, different. Not how you used to."

How he was kissing her pulled memories to when they were watching Phil and April nearly swallow each other. She remembered how they'd laughed about it. Now it wasn't so funny. She wondered if Phil had been giving him pointers.

Or what if…?

Doug's talking interrupted her thought before it could fully register. "It's the same old me, so what if I'm just trying to change up my routine some. You know, keeping things fresh."

"I liked your old routine."

"How about I mix it up some? Giving you a little of each?"

Heaving a sigh, Jenny didn't like his answer. "Fine."

"Let's get in the backseat."

She'd known this was coming. And she wanted to go back there with him, have some fun, because it might help her feel better. But she also *didn't* want to. Checking the clock in the instrument panel, she saw they had enough time before she had to be home. If she was a minute late, Dad would snap.

"I can't go home late tonight," she said.

"You won't be."

"My dad will kick my ass."

"Nah. He seems like a pushover, you can talk him out of it."

That comment did nothing to sway her, but it did plenty to make her feel lousy for how she treated her dad. Doug was right. She could get out of any kind of punishment from her dad, and it took Doug's comment to make her realize how much she took her father for granted. And her mother, for that matter.

"Doug..."

"Come on," he said, thrusting his head toward the back.

"I can't fuck things up..."

Doug groaned. "How will getting in the backseat for a little bit fuck things up? I'll have you home before your curfew."

"It's not that, Doug. Can't you tell I've got a lot on my mind? Don't you understand?"

Doug flopped down in his seat, angry. Jenny sat up, adjusting herself, fixing her bra. It really was a tight piece, maybe too tight. It crushed her tender nipple, sending a stinging pinch through her breast. She pulled her skirt down between her legs. Why did she always wear such short skirts? Surely she owned something that could easily cover her.

Looking at her grouching boyfriend, Jenny figured he probably thought all this was about the sex and kissing. And, some of it was, but the point she wanted to make was that she was going through some stuff and all she wanted—*needed*—to hear was that he was there for her. That he understood. That he cared. From the frowning scowl on his face, she knew she wouldn't be getting any kind of consoling reaction.

"Now you're mad at me," she said, throwing her hands up and letting them drop.

"Well...what do you expect? Do you think I'll be all smiles after you say something like that?"

"I don't know..."

"We used to be really hot and heavy into each other, but now we're just weak sauce."

"*Weak* sauce?"

"Yeah. Maybe I *am* changing up the way I kiss, hoping it'll make you want me like you used to."

"I *do* want you."

He looked at her. Half his face was washed out from the moonlight coming in through the window. The other half was wiped with darkness. He looked eerie, and a hint of sinisterly romantic.

"And you don't have sex with me anymore," he declared.

"That's not true. I still have sex with you."

"Yeah...sure. Last month sometime."

"My parents are really stressing me about school. My grades are starting to suck and if I don't get them up, I'm screwed for the whole summer."

"I get it. You're stressed—"

"*Very* stressed, Doug."

He raised an eyebrow. His lips curved into a smirk. "And you have said that sex with me relieves your stress."

"I never said that."

"It's what you meant."

It had been one of their better times. His parents had gone outside to grill hamburgers, leaving her and Doug alone inside. So, they'd snuck off to the bathroom and done it on the floor mat. It was quick, but so much fun and impressively satisfying. She'd had a bad day and had made the comment, *That just made me forget all about my day.*

Should've kept my damn mouth shut.

"So what?" she said finally.

"So…let's get in the back seat." His hand landed on her thigh, high up, his fingers just nipping under her skirt. "And all this stress goes bye-bye…"

It felt good having his hand there, so close to touching her panties, but not making any attempt to do so. Just the gesture made her *want* him to touch her. She looked at him, glanced at the backseat, and then back to him.

"Ready?" he asked.

"Yeah," she said, climbing over the seat, making sure her rump brushed his face.

"All right!" he hollered, following her back there.

As they started pulling at each other's clothes, Doug's phone vibrated from the front seat more than once. They didn't notice as his pants came down, as Jenny removed her panties and Doug mounted her.

But Jenny paid no attention to the phone as Doug lay on top of her, thrusting wildly.

CHAPTER 23

Henry Conner was unboxing the microscope he'd borrowed—*stolen*—from the blood lab at the clinic when his doorbell chimed. Glancing at the clock, he saw it was nearing ten.

Who would be coming by so late?

Probably one of the Heymans. They'd been coming over a lot, especially since the detective had visited them. He'd visited Henry, too, but the Heymans were a paranoid pair and thought the detective suspected them of something. Henry couldn't blame them for thinking that way, not after all they'd been through. But, his personal opinion of Detective Garner was that he was an idiot. Even if he were to suspect something was awry, he doubted the man had the brains to properly decipher what it was.

That still didn't explain who might be visiting at this hour.

Henry stepped away from the desk, giving it a final quick glance. He nodded, approvingly. The microscope was attached to a desktop computer with a line running out the back that connected to a Hi-Definition Camcorder. He was almost satisfied with his set up, but knew it could only be a temporary workroom.

The doorbell chimed a second time. Henry left the room, hurried through the hall and down the stairs, and made his way to the front door. He put his eye to the peephole. All he saw was solid black. Someone was deliberately blocking his view.

Trying to be secretive, are we?

"Who is it?"

A short pause, then a woman's voice said, "Hawthorne sent me."

"Hawthorne?"

"Yes. Open up, please."

How did Hawthorne find him?

It couldn't have been too hard. The Heymans found me easily enough. Guess I'm not as good at hiding as I thought.

Sighing, Henry snatched back the deadbolt, then unlocked the knob. He opened the door.

"Henry Conner?" asked the passably attractive woman on the other side. She lowered the hand she was using to cover the peephole.

"And you are?"

"Denise Harper. We need to talk."

Sitting in his chair, a glass of bourbon in his hand, he stared at the young lady who now occupied his couch. The thick fluffy cushions looked to be trying to swallow her as she sank down into their soft padding.

A college student, most likely. Hawthorne liked them young, usually offering grants to the pretty ones willing to show him *appreciation* for allowing them on his team. Henry didn't doubt this girl was one of those many.

The thick black glasses with ultra-thin lenses slipped down her nose. She shoved them back into place with a finger.

"I told Hawthorne to let me handle this," he said. He took a heavy gulp of drink. It singed the back of his throat.

"He thought you might need some assistance."

"I don't."

"He disagrees."

"It's not his decision."

Denise smirked, her upper lip arching slightly. "You're wrong about that."

Leaning forward, Henry sighed. "He's planning to just come right in and take over, isn't he?"

"Only if I say he needs to."

"And do you think he does?"

"You haven't shown me anything to say either way."

"And I'm not planning to. I'm sorry Ms. Harper, but you've wasted your time. And mine. You may leave now."

She offered a single cold laugh. "I'm not leaving."

Standing up, Henry slammed the glass down on the coffee table.

Holding his stare, Denise made no effort to move. She spoke louder, firmer. "Hawthorne is ready to come back on board. He is willing to supply you with whatever you need to study the specimen. Crack him open…"

"The parents would never agree to those kinds of tests. They wouldn't want to see the kid put through any kind of pain."

And neither would Henry. Not unless he absolutely had to hurt Gabe to learn from him.

Denise uncrossed her legs, trading her position and throwing the other leg over the opposite knee. The dim lighting threw glossy streaks on her smooth skin. "Then you need to think of something."

He wondered if it was her idea or Hawthorne's for her to wear such a short skirt. Didn't matter, he liked what he saw but he wasn't the type of person who'd allow it to influence him. "I will think of something, but I'm doing it my way."

"With *my* help."

Henry nearly exploded but swallowed the bubble of rage back down into his gut. His stomach felt as if he'd just eaten a boulder. Dropping back down into the chair, he pushed his head into the L of his hand. His thumb rubbed his temple. "You're not going to let up on this, are you?"

Denise smiled. "Now you're starting to understand. Hawthorne doesn't pay me what he does for me not to get him what he wants."

Henry sighed. "What do you suggest? If the parents learn you are involved, they will run. There's no doubt in my mind they will take the kid and hit the road, disappearing again."

"Then they won't know about me. Do what you have been doing. I'll bring some more equipment over here and set it up. We can do minimal examinations for a little while, but eventually we'll have to get the kid in the lab."

"Where *is* the lab?"

"You'll learn that in due time."

"The parents won't allow us to take him anywhere."

"The parents are expendable."

Henry stared at her, shocked by what she said although he shouldn't have been. "The parents might be the key to why the kid wasn't a failure like the rest."

"Then maybe we will keep *one* of them, that is, if *both* aren't willing to cooperate."

Henry felt like he was falling although he was still sitting in the chair. Her words trundled through him like a stampede of razors.

"You weren't the only one who got burned back then," she said. "Hawthorne lost millions trying to cover it up. When I came on board a couple years ago, he was still trying to clean up your mess. I'm going to make sure that doesn't happen again."

Henry opened his mouth but the words seemed too frightened to come out.

"Keep the light on for me," she said, standing up. "I'm going to go get my things and will be back in a little while."

"What do you…?"

"I'm moving in. We're going to be roomies!" She clapped her hands, hopping up and down like a preteen at her birthday party.

Henry's stomach clenched, wringing the bourbon back up the way it had come in. Quickly, he shot out of the chair and ran for the bathroom. Leaving the door open, he dropped to his knees and vomited into the toilet. The puke splashed into the water, burning his throat as if he'd guzzled battery acid.

In the background, he heard Denise tell him bye and to drink some Pepto. She'd pick up some Ginger-Ale on the way back.

Henry regretted he'd ever called Hawthorne, but deep down, he knew the only way he could accurately examine and study Gabe was with the callous man's help. This time wouldn't be any different than their first collaboration. He'd only hear from Hawthorne by phone or email, never meet the guy face-to-face, but his lab techs would be everywhere.

Maybe he should let Denise Harper know the risk of working for a man like Hawthorne. Usually if things went sour, you died. After Project: Newborn failed, and it was discovered what they'd really been up to, Hawthorne had set it up to kill everyone involved.

And I come out of hiding and make that phone call. That was how Hawthorne found me. Calling him from a blocked line hadn't been enough security, so he'd probably had his computer wizards hack into an IP address somehow and hone in on my location.

Henry might as well have shot a signal in the air of a giant arrow pointing down at his house.

Idiot.

The soft bump of his front door closing resounded faintly in the distance. Reaching above, Henry found the lever and flushed the toilet. Watching the vomit swirl down the drain brought back the visual of blood swirling down the drain in the labs. That took his thoughts to Hawthorne's phone call those years ago, telling him the lab was going to be eradicated, and to disappear.

Should've stayed invisible...

He hoped he hadn't sold his soul to the devil again.

CHAPTER 24

Detective Frank Garner left his car where the short drive of Sunwalk dead-ended, then toddled back toward Betty Andrews' house. He'd looked around the grounds for a short time, confirming nothing had changed and there was no evidence he'd overlooked. Then he'd decided to take a gander at the private community. He hated to say, but his investigation had gone cold, though he'd only admit it to himself if he'd been drinking. Which tonight, he'd been drinking copiously. The Andrews family, however, thought he was following possible leads, when really he had *nothing* to go on. And hadn't had anything of much interest at all from the beginning.

So why did I come here tonight?

He had no clue. Just a hunch in his gut told him the resolution was right in front of him. If only he could see it. Couldn't see shit right now, though. It was too dark and being a cloudy night with the possibility of thunderstorms, he didn't even have stars or the moon to piss by. That was why he'd peed on his shoes when he'd been aiming for the bushes in Betty Andrews' back yard. Not because he'd had too many beers at Haps.

Garner couldn't even remember a decision to drive out to Sunwalk being made. All he recalled was staggering out of the bar, getting in his car, and driving out here a safe fifteen miles below the speed limit. He figured he was a pro at driving after a few beers, but the scratches on his car would suggest otherwise.

The idea to go back to his car and grab a flashlight lasted only a moment before he decided against it. If someone was to see the track of his light capering back and forth, they'd call the cops. The *sober* cops. And he'd get in trouble, again. He'd been lucky the last time hadn't cost him his job. He might have been lieutenant by now. He doubted they'd take pity on him a second go-round, especially since he couldn't use his wife leaving him as an excuse. That was two years ago, surely a man would be done with the pity parties by then.

But he wasn't a man.

Don't start the feeling sorry for yourself shit again. Go down that route and it's hell getting back.

Walking on the side of the road, he eyed the houses. Dark for the most part, some had their porch lights on as if expecting someone to visit. Most of the windows were lightless, while others had dim smolders of orange faintness from nightlights or lamps. Looked as if Sunwalk was asleep.

All was quiet through the house, not a creature was stirring, except for Detective Garner.

He giggled, quickly allaying himself. His shoes made moist squishy sounds in the grass as he walked carefully, overly concentrating on his balance. With the ditch on the other side of him, he didn't want to slip and fall. He'd never be able to crawl out. Someone would find him in the morning while walking their dog. He might even wake up to a cocked leg and warm yellow splashes on his face. No, falling in the ditch could not happen. And it felt like it might at any moment from how bad everything seemed to be tilting all around him.

He stopped in front of the house that hadn't left him since he was here drinking sweet tea served to him by the most gorgeous woman he'd ever seen. He still remembered her name. *Sheila.* So lovely that it caused him to describe her as exquisite. Garner wasn't even sure what that word meant, but it sounded good. Gazing up, he wondered which dark window was her bedroom.

And the bed she shared with her husband…

Garner hadn't liked the husband. Greg was his name. Greg and Sheila Heyman. There had been something off about them both, and it wasn't their quirkiness. That kind of personality could be understood and even tolerated. No, this couple had secrets, probably a rack of skeletons hanging in their closets. They didn't come across as people apt to hurt someone though, even an old tetchy hag like Betty Andrews. Still, he wouldn't put it past anyone these days.

He looked to the house next door, beyond the fence to the dark section of yard where the Andrews mutt was devoured. At first, he'd been quick to put the blame on coyotes. Now he wasn't so sure. During his quest, he had yet to spot one coyote or evidence there had been any in the area. Other than the dead one he'd seen on the side of the road on his way in, of course.

The daughter and her friend had reported hearing growls when the dog was killed, and Garner believed them. He didn't suspect the girls or the parents of any involvement either. Todd Parker seemed like a down to earth kind of guy and his wife was super sweet. Going against what the neighbors said, being a horror author didn't make Todd

Parker a pet-slaying, devil-worshipping maniac.

Still…

Garner wished he had at least an inkling of probable cause to search the grounds, but he had zilch. That wouldn't stop him from taking a quick stroll around the house, though. Just the outside, maybe the back yard, then he'd make his way through the Heymans' back yard and return to his car. Unless he found something, of course.

The Parkers didn't own a dog, so he didn't have to worry about barking or biting as he crept alongside the fence. It was even darker in this spot, the fence blocking out what light there was from the power poles. Overhanging boughs, thick with bushels of leaves strangled out the rest. He could have been walking with his eyes shut. Blinking to make sure they weren't, he shortened his stride. The house to his right, the fence to his left, trees in between, he figured he had enough cover. His clothes were dark and blended in with the curtains of shadows. No one should be able to see him out here.

Felt like the house stretched forever. Seeing it from the front, you'd have no idea it was so big. Just kept going and going. He stepped away from the fence, seeing a tree ahead. Shoulders hunched, he scurried over to it, shoes swishing through the damp grass. He stood underneath. From here, he had a nice view of the house's backside. Things always looked different at night, but if his memory was correct, he was right near where the dog was found. Several feet to his left, he thought.

Garner's eyes searched the darkness. He couldn't see the Heymans' house from here. But he could see plenty of the murky woods where the fence ended and the trees girdled the yard in a fortress of seclusion.

He wanted to rifle around over there, but figured it was a

waste of time and way too risky. Without any light, he could seriously hurt himself. Trip over a jutting root, get his foot snagged in a rut or hole. No way. He still had some scouring next door yet, so he needed to get going. And, it was late, but at least he was off tomorrow and could sleep in.

Scuttling noises above arrested his attention. Little ragged chips chinked down on his head, severed leaves drifting over his shoulders.

Garner looked up. Couldn't fathom what he was seeing: a figure straddling a branch. He saw shadowy movements of a leg as it squatted. His eyes began to focus, and he could make out features.

His mouth shot open to scream.

Then the creature in the tree dropped down, pouncing on Frank's chest. Two claw-edged hands gripped his throat, tearing through the flesh and spraying hot bursts of blood onto its hideously deformed face. An elongated forked tongue lapped at the sticky-red jets. The pain was awful, like cold knives digging into his throat.

Then he felt himself being hoisted upward, his back slamming against the rough texture of the tree bark. It scraped him as he climbed.

Garner's mind quickly shut down, granting him a moment's break from the madness before death took him forever.

CHAPTER 25

Henry Conner's first thought was an earthquake had hit. His whole body was shaking, the mattress underneath him bouncing and thrusting. Trying to sit up, he felt pressure on his shoulders, so he started swinging his arms in an effort to free himself. A fist struck something hard and fuzzy.

A sharp cry. "Ow!"

Then he felt a heavy blow on his bicep like he'd been hit with a baseball.

Now he was awake. His wild, confused eyes darting. The room was dark except for a dim scabbard of light swilling in from his opened door.

"Get up!"

He looked to his left and saw the dark form of a woman rubbing her head. Tangles of hair bowed out.

"Denise?"

"Duh shit…someone's ringing the hell out of your doorbell. Can't you hear it?"

Now he could, an unrelenting chain of clangs. Reaching behind him, he felt the cool smoothness of his bourbon bottle. He slid it under the pillow. If Denise saw it, she would realize it wasn't the same one he'd been drinking out of yesterday. That one he'd stuffed down into the bottom of the trash can. He didn't want her knowing how quickly he chugged through them.

"What time is it?" he asked.

"It's after one in the morning. Get up and see who it is."

Henry went to throw the sheets off his body but found they weren't there. His sticky skin looked pale and damp in the swath of light. Then he realized he was naked.

"And you might want to put on some clothes," said Denise, confirming she'd noticed.

Dressed in a robe and standing downstairs, his eye squinted against the peephole, he wasn't surprised by who he saw at his threshold. Sheila Heyman. She looked as if she'd just hopped out of bed and ran right over. She wore a tank-top, and because she had on no bra, Henry could see the faint impressions of breasts through the wispy fabric, as well as the tiny juts of her nipples, thanks to the mild night. Her shorts could barely pass for it, and looked more like panties that barely covered the lower cambers of her buttocks.

His hand curling around the doorknob, he glanced behind him. Denise stood halfway up the stairs. He thrust his chin at her. Taking the hint, she nodded, then turned and ascended the stairs. He watched her rump flex in the tight black panties that clung to her like thin dark skin. When he could see her no more, he faced forward and opened the door.

"Thank God!" cried Sheila. Not waiting to be invited, she rushed in.

Henry flung the door shut. "What's happened?"

"Guh-Gabe...he..." Unable to finish the sentence, she started to cry. Pushed her fists into her eyes.

"It's okay," he said. He reached out, putting a hand on her shoulder. Her skin was cold and smooth, little bumps of goose flesh felt like rice against his fingers. "Let's go sit down." He felt the brush of her hair as she nodded. He guided her into the living room. There were no lights on, but he could see the soft shapes of his furniture from light leaking down from upstairs. Taking her to the chair, he helped her down. She made no attempt of taking her hands away from her face. Continuing to cry, her shoulders bopped, hair bouncing.

"Want a drink?"

"Please..."

"Okay." He hurried to the bar. His hand rummaged across the counter as he searched for the lamp. His fingers grazed the tip of the drawstring. Pinching it, he yanked the skinny cord down. A puddle of dim light threw glossy blotches in the surface. "Any requests?"

"Something with a punch."

"Hmm..." He looked at the shelves on the wall behind him. The first bottle his eyes landed on was skull-shaped. "Vodka?"

"Straight?"

"I could mix it in something. I have orange juice in the fridge."

"No thanks. The vodka will do."

He nodded despite the fact she couldn't see it from pressing her fists into her eyes. He brought down the bottle, unscrewed the cap and filled a shot glass to the rim. He was about to take it to her when Sheila flopped down on one of the three barstools. "Hit me, barkeep."

Henry slid the drink in front of her. "What happened?"

Sheila tossed back the shot, grimacing as she set the glass

down. "One more. Greg would kill me if he knew I was taking shots...but dammit, I need them."

He gave her another. "We won't tell him. You can say I took a long time answering the door."

The second shot looked easier to handle than the first. Still, she couldn't stop the horrible crumpled-up facial expression when she was finished.

"That's some...strong...whoa!"

Henry took the glass from her and hid it under the bar. "All right. Now tell me what Gabe did."

Nodding, she wiped her mouth with the back of her hand. "He attacked someone..."

"Oh shit. Who?"

"That detective..."

"Holy *shit.*" Henry brought the shot glass back, refilled it, and instead of sharing, he swallowed the blazing sour fluid himself. Burning air gusted through his lips. "You mean the one that's been all over the neighborhood?"

"Yeah..." She pushed her hand into her hair, shaking it. "Of all people, it had to be him."

"He was looking for Ms. Andrews..." Henry raised an eyebrow. "At least now he won't know Gabe killed her too."

"Ms. Andrews?" Henry nodded. "I did that."

Henry's substandard response seemed to bother her. She squirmed uncomfortably in her seat as if he'd reacted with an expounding outburst. "Greg took care of it."

"Why didn't you tell me? All this time I thought it had been Gabe..."

"We didn't want to scare you away. We thought if you knew I—"

"—it's going to take a lot more than that to scare me away."

"A murder doesn't?"

"No. *Two* murders won't either, in case you're wondering."

"I was."

"Where's Greg now?"

Greg stood under the tree, looking up. He could see the eerie shape of an arm sagging over the limb. A cold droplet of blood dripped onto his forehead. Flinching, he reached into his pocket and removed an old tissue. He used the crumpled wad to wipe off the blood. He felt another one drip into his hair. Then another.

Another.

Shit!

Looking down at his feet, he saw he was standing in grass speckled in the red dewdrops. Blood was drizzling down from the detective's body in a gentle but steady dribble. Like the faucet of a shower right after it has been shut off, the water just continues to trickle a short while after. He wondered how much had been splattered and where.

No time to focus on that. Get the body.

That was why he was here. Clean up would have to wait.

He patted his back pocket. Garner's wallet was still there. He'd almost missed it when Gabe had first showed them the massacre. Tucked in a patch of grass that was higher than the rest, the leather folder nearly blended in. Luckily he'd seen it, or all this work they were about to embark would be for naught. His heart had thrust itself into his throat when he saw the detective's badge and ID.

Of course it has to be him…

He began to climb.

"I'm going with you," said Denise.

"Not a chance," said Henry.

Sheila had only been gone thirty seconds when Denise hopped down the stairs, dressed in dark clothing and wearing an eager grin.

"Yes, I am."

"No."

"Think about it. You're going to dump a car, right?"

Henry sighed. "Right."

"You're gonna want to drive a long ways off, right?"

"I imagine. The smart thing to do would be to take it out of town, dump the car somewhere no one will think to look."

It sounded like a good plan in his head. He'd volunteered to handle the car for the Heymans while they handled the body. Sheila had told him Greg's plan on keeping the human meat for Gabe. He wasn't sure doing that would keep Gabe in line, but it was worth a shot. The kid wanted the meat fresh and juicy, maybe even needed the thrill of the hunt, and the kill.

Denise crossed her arms, her bottom lipped pursed as if considering his plan. "It's great. You've thought it through."

"Thank you." He grabbed his keys off the rack next to his door. "I'll be back."

"How are you going to get back?"

He paused at the door. "Excuse me?"

"I see no problem in your strategy in getting out there. However...you dispose of the car, and then what? Walk back? Take a cab? A bus?"

"I get your point."

"I'll follow you, in your car."

As much as he hated to acknowledge it, she was absolutely

right. Why he hadn't thought of that beforehand, he had no idea.

It's not like I have tons of experience in this.

He wondered if Denise did. She seemed to know a lot more than him.

But he hated his ignorance in the matter. He blamed the booze. He'd ingested way too much in the past couple days.

The past week.

Month.

Stop!

"Let's go," he said.

Excitedly, Denise clapped her hands as if he just told her he got her a puppy.

After Greg had gotten Garner in the basement, he'd gone back outside. There was no decision reached on how to clean up the blood left behind. But there had been no need.

Rain cut wet slashes in the dark. Greg saw the backyard momentarily in a starburst of lightning. He smiled. The rain should wash away the blood. The first big storm of the year had hit, a whopper, and he couldn't be happier. Relief washed through him. He turned away from the yard, and began his journey to the back door. Inside, he closed the door, locked the useless deadbolt, and was on his way to the living room when he noticed the kitchen table.

A chainsaw sat on top, its yellow clunky body tilted back, the jagged teeth of the blade pointing upward.

He'd asked Sheila to find him something to cut the body up with. If he used the ax inside, he'd probably whack chunks out of the concrete floor in the basement. And they'd lose their deposit. Plus, the ceiling was too low, and he was too tall. Floor beams would catch the ax in mid-swing.

Walking over to the table, he studied the chainsaw curiously.

"It was all I could find."

Turning back, he saw Sheila standing in the doorway. "There's a hacksaw somewhere..."

"I saw it. The blade looked dull. I found this in a trunk. Must've been left here by the last tenants. Don't know if it works..."

"Does it have gas in it?"

"Something was sloshing around in there."

Nodding, Greg couldn't restrain the fervor to touch the saw cascading through him. Something in him hoped more than it should that the saw worked.

"It's raining?" she asked.

"Yeah...storming like hell."

"Good."

"Should clean everything up for us."

She heaved a reassured sigh.

"Before I get started on Garner, we better go talk to Gabe."

Sheila nodded. "What are we going to say?"

"I think..." He paused. He noticed the worried look she was giving him, "...we have to stop talking."

"No, Greg. Not that..."

"We've tried time-outs, grounding, taking things away...and none of it works."

"Greg...we agreed from the beginning that we would *not* punish him physically."

"That was then, this is now."

"But, Greg...his *condition*."

"Condition or not, Sheila, he's our son. Doesn't matter how big he is, or even how strong he is. I am his father, and you are his mother. He is *our* responsibility. If we don't show him this kind of behavior won't be tolerated, he'll keep doing it."

"He can't control himself."

"That's a load of bullshit. *I* don't think he's trying."

"Greg..."

"Do *you* think he's trying?"

She raised a shoulder, but said nothing.

"He's pretending to, and that worries me. He's starting to lie to us, and he's acting different. Something's going on and he won't talk to me about it. I can't help but wonder if I'm failing him as a father."

"You're not..."

"Well, I'm doing something wrong."

"It's not you, it's me. Sometimes I won't...I can't nurture him the way he needs to be nurtured."

"You do fine."

"I don't do enough. I guess I got that from..."

She stopped before allowing the sentence to suggest her mother. Greg had listened to Sheila on several occasions, as he held her tightly in bed, maliciously curse her mother, then held her even tighter when she cried about it. He didn't know everything, but he didn't *want* to know, either. What little Sheila had divulged was enough for him to know her mother was not a kind person. A domineering, officious witch, he'd probably go as far as calling his mother-in-law evil. He was grateful she'd died before he and Sheila met.

Sheila finally spoke again. "You're right. Something's going on."

"We'll talk to him about it tomorrow. But, right now..." He reached for his belt.

Sheila's eyes grew as a slight panic began to develop.

"Greg...*please...*"

"Sheila. There's no debating it."

Her panic faded. Now she was mad. "Then you'll have to do it by yourself. I want no part of it."

"Fine. I'll handle it."

He walked away, leaving her behind. He could feel her pleading eyes on his back, hoping he would turn around and tell her he'd changed his mind. That wasn't happening. He was going through with the spanking.

It's not like I'm thrilled with the idea...

He was dreading this more than taking a chainsaw to the detective's body. But just like that atrocious chore, this had to be done. If he didn't show Gabe how serious he was, his son would keep walking all over him.

As he slid the belt out of the loops of his pants, he wondered how long Sheila would stay mad at him. Thinking back to the resentment she'd shown him caused his neck to sweat. He couldn't believe she was just going to *sit this one out.*

Let me do all the mean stuff...

Then she can be the one to console him later, snuggle with him, and protect him from the mean, spank-happy daddy.

At the top of the stairs, gazing down the hall to Gabe's room, he was contemplating not doing it at all. Maybe showing him the belt, telling him what will happen if he does it again, would be enough. Standing there, he knew it wouldn't work. He had to actually put the leather strip to his son's bottom. And knowing that made his throat tighten. His chest felt like it was trying to sink in.

Get in there and get it over with.

He started forward. It felt like he was wearing iron shoes, trudging through the hall. Stopping at the door, he took a deep breath. Opened the door, letting it swing inward. Blue light spilled into the hall.

The bed was empty.

Dammit!

Greg rushed into the room. He didn't see Gabe anywhere. Not on the bed. Not playing with his toys on the floor. Not behind the chair...

Wait a second...

Straining his eyes, he began to make out the fluffy shape of Gabe's hair in an unlit corner of the room. A dark, fuzzy form against the shadows. Two orbs slowly faded in, reddish egg shapes glowing.

Greg felt bad he'd automatically assumed his son had snuck out, but who would really blame him for thinking so? After all the times Gabe hadn't listened, Greg was bound to think the worst.

"Gabe?" he said.

His son's eyes fixed on the belt dangling from Greg's hand. He looked up, suppliant eyes getting bigger. A squeaky whine escaped.

Greg felt himself deflating inside. All his courage seemed to shrivel up like a tire with a slow leak. His arm holding the belt became weedy, as if he couldn't even lift it to put the belt back on. He didn't want to use this belt on his son. Even though he should, he didn't think he could.

"Why won't you listen?" he asked.

Gabe grunted once, then lowered his head. He had no reason.

"Don't you want to talk about it?"

Head shake.

"Why not?"

Another head shake.

"Gabe..." He was afraid to ask this next question, but knew it needed to be addressed. "Have you done things your mother and I don't know about?"

His son flinched as if someone had tried to strike him. Greg knew right there Gabe was hiding even more than he already knew.

"Do you have secrets?"

Gabe cowered even lower. At this angle, Gabe looked less like his son and more like a frightened stray animal.

Greg walked deeper into the room, stopped at the bed, and sat on the side nearest Gabe. "Gabe...we don't have secrets in this house. You know that."

He waited for Gabe to respond with either a nod or some kind of identifying grunt. He got neither. This worried Greg even more.

"Booger? Look at me."

Gabe crumpled himself up even tighter.

"Booger?"

Gabe raised his head but didn't face Greg. He looked away.

And Greg felt his heart burst, raining into his gut. Pin-like tingles fluttered in his stomach. Tears welled in his eyes. Doing nothing to stop them, they spilled out, sliding down his cheeks.

"That's how it's going to be?"

Gabe acted as if Greg hadn't spoken.

"You're not going to talk to me, to tell me what's wrong?"

A growl. Not foul or threatening, just a response to let Greg know he heard him but he wasn't going to cooperate.

The belt felt like a dead leathery snake in Greg's hand. His fingers were cramping from holding it so firmly and his palm was itchy and damp. He switched the belt to the other hand, wiped his hand on his pants, and then returned the belt.

He'd hoped a long talk with Gabe would have treated the matter. Now he understood this was a test. Gabe had noticed the reluctance in Greg, and now wanted to see just how far he could push him.

So, the belt *would* have to be used.

God, I don't wanna do this!

But gazing at his son as he looked around the blue-tinged room, giving each object—except for Greg—equal attention, he knew there was no getting out of spanking Gabe.

"Come here," he said.

Now Gabe could suddenly hear again. Looking at Greg, his eyes returned to their anxious manner. He shook his head.

"Now, Gabe. This is not up for discussion."

His back to the wall, he used his feet to push himself up. His shirt made slight swishing sounds as he rose. Gabe nervously picked at his pants with clawed fingers. If he kept at it, he'd slit the gauzy fabric of his pajama pants, then he'd be down two pairs.

He made no effort to walk the short distance to the bed.

Greg slapped his thigh. "Now!"

Gabe bumped against the wall. Greg's sudden rise in volume had scared him. He almost lightened his approach, but when he saw his son timidly coming closer, he didn't. It was working. Gabe was taking him seriously again.

When Gabe was standing in front of him, Greg patted his legs. "Pull your pants down and lean over my legs."

Gabe started to cry. Mucus-colored tears streamed from his eyes. Shaking his head, he covered his bottom with both hands.

"I don't want to, Booger. You know that, don't you?"

Gabe nodded, and Greg believed him. It helped him feel

slightly better but not enough to make a difference.

"I love you," said Greg.

"Uh uhhh ooooh..."

Greg was now crying, his throat clucking as he tried to hold it back. "Do it, Gabe. Let's get this over with."

Still crying, Gabe tugged at his pants until his underwear was out in the open. Greg recognized the teddy bears decorating the seat of the briefs. Their colors were starting to fade from frequent washes.

"Come on," sniffled Greg.

Nodding and crying, Gabe stepped around Greg's knees and slowly took position. His stomach bent over Greg's thighs, with his butt poking upward. Greg could feel his son's trembling down to his feet.

Get it done, so this can stop!

Greg held up the belt. It fell against his arm like a dead snake. Trying to remember how his own father held the belt when it was Greg where Gabe was now, he realized he was doing it wrong. He quickly held it out, folded it back, and gripped both ends. The belt was now a loop at the striking end.

That looked right. But felt terrible.

As he raised his hand into the air, Greg hoped this wouldn't make Gabe afraid of him, or even worse: hate him.

I love you, Gabe...

He brought the belt down.

CHAPTER 26

"That was fun," said Denise. She was leaning back in the driver's seat, one arm on the steering wheel, her wrist bent over the top. She casually drove as if they were enjoying a scenic drive.

"Are you insane?" asked Henry.

He looked at her from the passenger seat. She shrugged, her demeanor not faltering.

"That was *not* fun," he added.

"Please. Don't act like you didn't enjoy it. Didn't it make you at least *semi*-hard?"

Her blunt question surprised him. "Excuse me?"

"I bet if I put my hand on it, I'd feel some wood."

She was right but he wasn't going to tell her so. He knew his arousal wasn't from disposing of the cop's car. The thrill of doing something bad...naughty...had turned him on. He wasn't proud of it, but he couldn't deny it. "Stop talking like that."

"I'll be honest, I'm gushing down there. If I was wearing panties they'd be soaked. I bet I have a wet spot on my pants." She attempted looking down, frowned, then faced the road again. "Oh well. Too dark to see." She looked over at him, grinning goofily. "Why don't you feel and tell me?" Her thighs parted, granting him room to reach over.

Henry almost did but shook his head. "You have completely lost your mind."

"I don't know how much was there to begin with."

"Probably not much."

"Ouch. Aren't *we* cranky?"

Henry wasn't going to give her the benefit of a response. He had every right to be cranky. The shit he'd done tonight just to ensure Gabe's well-being called for a drink. Maybe that would kill his own excitement. As much as he wanted to check Denise's pants for damp spots, he didn't think it was a good idea.

An image of the detective's car sinking into the swamp, its taillights vanishing under capes of murky aerated water, wouldn't leave his mind.

Should've had the body in the trunk...

Denise had disputed that idea from the start, saying if someone found the car, the body would exhibit all the signs of Gabe's slaughter. It would be enough to get the kinds of people involved they didn't need.

Unless they burned the body first.

She was right but he would feel better knowing the body was at the bottom of the swamp, instead of stored away in the Heymans' freezer to be used for some kind of grotesque kid's meal.

Denise groaned from beside him. "We might have to stop by my apartment."

"Why?"

"Pick up my vibrator."

"Jeez..." he muttered.

Her thighs wouldn't be still. They kept flexing and

pressing together, rubbing, squeezing tightly.

She's really horny…

So was he and hated it.

"Henry?"

"What?"

"Let's fuck."

A surge of provocation itched through him. His penis swelled, throbbing against the zipper of his pants. "Denise…"

"Don't make me get my vibrator and *please* don't make me take care of it with my finger. Just a little quickie. Come on, you know you want to."

He decided not to argue, and just go along with it. "Fine."

Denise stamped the brakes. The car skidded, tires squealing, as they bounced to a halt on the verge of the road. She threw the gear into park.

"What the hell?" he shouted.

Denise already had her seatbelt off and was pulling down her pants when she said, "Get 'em down." She nodded at his pants which were still snugly on him.

Looking around, Henry thought where they were appeared isolated enough. Pastures on each side of the road, and they hadn't seen a car this entire trip.

So far.

He would bet once they got started one would just come zipping right along.

"Henry!"

"Oh…right."

He'd gotten his pants down to his knees when Denise climbed onto his lap, putting a knee on each side of him. His stiff penis titled against her right thigh.

"Hawthorne would kick my ass if he knew." She reached between her legs, gripped his penis.

"Our secret," said Henry. He leaned up to kiss her but she pushed him back down.

"What are you doing?"

"Kissing you..."

"Ew, Henry...that would be weird."

He didn't have time to ponder the absurdity of her statement. She was already impaling herself on top of him. Head leaned back, she gasped at the roof of the car. She sheathed him, tight and slippery.

Henry clawed at the side of the seat. Finally he found the lever and pulled it back. The seat dropped down. Denise landed on top of him, squealing in surprise.

Then she began to grind her hips.

When they were finished minutes later, Denise sat behind the wheel, panting. She hadn't bothered to put her pants back on. A hand gripped the gearshift, the other loosely hanging onto the steering wheel. "You're pretty hot for an old guy," she said.

Henry smiled. That was as good a compliment as he would get from her. And he'd take it. "Thanks."

"We just might have to do that again sometime."

"I'm game if you are."

"Oh yeah. Definitely." Laughing, she pulled the gear down to D. "Big time."

Henry couldn't believe he felt pride over that, but he did.

The chainsaw worked but was constantly jamming up. The toothy chain would snag a section of clothing and shut off, pulling against Greg's wrists and making them hurt. He finally had to strip the detective. Once the clothes were out of the way, the chainsaw had no trouble.

Messy, but it ran like a champ.

He'd prepared by making a little shelter around him out of plastic and draping the floor in a sheet as well. He'd cut two slits in the plastic shield, and slipped his arms through. Whatever gore the chainsaw threw back at him, it was deflected by the plastic wall.

He'd concocted a table out of an old door propped on two sawhorses. The body was on top, in sections. Blood left pooled trails between the dismembered parts. Shutting off the saw, he set it down on the plastic flooring.

"That was awful..."

Gasping, Greg spun around to find Sheila standing at the foot of the stairs. She looked pale, as if she'd put on a heavy layer of white face paint.

"How long have you been standing there?"

She shook her head. "I can't believe...awful..."

"Honey, you shouldn't have watched me...you know? That's why I told you to stay upstairs."

"What?" She looked at him as if he'd said something vulgar. "No. I'm not talking about *that.*" She thrust her chin at the table, indicating the dismembered spectacle. "I'm talking about what you did to Gabe. It. Was. Awful."

Greg stepped away from his gore-defense cubicle, approaching her cautiously. She had a look about her like someone about to snap. "It had to be done, Sheila. You should have seen him up there. He acted like he didn't even care that we were upset with him."

"He does."

"I know that. But, he was trying to get away with something he knew was wrong. And, he's keeping secrets."

"What kind of secrets?"

"I don't know. He wouldn't tell me. I'm going to try to work on him some more tomorrow."

"Maybe Dr. Conner can help."

"Maybe. I doubt it, though. This isn't where a scientist needs to offer his opinions. This boils down to good old-fashioned parenting."

Sheila sighed. "I guess you're right."

He studied her colorless face: the purple crescents under her eyes were swollen and puffy. "Are you feeling all right?"

She shrugged. "Stress, I'm sure."

"You don't look like you feel well."

"I got a little sick earlier, but I'm okay now."

"Well..." He frowned. "I'm done with all the loud stuff down here. Why don't you go to bed and I'll clean up and stock the mea—the stuff."

"You don't mind?"

Smiling, he shook his head. "No, dear. Take something for your stomach, and then get to bed."

Sheila groaned in relief. "*Thank* you." She walked over to him and wrapped her arms around him. "Thank you."

He hugged her back, although knowing she'd been vomiting made him squeamish. She might be contagious. So, instead of kissing her on the lips, he just gave her a quick peck on the forehead.

"I can help you if you need the help," she said. Her voice was muffled against his shirt.

He really wanted her help, but would never forgive himself. If he asked her to stay, she would. And, she'd assist him until there was nothing left to do. She needed her rest, and if she was getting sick, she shouldn't be down here in a cool, damp basement.

"No," he said. "I'll be fine. Shouldn't take me much more than a couple hours to finish up."

"Okay." She squeezed him one more time, then pulled

away. "Wake me up when you come to bed."

He never understood why she always asked him to. She never remembered the next morning, and would ask him what time he finally came to bed. Greg supposed it comforted her in the moment, but it was quickly forgotten once she was back asleep.

"G'night," he said. "I love you."

She stopped nearly halfway up the stairs, turned back, said, "Love you too." She parted her lips for an exhausted smile. Then she ascended the rest of the way.

The door clapped shut.

On his way to the table, Greg took another pair of yellow rubber gloves out of the package and pulled them on. He flexed his fingers, wiggling the digits into the slots. Once they felt comfortable, he grabbed the box of meat paper. He rolled out a lengthy sheet, and ripped it across the tiny teeth.

Then he began wrapping the meat.

Sheila was going to check and see if Gabe was sleeping when her stomach suddenly felt like it was being rung with arctic hands. She detoured to the right, dashing for the bathroom. She'd barely gotten the toilet seat up before vomit burst out of her mouth. Thankfully she was slightly bent over, and the brew splashed into the toilet. Dropping to her knees, she gripped her hair and held it back as she unloaded what remained in her stomach.

A few agonizing minutes later, she trusted her stomach was done, and reached up to the lever to flush. She used the bowl's rim for support as she stood. A sheet of gelid sweat was on her brow. She wiped it with a clammy hand, then went to the sink and washed her hands. Once they were clean, she cupped them together. Letting the water fill them, she raised them up to her mouth and guzzled it down.

What's wrong with me?

Nerves, most likely.

Sheila thought that might be some of it, but she doubted it was all of it. She didn't *feel* sick, but she definitely didn't feel like her usual self.

How can I?

With everything happening, she should be grateful she hadn't completely lost her mind.

Maybe I have. Now I'm losing control of my body too.

She didn't believe that, either.

Pulling the lever down, the faucet stopped spewing water. She took the towel from the rack and buried her face in it. She'd just put it on the bar a short while ago after her last visit to the toilet, so the cottony touch felt soft and great on her skin.

Done drying her face, she chucked the soiled cloth into the hamper on her way out.

She poked her head into Gabe's room. She could hear the soft snores of him sleeping. Before much longer, those soft snores would grow to loud bores. That was fine by Sheila, since she'd grown so accustomed to the sound.

Sheila left Gabe to sleep, then went to her bedroom. Bumping the door with her foot, she was pulling her shorts off before it closed. Her shirt and bra came next. Leaving her panties on, she crawled into bed. The sheets were cool and smooth against her as she snuggled against the pillow.

Sleep came quickly.

CHAPTER 27

Todd Parker reached the end of the article, exhaled heavily, and folded the newspaper. No news on the disappearance of Detective Frank Garner. Over a week had passed since he'd left the bar, and the planet, for all the authorities seemed to know.

He glanced at the lamp table, the new paperback he'd started on last night waiting to be opened again. As much as he would like to do some reading, he knew he wouldn't be able to focus on the words. He wished he could say he was too distraught over the two disappearances this month. Both were people he'd had recent contact with before they'd vanished. The entire neighborhood seemed to be affected by it and that, he supposed, was partly what had him so edgy. But, the real source of his chaotic nerves at the moment was the Mustang sitting at the mouth of his driveway.

Approaching midnight, it was too dark for him to see what they were doing. He might be able to make out something if he gawked long enough, but they'd probably see him from the road, watching. Jenny wouldn't like it and she'd let him know.

I'm her father. I have the right to march right out there and plaster my face against the window if I want to.

That was true. He could do that. He wouldn't, but he *could.* Glancing at the clock, he thought he just might make a trip outside if Jenny wasn't in soon.

Sighing, Todd kicked down the footrest on the recliner, and groaned as he stood up. His knees popped, then his lower back. He stretched, shoulders strained back, and this produced another round of cracks from his spine. Lisa had been on him for a couple years now to see a chiropractor. She'd told him years of sitting hunched over a keyboard were hell on his back. Lately, he was prone to believe her. His back, especially the lower region and hips, always seemed to ache.

Maybe he should see one.

On his way to the kitchen to get a beer, he knew he'd avoid the chiropractor at any cost. It'd take his back going completely out before he'd even truly consider letting anyone grope all over him like that.

The light above the stove was on, throwing a small neutral slice of light across the counter and floor. They usually left this light on during the night in case someone wanted a late night snack or drink. No one ever did, except for Todd, if he was doing some third-shift writing, imminent to a deadline. He'd sneak down the stairs and either treat himself to a large bowl of ice cream, or drink a few glasses of chocolate—or strawberry—milk. And on those nights where the words were being stubborn by not wanting to come out, he'd make a large sandwich. Double stacked with ham and turkey, some lettuce and tomato on toasted bread. Even pickles, if he felt daring.

His stomach grumbled to advise him it wouldn't mind a

little snack right now.

With the fridge open, he took out a bottle of Bud Light, then opened the meat drawer. The sandwich meat was on top. He grabbed the ham and the turkey, holding them between his fingers. Sticking them under his arm, he grabbed the cellophane-wrapped lettuce. Whenever they got a new head of lettuce, he liked to tear off some leaves for sandwich usage. Sometimes it became stale and soggy before he used it all. But, this batch was fresh and crunchy.

On his way to the counter, he heard the front door open. It slowly closed as if Jenny was trying to conceal her entrance. He set the sandwich materials on the counter and listened.

The soft rustling of clothing as she entered the living room. A pause. Then a sigh of relief.

Hearing her little lament made his chest feel tight. His daughter was actually *thankful* he wasn't in the living room. She must have thought he was already in bed. Apparently she wanted to avoid any kind of communication with Todd tonight.

He stood there, listening to her leave the living room. The muffled sounds of her tread came from the stairs, heading up. Todd looked at the sandwich meat. As delicious as it all looked, he no longer wanted to eat.

Jenny closed the door in her bedroom, locking the knob. She shrugged out of her pocket book. It landed on the floor with a clinking bump. Her sandals were next. Kicking them off as she walked, she left them where they landed.

As she neared her bed, she smacked her lips, glided a finger across their soft edges. They felt numb and rubbery. Doug had been kissing weird again; this time was the worst of all. His mouth was like a wide-open chasm with a plushy serpent lashing at her face. She'd tried dodging its moist touches, but it was a fight she couldn't win. Finally she'd slapped him. Not on the face. She'd gotten him on top of his head as he'd moved for her breasts with that licking monster.

He'd looked up at her, insulted, hints of boiling anger in his eyes. "What the *hell* was that for?" Rubbing his head, he seemed determined to find a lump up there.

"Who are you?" she asked. "Where are you right now?"

Confused by her questions, he'd made squally sounds while trying to speak. Finally, he managed a response. "What's that even supposed to mean?"

"You're not *you* right now. And obviously, it's not me you're trying to kiss, because I don't kiss like that!"

Groaning, Doug slammed his fist down on the seat between them. "I'm getting real tired of this, Jenny!"

His outburst had mildly surprised her, left her feeling a little bit scared. She'd never heard him shout like that.

"You've got me so confused..." He grabbed both sides of his head. "I can't even *think* straight!"

Had she really been screwing him up that bad?

No. He's screwing me *up! He's a totally different person every time we get together. I never know which Doug I'm gonna get!*

A little dramatic, she realized, but the point was on the mark. "Doug...what kind of girlfriend do you want me to be? Last year, I was fine the way I was, and everything...the sex stuff...was fine too. What changed?"

Doug was huffing. She could feel the heat of his breaths making the car stuffy. "Nothing changed."

"Doug." He finally looked at her. "Everything's changed."

She saw the anger finally break. His eyes started to look normal once more. "No...it hasn't."

"Then what has?"

"*You* changed," he said. Jenny opened her mouth, but Doug was already talking again before she could say anything. "You're too uptight now. It's like you don't want to have fun anymore."

"I don't like screwing all..."

"I'm not talking about how much we have sex. I mean—yeah that's part of it, but not everything. You always walk around with this pout on your face. Like you're sad *all* the time. You know what? You've got it better than most. Look at the damn house you live in. It's the biggest in the whole neighborhood, maybe the whole town. You even have your own car, but you never drive it. *I* drive you everywhere. Your parents seem like cool enough people. Hell, they're a lot cooler than mine. Phil's dad is a fucking drunk that can barely get off the couch long enough to piss, so he usually just pisses in his pants instead. Your parents come to all the school functions, your dad speaks in the Literature classes. My mom *adores* your mom."

He was still lecturing her, although she'd stopped listening. What he was saying made sense, and she figured he wasn't the only who thought this way. She'd bet it also explained April's attitude around her lately as well. They were looking at her like a spoiled little brat who took everything for granted. She wasn't that way at all. She could still remember what it was like before Dad's books really started to sell. It was hell on her parents, and it had nearly ruined them. Not just financially, but emotionally. She remembered having to stay at her cousin's house once a week for several months. Her parents told her they had a class to go to. Really, it was marriage counseling.

She was very appreciative of everything she had in her life, including Doug. What bothered her was the future. She was terrified of what was going to happen at the end of the summer. Her inability to accept things, to let them develop naturally, was her downside. Jenny Parker was the kind of person who fought hard to change the things she had no control of.

"...split up for a while."

That last part jerked Jenny out of her fuzzy thoughts and right back into the car. "What'd you say?"

"I said...we need to split up for a while."

"You're breaking up with me?"

Doug's eyes closed, his lips tightened. Then he nodded, quickly adding, "Just for a little bit."

"Why?" Her voice was thick and high-pitched.

"I need some space."

"But you said I don't give you enough attention..."

"I'm saying I need time away from you."

Jenny felt like a frozen dagger had punched her in the heart. Her skin went cold and crawly, her stomach was nauseous.

Back in her bedroom, Jenny collapsed onto her bed. Not bothering to get under the covers, she just pulled one side over top of her, binding herself in the blankets like an egg roll.

Graduation being two days away, the planned beach trip in a little over a week, all she could think about was how much she dreaded all of it.

CHAPTER 28

Jenny stared at the paper tacked to the bulletin board outside her Literature Arts class. Her mouth was stuck open, a lump clogging her throat. Out of the twenty-two students in the class, she was the only person who'd failed the exam. And not a small, hardly noticeable blunder, she was in the lowest regions of a bad grade. To make matters worse, Ms. Sanderson always highlighted the flunkeys in the list, and her name was an emphasized gaudy green line.

Dad's going to kill *me...*

The few other students gathering in front of her naturally looked at the bright line first before searching for their own name. They read the name, glanced back at Jenny, and started snickering. She heard their soft, whispering chatter as they most likely made fun of her.

Having enough of it, Jenny turned away and hurried down the hall as the tears started to flow. She needed to stop by her locker and finish cleaning it out. For the final time. The realization dawned on her. It made her hasty retreat turn sluggish. Coming to her locker, she looked at it like an old friend about to leave. She would miss this damn thing more than she wanted to admit.

Grabbing the lock, she began to spin the dial: 10-25-10. Then she pulled down. The latch unhitched, and she pulled it out of the slot. The door vibrated when she opened it. Seeing the vacant spaces inside, it looked as if April had already emptied out her half of the contents. All that remained were Jenny's notebooks, pencil box, and the mini-posters and pictures she'd taped up at the beginning of the year to replace last year's. Those could all be thrown away.

She'd have to turn the combination lock in before she left. Wiping her tears, she decided she'd just sit the lock on the shelf in the locker. She didn't want to stop by the office.

A couple students passed her. Two guys and girl having a conversation about what they were going to do this weekend. She wondered where April was. She'd texted her this morning and told her about Doug. It had been three pages worth of sent messages. And, April hadn't replied. Maybe she was still sleeping. April's last exam had been on Tuesday so, other than getting her diploma, she was done. Jenny doubted she would come to school just to kill time. Jenny would have if it was her, just to spend some time in the library. She loved that place. Sometimes when she was in there, surrounded by all those books, she contemplated the notion of writing a story. She never told her dad that, though. He would become obsessed with the idea and push writing onto her any chance he got. She wanted to develop a natural affiliation with it, not something that was guided with his help.

Taking what little she planned to keep out of the locker, she stuffed it all into her book bag. She shouldered the pack, then tore down all the decorations. Wadding them into a ball, she walked over to the nearest trash can and dropped them in. She gave the locker a fleeting glance as she walked by.

Take care of yourself, old pal.

Four years she'd used that locker. Even something as trifling as a storage space would be missed greatly.

Jenny checked her phone again. Still nothing from April. She briefly considered driving over to her house, but decided not to. She wanted to get facing her dad out of the way. She was not looking forward to his backlash, even if she deserved it.

Maybe it wouldn't be as bad as she was building it up to be.

That was a load of crap and she knew it.

Henry Conner was reviewing the program Denise had created. All of it was based on Gabe. She had their tests organized by date, the progress or lack thereof all stamped in the side. On the days they had videoed the experiments, she'd attached a video file. All of them were loaded with audio files of his vocal notes and monitoring records. He was impressed by the amount of work and detail she'd put into it. A great job and he told her so.

"Glad you like it," she said. "Software design is my second passion."

"I can tell. You have a talent for it."

Her cheeks flushed. "Thanks."

They were in the office, which lately had started to resemble more of an upper class meth lab from all the beakers, flasks, burners and tubes stretched throughout the room. It was even starting to smell like a lab: heavy ammonia-like odors that singed his nostrils and made his eyes water.

Denise hadn't bothered getting dressed today. She sat in the other office chair, legs crossed, her foot slightly turned to the side. Since they weren't dealing with any chemicals today, there was no need to cover herself. Henry was grateful. She had a great body that he enjoyed ogling. He wasn't quite comfortable enough to walk around naked just yet, so it was a T-shirt and shorts day for him. The weather outside was supposed to be hot and humid, so he planned to spend as much of it indoors as he possibly could.

Since that night on the side of the road, things had been different between Henry and Denise. They had sex frequently, and Henry had started to detect feelings becoming involved. Not love, but definitely approbations of some sort. He saw it in the way she acted toward him, and could feel it even inside himself when it came to her. The two of them definitely liked each other, and that was obvious to them both.

They made a good team, even Denise said so constantly.

"We're perfect partners," she'd said.

"I think so too."

"I mean…I've admired your work for so long, getting to be with you like this, and working on this project, all secretive and stuff…is such a dream come true."

"You've admired my work?"

"Yes! Hawthorne gave the rundown of all you've accomplished in your life, and it's inspirational."

She'd talked to him like a groupie to a rock star, with that same infatuated gleam in her eyes.

Henry glanced at her, enjoying the smooth slopes of her breasts as she brought up another page on the newly created program. A look of concentration had slightly pinched her brow, narrowed her eyes. She looked determined and precious, all at the same time.

With the detective almost forgotten to both of them, they'd returned their focus to the Heyman kid in full force.

"Guess it's about time for an update, huh?" she said.

Henry's good mood dwindled. "I guess."

"You don't look thrilled."

"Neither do you."

Denise shrugged. Her nice breasts jiggled slightly. "It is what it is."

A saying Henry hated but one he agreed with. "All right. Let's get it over with."

Hawthorne had shipped them a special IP phone, a device that worked through the internet. Though it worked like a regular phone, its signal could be routed through multiple servers which made it nearly impossible to be traced. Hawthorne had demanded their voice conferences be conducted this way, just in case.

Just in case he sends out goons again.

He wondered how much Denise truly knew about Hawthorne. More than Henry? Doubtful. Not that Henry knew much himself, but he'd dealt with the mysterious benefactor before and was well aware of the wickedness that came with the association. If it hadn't been for Dr. Vanhoy pulling Henry into the project to begin with, his life would have been Hawthorne-free.

And Gabe free.

Maybe that would have been better for them all. He wondered where he'd be now had he not joined Project: Newborn.

Henry saw movement in the corner of his eye. Someone was rushing through the doorway. He jumped in the seat as he turned to face them.

It was Denise.

She had on athletic shorts and was pushing her head through a clingy T-shirt. Her face behind the clothing, she hadn't seen his reaction. *Thank God.* He'd been so engaged in his thoughts, he hadn't even noticed her walk out.

Her getting dressed disappointed him.

She noticed.

"Only temporary," she assured. "I'd feel too slimy talking to Hawthorne naked, even if he can't see me."

Henry grinned. "Promise it's only temporary?"

She drew an X over her left breast. "Cross my heart." She puckered her lips, kissing at him.

His chest felt warm and bubbly. He'd never had a girl stay with him for more than a night, and Denise had been here for almost two weeks now. Thinking back to when she first showed up, he couldn't believe he'd actually tried to send her away.

But I didn't know we'd start…

How could he have known? Still didn't feel like it was really happening even now.

A pop, followed by the drone of a dial tone snapped him out of it. He looked toward Denise as she started dialing the number.

Hawthorne's number.

His stomach gurgled. Fizzy acidic trickles rose to the back of his throat.

The call was answered on the first ring.

"What's new?" asked the deep, portentous voice.

"More of the same," answered Denise. "The kid shows continuing signs of maturity, just as Dr. Conner has suggested."

"Oh?" said Hawthorne. "Still?"

"Yes," she said. "At this rate, he's well on his way to development."

"What *kind* of development?" he asked.

Henry cleared his throat. "We don't exactly know, and making a guess of any kind would be incompetent on our part. We're dealing with an unpredictable species, so trying to predict any of his evolution is not logical."

"I see," Hawthorne said. "And where does that leave us?"

Denise and Henry shared a reluctant look. She nodded, telling him to go on and say what needed to be said.

Henry cleared his throat again before speaking. "There's not much more we can do here as far as examination and research. I mean, I can take some more blood samples, skin and tissue samples, but I'm sure the parents are getting tired of the same tests over and over. The equipment I have access to here is inadequate to what we need."

"Then it's time to move on," said Hawthorne. "He must be brought to the labs."

"That's impossible," said Henry. "The family wants to—"

"I don't care one iota for what the *family* wants!"

Denise winced at the sinister growl. Henry rolled his chair closer to her, grabbing her hand. She squeezed him. Her fingers were freezing.

"Hawthorne," began Henry, but that was all he was allowed to say.

"Listen to me, Conner. You do whatever you have to do to get that kid. When he is in your possession, call me, and I will arrange for you all to be picked up and brought to the labs. I have already assembled a team to assist you, and they are on standby, awaiting orders."

"Hawthorne, what is it you're suggesting I do?" he said.

A chilling harrumph came from the phone's distorted speaker. "Whatever it takes. But make sure *no* one can stop you from bringing the kid to me. Understood?"

Henry felt sick. His brain was being pricked with daggers.

Mouth dry, it was hard for him to swallow.

"*Do* we understand each other?" asked Hawthorne.

Henry could feel Denise staring at him, no doubt wondering how he would respond. It caused globules of sweat to pop up on the back of his neck.

Too much time passed, so Hawthorne started talking again. "Conner, I will *not* repeat myself. Understood?"

"Yes," he said, his throat a croaky gasp.

"So…you know what has to be done. If the parents will not cooperate, then we proceed without their involvement. Catch my meaning?"

He not only caught it, but was punched by it. He ached all over. "I understand…"

"You have forty-eight hours until I require another update."

The call was ended. The dial tone returned. Denise quickly pushed the button on the phone's base, silencing the annoying sound.

No one spoke. It seemed like minutes passed before Denise finally broke the silence.

"Well…" She stopped, at a loss for words again.

"Yeah. *Well.*"

"What are we going to do?"

"He wants Gabe," Henry stated.

"Of course he does. You had to know this was coming. You called *him* remember."

"I know I did."

"Why *did* you call him? You had to have known it was going to come to this."

"Do you think I really wanted to? If I thought I could handle it all from this room, I would. They want me to cure him, and damn it, there are moments where I think I really could. It might be best for everyone involved. Then there's the flip side to the coin, the one where I am nearly obsessed with learning more about Gabe. This all started with a mutated egg I implanted into the mother. And what it eventually became is mindboggling, even to me." He noticed how one of Denise's hands were gripping her breast through her shirt and squeezing it, kneading it. She was getting off on his tirade. "Bottom line is this, I need his resources. I can't do much of anything without them..."

"Yeah, but I mean, you seem so...I don't know...troubled by what Hawthorne told you."

"He wants me to *kill* them, Denise. Don't you understand that?"

"I understand it just fine."

"But..." He shrugged.

"You like them."

"No, I don't."

"Yes, you *do*. You got rid of that cop's car for them."

"I didn't want them to run away."

"That was part of it, sure. But there was more to it than that. Deep down, you like the family. You like the kid too. You've all bonded over these past few weeks. It makes sense. You're all working together on a common goal, and that's Gabe's well-being."

He supposed she was right, but he wasn't going to tell her that.

Denise continued. "But, if doing what Hawthorne wants will get the kid in our possession, then so be it. We get rid of the parents, get the kid and head to Hawthorne. Just think of the potential then. All that we can do without worries of offending the parents and sending them fleeing back into hiding. How *great* would that be?"

Admitting that he agreed with what she was saying would make him as much a monster as Hawthorne. And Denise's willingness to go along, without any indication of remorse, was also somewhat unsettling. He hoped he hid his feelings well, because he was trembling on the inside. He was cold, but sweat still slid down his sides, tickling him.

"Want to take a shower with me?" asked Denise.

He looked at her. She was standing up, pulling the shirt off as she rose. Her breasts appeared from behind the shirt. They weren't huge, but they also weren't small. Two springy humps with small pink nipples. A perfect set.

A shower sounded nice, and he told her so.

Smiling, she said, "Meet you there!" Then she pranced out of the room in a hopeful trot.

He hoped the warm water would kill the chill that had lodged in his spine.

CHAPTER 29

"You failed?" said Todd, louder than he'd intended.

Sitting at the corner of the table, Lisa sat across from him with Jenny at the head. His daughter looked sick with worry. And he could understand why, bad grade notwithstanding, this arrangement resembled an interrogation more than an actual discussion.

When Jenny had come home, Todd was just finishing up a chapter on the new book. It was lunchtime and he was ready to eat. They'd run into each other in the kitchen, where Lisa was putting together sandwiches for the three of them. He'd been able to tell by Jenny's behavior that she had something to tell him, and whatever it was, she wanted to avoid.

He'd asked her what was on her mind, and she'd told him he might want to sit down. He knew then that she'd failed something.

Literature Arts.

Of all subjects, it had to be that one. She'd barely managed a C all year, and with such a pitiful grade on her final exam, she would get a flunking grade for the semester. Todd was so disappointed, but he wanted to hide just how much.

"It's not that big of a deal," said Jenny.

"You know how dumb that sounds, right?" Jenny nodded. "You maintained a certain grade point average throughout high school, until this year. Now it's going to show on your academic record, for the rest of your life, that you pissed through Literature in your senior year."

Jenny gulped. "I can make it up, I know I can. I'll talk to the teacher and see when she's doing the retakes."

"I hope she'll let you," said Lisa. "Sometimes the teachers aren't willing to hand out another chance if they don't feel the student gave it their best."

If Jenny's head lowered any further, her chin would be resting on the table. "I'll ask her tomorrow before the cap and gown pictures…"

Todd blamed himself for her grade. Literature—in a sense—was his career. And there were instances where he had probably been extra strict on her when it came to reading, grammar and punctuation. Actually, he knew there had been more than one occasion when Jenny was little he'd lost his temper whenever she mispronounced a word that he felt she should know. Anything associated with Literature had been her weak spot from early on, and he wondered if it was because she'd stopped caring about it a long time ago, thanks to him.

Seeing Jenny now made him believe that was exactly what the problem was. He'd been too hard on her. And she'd been too stubborn to give it her all like she did to everything else she attempted.

She looks like she feels bad about it, though.

Head down, watery eyes, and a jaw that couldn't stop quivering, it was obvious. But, he still had to stay true to his threat. He didn't want to, but he had to or she would never learn anything from this experience, whether she was able to retake the exam or not.

Todd sighed. "Well…in the meantime, I have no choice

but to ground you."

Jenny sank in the chair, her arms going limp. Her head fell back. "Dad, please don't."

"I have no choice," he repeated. He noticed Lisa giving him a pleading look as well. He repeated it one more time for her sake.

"April and I are supposed leave for the beach on Monday."

"Correction. You *were* supposed to leave for the beach on Monday. Not anymore. I warned you if you failed any of your finals, you'd be grounded all summer. I'm sticking to my guns this time. You might be starting tech school at the end of the summer, but you're still my daughter, and I can still ground you. And, yes, I know this bad grade doesn't mean you'll never amount to anything, and that college isn't ruined, but it's the principal, Jenny. You can't peter around with something, anything, that's this important. Everything should be given your all, no matter how much you don't like it, or how much you think it'll piss me off."

"Please," Jenny whined. "I need to go to the beach, you don't understand..."

"You're right. I don't understand. I don't understand what's gotten into you lately. You're too dependent on Doug now. Before, he was an addition to your life, now he *is* your life."

"Not anymore."

Todd looked at Lisa, wondering if she knew anything about this. Lisa shook her head, just as confused as he was.

"What do you mean by that?" asked Lisa.

"He dumped me last night."

Todd remembered seeing them outside, and how the car had sat parked out there for a long time. He'd assumed they were doing things couples do and had forced himself not to dwell on it for fear of images manifesting. But had he known that jerk was out there breaking his little girl's heart, he'd have dragged him out of the car and beaten the shit out of him.

"I'm sorry, Jenny." Todd took a deep breath, letting it huff out. "I didn't know."

"I know you didn't."

"It doesn't change things here, though."

Groaning, Jenny stood up. "I wasn't telling you to get pity. I was just letting you know."

"Sit down," said Todd. "We're still talking."

Tears filling her eyes, she quickly wiped them away. "No. I don't need to hear anything else. You've already made the decision, so what's left to hear? Gonna talk more about how I need to apply myself, then tell me all the hundreds of ways *you* did it?" Mocking him, she said, "Because if I hadn't disciplined myself and worked really hard, I never would have sold a novel and would probably be working somewhere I hated right now..."

"Jenny," he said.

Still using that deep, irreverent tone, she said, "You know I did this, I did that. You should do what I did. Do this, because I did it."

Todd could feel his skin heating. "Sit down."

"I'm the best-selling author Todd Parker, I don't fuck up. Never have, never will."

"That's enough!" he shouted, slamming both fists down on the table. Lisa gasped from across him. Jenny recoiled back a step. "Enough!"

The room was heavy with uncomfortable silence before Jenny finally said, "I'm going to my room."

She walked away from the table. Slow at first, but her

stride quickly became a run as she went up the stairs. Todd thought he heard the soft sounds of her sobbing. A moment later, a door slammed.

Todd sighed. He looked at his wife. She sat there, hand to her chest, tears dotting the corners of her eyes. She looked upset with him, maybe even a little scared.

"I know," said Todd. "I shouldn't have lost my temper."

"She left you no choice there."

"Was I too harsh with her?"

Lisa slowly exhaled through pursed lips, like someone about to attempt something dangerous. "I don't know if you were too harsh or not, but I think it was too much at once. You go from practically letting her walk all over you to laying down a strict law that you will not, even for a moment, consider negotiating. How do you think she's going to react?"

Todd leaned forward, putting his hands together. He put his mouth against the ball of fingers. "I don't know. I hoped she would have just passed the damn class so I wouldn't have to lay down *any* law." He groaned. "Think what she said about Doug was true? Think they're really broken up?"

"I do. The hurt I saw in her eyes was real."

"Damn. No wonder she's been so different lately. The kid was messing with her head, I bet."

"Maybe, maybe not. But, your firm sentencing might have come at a bad time. Maybe you could have thought on it a little?"

Now Todd felt lousy. He'd just been doing what he thought Lisa wanted him to do, what any parent would do in the same situation. "Lisa, you always say I'm never firm enough with her, and then when I am, you say I shouldn't be."

"That's not what I'm saying at all. I'm sorry. Please don't

take it that way. I'm just saying…well…" She shrugged. "Your timing sucked."

Todd wanted to keep a stone face going for dramatic effect, a way to prove his point. He couldn't. His grin gave him away.

"There's that smile," she said.

"Enjoy it while it lasts. If today was any indication as to how this summer's going to go, I doubt I'll be doing it much."

"We should talk to her again."

"Yeah," said Todd, starting to stand.

"Not *now*," said Lisa sharply. "Later."

Sighing, Todd dropped back down, leaned back in the chair.

"You have to understand the mind of a teenage girl, Todd."

"I don't. That's the problem."

"I'm a little out of touch myself," said Lisa. "I'm afraid I've forgotten how their minds work."

"Maybe we should get a book."

Lisa frowned. "She's not a dog, Todd."

"Your right. Let's go for a walk and talk it over."

"Sounds good to me."

Todd put his hands flat on the table and pushed. The chair scooted back. He stood up. Lisa was already on her way to the door. He watched the swerving of her rump as she walked. Wearing yellow shorts that made her look like a softball player from the eighties, they clung to her hips and buttocks. He liked it. A lot. They must be new because he didn't remember ever seeing them before.

She looked back at him over her shoulder. "Coming?"

A dozen inappropriate remarks swam in his head. Any

other time, he would have picked one and said it for laughs. Not now, though. Just wasn't a good time. Maybe if the walk went well he'd try to be sly then.

"Yep," he answered.

"Why aren't you moving?"

"Enjoying the view."

Even after all these years, he could still make her blush. Her pinkish cheeks proved it. "Todd..." She tried to peer over her shoulder to see what was so fascinating.

"Like the shorts," he said.

Laughing, Lisa poked her rump out and gave it a little jiggle.

Tingling heat flowed into Todd's abdomen. "Wow, they look good on you."

"Oh? Hmm. I thought maybe *I* looked good *in* them."

"You make a great team."

Lisa laughed again. Todd felt a gush of relief seeing her starting to lighten up. He had been a bit worried that she was angry with him. And she probably was, but thankfully her current attitude showed signs it would probably pass quickly.

Lisa turned around and faced him. "Walk with me and I might show you the new panties I'm wearing under these shorts later."

"Forget the walk. Show me now."

Lisa crossed her arms. "We need to talk about Jenny."

His excitement started to act in reverse. Although the walk had originally been his idea, it didn't sound as fun. He would accompany her regardless, because bottom line—she was right. "Okay. Let's get going."

They went outside. From the comfort of air conditioning inside, the heat felt like a blanket straight from the dryer dropped onto them. Todd wished he'd put on shorts before coming outside.

Lisa must have noticed his nose wrinkling into a grimace. "Want to go change?"

He was tempted, but said, "Nah. Let's just walk."

"Think you can handle it?"

"Who are you talking to?"

"A guy that would never admit he *couldn't* handle it."

"Exactly. Let's go."

They took their usual route, going in the direction of the dead end. Once the road ended, they'd turn back, possibly going to the entrance of the community before walking back home. Some days they would go through the field and hike the paths in the woods on the far side. Not today. He wasn't dressed for it.

Approaching Ms. Andrew's house, Todd was glad he'd worn pants. They hid the goose flesh prickling his skin. Lisa avoided looking in that direction. Todd tried to. Unfortunately, he'd already gotten a decent glance, and although he was looking straight ahead of him, he could still feel it off to the side, stalking him from behind its dusty windows. Betty Andrews had only been away for a few short weeks, but the house looked as if no one had gone near it in a year. Todd would swear the paint had faded drastically, and the shutters looked loose on their hinges. The weed-choked lawn needed to be cut, the mailbox lid hung open—a weather-damaged, crumpled stack of sales papers inside.

Why hasn't anyone come and checked it?

At least they'd taken down the yellow tape. Like ghastly scars, the caution line drew attention, letting you know something bad had happened. But, since the property hadn't technically been a crime scene, there was no need for it, so down it came. He hadn't seen Rebecca, Betty's only daughter, since right after the disappearance. He supposed she didn't want to be in the house without her mother. Todd understood that. He'd be the same way. Why stay in a home the owner wouldn't come home to?

"You're quiet," said Lisa.

"Sorry."

"Ms. Andrews?"

"Yeah."

"I know. It's awful. Still bothers me. I mean—I was one of the last ones...who..." Her voice sounded like she was about to cry.

Todd quickly put his arm around her. They'd come out here to talk about Jenny. He didn't want Lisa to feel guilty because of Ms. Andrews as well. She'd been carrying around that grief since the detective had showed up that first time.

And he's missing too.

Don't think about it.

"Oh my God," said Lisa. Appalled.

"What's wrong?"

Looking at his wife, he saw the contortion of her face. She was looking to his right, so he turned to see what had her so bothered.

He saw it right away.

Dr. Conner's house looked as bad—worse—than Betty Andrews'. The lovely terrain of floras that usually made his house stand out like a magnificent photo from a gardening magazine were all dehydrated, drooping and faded to deathly grays. The green grass that looked as fine as lovely hair had turned brown and tall like a wheat field.

"What the hell?" he said.

"Is *he* all right?"

Todd tried to remember when the last time was he'd seen

Dr. Conner. Yesterday morning. He'd seen him drive by the house and he'd thought someone was with him but he wasn't sure. "I think so."

"How could he let all his work…just go to crap like that?"

"Does he not come into the store anymore?"

"I don't know. But you better believe I'm gonna ask Gladys when I'm there doing the books."

Seeing Conner's yard put a cold, tight squeeze in Todd's back. Somehow the degradation of such a faultless yard was scarier than the abandoned Andrews house.

Lisa started walking again. Todd joined her.

"So, this weekend is the big weekend, huh?" she said.

Todd sighed. "I don't know how big it's going to be now. Jenny will probably be the only graduate frowning in the pictures."

"Not that. I mean *your* big weekend."

At first Todd wasn't sure what she was talking about, but then he remembered. *The convention.* Saturday he would be signing books all day at the horror convention in Charlotte.

"Damn. I guess it is. I forgot all about it."

"Is Greg still going with you?"

"I…" Greg hadn't told him one way or the other. "I'll have to check. He hasn't said."

"I hope so. It'll be good for them both. I bet people would love him. I haven't talked to Sheila in a few days. I'll give her a call later and check in. You *do* want Greg to go, don't you?"

"Of course. If *I* go. I might need to cancel."

"Why?"

"I'd forgotten all about it. I haven't gotten any books from my publisher to sell."

"Todd!"

"I *know*. I just forgot."

"Call them when we get home and see if they'll overnight you some."

He supposed that would work fine, but it was going to be expensive. His fault, though. He should have taken care of the preparations weeks ago. That was Todd, always waiting until the last minute for everything. Canceling his appearance was tempting, but also very unprofessional. He'd piss off so many of his readers, as well as the event organizers. He was positive his publisher would have something to say about it as well.

"All right. I'll call them. And take the lashing I'm probably going to get."

"They're not going to lash you," said Lisa, laughing.

"Well, they'll pick on me."

"They better. Might help you remember to have these things finished in advance."

Todd laughed. "I doubt it."

"I doubt it too." She put her arm around his waist. "But I love you, so it's fine."

"Damn right it is."

Todd was glad the tension had dispelled. Lisa seemed like her normal self, and so did he for that matter. However, he knew it would all come back once they walked past the houses again, returning in full force once they were home.

CHAPTER 30

Saturdays used to be Henry's longest day in the yard, especially during the summer. Saturdays had always been his mowing day. He'd take the lawn tractor twice over the front and backyard in first gear, making sure the grass was evenly cut. Afterward, he got the Weed Eater and vanquished any sprigs of grass starting to jut up around the bush stalks. By the time he was finished with those chores, it would be lunchtime. He'd eat it on the back deck, enjoying the moist scent of fresh cut grass. Then he'd move on to weeding his gardens and giving them healthy doses of plant food.

Not this Saturday, though, nor had he for the last several. Today, Henry Conner was in Gabe's room. And he'd just lost another round of tic-tac-toe. Gabe had become a whiz at the game, this time beating Henry in under a minute. When they'd first started playing, Henry let the kid win, out of fear of angering him. Now he tried with all his wit and skill to beat Gabe and couldn't do it. He'd won only once, nearly shouting in triumph. Instead, he'd pretended to be humbled by the win, but on the inside was crying: *In your face!*

The camera sat on the tripod in the far corner of the room,

pointing at them. It was on, although he hadn't recorded a single second of footage. He just wanted to give the impression to the Heymans that he was still documenting Gabe's progression. Tonight being the end of Hawthorne's deadline, he didn't need any new footage. He'd have the star of the all the videos in possession soon enough. He was only here this morning because he'd promised the Heymans earlier in the week he would be. So, he had an act to keep up.

I can't do it.

He would have to.

Warn them. Tell them about Hawthorne so they can get away.

Then where would that leave *him?* Hawthorne would pursue them, probably killing him and Denise because they knew too much. He *had* to bring Gabe to Hawthorne.

Hawthorne will probably kill me anyway.

Henry sighed. Gabe sensed his troubled nerves. He could see the kid feeding off his nervous energy. Patting Gabe's hand, he hoped it would convince the kid all was okay.

"Can I talk to you in private?" asked Greg.

Henry's stomach pinched. "Sure." The last time they'd talked in private, Greg had nearly punched him. He'd admitted he didn't have any new schemes on how to help Gabe, and Greg wasn't happy with that answer.

Greg nodded. "We'll head into the kitchen." He turned to Gabe, saying "I'm going to borrow Dr. Conner for a minute, okay booger?"

Gabe whined a grunt, then nodded without any zest.

Henry felt something touch his heart at that. When they'd first met, Gabe had hated him. He'd realized this right away and had been nearly too scared to continue contact out of fear the kid would physically display his aversion. But the kid's allure had kept him coming back. Now he could tell Gabe legitimately liked him, and Henry had to admit, he liked him back.

"Be back soon," said Henry.

Gabe smiled. Lips curling back to expose a tight-fit grille of razor-sharp teeth. Didn't matter how much Henry liked the kid or vice versa, seeing those teeth made him hurt inside.

Standing up, Henry's knees popped. He stretched as he turned around. Greg walked backward out of the room, then held his arm out to signal Henry to follow him. He did. On his way out, he shut off the camera.

They made their way up the hall, and Henry followed Greg down the stairs. Entering the kitchen, Henry saw Sheila sitting at the table, a cup of coffee in front of her. She was fingering the side of the cup. She looked up when she noticed them.

"How was your time with Gabe today?" she asked. There was a hopeful yearning in her eyes.

"Good. Same as it has been."

"Do you think his urges have passed?" she asked.

Henry doubted it, even though it had been many days since Gabe had last attacked anyone. But to put her at ease he said he thought so.

She gusted out a relieved breath. "Thank God..."

"All right," said Greg, pulling out a chair for Henry. "We really need to talk about what to do from here. Gabe's behaved for a little over a week now. The meat seems to help him but it's not completely stopping his cravings. I can tell he *wants* to go out. Even after I installed that expensive lock, I found out he had started getting out through the basement. I've got the windows bolted shut and another lock like the one up here on the door that leads outside. It's kept him in so far, but once the cravings become too strong for him to bear, he'll find another way out. We've been lucky no one's...well...frankly...that no one's suspected us. But, it's only a matter of time before someone else goes missing and someone realizes it all started shortly after the new neighbors arrived." Greg breathed in heavily, having gotten all he needed to say out in one breath.

Then he patted the back of the chair, indicating he wanted Henry to sit.

And Henry didn't want to sit. Especially with Greg lurking behind the chair like that. The fear that Greg would suddenly wrap a wire around his throat helped him decide to remain standing. "Nah, I'm good. I need to stand up for a bit. Got a little achy being on the floor for so long."

Greg nodded, apparently satisfied with that answer. "So, what we want to know, *need* to know, is where do we go from here? You've studied him, interacted with him, gotten blood, video—which I still don't like by the way—and we're still exactly where we were the day I brought you over here."

"Well, Greg, you have to understand that what I have access to is very limited. This isn't something I can analyze once and have a fix for. I've needed to study him countless times, and to the abilities of the instruments and technologies I have within reach, which isn't much. And, I know you don't want to take him anywhere..."

"Out of the question."

Sheila nodded her agreement.

Henry almost told him about Hawthorne but stopped himself. "There's not much I can do beyond what I already am. Gabe is still new to me. Had I been able to accurately monitor him more as an infant, I might have been able to move faster on a solution."

Greg's forced composure dropped off entirely. Anger was clearly visible on his face. His body tightening, hands gripping the chair, red blotches worked their way up his neck.

"What do you suggest I do, build a laboratory in my basement? I'm sure we can head to the toy store and buy a science kit that'll take care of the problem." Sarcasm wasn't what Henry had intended, but his frustration with his inability to please the Heymans and Greg's obvious anger made his aggravation grow.

"Don't be funny with me," warned Greg. "I'm not in the mood."

Henry could see that, so he stopped being sarcastic. "I'll be honest with you for a moment, Greg. When we first started this, I thought there was no chance in hell that anything could be done with Gabe. I just went along with it, because I was scared not to, honestly. I think I might be able to help in some way, but I can't do that with what I have at my disposal. Do you understand?"

Sheila reached out, touching Greg's hand. He flinched. Then he noticed who had touched him and relaxed. She said, "Maybe we should see what our options are."

"We don't *have* any options, Sheila, you know that."

"Maybe we do. I mean, Dr. Conner probably has someone he can call..."

Too late, he thought, but said, "I do. I can call him right now."

"No," said Greg. "The last time your friends got involved, we were almost killed. Not again."

"Then what do *you* suggest, Greg?" asked Henry. He really wanted to know, because he had no clue how to proceed. He definitely didn't want Greg losing his cool this close to the end.

The end. Knowing what was undoubtedly coming sent a scurry of chills up his spine. He hoped they wouldn't notice him shaking.

How far away are Hawthorne's drones?

From where he stood, all he could see were the kitchen windows. He scanned them, checking for masked mercenaries shuffling around outside. He didn't see any.

Surely he'd let me know before they were supposed to attack.

Henry shivered.

Greg sat down in the chair he'd tried to get Henry in. Seeing that, Henry followed, sitting in the one at the head of the table.

Leaning on his elbows, Greg's head hung low. "I don't know, honestly. I had just kind of hoped..."

"Kind of hoped what?" asked Henry.

"That you would have proven *nothing* could be done. That way we could stop worrying about it and move on."

"Greg," said Sheila, a bit of a gasp in her voice. "What do you mean by that?"

"Come on, Sheila. You know as well as I do that if we thought someone could just wave a magic wand and make Gabe normal again, we would search the whole planet until we found him. Am I right?"

Sheila didn't respond, but Henry judged her behavior, and it told him yes.

Greg continued. "I'm happy to hear that Dr. Conner thinks he might be able to help Gabe, but it puts us right back to where we were before we got here. Just a hope and a prayer, with nothing concrete to support what he's saying. And the only way to know for sure would be to take Gabe somewhere so people can examine him. Do you know the kind of examinations they'll do?"

Sheila nodded. "The bad kind."

"Exactly." He looked at Henry. "Could you guarantee that if we allowed you to take us to someone, they'd treat us with respect and compassion like you have?"

Henry felt cold inside as he lied to them and said, "Yes."

Greg seemed to consider it a moment, then said, "I don't believe you. I *want* to believe you, but I don't."

Sheila sighed. "Greg. I don't understand what's going on in your head. Please, tell me."

"Me too," said Henry.

"I just want this to end." He sat back in the chair, defeated. "I'm tired. I can't keep this up much longer."

"Keep what up?" asked Sheila.

"The hiding, the running, the hope, the disappointment. All of it. It has to end."

"That's what I'm telling you," said Henry. "I think it *can* end, but you have to trust me."

"I do trust you," said Greg. "More than I've trusted others. It took me some time, but after getting to know you, it's helped me trust you. But, it's also helped me know when you're not being completely honest. And, you're not right now. I think you're just as hopeful as we are, and you *hope* Gabe will be safe if we go with you where you want to take us. You know, though, that it's just not possible."

Henry figured his face showed Greg how right he was.

"What I'm saying is that we stop putting Gabe through this. We just make our home here, and be done with it."

Sheila's nose wrinkled. "Have you gone bonkers?"

"I think so," said Greg.

"We can't stop, Greg," said Henry. "There's so much more about him that we need to learn."

"I agree. I'm saying we just need to stop being hopeful you can cure him, and just be glad that we have a doctor who can help us *treat* him."

Henry let that stew in his mind for a moment. Greg made so much sense that Henry felt elated. Stop trying to make Gabe something else, and learn how to coexist with what he already was. That would be a great strategy. They should have been doing that from the beginning.

How would Hawthorne react to this? Maybe he could convince him to hold out for a little while longer. That would give him time to come up with a way to severe his ties from the rich lunatic.

"I'm in," said Henry. "I think you're right."

Greg turned to his wife. "What do you say?"

"But, Greg, his cravings...what if he starts sneaking out again..."

"It's going to happen, I'm sure. But maybe Dr. Conner can help us come up with a way where one day it won't."

"I don't know, Greg..."

Henry chimed in. "He likes to hunt at night from what I've gathered. Use that tranquilizer I gave you on him when he goes to bed, and then in the mornings have some fresh meat thawed and ready. That should sustain his appetite for a while, at least. Give me some time to come up with a better plan."

"Okay," said Greg.

Both men turned to Sheila who sat in her chair, frowning. Her brow was creased in deep concentration. No one spoke, silence engulfing the room until it was interrupted by the chime of the doorbell. All of them jumped.

Greg paled. Sheila gnawed at her bottom lip.

Henry understood why they suddenly looked so scared.

Hell, he felt it, too, now that he'd participated in one of their Gabe cover-ups.

"Don't worry," Henry told them, wishing he could take his own advice.

"What if it's someone looking for the detective," said Sheila.

Greg held out his hand as if patting the air. "No one knows he was here. The news said he left the bar that night and hasn't been seen since."

"Maybe they figured something out."

Hearing Sheila panic like that, Henry decided he would write her a prescription for valium. She needed it. And, it probably wouldn't hurt for Greg to be put on some kind of anti-depressant to help with his anger. "Let's all go to the door together."

Greg nodded. Sheila did as well. Together, the three of them stood up, and headed out of the kitchen. Approaching the door, it chimed once more, making the trio gasp.

Henry wondered if it was just his nerves, or if the bell was really as thunderously loud as it sounded. He figured it was a combination of the two.

Henry and Sheila stood back as Greg opened the door.

The Parkers waited on the other side, smiles stretching their happy faces.

"Hi!" squealed Lisa.

Sheila's apprehension vanished. A smile nearly as big as Lisa's split her mouth, flashing blindingly white teeth. "Hey!"

Lisa rushed in. She and Sheila met halfway, hugging.

Todd said hello to Greg, then added, "I'm happy to see you, man, but I don't know if I can do what they're doing."

"Thank God," said Greg, laughing.

They shook hands. Greg closed the door behind the

Parkers and started leading the group into the kitchen. Lisa said hello to Henry, then Todd did the same.

"Hope you don't mind us dropping in on you like this. Seems like we always come by unexpectedly, but we tried calling first, I promise. Something's wrong with your phone."

Henry shrunk inside. Hopefully the Heymans hadn't paid their bill and no one had cut the line.

Greg looked confused. "Really?" He walked over to where a phone was mounted on the wall. Taking it off the cradle, he put it to his hear. Frowned. Then he tapped the button repeatedly before hanging it back up. "That's weird."

"Did we pay the bill on time?" asked Sheila.

"Who knows? I'll call from my cell phone later."

"Anyone want some sweet tea?" asked Sheila.

"Sure," said Todd. "I'll have a glass."

Henry wondered why they hadn't offered him any sweet tea before now. "That sounds good."

"I'll help," said Lisa.

Sheila and Lisa left the men to sit at the table. They went over to the dishwasher. Lisa started taking glasses from the top rack while Sheila fetched the tea from the fridge.

Todd turned to Greg. "Given anymore thought to my offer?"

The comment confused Greg, but then it dawned on him. "Ah..." He leaned his head back, shaking it as if embarrassed. "I completely forgot. It's tonight, isn't it?"

Todd nodded.

"Damn. It completely slipped my mind."

"Don't feel bad," said Lisa from the counter. "Todd forgot too, until I reminded him yesterday."

"What'd they forget?" asked Sheila.

"You, too?" said Lisa, surprised.

"I'm not sure I ever knew so I *could* forget."

"Sorry, honey," said Greg. "I was going to tell you after I thought it over some, but then, you know, things got a little hectic."

"Okay," said Sheila, still confused.

"Don't keep us in suspense," said Henry. "What did you guys forget?"

"I'm signing books tonight at a convention in Charlotte from six to nine and asked Greg to go with me so I could introduce him to the comic book guys. They're always looking for artists. There's a VIP party, and I thought it would be a great chance for Greg to mingle with these people. I had to get copies of my books overnighted, and there was a fear they wouldn't arrive. If they didn't, I was going to rethink going, but they got here a couple minutes ago, so we came right over to see if you were still coming along. I would have asked last night, but with Jenny's graduation and dinner afterward—well, we got home pretty late. This is the first chance we had to walk over. But Lisa's been calling all morning."

Henry nodded, then looked at Greg. "And you're not going to go?"

"I don't know."

"Why not?" said Sheila. "You should."

"I don't want to leave you here to handle Gabe alone."

"I'll be fine," said Sheila.

"She won't be here," said Henry. "I'll watch the kid."

"Oh, that's fantastic news!" cried Lisa. "Then I'll go with Todd. We can walk around while the boys do their thing."

"Walk around? What's there to see at one of these things?"

"Oh, it's just so much fun seeing people dressed up. You feed off their energy. They're having such a good time, you can't help but to enjoy yourself."

Greg looked at Henry, his eyes narrowed. "You don't mind hanging with Gabe?"

"Not at all." Henry struggled to contain his anxiousness. If Greg noticed the fervent excitement, he'd stay home and put an end to this new development. It was so perfect that Henry was nearly bouncing in the chair.

If the Heymans weren't home, he could just simply take Gabe. They would come home and find the kid gone, Henry gone, and his house cleaned out. And, the best part was no one had to die. He couldn't wait to get back to the house and tell Denise.

"All right," said Greg. "If you're sure..."

"I'm positive."

Greg and Sheila shared a look, talking to each other with their facial expressions. Finally, in unison, they told the Parkers they would go.

There was a celebration of animated cheers, but Henry was too busy planning out the evening to hear what the rest of the group was discussing. He sipped on his tea, noting that it was the best he'd ever tasted.

CHAPTER 31

Once the Heymans' house was out of sight, Henry ran. The camera bag, hanging from his shoulder, rebounded against his back as he rushed along. He didn't stop until he reached the front door of his house. Clawing at the knob, he finally managed to get his sweat-slick hands to latch on. He went inside. From the brightness of the sun, he viewed his living room as if he had sunglasses on.

Then he remembered he did.

Taking them off, he could see much better, even though it was still pretty dim. He looked up at the ceiling. There weren't any lights on.

Was Denise still asleep?

"Denise?"

He dropped the camera bag on the couch, looking around. He called for her again. No response. Maybe she was in the kitchen.

He ran like a kid who couldn't wait to tell his mom he had a girlfriend, feet smacking the hardwood.

She wasn't in the kitchen, either.

Odd.

Maybe she was in their makeshift lab. He took the stairs two at a time, almost leaping his way to the upper level. Hurrying up the hall, he hung a right to enter the office.

It had been cleaned out. All the equipment had been packed up, leaving the desk and tables bare and glossy. Nothing had been left. Apparently while he was gone, Denise had been disassembling their lab. He pictured her car stuffed full, and wondered if that was where she was: in the garage packing up the car like they were about to go on a trip.

He wished they were going on a trip, a real one. Not the purported adventure they were about to partake of. Something fun. A beach trip would be good. Maybe they could later, once things slowed down.

Henry made his way into the room to give it a final look over to make sure she'd gotten everything. Something crinkled under his feet. Looking down, he saw he had walked onto a sheet of plastic. The clear cover blanketed the rest of the floor. It wasn't quite wide enough to spread over all of it, so there was another sheet draped across from another direction.

Confused, Henry tried to think of a reason why it would be here. Then he sensed he wasn't alone in the room anymore. He turned around. Denise was entering the room. Like most days, she didn't have on a lick of clothing. She approached him with her right hand behind her back.

"There you are," he said.

"Yep. Took you long enough to get home."

"Sorry about that. Some things came up and I've got great news. Have you heard from Hawthorne today?"

There was a flicker of something on Denise's face. It didn't last very long but Henry thought it was regret. She nodded. "I did."

"Great. Let's call him back. You won't believe what's happened. Things are going to be much easier now."

Denise stood in front of him, so close that Henry could see the faint dots of the freckles on the bridge of her nose. "Won't be necessary."

Henry frowned. Something was wrong. "Denise..."

"Hawthorne told me what I have to do. I don't like it, but I'm going to do it because it's what he wants."

Again, he noticed the arm behind her back. "What have you got hidden back there, Denise?"

She showed him. Henry shivered. His testicles retracted, trying to imbed themselves into his abdomen.

It was a pistol. At first he thought it had an elongated barrel, but he quickly realized it was a silencer that had been screwed on. "Remember when I said I was a soulless bitch?"

"I didn't believe you," he said.

"Yes you did. And, it's true."

"No, it's not."

"It is. Why else would I be doing this?" She pointed the gun, leveled at his chest. "Huh?"

"You don't have to."

"Yes. Hawthorne..."

"Listen. The parents aren't even going to be home tonight. I volunteered to babysit for them so they could go to some dumb thing with their neighbors. They trust me. I've babysat for the kid before, so they don't mind me doing it."

"That's great, Henry. How much do you charge an hour?"

"*Listen* to me. We don't even have to go in there and kill the parents and take the kid. There doesn't have to be *any* bloodshed. I'll tranq the kid, then we can shackle him, load him up, and get the hell out of here."

Denise pursed her lips, considering. "That could work..."

"See?"

"But, Hawthorne said to kill you, so that's what I have to do."

"Why? Why does he want you to do this?"

She shrugged a shoulder. "Liability? Who knows? He wants that kid, no matter what. He's been working on this project nonstop, even after the incident in the lab back then. He's never *stopped* working on it."

"That's why he needs us..."

"No. He needs the kid and your research. I can get him that. You've..." A sob tried to break loose. She held it back. "You've become too attached to them, Henry. Dammit, you care about that family too much to do what *needs* to be done."

"Don't do this..."

"I'm sorry." Her finger started to squeeze the trigger.

Henry was fast. He slapped the gun away. There was a whistling pop, and he heard sheet rock crack behind him. He lunged, wrapping his arms around Denise's tiny frame. He felt her breasts squish against his chest. Keeping one arm hugging around her, he gripped the equipped hand by the wrist.

And squeezed.

He felt bone starting to give, heard soft cracking sounds. Denise cried out, releasing the gun. It fell to the floor. When it landed, he quickly kicked it away from them.

Denise struggled out of his hold. Her breasts shook as she grabbed her hurt wrist. Leaning over and huffing, she looked at him. Her hair had fallen into her face. She flung her head back; the hair went with it and stayed. "You asshole, that hurt!"

"You were going to *shoot* me!"

"Dammit!"

She took a slight step back, then sprung her foot up. The heel caught Henry under the chin. His teeth clacked together. Everything went black for a moment, then slowly fizzled back in. He felt gritty bits of teeth on his tongue. Before his eyes could completely focus, he saw the blur of Denise planting one foot down. She spun. Then he felt another foot wallop the side of his face.

The blow sent him to the floor.

Henry's head throbbed. Tight cramps of pain traveled down his neck. He tasted blood filling his mouth.

"Do you think I *want* to do this?" shouted Denise. He felt another kick at his ribs. Something popped in there, stabbing his insides. "I don't!" Another kick.

"Then…stop!"

"I *can't!*"

Through tear-drenched eyes, he could make out the shape of her. She was circling around the front of him, to give him a kick to the face, he figured. He saw the pale-colored smudge flying at him. Throwing up his hands, he caught her foot just before it struck him. Toes tickled the tip of his nose.

"Yah…!" shrieked Denise as Henry yanked up, pushing her foot back to her.

He heard the carpeted bang when she hit the floor. Now was his chance. It would take her a moment to find her bearings. He needed to move quickly.

He couldn't. He was way too dazed and hurting. By the time he was on his feet, so was she, both hands balled into fists.

She swung. He shot his head back, feeling the wind of the narrowly avoided punch. As he brought his head down, her other fist got his jaw. The hit rocked his head to the side.

Henry understood that he needed to stop holding back and retaliate. But, he also realized that she was a lot younger, had more agility, and as much as he hated it, she was stronger. Still, he needed to give her some kind of competition, at least. There was one way he knew for sure to do that.

Fighting dirty…

It helped him when he was younger on the playgrounds, in the bathrooms at school.

Denise charged. He dropped to his knees, swinging his arm up. In midstride, her legs slightly parted, his fist slammed against her groin. He knew she didn't have the extras down there that he had, but he suspected a punch in that region would put anyone down.

He was right.

Denise twirled over his shoulder, slamming on the floor. She rolled away from him, hands clutched between her legs. Her face wrinkling in pain, lips peeled back and teeth bared like a snarling dog.

Groaning, Henry got to his knees. He took a heavy breath and his body lit up, aching all over. Tonguing the back of his teeth, he felt a few wiggle. Then something pricked the plushy tip, a jagged chunk jutting up from bloody gums.

He looked around. Denise was still rocking from side to side on the floor a few feet away. Still groaning. He crawled to her. As he neared, she kicked at him.

"Stay back," she cried.

Henry swatted a fist at her. Missed. He tried again. Missed. She brought her other foot up, connecting with his wrist and knocking his arm out to the side. This brought him down again. His chin hit the floor, shooting even more pain into his head.

He started to cry. There was no way he could beat her in a fair fight.

An image exploded so vividly in his mind, he hated that it wasn't real. In his mind, he saw himself go for the gun, grabbing it and pointing the weapon at Denise. Her eyes were closed in agony, so she didn't see him fire.

But he was still on the floor, dodging her kicks. He needed to put this fantasy into motion. And, he did. Not necessarily how he'd envisioned it in his mind. There, he'd made a fervent dash, snatching the pistol off the floor, rolling to his side like Mel Gibson and firing two quick shots. In reality, he didn't have the strength to crawl, so he dragged himself on his elbows like a wounded a soldier. He *was* wounded, but he definitely ranked nowhere near the soldier category. Unless sniffling and being beaten up by a girl qualified.

The gun seemed miles away. He thought he would never reach it, but he kept trudging on, pulling himself. Why was he *so* heavy? Couldn't he have watched his weight at least a *little* bit? Eaten better? Worked out?

He hated gyms. Hated lifting weights.

Still, there were other ways to stay in shape. If he was able to later, he would do something to maintain a healthy weight.

The gun was much closer when he blinked the tears out of his eyes. He heard someone laughing wildly and realized it was himself. He didn't care. There was reason to celebrate. He was so close, almost there, his hand just inches from the barrel.

Denise's foot stamped down on his hand, breaking it. Screaming, Henry tugged at his hand. Her heel kept it planted there as she leaned over and coolly picked up the gun. Henry followed her movements. Down when she grabbed the gun and panning up when she stood up straight. Breathing heavily, she winced slightly. A hand reached down, gently touching her groin.

"That was dirty. That *hurt.*"

Henry shrugged, groaning from the pain it caused his hand. He thought about trying to grab her calf and pull her leg out from under her. It wouldn't work. He was a smart enough man to know when he'd been defeated. And, that moment had occurred several minutes ago.

"So..." he huffed. "This is it?"

Denise stuck out her bottom lip in a pout that almost looked real. He supposed to extent it was. "I'm afraid so."

"Damn."

"Yeah." Her eyes were full of moisture. He wondered if it was tears. "But, hey, we had some good times, right?"

"We did."

She laughed. "Yeah. Can I tell you a secret?"

"Not like I'm going to be able to tell anyone."

"I guess not. Well...that night in the car? Our first time?" He nodded. "I've never done anything like that before. I just wanted it so bad and you definitely gave it to me."

"Glad I could help."

"I'm gonna miss you, I hope you know."

For some reason, that made him feel really good to hear. "Thanks."

"Don't mention it."

"Couldn't if I wanted to."

"Right," she said, her voice turning to a whisper. "Well...I guess you'll know soon what awaits us on the other side. Either a bright light or...nothing."

"I'll let you know if I can."

"You do that." She pointed the gun. Looked like it was aimed right at his head. "Have a nice trip."

"You too."

Henry was mostly disappointed because he wouldn't be able witness the progress with Gabe. But, he felt like the biggest idiot because he hadn't once considered Hawthorne would use Denise this way. He'd expected a small team of masked goons to raid the Heyman home, dispatching Greg and Sheila quickly and abducting Gabe in a silent seize. That was sloppy of him, but his mind hadn't exactly been where he'd needed it to be.

Booze. The kid. And of course, Denise.

He'd been doomed from the start.

The gun's pop was a sharp gusting chirp.

CHAPTER 32

Jenny, lying on her stomach, had her head buried in the pillow. She'd barely moved from this spot since coming home from graduation last night. Since she was grounded, she wasn't able to go to any of the parties afterward, and instead of joining the graduating class for dinner, she'd had to go with her parents to a steak house. Her friends went to the Blue Thunder Drive-In, a 50s spot where the cars drove up to the menus and ordered their food through tiny speakers. A few minutes later someone on roller skates brought the food out, balanced on a giant tray that Jenny couldn't grasp how they managed not to drop.

It had been packed when they'd driven past it, and she'd wondered if Dad had taken that route on purpose just to taunt her. Probably not, but she also wouldn't put it past him. Eating with Mom and Dad had been a strained civility. Dad had tried once to start up a conversation, but it hadn't done any good. No one was in the mood to talk, not even him, so he'd quickly given up hope.

There was a knock on her door. She recognized its tone and depth as belonging to her father.

"It's open."

The door opened. She heard her Dad sigh. "Hey kiddo."

"Hey." Her tone was pouty.

"Still upset with me?"

"Why should I be upset? You told me what would happen if I wasn't careful. I wasn't careful, so it happened. I can't be mad at you."

"But you are."

"So what if I am. I'll get over it, I'm sure."

"Will you?"

She wondered about that and assumed she probably would, but it would take passing her retake exam before she could even consider it. "Probably."

"How did April take to the news about the beach trip?"

Jenny had finally talked to April briefly in the auditorium during the rehearsal yesterday and informed her that the beach trip was off. She wondered if April's disappointment was from the fact they couldn't go together, or that *April* couldn't go without Jenny's money. All along Jenny had assumed she would be picking up the bill for the majority of the trip, but now she realized April had expected her to cover it all.

Not happening. Too bad for her.

And too bad for me, she realized.

Did Jenny have any friends? Any *real* friends.

April is a real friend. She's just mad. And spoiled.

"How do you think she took it?" she asked her dad.

He sighed. "Probably about as well as you did, I suppose."

Jenny nodded, her hair making whispering sounds against the pillowcase. She glanced at the clock and saw it was a little after four. She looked at her dad over her shoulder. "Aren't you supposed to be going to that convention or something?"

"Yeah. I need to get going in a little bit. That's sort of what I wanted to talk to you about."

Oh God...please don't let him ask him me to go.

She used to enjoy those conventions when she was younger, but now they were more hassle than fun. Long lines, expensive food and sodas, weirdos all over. Older men who always hit on her, women too, and lots of costumes. Used to be fun, but it just wasn't her thing anymore.

Dad kept going when he realized she wasn't going to respond. "Well... Your mother's going with me and we were going to bring the Heymans with us. Remember how our neighbor is a comic book artist?"

"Yeah." And how she'd been excited to tell Doug about it. She realized she'd never gotten the chance to introduce them.

Guess that won't happen.

"The Heymans were going to go with us so I could introduce Greg to some folks that might want to hire him."

"That's...cool?" She wasn't sure why he was telling her any of this.

"Well, Dr. Conner was supposed to babysit for them, and he hasn't shown up. They told him to be there at four and he's late, not answering his phone, so they called and canceled on us."

"That sucks. But Dad, I don't want to go in their place. I'm not in the mood to mingle with those kinds of people tonight."

"Fair enough. But are you in the mood to babysit?

Jenny sat up in a flash. "What?"

"Will you babysit the Heymans' kid so they can go with us tonight?"

"Isn't he sick or something?"

"Yes. But I think you'll be able to handle it."

"He's not contagious, is he?"

"No, Jenny. Not that kind of sick. A skin disorder that keeps him in his room."

"And they're okay with me doing this?"

"We haven't run it by them yet. Wanted to get you on the fence first."

"Dad...I'm not the person you want for this."

"Listen, if you babysit Gabe for the Heymans tonight, I'll reconsider your beach trip."

Excitement buzzed in Jenny's stomach. "Are you serious?"

"Under a few conditions."

"Okay..."

"You postpone it a week, retake that exam next week and pass with a high mark, so your transcripts show you were on honor roll for this semester. If you don't make at least a high A on the exam, you can't go."

"Even if I babysit?"

"Even if you babysit."

"Why does this exam matter to you so much? I've already registered at the community college..."

"Aren't you planning on transferring later?"

"Well...yeah..."

"Then you'll need this grade. You might not think so, but you will."

Especially if she pursued the idea of taking creative writing courses. A flunked Literature Arts class wouldn't help her any. "Okay."

"Do we have a deal?"

"This is blackmail."

"I'm not confirming that."

"Are you denying that?"

"I'm not at liberty to say."

Jenny felt a smile trying to break out on her face. "Okay. I'll watch the kid so you all can go out."

Smiling, Dad crossed the room, scooped her up in his arms like he used to when she was little, and kissed her on the forehead. "You're a pretty good kid, you know that?"

"That's what I hear."

One more kiss on the forehead, and he set her back on the bed. "Get ready quick. We'll call the Heymans and let them know."

"Okay."

He hurried back to the door. "Love you!" He waved and was gone.

Sitting there, hopeful about the beach trip, and a little confused by her father's behavior, she smiled. "Love you too," she muttered.

CHAPTER 33

Sheila had half of a broken pill capsule and was pouring the powder from inside into a glass of chocolate milk. This was number four, and Sheila told him she was worried they were giving their son too much. But Greg wondered if even this many would be enough. Dr. Conner had sworn one of these tranquilizers would knock Gabe out. But Greg had witnessed Gabe being unaffected by just one. It had made him a little a groggy, but other than that he was impervious to the drug. Sure, it was a smaller dosage, but he didn't want to chance it.

"I can't believe we're doing this," she said. "Are we bad parents?"

She asked this question so often he was starting to wonder if they were. "This is definitely in the book of bad parenting."

"God. We're going to Hell. There's no doubt now."

They'd done even worse things recently, but he didn't bring that up. "I told you we don't have to go."

"We have to, Greg. You might not get another opportunity like this."

"I can submit my sample pages to the companies like I

always do, by email."

"But they make you wait for months before giving you an answer. We might not have months to wait. Besides, with Todd being there to be the go-between, you can bypass all that bullshit. You might even be drawing for someone by this time next week."

Greg knew it didn't work like that, but he understood her point. "Okay. But we never do this again, Sheila. We don't even speak of this again, okay?"

"Believe me, I already want to forget this."

Half an hour later, they were standing beside Gabe's bed. Greg had just laid Gabe down, and Sheila stood back, his blankets in her hand. Once Greg had their son situated, Sheila spread the blankets over him, tucking them under Gabe's chin. He looked so cute lying there that Sheila started to cry.

"I feel like such a piece of shit," said Greg. "Can't believe we drugged our own kid."

"It's the only way we can ensure he'll be good."

"By drugging him?"

"People do it all the time," she said. "Hyper kids all over the world are on all kinds of drugs to keep them calm."

"Not like this."

"I doubt we're the only parents ever to sneak their kids any sedatives. At least, I hope not." She could still feel the chalky residue of the tablets' insides on her fingertips.

Greg looked at her. "We can still change our minds."

Sheila was tempted. She was really tempted. But, by doing that she would become the unsupportive wife in her husband's moment of opportunity. She didn't want to be that, didn't want to be her mother. Greg was very talented, an incredible artist, and any chance that came his way, she wanted him to grasp. After all, she loved him. Deeply. And he would want the same for her; she knew that with all her heart.

"No, honey," she said. "We have to do this. If we're going to make it work here, then we have to take risks. It's not like we're leaving him alone. Jenny will be here."

"But we're locking the door to keep her out. Don't you think she's going to find that to be a little weird?"

"We'll tell her he came down with a bug and to stay out of his room."

Greg seemed to consider that. "I guess we'll have to."

"Do you think this will be worth it?"

"I hope so."

They stared down at their son for a moment longer, saying nothing. Then Sheila said, "Do you want to do it, or do you want me to?"

Greg shook his head. "You put the medicine in his cup... I'll do this."

He crouched next to the bed, hidden from the shoulders down. She could see him slightly moving, could hear the quiet muffling of him digging around. He stood back up, in each hand was a shackle attached to a leather strap. Such all-consuming guilt made his face appear twice its age. Looking down at Gabe, he said, "I'm sorry, Booger. It's not your fault, okay? We *have* to do this to keep you out of trouble. We know you can't help the way you are, and neither can we...but we have to take these...precautions."

Greg began shackling their son. He clamped a restraint around Gabe's narrow wrist, then brought it down behind the headboard, tying it tight to the leg. He did this on the other wrist as well. When he'd finished with that, he moved on to the ankles.

Like usual, it felt like it took Greg hours to complete binding Gabe. Mercifully, he finished and joined Sheila on her side of the bed. Gabe was shaped like an X, looking pitiful in his pajamas, and tied up in a position that used to bring Sheila such joy when she was displayed like that. The bondage set belonged to Greg and her, and on certain occasions they liked having some fun with it. After the first time they'd used it as a means to bind their son, she'd lost her love for it. Apparently, so had Greg, since he hadn't suggested they utilize it since.

The doorbell rang. Sheila's stomach pitched. It felt tight and gritty, as if a load of rice were on a spin cycle in there. She and Greg stared at each other nervously.

"Here it goes," he said.

"Okay."

CHAPTER 34

"You have a really nice home," said Jenny as she entered the living room. She did a small twirl, taking it all in. It wasn't as big as her house, but she really liked the layout. Sometimes she felt where she lived was too big for just the three of them.

"Thanks Jenny," said Greg. "You know what's ours is yours. Have a seat." He motioned for her to sit in the chair.

Everyone sat, Greg and Sheila taking the couch. Jenny shrugged out of her book bag and set it on the floor by her feet. The material felt stiff and scratchy against her calves. She crossed her legs, realizing that at this angle, the Heymans could see right up her skirt if she wasn't careful.

Should've worn shorts. What was I thinking?

She'd been thinking about inviting a certain someone over who shouldn't be coming over, and that was why she'd worn this skirt. It was one of his favorites. Showed plenty of skin.

I'm going to come off as desperate.

Wasn't she?

Sheila smiled. "Thanks for coming on such short notice. I'm sure you have plenty of other places you'd rather be on a

Saturday night."

"Well, my dad kind of grounded me for flunking one of my finals, so it's not like I had a whole lot of plans."

Sheila gasped. "Oh, no."

"Sorry to hear that," added Greg. "But an education *is* important..."

Shrugging, Jenny said, "It's all right. I hope you're okay with me watching your son. I'm sure my dad just threw it on you, putting you in one of those situations where you couldn't say no. He does that, but...he means well."

Greg's laughter confirmed Dad had done just that. She'd figured as much. "It's fine. Is that bad grade going to affect college?"

"I'm retaking the exam next week. Brought some things over to study while you're gone. I should be okay in the long run."

"That's good," he said. "With Gabe already asleep, you should have plenty of time for studying."

"Wow." Jenny checked her watch. "He's already asleep?"

"Yeah," he said. "Easy money, huh?"

Everyone laughed. Greg's chortle was unnaturally loud, almost booming in the small room.

"Besides," Sheila said, "he wasn't feeling well. We gave him some medicine. He'll probably be out for the rest of the night. So, really all you have to do is make sure ninjas don't invade the house or anything."

"Oh?" said Jenny. "It's a good thing I've trained with some of the best.

Sheila pretended to wipe sweat off her forehead. "Phew! Thank goodness."

Jenny laughed. "Gabe's six, right?"

"Yes," Sheila said.

Jenny frowned, trying to be delicate in her wording. She knew this little talk was more of an interview procedure to ensure she was capable of babysitting their son. She understood that. But this was also a chance for Jenny to be briefed on what she was getting into. "What should I do…if he wakes up?"

"Okay," said Greg. "Maybe we should tell you a little about Gabe. Just in case."

The last three words made the back of her neck tingle. "Just in case?"

"Oh—in case he wakes up."

Sheila turned to Greg. "Greg…you're scaring the poor girl."

"I'm not meaning to."

Sheila turned to Greg. "What Greg's trying to say is that Gabe is a little…*active*."

"Active?"

"A bit *hyper*active. Sometimes he can be a real demon."

"Ah, a hell child," said Jenny, laughing.

"Yes…something like that."

Jenny's nose wrinkled. "Why are you telling me this…if he's probably going to be asleep the whole time?"

The Heymans gave each other a quick glance. Then Greg said, "Making sure all the ground's covered, I guess."

"That makes sense."

"But, what we're saying," he continued, "is he can be a bit of a spazz at times, and that makes it hard. We rarely have anyone babysit him…"

Sheila added, "With his skin condition, it just makes things even worse."

"I see," said Jenny, nodding. "I'll be sure to let him sleep. But…if he wakes up?"

"Our number's on the fridge," said Sheila. "Call us and we'll tell you what to do."

"And we'll head home," added Greg.

"Okay," said Jenny.

Sheila patted Greg on the shoulder. "We should get going," she said.

"Right." He turned back to Jenny. "Real quick, let us give you a few rules to abide by while you're in our house. Number one, which we've already established, be very quiet. You don't want to wake Gabe up. Number two, you can help yourself to anything you want in the kitchen as long as you clean up after yourself. Just stay away from the wrapped meat in the freezer. And number three, no guests, at all."

Jenny nearly cringed. She felt pretty lousy, since Doug coming over was her plan. But she also realized she would feel worse after she called him and asked him to, either from breaking the rule or the disappointment of Doug rejecting her.

"I promise," Jenny lied.

"Good," said Sheila, as she and Greg stood up.

Greg walked to the door, grabbing a leather bag off the floor. Most likely his artwork was inside. Jenny wondered where his office was. Maybe she and Doug could find it and look at some of the drawings.

If *Doug comes over.*

Jenny escorted the Heymans to the door. Greg opened it, allowing Sheila to exit first, then he joined her. Jenny stood at the threshold, a hand on the door.

"Just let Gabe sleep," he repeated.

"Everything's going to be fine."

Greg and Sheila lost their smiles.

"We hope so," said Greg.

They told her bye and walked away, heading toward Jenny's house. She shut the door when they crossed the property line.

Jenny leaned against the door, letting the air slowly waft out her nose. Alone, in a large home with a sick boy, the only sound being a clock ticking from somewhere, she couldn't help feeling a little spooked.

The ceiling groaned faintly. She looked up. It repeated. Was someone walking around up there, or was it just the house doing its best to scare her?

She pushed off the door with her shoulders. She walked to the stairs, pausing at the bottom, and looked up.

Up top was much darker than down here. Sunlight splashing through the windows threw sideways bars across the upper wall, making it look much later than what it really was.

The floor popped. Definitely someone was moving around up there.

Great. So much for sleeping the whole night. The parents haven't even gotten to leave yet.

This was good, though, they could come back and handle it.

But what if it isn't Gabe?

Who else could it be? If it wasn't then she should definitely call someone.

Just check real quick, to be sure.

Jenny started to climb the stairs, letting each foot down softly on the heel to be quiet. She wasn't sure why she was taking such measures to silence her movements, but she just felt she should be.

She put a hand on the rail. It felt icy under her already cold hand. She brought it back, balling it into a fist, and putting it against her chest.

At the top of the stairs, she looked around. She realized she had no idea which room was Gabe's. That was something she should have asked before they'd left.

Screw that! They should've told me.

From what she gathered just by her transitory glance, there was only two closed doors. A narrow one next to the bathroom that she assumed was a broom closet. It didn't have the traditional knob like most doors had, but a latch. Probably contained towels, wash rags, maybe a vacuum cleaner. Not a sick kid.

The door to her left, tucked in a dark corner as if meant to be hidden, had to be Gabe's. The windows couldn't reach it, so the shadows were a heavier curtain on the pale white surface of the door, the knob a shiny bulb winking in the black.

Jenny gulped. Her lungs began to throb, pointing out that she'd been holding her breath. Taking in a heavy breath, she shook her head at herself. She couldn't believe she was so…so what?

Scared? Of a closed door?

She'd never admit that. And she was going to prove it.

To who?

Herself.

How?

By marching right over to the door, opening it and making sure the kid was in there.

And if he's not?

Call the parents and tell them to get back over here and put his little ass back in bed.

Sounds like a plan. Get to it.

Jenny remained where she was, staring at the door.

Another minute of vigorous inner encouragement and she

managed to put a heavy foot forward. Felt like she was walking with the blood cut off in her legs.

She stopped right outside the door. Leaning forward, she put her ear against it. She winced at the chilly bite of the door upon her ear. On the other side, she could hear a quiet constant buzz, like one of those bug zappers.

Her hand found the knob and started to turn.

It was locked.

"Wha...?" she whispered.

She tried turning it the other way, even though she knew it wouldn't help. It was locked in that direction as well.

Why would they lock the door? She shook her head. They wouldn't have done that, would they? Maybe the kid locked it? That could have been the noises she heard: him moving around, maybe using the bathroom, then locking the door to the strange girl downstairs.

She was tempted to call his parents but decided not to. It was just a locked door. No big deal.

Jenny turned around and hurried down the hall. She gave the kid's door one last look before trotting downstairs.

CHAPTER 35

Denise waited five minutes to make sure the girl wouldn't come back before reaching up and blindly pawing for the door latch. She found it. Gently, she eased it down. There was a soft click, and the door opened a smidgeon. A horizontal bar of light dropped down on her. Through the little gap, she could see out into the hall. Deserted. She listened a moment and could hear the faint scuffling sounds of Jenny moving around downstairs.

Good. She could come out.

Scrunched up under the bottom shelf, Denise wriggled her way out into the hallway. Once she was clear of the closet, she stretched. When her muscles were good and relaxed, she stood up. Thank God she was flexible. If she wasn't, there was no way she could have squeezed herself into such a small space. Remembering Henry's reaction when she'd bent her legs behind her head brought a smile, and a tight tug in her chest. She shook her head to stop the guilt from manifesting.

Thankfully she'd worn pants that would stretch with her: a pair of old black jeans that were more than just broken-in. If she hadn't needed the pockets, she would have worn her Yoga pants. She also had on a black shirt and matching vest on top of it. She wished it was one of those heavy-duty vests with all the pockets. It wasn't. This one came from the discount rack at Marshall's because she thought it was cute.

Denise pranced on the tips of her toes to the kid's room.

She knew where it was because she'd scoped this house multiple times throughout the past few weeks. She'd constructed two scenarios and, so far, the first one was working fine. Last night she'd come over after Henry had fallen asleep and killed the phone and internet, severing the Heymans' ties to the outside world. She could have waited until today to do it, but she was already here last night doing one more reconnaissance, so she had decided to get it over with to save some time.

After wrapping up Henry's body in the plastic she'd laid out and stuffing him in the trunk of her car, she'd snuck in through the parents' window when they were both downstairs talking with the babysitter. She'd climbed up the gutter outside, pried the window open and let herself in. She'd been tempted to pluck them off then, but to save herself the task of cleaning up the mess, she let them talk instead.

She'd been on her way to the kid's room when the girl had decided to come upstairs. The linen closet had been a spur of the moment idea, and luckily it had worked. She should have killed the girl. Cleaning up one body wouldn't have been as much work as three, but she was feeling sympathetic because of Henry. She didn't feel like killing anyone else today.

But if the girl came up here again, she would do it and suffer the extra guilt later.

Denise tried the kid's door, but it was locked. *Figures.* They wouldn't want the girl coming in and seeing what the kid really looked like. He was probably doped up on Henry's tranquilizers, which would make her job that much easier.

Getting the kid out of the house would be the hardest part. She'd already decided that exiting through his window and climbing down the tree outside with the kid in tow would be the easiest way to go. If he was already asleep, that would save her from having to tranquilize him herself.

But the door…

She let her hand drop away from the knob.

No problem.

Reaching into her back pocket, she removed a tiny case. Inside were her lock-picking tools. She crouched in front of the knob, then removed the utensils from the case. She slipped the unfolded paperclip into the slit. Sure, it was a provisional tool, but she'd picked numerous locks with them. Once it was in place, she took the smart key and wedged it into the crevice on top of the paperclip. Then she began to wiggle them, waiting for their tips to catch. It took a full five seconds before she felt them click into their appropriate spaces.

Turning the picks simultaneously, the lock pulled back with them. She smiled at the tinny click. Done. She removed the tools, put them back in the case, and slipped it into her back pocket. She stood up and turned the knob. It opened without any trouble.

The damp odor of an aquarium hit her. It reminded her of the fake caves at the zoo. Dark and humid. The only light in here came from small boxes attached to the wall. The bulbs behind the metal netting gave off a blue hue and buzzed like a beehive. She quickly shut the door behind her. Although the lock was broken, the door latched into place fine.

From the light out in the hall, she was practically blind in the murky room. She could hardly see the floor. The furniture was only shapes spread throughout the room. She saw a black rectangle on the far side wall. The window. She hurried across the room, bypassing the dark shape of the bed to her right.

The glass was blocked by wooden blackout blinds. She pushed her hands underneath and found the grooves on the pane. She lifted. Her hands slipped off the unmoving window, jarring her shoulders.

Ouch, dammit!

Sucking back the pain, she pulled her hands out and stuck them through the slats. She found the lock, twisted it, then tried opening the window again. It still wouldn't budge. She felt around the sill. Her fingers found a smooth line going across the window where the small gap between the sill and pane should be.

It had been glued shut.

Denise stifled a groan. No worries, she still had the wedge she'd used to open the other window. She'd just use it here as well. She reached into her vest, fingered the wedge, and pulled it out. She set it on the sill so it would be ready when she was.

Now to check on the boy.

She walked over to the bed. The blanket covered everything, pulled up high to conceal the kid's face. With him in a state of catalepsy, there was no need of being modest. So, she yanked the blanket back.

And gasped.

The bed was empty. Broken shackles lay rumpled on the mattress. There was a ruffled depression in the pillow where his head had been.

Denise eyed the dark room. So many places for him to hide. "Gabe?" Her voice sounded dry and croaky. She cleared her throat and tried again. "Gabe? I'm Auntie Denise, a friend of Dr. Conner's. You know Dr. Conner, right?" She walked over to where an inflatable chair was. He wasn't behind it. She tried over by the bookcases next. It was also clear.

Her skin felt cold and too tight. Her shirt was strangling her. She went to tug at the collar and felt the smooth slant of her neck, then remembered it was a V-neck. The asphyxiation was from her constricting throat. The vest was suddenly uncomfortable and heavy on her shoulders.

She saw the wedge glimmering in the blue light. She rushed to it, snatching the metal hunk up. Holding it high by her face, she turned back to face the room.

"Come on out, Gabe. I won't hurt you."

Unless you make a go at me first.

"I'm a friend. Dr. Conner sent me to get you. He wants to take you for a ride. Doesn't that sound fun? A car ride?"

She continued to search the room, including the closet, and each place she checked, she didn't find him. The dread accelerated, making her heart thump against her chest. Her throat made hollow clucking sounds. Her eyes watered. She thought she felt something crawling on her and quickly slapped her hand. Nothing was there.

Now she was getting angry. She wanted to shout but was afraid of provoking hostility from the kid. She strained even harder to be polite as she walked back to the bed.

"Gaaabe? Come on out. Are you hiding? Am I supposed to find you, is that it? Well, I've looked everywhere, Gabe." Her knee bumped the bed, making her squeal. She jumped back. Put a hand against her chest and could feel the thump of her heart against her fingers. Laughing, she let her head droop.

Then something clicked in her head.

Under the bed.

It was the only place he could be.

Getting down on all fours, Denise lowered her head down to the darkened aperture between the frame and floor. "Gabe. I know you're under there. Why don't you come on out, huh? Give ol' Auntie Denise's knees a break." She pulled back the bed skirt to peer behind it. More darkness. "Gabe?"

Eyes slowly lit up, glowing. Each one had a vertical slit of a pupil.

A growl sent dull tremors through the floor.

Denise was about to scream but a fuzzy hand shot into her opened mouth. Claws and knuckles lodged into her throat, slashing and tearing. Blood began to fill up what little space the hand hadn't blocked.

She was choking, couldn't breathe. She pulled back, trying to tug her head away from the carving fingers. She couldn't get free. His grip was too tight.

Denise could feel herself being slowly pulled under the bed. Her hands slapped and pawed at the metal frame but couldn't grab on.

She went all the way under.

CHAPTER 36

On the couch, lying on her back with her legs draped over the arm, Jenny clutched her cell phone to her ear. Her stomach was a fury of tiny grenades. She wondered if Doug would pick up this time. She'd tried calling him twice already, but he'd ignored the calls. If he were smart, he would have let the voicemail pick up on its own, but it had only been on the second ring when his outgoing message suddenly cut the ring short.

That meant he'd looked at the screen, saw it was her, and hit Ignore.

Asshole.

So she had planned to call from the Heymans' phone, but it wasn't working. She'd never attempted blocking her number before and wasn't sure it would work on a cell, but she gave it try. She shouldn't bother. But Jenny had to know for sure if he would answer the phone not knowing it was her calling.

The trick must have worked. The blistering loud ruckus of Megadeth burst in her ear, distorting the earpiece. She held the phone away from her.

"Who's this?" he said without a greeting.

"Hey," she said.

There was a short pause. "Jenny?"

"Yeah."

She thought she heard him sigh, but she told herself it was the wind. "Where are you calling from?"

She was tempted to tell him she'd blocked her number but decided not to. "The Heymans'. I'm babysitting."

"The who?"

"Our neighbors."

"Babysitting? You?"

"I know, weird huh?"

"Never would have taken you for a member of the babysitter's club."

Jenny smiled, although she hated herself for it. "Guess I'm an honorary member for the moment. So, what are you doing?"

"Me?"

She almost said something snarky but refrained. "Yes."

"Oh…hanging out."

"Alone?"

"No. Phil's with me."

"Oh. Tell him I said hello."

"Uh-huh…"

She waited. "Well, tell him."

"I did."

"Oh… I didn't hear you. Music's too loud."

"Hang on and I'll cut it down." The music's volume lowered greatly. "Better?"

"Much. Thank you."

"No problem."

"Are you okay with me calling?"

"Sure."

"Then why didn't you answer when you saw my number the other times?"

"I don't know."

"If you don't want to talk to me, we can hang up. I won't bother you anymore."

"Well… I just didn't know what to say. And I was a little surprised. I wasn't expecting to hear from you."

"I guess not. I just wanted to talk to you."

"Okay."

"Do you want to talk to me?"

"Of course I do."

"You could've called anytime. I wouldn't have minded."

"Just giving you some space," he said. "And me some too."

"Yeah." She hesitated.

"What's wrong?"

"I miss you."

"Really?" There was true shock in his voice.

"Yes, really. Why do you sound so surprised?"

"I don't know. I guess I never thought… I don't know."

She realized he'd never assumed he was the kind of guy she could miss. "Well, I do miss you."

"I do too."

Her throat felt like it was swelling. "Would you want to…I don't know…I wanted to see if you…" She couldn't get the words out. They kept lodging behind her teeth.

"What?"

"If maybe you wanted to come over?"

Another pause. "When?"

"Now."

"To your neighbor's house?"

"I want to talk to you about some things."

"What things?"

"Us. You're just hanging out with Phil anyway. Drop him off with April or something and come over."

"Where's the kid at?"

"He's already asleep. He'll be down for the rest of the night."

"Jenny..."

"Please, Doug? *Please?*"

His sigh was unmistakable this time. There was no passing it off as the wind. But she got the answer she wanted when he said, "Okay."

"Promise?"

"I promise. I'll be there in about forty-five minutes. What time will the neighbors get home?"

"Late. They're off with my parents. Oh, and Doug?"

"Yeah?"

"It's the neighbor that draws comics."

"No shit?"

"Nope. Maybe we can look at his drawings."

"That'd be awesome."

She smiled. "See you soon." She pushed the "off" button before he could respond.

Smiling, she thrust herself off the couch and rushed for the bathroom. She wanted to make sure everything on her was in order.

Doug set the phone in the drink holder. He groaned.

"What the *hell* was that, Doug?"

As Doug braked at a stoplight, he glanced over to his right and saw a pair of silky legs, pale in the dark car. The light from the instrument panel bounced off their glossy surface. An image of Phil wearing a skirt as short as the one April had on tried to appear in his head. He quickly shook his head, knocking that image away in a hurry. "I didn't know what else to say."

"You could have said, I broke up with you, so no, I won't be coming by tonight."

"I felt like I *had* to tell her I would."

"You still care about her, don't you?" April crossed her arms.

"Listen to you. You sound like such a bitch right now. She's your friend, for godsake."

"And you're still the man of her dreams. I think she's starting to suspect us."

"Wait, you said she thought I was cheating. You didn't say she knew anything about us."

"I don't know if she does, but I got this feeling."

April's ringtone suddenly began to play. Doug knew who it was without having to ask.

"It's Jenny," she said, confirming.

"Are you going to answer it?"

"Shut up so she won't hear you." She held the phone out and turned it on speaker. "Hey girl, what's up?"

"You answered."

April closed her eyes. "Of course. Why wouldn't I?"

"You've been avoiding me."

April gave Doug an ashamed glance. "I've just been busy…"

"It's okay. I understand."

Collapsing back into the seat, April stared at the ceiling. "So, what's up?"

"I just called Doug."

"You did?"

"Yeah."

"How'd that go?"

"Pretty good, actually. I'm babysitting, but he's going to come over so we can talk."

Doug felt crummy listening in like this. She sounded excited, anxious and happy. Squirming in his seat, the car felt overly small and cramped.

"What are you going to talk to him about?" asked April.

"I don't know…"

"Yes you do."

"Things. So will you do me a favor and let him dump Phil with you for a bit?"

"I'm not Phil's babysitter."

"April, that's not what I meant."

"I was about to go…"

"I mean, I understand that you're upset with me because of the beach trip. And, you and I need to talk about some things as well, but tonight I just want to get a few things straight with Doug and don't need Phil around while we do that."

Doug noticed concern on April's face. He assumed she was wondering what Jenny wanted to talk to her about. Maybe she suspected things after all.

Great.

April scratched her head. "Oh, well…they were actually on their way over to pick me up."

Doug's head whipped toward her. Why was she saying that?

"They were?" asked Jenny, disappointment heavy in her voice.

"Yeah, Phil and Doug are hanging out tonight and I wanted to tag along. They can't come here because my parents are home, and they hate Phil. You know that."

Jenny laughed. "They can't *stand* him. My Dad's not too fond of Doug, either."

Doug knew she'd been lying all this time about how her Dad felt about him. He just wasn't expecting it to hurt so bad learning it.

"Think of something," said Jenny. "Please. I wanted to talk to Doug alone. Face to face."

"I gotta go, Phil's beeping in."

"All right," said Jenny. She was starting to say something else when April ended the call.

"Was Phil really calling?"

"No. I just told her that so I could get off the phone. I *hate* lying to her. I *hate* it. I'm such a terrible friend."

Doug said nothing to dispute her statement. "So, am I dropping you off?"

"Are you high?"

Right about now, Doug wished he was. Might make this night a little easier to handle.

"I think she wants to get back together with you."

Doug wondered if that was so bad. Since dumping her, there had been several times where he thought he'd made a mistake. Jenny was the kind of girl any guy *needed* in his life. Hot, loyal, and she actually cared, had a good heart and brain.

But April...well, April was a freak. And that was a girl every guy *wanted.*

"Do you want to get back with her?" asked April.

"Not really."

"Well, you need to tell her."

"When?"

"Tonight is a good night."

"I can't talk to her about this shit while she's babysitting."

"You still like her. That's why you won't do it."

"I've told you, it's complicated."

"You were screwing me while dating her, now you're broken up and are still screwing me. What's complicated about that? If you cared about her at all, you wouldn't be."

"So, I take it you don't care about her."

"I love her like she's my sister."

Doug wanted to grab April and shake her until she made sense. "Then why are *you* doing it?"

"I can't stop myself. *I* like you, Doug. A lot. I've been with other guys and it's just physical and even with that, I don't get much of a thrill. It's different with you. *Very* different. You just do everything right. I wish I could stop myself, but I can't."

"I can't either." And it was true. April had this hold on him that he couldn't break free of. Even now, as he knew ultimately that being with April would only bring him harm, he was still here. If Phil ever found out about them, he might kill Doug.

"Here's what we'll do. Let's get Phil and the three of us can go over there. She'll never talk to you about getting back together if we're all there. It'll buy us some time, anyway. How will it look if you drop me off at Phil's house?"

Not good.

"You can't take me back home. My parents are still up, and if they see you dropping me off *without* Phil, they'll think it's weird."

"They were there when I picked you up."

"No they weren't."

"Oh…"

"So, all of us going to see Jenny will be the only thing that'll work right now."

"She'll get pissed."

"We'll deal with it. Plus, we *have* to have Phil with us, just in case she ever bumps into him and asks what you two were up to tonight."

"Shit," he muttered. He hadn't thought of that, either. April was so good at deception, it scared him. "All right. What are we going to tell Phil? Aren't you supposed to be going off with your parents tonight, who really aren't going anywhere?"

What if Phil calls and they say, "Phil, we thought she was with you!"

Shit. He hadn't considered anything like that ever happening. He doubted Phil would ever call to check up on April, but now Jenny's unexpected phone call had his paranoia raging.

April sighed. "I'll suck him off and he won't worry about a thing." She'd said it as nonchalantly as if she was going to wash her hair.

"I wish you wouldn't say shit like that around me."

"You're going over to talk to Jenny about getting back together. How do you think that makes me feel?"

"Probably as good as knowing you and Phil are *still* together. I broke up with my girlfriend, remember? You haven't broken up with Phil yet."

"I will. He leaves for Basic Training in two weeks. We'll just have to hold out until then."

Doug shook his head.

"Don't worry. I'll suck him off, but you're the *only* one I'll have sex with."

"That makes me feel so much better."

Again, he questioned why he was wasting his time with April. Then, when she parted her legs so he could see up her skirt to the shadowy band between her legs, he remembered.

CHAPTER 37

Whenever Jenny got nervous, she had to eat. She'd worried about this issue a lot, fearing one day it would cause her to get fat. This fear explained her obsession with keeping her body fit. So long as she exercised, the weight wouldn't be able to pack on.

But she needed something to calm her growling stomach. Nothing major, something small would suffice.

In the kitchen, she sieved through cabinets, looking for the snack supply. She finally found it and was surprised by how well-stocked it was. She dug through bags of chips, cookies, beef jerky, trying to decide which to pick.

She settled for the Cheese Puffs. It was a fresh bag, still sealed. She grabbed it, the plastic crinkling loudly as she took it down from the cabinet. On her way back to the living room, she stopped by the fridge and got another can of Dr. Pepper Cherry. Being her second one, she decided it should be her last or she'd be peeing all night.

Jenny popped the tab and guzzled a couple heavy gulps. A burp tore through her. Laughing, she said, "Whoops." Another swallow, then she headed for the living room.

She sat down on the couch, dropped the bag of Cheese Puffs next to her, and leaned over to put her can on the coffee table. The remote control was there, so she grabbed it before leaning back. She was about to cut it on when she heard the patter of little footsteps followed by the squeaky laugh of a kid behind her.

Gabe ran away from the couch. It really was her! He'd had to see to be sure. He'd smelled her, but he hadn't been certain she was actually *in* the house. She was! He couldn't understand why, though. That mean woman had come in his room. He'd been able to smell Dr. Conner's blood in her skin. She probably didn't know his scent was on her, but Gabe detected it as if she had bathed in it. She was going to hurt him. He could always tell when they were going to hurt him. So, he hurt her first.

But why was Jenny here? Where were his parents? He'd tasted his medicine in the milk. They didn't think he could, but he could tell the difference when it had been added. That meant they'd wanted him to sleep, but they didn't know the medicine didn't work for long.

Now they weren't here. But Jenny was. He was excited at first, couldn't contain his laughter. But as he rushed back into the shadows, he began to wonder if Jenny had made his mom and dad go away.

"Little shit," muttered Jenny, heart in her throat. She turned around, getting on her knees and peering over the back of the couch. He wasn't there. He had been just a second ago, but the little plodding steps had been him running away.

And the laughter. Something had sounded so odd about it. Like a woman with a three-packs-a-day smoking habit trying to sound cute.

Eerie, if Jenny wanted to be honest about it.

"Gabe?"

She looked from right to left. Saw nothing, heard nothing. Frowning, she scooted back and stood up. She walked around to the back of the couch on wobbly legs. Either it was from being on her knees for too long, or the alternative: the shakes. But why would she be scared? It was just a kid.

Maybe it was the possibility of seeing him. All she'd been told from the get-go was he had a skin condition. What if he looked like some kind of freak? Like a kid version of the Elephant Man?

Oh God, please don't let him be gross-looking.

She wouldn't know how to react if he was.

"Gabe? Are you in here?"

Jenny looked up at the ceiling as if she might be able to see through into Gabe's room. He would be scared of her, too, she realized. He didn't know who she was, and yet, she was in *his* house, and his parents were nowhere around.

Great.

He'd probably cry. Maybe she should go on and call the parents.

No. She needed to check on him first. The parents would ask if he was okay, so she should have that verified *before* calling them.

The stairs were ahead of her. Only a dim glow of light resonated up there, most likely from a nightlight of some kind. Now that the sun had set, the entire house was gloomy and shadow-ridden. On the wall to her right was a light switch. Hopefully it went to the stairs. She put a finger under the switch, flipping it up. Light blared down on the stairs, another one clicking on at the top, illuminating the hallway.

With its low wattage bulb bouncing off the walls, it gave everything a pale green complexion. Like walking into a bar or club.

Gradually, she went up the stairs. At the top, she stood at the mouth of the hallway where it split into separate directions. The bathroom light wasn't on, so he wasn't in there going potty.

But his bedroom door was open part way, a blue bar of light thrown on the floor. Swallowing the nervousness down, she moved forward. She went to the door, giving it a gentle push. She stood in the doorway, putting on a false smile. She pushed down the anxiety, forcing it away. "Gabe? Are you in here?"

First thing she noticed upon entering was the odor. Musty and a little damp, like wet dog, but not quite. Then it clicked. April used to own ferrets, and if their cages weren't cleaned often enough, they began to smell how this room smelled. Awful. Slightly rotten with a hint of humidity.

The room was washed in blue light coming from small tubes in a box on the wall. They hummed like safety lights atop power poles. She spotted the empty bed. The blankets were a mess, bunched up in a ball on top. So, he was definitely up and around here somewhere.

"Gabe? I'm Jenny. I'm your babysitter. Your mommy and daddy are with my mommy and daddy. So, it's just us two kids hanging out." She went over to the bed. "Are you hiding under there?"

Getting down on her knees, she leaned over. The carpet was stiff and scratchy on her skin. "It's okay. If you're under there, you can come out."

She figured checking under the bed was unnecessary, but she wanted to be sure he wasn't hiding under there. If he was, she would just let him stay under there and go call his parents to get him out.

"Don't be scared, Gabe. I'm your babysitter. I'm your friend."

In the process of pulling back the liner, growls erupted from downstairs. Jenny screamed, letting the liner drop. It sounded like a dog was viciously attacking something down there: plastic tearing, crunching, wet chewing sounds.

"What the *hell* is that?"

Jenny jumped to her feet, ran out of the room. She rushed down the stairs, taking them in giant leaps. Charging into the room, feet slapping the hardwood floor, she halted at the sight of a massacre. A Cheese Puff explosion of torn plastic and puffy orange chunks littering the couch and spilling onto the floor. Crumbs and bits were everywhere.

Grimacing, Jenny stared at the mess in disgust. "What happened in here?"

She slowly approached the mess, picked up the bag, and examined it. The bag looked like Freddy Kruger had tried to eat the puffs with his gloved hand.

Someone grabbed her shoulder.

CHAPTER 38

Todd's hand was starting to cramp. And he was nearly out of books to sell. He hadn't anticipated the crowd being as large as it had been tonight. He'd made some new fans, met some of his die-hards, and had a good time chatting with them all.

Greg had already had two job offers for single run comics and two phone meetings set up for next week, based on his portfolio work alone. The man hadn't stopped smiling. And Lisa had done a great job keeping Sheila company. They seemed to be having a blast.

All in all, it had been a good night.

"Can I get a picture with you?" asked a young girl who couldn't have been any older than thirteen. She had on glasses that Todd guessed weren't prescribed since they had a 3D logo imprinted on the frames.

He glanced at a proud mother standing behind the petite girl and got an approving nod. He supposed since she allowed her daughter to read his adult-oriented books, then she wouldn't mind her getting a picture with the author.

"Sure," he said. "That would be great."

The girl's eyes widened as she gasped. "Really?"

"Yeah. Just let me come out there."

Greg scooted his chair closer to the table to allot him the space to pass by. Coming around to the front, Todd held his arm out. The girl snuggled against him, resting her head under his arm. The mother held out her smart phone and told them to say cheese.

The phone beeped, then the mom checked the screen. "Looks good," she said.

"Thank you so much!" cried the girl. "I'll upload it to Facebook and tag you in it."

Todd didn't have a real Facebook account, just one of those pages where people had to click "Like" to be a member of.

"Please do," he told her. "I can't wait to see it."

The girl hugged her newly autographed books to her chest. Then she left with her mother, giving Todd glances over her shoulder.

"Think she has a crush," said Greg.

"Nah."

"Starstruck maybe?"

"I'm hardly a star," said Todd, making his way back to his seat. He counted what remained of his books. Three trade paperbacks of Psycho Trip, one out-of-print mass market edition of Digger, and one limited hardcover of Sweet Skin.

"To that girl, you're a star," said Greg. "Should make you feel good."

Shrugging, Todd sat down in the folding chair. His ass was starting to hurt from the unyielding seat: a sheet of hard aluminum that seemed to cram his butt bone up his spine. "It does, but it's still a little overwhelming."

"I would imagine so."

"You must get that, too, right? I mean, whenever you meet a comic book fan."

"If I ever met them, I might." Greg laughed.

"Well, you will soon enough. Do enough of these and they'll be lined up to get *your* John Hancock. You make a decent amount of money from these things, and the best part, you can write off this stuff on your taxes. It's a win-win situation."

They laughed.

"Did we miss the funny?" asked Lisa.

Lisa and Sheila approached the table. Lisa was carrying a cardboard tray of hot dogs, which she set next to his books. There were two smaller plain ones, then four ogre weenies loaded with chili. Todd assumed those were meant for him and Greg. Sheila placed another tray down. There were four giant sodas planted in the grooves.

"Perfect timing, dear," said Todd. His stomach growled in agreement. He had forgotten about eating. He'd been too busy to even think about it. Thankfully, Lisa was here to make sure he got some kind of food, even something as greasy as a hot dog.

"I figured you guys were probably getting hungry," she said.

"I don't know about Greg, but I surely am."

"I could probably eat that hardback book," said Greg.

"Well, the hot dogs probably aren't any healthier than ingesting all that ink and paper, but it probably tastes better."

"We'll see, won't we?"

Todd grabbed a soda. "What do we have here?"

"They're all Cokes."

"Great." Todd took a cup out of the tray and set it in front him. Sheila handed him a straw on her way to the chair beside Greg. "Thanks."

"No problem," she said.

Todd stabbed the straw through the plastic X on the lid, raised the cup, and sucked. The soda hit his tongue, tingling and cold. It burned a little on the way down, eradicating his thirst. It tasted sweet and good.

The hot dogs never stood a chance. There was nothing left by the time they were done eating.

With everyone in a good mood, Todd thought it might be a good time to suggest getting together for Fourth of July weekend. He'd already rented a cabin in the mountains and he wanted to invite the Heymans. He knew their son's illness would probably make them say no, but he wanted to at least offer.

Whenever Todd had these ideas, the realization that he'd never met the Heyman kid always came about. It was a little strange to him that they kept their son such a secret, but he could also understand why they did. They'd come from years of mistreatment, and the last thing he wanted was to augment it. He figured they'd let him and Lisa get to know the kid whenever they felt the time was right.

"Just throwing this out there," said Todd. "I know it's still over a month away, but I wanted to mention it now so we could attempt to plan it out."

"Uh-oh," said Lisa. "Todd's gears are turning. I can hear them. They need oil."

Sheila laughed.

"Ha ha," said Todd. "I rented a cabin in Black Mountain for four days around the fourth next month. I'd like for you guys to come too."

"Wow, Todd," said Sheila. "That's very kind."

"I would like for *all* of you to come. If you can arrange it.

If not, I understand, but I just want you guys to at least think it over."

"You mean," said Greg, "bring Gabe with us?"

"Yes. If you feel comfortable. A skin disorder doesn't bother me."

He felt Lisa rubbing his back. He could tell she was proud of him for offering, whatever the outcome might be.

Greg and Sheila looked at each other, nodded, then looked at Todd.

"We'll see what we can work out," said Greg.

That was as close to a yes as he would get, but Todd was glad to have it.

CHAPTER 39

Screaming, Jenny flung the bag up in the air. Cheese Puff remains rained down on her, flaky bits of gritted cheese embedding in her hair. She started slapping at the arm clutching her shoulder.

"Jenny, calm down, it's me!"

She stopped screaming, her hand freezing in mid-swing. "Doug?" He stood before her, bent back, an arm held in front of him to block her hits. "*Dammit,* Doug! You scared the *shit* out of me!"

"You scared me, too! Screaming like that, trying to hit me!"

"You deserved it! How'd you even get in?"

Doug lowered his arm, putting his hand flat on his chest. "The door was unlocked, so we just walked in. Didn't want to ring the bell and risk waking up the kid."

"We?"

Doug lowered his head. "Uh...yeah..." He extended his thumb and pointed behind him. Jenny looked around Doug's burly arm to find Phil and April standing by the front door. Phil's arm was around April, whose face looked guilty of something.

Jenny nearly screamed her frustration but held it back. "Oh...hey guys. I wasn't really expecting *all* of you to...well...never mind."

"Sorry, Jen," said Phil, noticing her aggravation. "I was caught by surprise too."

"I didn't know where else to take them," said Doug, as if they were kids with nowhere to go. In a way, Jenny supposed they were. "We were all planning to go out tonight."

Phil started to say, "The first I heard about these plans was twenty—"

"What's going on here?" asked April, stepping all over Phil's sentence as she entered the room. Noticing the decimated puffs, her face creased into a grimace. "Gross."

"I think Gabe did this."

"Gabe?" Doug's voice deepened, showing authority. "Who the hell is Gabe?"

Jenny crossed her arms. She couldn't believe he felt he had the right to take that tone with her. "Gabe's the *kid* I'm babysitting. I think he's playing some kind of game."

Doug's stern expression softened as the jealousy faded.

April laughed. "How is that even possible? Didn't you say one time that he's like four or something?"

"He's five or six. *And* he's sick. He should be in bed, not out running around and tearing shit up."

"If he's sick," started Phil, "then why are we here? I don't want to catch a virus or anything."

"It's not that kind of sick," said Jenny. "He was born with it."

"Well, that's just great," said Phil, shaking his head.

"I thought you said he was asleep," said Doug.

"He was. But now he's awake. It happens, you know."

Doug scowled at her comment. Jenny took a deep breath. Sarcasm was not needed right now, so she should cool it.

"Are you sure it's him?" asked April.

"Yeah."

"Did you see him do this?"

"No, but he's not in his room, so it had to be. But…" She stopped.

"But what?" asked April.

"Nothing. It's just…interesting, is all."

"You're starting to freak me out."

"Well…" She hoped she wasn't making a mistake by telling them this. "His door was locked earlier. So, I couldn't even get in to check on him."

"Like the parents locked him in?" asked April. Her nose wrinkled, teeth bared.

"Maybe. He could have locked it himself, but they said he was asleep when they left, so I don't see how that's possible. It's unlocked now, which is weird…"

"I think you're spooking yourself," said Phil.

"Probably," she said.

"Stop it," he told her. "You'll start freaking April out and that'll be the end of it."

"Too late," said April.

"All right," said Doug. "We're here. So, what do you need us to do?"

"Get out of sight. If he sees you and tells his parents that you were here, they'll tell *my* parents, and after that, my life will be *over*."

"We can help you find the little guy," said April.

"Didn't you hear me? I said you're not supposed to be here."

April's voice took on a snotty quality. "Well, you

shouldn't have invited us."

"I didn't invite you, I invited Doug. If I would have known he was going to show up with a crowd, I wouldn't have." She ran a hand through her hair. "No offense."

Phil shrugged.

"Well, you've got us here," said April. "I have to use the bathroom anyway, so we might as well make sure you find the kid okay. If word gets back to your parents, we can just tell them that we called you to come hang out, and you told us you were babysitting. So, we stopped by, *uninvited,* and you were freaking out because the kid was hiding, and you couldn't find him. And we stayed around just in case you needed us."

It was unnerving how fast April could whip up such a convincing lie. "It won't work," said Jenny.

"Why not?" she asked.

"Because it won't."

"It'll work," said Doug.

"Yeah," agreed Phil. "Plus, April isn't the only one that needs to make a pit stop. I drank a lot of sweet tea today."

Jenny groaned. "Fine. After we find Gabe, all of you have to leave. Right away. Got it?"

They understood.

"So what's the turd look like?" asked Phil.

"I told you his bedroom was locked, so I have no idea. But I know he has some kind of skin thing, and it must be pretty bad since he's in his room all the time. And there're these weird light bulbs in there that make everything look blue."

"Fan-fucking-tastic," said Phil. "A little monstrosity running around here. I'll probably shit myself if I see him."

Jenny pointed at Phil. "Don't you *dare* scare him if you do find him. Don't scream, or anything like that. Just come tell me where he is, and I'll call his parents."

"Okay, *jeez!*"

"We won't scare him," assured April. "Right, everyone?"

Doug and Phil agreed.

"Thank you," said Jenny. "And I'm sorry I'm acting like such a shit right now, but I'm stressing."

"It's okay," said Doug. He gave her that look that always made everything feel a little better. "We understand."

The look wasn't working this time.

"We'll check upstairs," said Phil. "And visit the lavatory."

"Don't steal anything," said Jenny.

Phil made a face as if he'd been wounded. "That hurt, Jen. That hurt."

"I know you, Phil. I mean it."

"All right. Scout's Honor that I'll keep my hands to myself." To April he said, "Come on, babe, let's find this whipper-snapper."

Pulling April away, he led her to the stairs. She glanced back over her shoulder as they mounted the stairs. Jenny followed where her gaze was aimed and saw it ended at Doug. And the worst part was that Doug was looking right back at her.

Everything seemed to fall into place. Jenny got it. And it had been so obvious she should have figured it out much sooner. Maybe that was why she hadn't. All the evidence was so plain and in sight, she hadn't noticed it.

Or she'd purposely ignored it.

April and Doug's odd behavior. Those bruises on April's neck from a mystery guy. Doug's sudden change in how he kissed and acted whenever they got sexual. Now she knew.

Marching over to Doug, she stood in front of him, staring straight through him.

"What the *hell* is going on?" she asked.

He gulped. "What do you mean?"

"You know what I mean."

"No, I don't."

"I'm not an idiot, Doug. I know what you've been doing all this time, I just need to know why."

"You're not making any sense."

"You're such a son of a bitch. A complete *bastard*."

"Why are you saying that? I don't know what you're talking about."

"And how you can just look me right in the eye and lie hurts me the most, Doug. I thought I knew you…"

"You *do* know me. I'm the same Doug I've always been. Nothing's changed about me. You've changed."

"Bullshit. You're not going to twist this around and make it my fault."

He reached for her like he wanted to hug her, but she slammed both hands against his chest, shoving him.

"What the hell, Jenny!"

"Stay away from me!"

Doug sneered. "You asked *me* to come over, remember?"

"Why, Doug? Why her?"

"Who?"

"Just go. Get away from me, now."

"Fine. I'm going to hang out in the kitchen."

"You would."

He walked toward the right, peeked around the corner, and nodded as if confirming the kitchen was that way. "I'll be in here when you're ready to apologize."

Jenny wanted to rush across the room and start clawing his face. Instead, she bit down so hard on her lip that she drew blood. The heartbreaking truth of who Doug really was wanted to break her down. She held it in as she began her own search for Gabe.

She hoped the poor child hadn't overheard the things said in here. All she needed was for him to be alarmed. He'd never come out of hiding then.

A part of her, deep down, wanted him to stay hidden. But it was hardly noticeable, and she wasn't sure why it had come about in the first place.

CHAPTER 40

"All clear," said Phil.

Peeking his head around the door frame, Phil glanced back at April. "We've got to check it out. He could be hiding in the closet or something."

"Whatever."

They entered the dark room. The only light came from a dim nightlight plugged into a corner outlet. Phil thought this searching bullshit was pointless. But he'd gone along with it just to keep everyone cool. He'd sensed tension downstairs, especially between Jenny and April. Any moment he'd expected them to attack each other, pulling hair and clawing their eyes out. Maybe they'd have ripped each other's clothes off and really tore into each other.

That would have been really awesome to witness. Just not now. Something had happened between the girls. He wasn't the idiot everyone took him for. He could tell whenever someone lied to him, tried to take advantage of him, but he never let on. Made it easier for him to manipulate them later, in his own way.

Take April for example. She cheated on him whenever she

got the chance. And she just kept going, thinking Phil was completely clueless. He was okay with that. When she found out he wasn't joining the army and was really moving to Boston in September after getting his CCNA certification this summer, to take a job at a security firm making over seventy grand a year, the joke would be on her. He'd already passed the pre-certification exam and that was what had gotten him the job. They wouldn't need him to start until the fall, when they took on four new network security analysts. This gave him plenty of time to become certified so he could start.

Smiling, he walked deeper into the cavern-like room.

"Have you noticed how dark it is in this house?" asked April. "It's creepy."

"Yeah. A lot of blue shades."

"What?"

"The lights. They cast a lot of blues. Nothing looks like natural light."

"Weird. Maybe the light hurts his eyes."

Phil wondered if the kid was an albino or something. It was the only reason he could figure to keep the lighting so dim. "See a light switch anywhere?"

"No."

Phil didn't care to circle the room, slapping a wall to find one. Plus, he'd gotten used to the dark. "I'll check the closet."

"How can you even see it?"

"I have excellent night vision."

"Yeah right."

"It's the darker shape against the dark wall over there. Looks big enough for two rolling doors."

"Aren't you the inquisitive type?"

Bitch.

To his surprise, he made it across the room without

tripping over anything. He pulled back the doors, folding them over each other on the tracks. Using his cell phone as a flashlight, he waved it over clothes that belonged to adults. The parents. One half of the bar was full of men's threads, and the other sported dresses and other female wardrobes.

The bottom was stocked with mounds of shoes, mostly women's. He checked thoroughly for tiny little feet that didn't belong with the larger sizes. He didn't find any.

"Closet's empty."

"Kay," said April, sounding bored.

Phil groaned as he stood up, his knees making soft popping sounds. Shutting the doors, he turned around and noticed April was sitting on the bed. She leaned back on an elbow, legs crossed, smooth and pale in the heavy darkness. Her skirt was so short she could have passed for naked in this lighting.

"What are you doing?" he asked.

"Sitting down."

"We're supposed to be looking for that kid."

"I don't care about finding some stupid kid."

"What the hell's with you? You're being a brat."

"I don't want to be here."

"I don't either, but you volunteered us to help."

April said nothing.

"Well, he's not in here."

April sighed. "That's great detective work you're doing there."

"That's great bitch work *you're* doing there."

He saw the dark shape of April's head shaking.

Probably rolling her eyes.

He looked at her legs again. Even in such darkness they were a nearly perfect set: full and curvy, thick thighs that tapered up to a plump yet firm rump. He reached out and rubbed her knee. She moaned.

"You know…you owe me something," he said.

"And that is?"

"You promised me a blow job in your text. It's time for you to pay up."

"Here?"

"Oh yeah. Here and now. And since you were being snappy and cold, I think you owe me a really good one."

April giggled. "I thought you promised Jenny you'd keep your hands to yourself."

"Hey. It's your mouth and my dick, my hands won't be involved."

"What makes you think I'm going to do it?" she asked, teasingly.

"Because I'm not asking."

"Oh? Are you demanding?"

Done with being coy and flirty, Phil snatched a handful of April's hair and jerked her off the bed. Gasping, she went willingly. He knew how much she loved being forced, so he was only obliging. Frankly, he didn't care one way or the other how he got it, as long as he did. She was panting as she fumbled with his belt. Her hands found the top of his pants and tugged them down with his boxers. His erection didn't drop with them, it pointed straight at her.

He moaned softly when her hand curved around his penis.

"Wait," she said. "What if someone walks in?"

"They'll have to wait their turn." He pulled her head forward, feeling the moistness of her mouth as her lips curved around his girth. "Do that thing with your tongue that I like so much." She did. He gripped her head on each side.

Her mouth full, she struggled to say, "You're using your

handsh..."

"Shut up and suck."

She did.

In the upstairs bathroom, Jenny slammed the door behind her. She'd pretended not to hear April's awful choking sounds coming from the other bedroom on her way in. She might have confronted her supposed best friend had Phil not had his penis stuffed in her mouth.

Gripping both hands on the edge of the sink, she broke down. Tears poured out of her eyes, streaming down her cheeks and dripping off her jaw. The droplets made little blipping sounds as they burst in the porcelain.

"That asshole," she gasped.

Her chin was out of control, trembling, making her teeth chatter. Her emotions continued to explode out of her eyes. She needed to regain control of herself. She did not want anyone hearing her sobbing through the walls, and she definitely didn't want anyone to know that she had been.

Jenny grabbed a section of toilet paper and yanked down. Instead of tearing off, the roll spun, dispensing a long strip of tissue. She slapped her hand on the roll to stop its spinning, then tore it off. Wadding up the tissue, she dabbed her deluged eyes, blew her nose, and dropped the soiled paper in the toilet. She got some more and repeated the process. Finally, she was calmer, but her eyes were red and puffy. Combing her hair down with her fingers, she tried to at least somewhat make herself look normal. Finished, she checked her reflection again. And frowned. They'd know she'd been crying.

Oh well. Screw 'em all.

She could feel a headache coming on. With everything

else, she didn't need a headache too. She didn't bring any aspirin or anything with her. Maybe she could find something to take. Then she realized where she was standing: in front of a medicine cabinet.

Jenny opened the mirrored panel. Prescription pill bottles lined each shelf, arranged in neat, organized rows. There had to be some Tylenol or at least a generic pain reliever amongst the mini drugstore before her.

She started reading over the labels, hoping one of them would be something she could use. Instead of finding any familiar brands, she read nothing but long names she didn't recognize. She took a random bottle and shook it. She could see the silhouettes of giant pills through the orange plastic tube as they rattled against the plastic. Putting it back, she continued snooping. More names she didn't know, nor could she even pronounce them.

Take two for anger. Light sensitivity. Depression. Anger, rage, dietary supplement.

The bottom shelf was stocked with a variety of sleeping pills. One of them stood out from the rest.

Horse tranquilizers.

She couldn't take anymore and slammed the door. The mirror vibrated against the compartment. "Jesus…"

Jenny hurried out of the bathroom, keeping her back to the bedroom as she made her way to Gabe's room.

From under the bed, Gabe watched them. The guy had his hands in the air, as if reaching for the ceiling, fingers flexing and clenching. The girl was on her knees in front, and all Gabe could see of her was golden hair, flopping as her head moved back and forth in a frenzied thrust. It sounded like she was quacking while slurping a milkshake through a tiny straw. He wasn't sure exactly what it was they were doing, but they were enjoying it.

They didn't belong here, either, and Gabe couldn't figure out how all these people got into his home. What had they done to his parents? What would they do to him next? His heart pounding in his chest, he slid out from the under the bed, digging his claws into the fluffy fibers of the carpet.

What was the word Dad used whenever explaining to Gabe about someone who didn't belong?

Strangers?

No. His parents always told him to keep away from strangers. But, the word Gabe was trying to recall was different, but with a similar meaning.

Creeping up on the man's bare butt, his cheeks dimpling and compressing, the word suddenly emerged as Gabe raised his hand, brandishing his claws.

Intruders.

And, Gabe had seen what his parents had done to intruders. The same as he'd done to that man under the tree that night.

The same thing he'd done to that woman in his room.

And he would do it now.

"Almost there..." said the guy, his voice thick and foamy.

"Mm-hmm," said the girl, as if trying to talk while eating a mouthful of peanut butter, smacking and slushing.

Gabe flicked his fingers, the dim light echoing off the sharp tips of claws. Then he thrust his opened hand forward. It vanished, claws first, between the man's cheeks, plunging deep. His arm moved easily, like digging through mud.

The man didn't scream but he made awful gagging sounds, whining as he tried to breathe. The girl made a *huh* noise, confused. More wet rips and then she was gagging and convulsing as Gabe's hand entered her mouth.

His hand kept traveling, not stopping until bursting through the back of the girl's skull. Brain, hair and chunks of bone were a gory mound in his palm. His attack lasted only a flash of a moment, but Gabe had savored the feel of warm flesh tearing apart, hot sticky blood trickling over his fingers.

Wrenching his arm free, the man fell forward, collapsing on top of the girl. It looked as if the man had gained two more legs and arms, the girl's face buried under him.

Gabe licked his fingers. The taste of blood sent a wild buzz through him.

He wanted more. Needed to kill. All of them. *Intruders.*

They would die.

And he would eat.

Rolling his tongue across his narrow lips, Gabe was antsy to continue.

CHAPTER 41

Jenny sat on the floor in Gabe's room, hugging her knees to her chest when she heard the rapid plodding of footsteps as they made their way down the stairs.

Good. They're done.

She sighed. The sounds coming out of there had been disgusting. But she supposed April must like that sort of thing. She'd always assumed April used her apparent nymphomania as an excuse for attention, the kind she shouldn't want. Now she was starting to wonder if there was truth to it.

Not my problem anymore.

After tonight, she was done with both April and Doug. She'd spent this entire year worrying more about what those two thought of her than what was best for her. Not anymore. While she had been succumbing to all their needs, they'd been succumbing to their own behind Jenny's back. They could have each other for all she cared now. It hurt just as much, but she'd get over it. Eventually.

She should get up, get back to searching.

She didn't want to. It felt too cozy here on the floor, her

back to the wall, feeling its cold smoothness through her shirt. The skirt had fallen back on her legs, showing the slope of her thigh as it met her buttocks. She couldn't believe she'd chosen to wear something so skimpy. She hoped the Heymans didn't get the wrong idea about her from this wardrobe choice.

All for Doug, she realized.

Not anymore.

Though she should feel freedom in knowing that, she only felt a cramp where her heart was. She imagined by the end of the summer she would be okay, but that seemed so far away.

Groaning, she pushed off the wall with her shoulders, and got to her knees. She was about to stand when her eye caught something by the bed. It tapered down from the bedpost, vanishing under the pillow. Now that she'd grown so accustomed to the shadowy room, she could see as if every light were on. The dark line by the pillow seemed to shout at her, it was so easy to spot. However, earlier, she'd been right at the bed and hadn't even noticed it.

What is *that?*

Jenny got to her feet, moving cautiously toward the bed. Something about where the line started, and the way it drooped down, was familiar. She'd seen it before and knew it shouldn't be in a child's room. When she arrived at the bed, she realized why she'd thought that.

There were four total, one on each bedpost. She shoved the bunched-up blanket aside and saw four shackles on the mattress. A bondage kit that most couples used to spice up their sex life was affixed to the kid's bed.

Her face contorted in horror as she lifted one up. The leather strap was cold and slippery in her hand. She let it go. It dropped onto the bed, bounced, the metal clasps jingling.

She couldn't pull her eyes away from it.

Doug sat at the kitchen table, drumming his fingers across its wooden surface. He'd been waiting a long time now, and he had to face the unacceptable truth.

"She's not coming in here," he muttered.

Doug sighed. Knowing that she wasn't begging him to take her back made him feel…lousy. Sure, it hurt his pride, but it really hurt his feelings. He'd made a mistake, and he realized that, but he also understood that it was too late to try and fix it. He'd fucked up. Let a really good girl go just so he could get his nut out with a girl that let him do anything to her.

What the hell was wrong with him?

His stomach grumbled, cranky it hadn't been fed yet. He and April were planning on going to get a movie from Redbox, grab a pizza and head to his basement to screw around while the movie played, unwatched, in the background when his phone rang.

Shouldn't have answered the damned thing.

No, he should have been smart enough to know that it was Jenny calling from a blocked number. She'd called two times in a row just a few minutes before the unknown number had popped up. He should have known.

A lot of should haves tonight.

Forget this. I'm raiding their fridge.

Getting up from the table, he went over to the fridge, and pulled it open. Light splashed him from inside.

Jenny walked around the foot of the bed. Her toe bumped something cold and hard. Looking down, she saw a wedge-shaped object on the floor. It was pale and about the length of a banana. Crouching, she picked up the object. It was heavier than she'd expected, its point thin and flat like a screwdriver, but its body thick like a crowbar. She wasn't quite sure what she was looking at. Perhaps a tool of some kind? Whatever it was, it definitely wasn't a child's toy.

She put it back down on the floor. Her finger dipped into something wet. It was only a dab in the carpet, but it clung to her finger, sticky like honey. She raised her pinky, examining the dark blot on the tip.

Blood?

She bent forward, elbows on the carpet. There were a couple more tiny splotches, leaving a trail as they disappeared under the bed. Curiosity outweighing common sense, she lifted the comforter once more.

And peered underneath.

"Nothing but raw meat in here," mumbled Doug. "No sandwich meat? How about a fucking bologna sandwich or something?" He slammed the fridge door, the items inside the door's shelf clattered.

He was ready to leave. He wanted to grab April and Phil, so they could head out, get some pizza like was originally planned and then find a way to ditch Phil before the rest of the night got away from them.

He was about to do just that when a scream ripped through the house. It prickled the hair on the back of his neck, making his skin pull back taut.

Sounded like Jenny.

"Jenny!"

"Doug!" she cried back, distant.

"Where are you?"

He turned around, starting to run. Movement to his right

stole his attention. A dark, hunched shape on top of the table, springing into a pouncing stance. He saw a flash of kid's pajamas just as the shape leaped from the table.

It slammed against his chest, throwing him back against the wall. He tried to push it off; the strength in something so small was unbelievable. Doug could do nothing to get himself free. Sharp stabbing pressure in his shoulder, and he glanced over to find claws imbedded in his flesh.

He screamed.

More bursts of pain in his stomach. He looked down and saw another monstrous hand digging into his gut, ripping it open, yanking out innards in vicious tugs.

My guts! Holy shit, he's tearing out my guts!

Then he felt teeth on his throat.

CHAPTER 42

The screams from downstairs drowned Jenny's own. She stopped, listened. They continued, rising to an agonizing pitch. Whoever they belonged to was in terrible pain. Letting the liner drop back down, blocking her view of the mangled woman's corpse, Jenny scurried back on her hands and knees. The carpet burned her skin as she scrambled to get up.

She was about to charge out of the room, then realized she had no means of protection. What would she find in a kid's room?

She looked down at the heavy tool on the floor and grabbed it. She felt a little safer, braver, knowing she had something like this in her hand. Now she ran out of the room. She hardly noticed the stairs as she bounded down them in lengthy strides. Her feet slapped down on hard flooring, nearly throwing her balance off. She regained composure as she continued to run.

The shrieks were much louder and coming from the kitchen. Shoes clapping, she ran that way. And bumped into someone. The impact sent her against the table. The tool flew from her hand, slid across the table, and fell to the floor with a jarring ring.

The front of her chest was soaked, her already clingy T-shirt plastered to her breasts. She looked ahead of her and saw Doug staggering toward her, his arm outstretched. His jaw moved as thick trails of bloody drool stretched down from the corners of his mouth. The other hand pawed at the large gorge where his throat should be. Stringy tatters of flesh jiggled in front of the large hollow, blood splashing out. His stomach was a basketball-sized crater, ropes of intestines trailing down, rubbing the floor and leaving murky smears behind him.

"Oh, Doug!" screamed Jenny. She wanted to go to him, hold him, but she was afraid of touching him. Even if she weren't, she couldn't get her legs to cooperate. They were leaden, planted firmly where she stood.

Doug dropped to his knees, slipped in his blood, and collapsed forward. He twitched a few times before going completely still.

Crying, hot streams of salty tears spilling down her cheeks, she screamed and shouted guttural bursts. Her fists pounded against her ears as she tried to block out the loudness of her reaction. She couldn't stop screaming nor could she deafen herself to the horrible noises she was making.

A child's laughter did it, silenced her completely as if operating by a switch.

Her frantic eyes darted about the room. The laughter came again, and this time she distinguished the pure enjoyment in its tone.

Gabe…?

Retreating footfalls resounded from the living room. More laughter.

"A game…?"

Jenny shook her head. This was fun to him. He was playing with her.

"You want to play?" she shrieked. She felt drips of sanity melt away. She heard more laughter and realized it was her own. "Okay, Gabe, we can play!"

She grabbed the tool before running out of the kitchen. Entering the living room, she heard thuds on the stairs, and turned, catching the backside of Gabe as he reached the top. He was larger than she'd expect a kid his age to be. The light she'd cut on up there was off. More movement, then silence.

Jenny rushed to the bottom step, reaching for the light. The switch had been torn out of the wall.

"Little bastard!"

Whoops and gobbles resounded from the upper floor that reminded Jenny of the sounds monkeys make. She bolted up the stairs. As she reached the top, turning for Gabe's door, it slammed shut.

The idea that he was intentionally leading her here wasn't lost with Jenny, but it was very distant in her mind. All she could focus on was her rage, and the blinding red sheets of hate in her eyes.

Jenny ran for the room, and instead of attempting the doorknob, she threw her leg up and kicked. The door burst open, tearing a chunk of wood out of the frame. Whipping inward, the door smacked the wall on the inside. There was a crunching sound of the knob stabbing into the sheetrock.

Jenny didn't care how much damage she caused the house, as long as she got the little shit.

"Gabe!"

She found the light switch, wanting to be done with the blue bulbs that barely lit anything. Flipping it, nothing happened. The switch didn't work.

Terrific!

She faced the room, the sharp tool by her side, turning in her hand.

Jenny saw him. He was behind an inflatable chair, crouched down, back to her. He had both arms covering his head.

For a moment, she began to consider the possibility that Gabe hadn't done that to Doug, that someone else was in the house, and for all the kid knew, she'd been the one to do the attacking. She didn't know where Phil and April were, maybe they'd killed Doug.

No way.

She knew for certain it was Gabe, although she had no proof or reason for it.

Jenny pinched the bottom of her shirt and pulled it forward. The blood glued the fabric to her breasts. It sounded like pulling a sticker off its paper when she peeled it off her skin.

She glanced at the shackles. The memory of what she found in the medicine cabinet came to her. It was starting to make a little bit of sense, not everything, but she could understand fragments.

The shackles were meant to keep him in bed. The door was locked to keep her out. The drugs are used on the kid to keep him calm and sedated.

So many precautions taken to keep her safe while she was in the house, and none of them had worked.

Gabe was a secret the Heymans had been trying to hide.

"Did you do it?" she asked him.

Gabe nodded.

"You killed Doug?"

Another nod.

"What about Phil and April, my other friends. Did you kill them too?"

Another nod.

"Why? *Why?*" She walked closer, nearing the bed. The chair was a few feet away. "Talk to me, Gabe! Tell me why!"

She kept moving, bravery building. Anger replaced her fear entirely. She trembled with it. Her skin felt as if it was on fire, felt as if popcorn kernels were detonating under her pores. Her head buzzed, feeling light on her shoulders.

Jenny was a couple feet from Gabe, who still hadn't turned around, cowering in the shadows.

"Look at me," she demanded.

He didn't.

"I said, *look* at me!"

When he disobeyed her order again, she slapped her free hand down on his shoulder.

He whipped around, teeth gnashing and mouth yawning wide. It seemed it would never stop spreading. Jenny jumped back, screaming at the hideous face. It wasn't human. No way could what she was seeing be human.

Blood was streaked across his face, splashy trails on his clothes. Little wiggly bits of flesh were stuck in his sharp teeth. A snake-like tongue lashed from his mouth. Beady yellow eyes glowed like sickly balls in the dark.

"Stay back!" she screamed. "Stay away from me!"

Again, Gabe didn't listen. He pounced. Landing on her, she went down to the floor, unable to support his weight. He tore at her, biting and clawing anything he could get—which was plenty.

He slashed at her face, leaving four narrow gashes down her cheek. Her shirt was ripped open, her bra. Claws slit her right breast. Jenny swatted and slapped his head. He caught her wrist in his mouth and bit down. Pain shot up her arm. Flashes of white overpowered her vision. She felt his mouth clamp down on her shoulder, his head wiggling, then snatching back as he ripped the flesh away. The tiny creature noisily chewed the chunk of meat he'd taken from her shoulder.

Jenny could hardly move. She began to grope the carpet around her, looking for the tool she'd dropped when she fell. She couldn't find it. Jenny's screams rose higher in pitch. Gabe seemed frozen above her, his hands on the floor at each of her sides as he savored the taste of her. His heavy breaths turned to pants.

She slammed a fist repeatedly down on his head, trying to get him off of her. She might as well have been punching a wall. It hurt like she was and was having the same effect.

With the other hand, she continued to explore the carpet to her side. As she was feeling hopeless, her fingers brushed metal. She cried out in triumph, curling her hand around the tool.

He swallowed. Licked his lips with that serpentine tongue of his. He was starting to come back from his haze. He'd crashed into the wall most junkies hit when they needed more. But Jenny could still use his stupefied state in her favor.

And she did, by punching the flat tip of the tool into his eye.

Shrieking, Gabe pulled back. He slashed at her again, across the chest, leaving trails of bleeding marks on her skin. Blood streamed out of his eye, coating her hand in the hot fluid.

Working against the agony that was her body, she yanked the tool out and thrust it into his shoulder. Blood splashed out, giving her a crimson facial. The kid jerked away from her, the tool jutting up from his shoulder like a spike.

He charged. Jenny thought he was coming for her, so she braced herself for the attack. It never came. He rushed by her, out the door and away.

On her knees, Jenny huffed, each heavy breath sending a wave of pain through her body. She looked down at the wounds on her chest. There were many she could see between the frilly halves of her torn shirt. Her right breast was a mangled hump, her stomach slashed and ruined. The bite on her shoulder was a clumpy cavity between her neck and poke of her shoulder.

But, she couldn't allow herself to slow down; she had to keep her adrenaline up so she could get out of here. It was hard to tell where Gabe had run off to, but she figured he'd be back to finish her off before long.

Jenny bit her lip to keep from crying out as she got to her feet. Hunched over, she moved toward the door, trying to caress her wounds, but there were just too many for her to cover.

CHAPTER 43

What a great night it had been. Putting his key to the front door, Greg couldn't stop smiling. Everything Todd had said would happen did. It was a success all the way around. Todd sold all his books, leaving with a huge wad of cash in his pocket, and used it to pay for their meals at the VIP dinner. Sheila and Lisa had a great time just hanging out, and Greg had four job offers and several meetings to contemplate before the weekend was over. It couldn't have gone any better if this had been his fantasy.

There were no phone calls from Jenny to report Gabe acting up, so he wasn't worried about coming home. In fact, he was a bit upset that the night had to end so early. It needed to though; he knew if he stretched his luck, it would snap. Tonight had reminded him what it was like to feel human. He'd had no idea how much he missed it.

"Send Jenny home whenever," called Todd from across the yard. He opened the door and let it sway wide.

Greg waved. "You got it, and thanks again for tonight!"

"It was my pleasure."

Lisa told them bye, then entered the house. Todd followed

her with a bit of stroll in his step. Once they were out of sight, Sheila spun around, hugging her arms around his neck. She kissed him. It was urgent and blunt. He felt her lips smearing across his. When she pulled back, she was smiling.

"Wow," he said.

"I'm actually not nauseous tonight. I say we get Jenny out of here and we hit the bed."

"After checking on Gabe."

"Right. A quick peek, then I'll meet you in the bedroom. And, this is a private meeting, so no clothes allowed."

Laughing, Greg kissed her again. "I'll be wardrobe free for sure."

"See that you are."

Arms around each other, they went inside. And immediately Greg knew everything was wrong. He caught the coppery scent of fresh blood. It hung heavy in the house like an atrocious fog.

"Oh God…"

"What's happened?" asked Sheila, hurrying away from him to the kitchen. She stopped at the doorway and screamed.

Greg ran over to her. "What's wrong?"

She pointed. He looked down at the man on the floor. Blood was splashed all over. Judging the size of this stranger, he was young, possibly a teenager.

"Oh shit…"

"Who is he?" asked Sheila.

Greg shook his head.

"Do you hear that?" she asked.

"What?"

"Listen…"

Greg held his breath as he listened. A soft dragging sound came from the living room. "Yeah, I hear it. Come on."

He took her by the hand and led her into the living room. Jenny was sprawled on the floor, pulling herself. A smeared trail of blood followed her from the stairs. More red splashes were spread out on the way to the upper floor. It looked as if she'd fallen halfway down and tumbled to the floor. She raised her head and began to cry when she saw them.

"I fell…down the stairs…I tried to get away…" Her lower lip puckered out into a pout. She sobbed.

"Oh my dear!" cried Sheila, running over to Jenny. She got down on one knee beside her. She went to grab her, but her hand hung in the air above her, as if she didn't know where it was safe to touch her. She sat down, cross-legged, and eased Jenny on her back, resting her head in the folds of her legs.

"What happened?" asked Greg. "Where's Gabe?"

"Attacked…he attacked…"

That was all Greg needed to hear to know the story. "Where is he?"

"Stabbed him…" She smiled as if proud. "I did…got him…"

Greg felt a pinch inside. "Where *is* he?"

Jenny slowly shook her head. Blood trickled down from the corner of her mouth.

"Find him, Greg!" screamed Sheila.

He ran upstairs, going straight for his son's room. "Gabe? Booger, where are you?"

He checked around, found another stranger's corpse under the bed, and moved on to their bedroom. On the floor were two more chewed-up bodies. The girl's head had been smashed, but the guy's face looked okay. By his features, Greg guessed the kid was around Jenny's age. He bet the one in the kitchen was too. The woman in Gabe's room was a mystery, though.

But where was Gabe?

What if he's…?

He forced that thought to stop. Gabe was fine.

I stabbed him…

Jenny's voice reverberated in his mind, saying over and over that she'd stabbed him.

Sheila stroked Jenny's hair. Such a pretty girl. She hated seeing her so hurt. It broke her heart, but she was more worried about Gabe. Why wasn't Greg back yet? She looked toward the stairs. He still wasn't on his way.

A part of her hoped Gabe was… *No.* She would not even consider that to be a blessing, not for a moment. He was her son. She gave birth to him, and she wanted him to be okay.

Jenny coughed, spitting up a phlegmy wad of blood. Sheila doubted the poor girl could hold out much longer without medical attention.

The thudding of Greg's feet on the stairs called her to look. Her husband was on his way down. "My God… What took you so long, Greg?"

"I found him hiding in the bathtub. She hurt him, bad."

"How bad?"

"He lost an eye…"

Sheila cried. "Oh no…no…"

"It already looks like it's healing though."

Sheila stared at Greg, her sobs on pause. "What?"

"Can you believe it? *Healing.*"

"I don't understand…"

"She stabbed him with a wedge. It was still sticking out of his shoulder, but his body was already pushing it out because the hole was closing up."

"Is he...?"

"...going to be just fine."

"Thank you, Jesus," said Sheila, crying. She reached over Jenny, holding out her arms. Greg got down on his knees and went into them, hugging her back.

"Our little booger," said Greg, "is a miracle. All this time we thought he was a curse, but he's a miracle..."

Sheila agreed. They'd spent so many years resenting Gabe for how he looked, and how hard he made their lives, when they should have been embracing him for the phenomenon that he was. That was what Dr. Conner had been trying to make them understand. If only they'd opened their eyes back then...so many years wasted. Their son was a blessing, a true gift from God. She didn't dare say that aloud, fearing Greg would scold her for speaking like a Catholic again. But it was what she truly believed.

Jenny shook her head. "No...he's a monster...he has...to...he tried to kill me..."

Greg looked down at Jenny, speaking over her whines. "When he's backed into a corner he attacks. He was scared, waking up to all these strangers in the house, to someone breaking into his room."

"What?" said Sheila.

"Yeah, a woman. I found her body in Gabe's room. Looked like she came in through our window and jimmied the lock on his door. That was how he got out."

Sheila was confused. Who would do that? Why? Greg was already talking again.

"Didn't we tell you, Jenny, that there was to be *no* guests in the house? Didn't we tell you?"

"Yuh-yes...but..."

"Not buts," said Greg. "Now we have to rethink this

whole situation. Everything has changed thanks to you. And you know what? We like it here, a lot."

Jenny was crying so hard she could no longer produce words.

"What are we going to do, Greg?" Sheila asked him.

"What do we *always* do when we're backed into a corner?"

"Attack?"

"Attack."

The blank look in his eyes told Sheila all she needed to know. So, when Greg took a pillow from the couch, she didn't question him. She didn't protest him pushing it down over Jenny's face. Sheila gripped the girl's wrists and held them above her head so Jenny couldn't get any leverage to fight back. Sitting on her legs, Greg leaned forward, holding the pillow so tightly his knuckles had turned white.

"Look at me," he said. Sheila did. "I love you."

"I love you," she said.

They stared into each other's eyes as Jenny bucked below them. Eventually her struggles weakened, a couple minutes later they ceased altogether. Greg kept the pillow over Jenny's face long enough to lean forward and kiss Sheila tenderly on the lips.

Greg stood up, leaving the pillow lying on Jenny. Sheila scooted out from under her, gently lowering her head onto the floor.

"Now what?" she asked.

"Take care of the rest."

Sheila felt a hollow space open up in her chest. "We really have to, don't we?"

Greg nodded. "I hate it as much as you…"

"I really like them, Greg…"

"I do too…I do too."

Sheila sat down on the couch, all the strength gone in her legs. She listened as Greg rummaged through Jenny's purse and found her phone. She heard beeps of him dialing…

"Todd? Hey…it's Greg. Can you and Lisa come over for a minute? Yeah, we need to talk to you about Jenny. No…she's fine. Are you on your way now? Okay. Good. See you in a few."

Tears swelled in Sheila's eyes when she heard the sharp scrape of a knife being pulled out of the rack on the kitchen counter. Greg had gotten to be too good at this. It worried her how quick he could dissect a rattled situation and come up with a plan that usually required people being killed.

She looked up as Greg took his place at the door, a chef's knife clutched close to his chest.

CHAPTER 44

Sheila's first thought when she opened her eyes the next morning was it had all been a bad dream. She looked around her bedroom, relieved and confused, but it quickly dissipated when she realized what she'd hoped to be a cruel figment of her imagination was her reality. Greg's spot in the bed was vacant, so that meant he was probably still in the basement, adding more meat to Gabe's menu.

She'd gone to bed angry at him for attacking the Parkers last night. He'd been merciful with Lisa, a quick slit of her throat, but Todd had put up a fight. For a moment, she'd feared Todd was going to get the upper hand, so she'd intervened by caving in his skull with a fireplace poker. Todd had dropped onto Greg, heavy and limp. She had to help Greg get out from under him.

After that, she let Greg do the rest. It felt like a lifetime ago that they had joined the Parkers at the convention, having the best night in recent memory. Coming home and finding what Gabe had done changed it all.

It wasn't his fault this time.

And it actually wasn't. It was hers and Greg's. If they hadn't left Gabe at home and gone out, none of it would have happened. She made herself stop dwelling on the ifs, though, because it would surely drive her mad. There was always an *if* to any situation. Didn't make it fair, but it was easier to handle.

Sheila got out of bed. The air was cool and nice on her tacky skin. She must have sweated all night from how clammy she felt. She stretched as she walked, taking long strides to loosen up her muscles. She glanced at the bloodstained carpet where those other teenagers had been, and quickly looked away. Holding out her arms, she arched her back until it popped.

She felt better.

Before heading to the bathroom, she peeked her head in on Gabe. He was still asleep. Good. He needed his rest. His eye looked even better now than it had when she'd gone to bed. By the end of the day, it would probably have grown all the way back.

It was still hard to fathom how he was healing. It would probably never make sense, so it was best not to try and ascertain how it happened and just be grateful that he could.

As she was about to leave, she caught a glimpse of the calendar hanging on his wall. It was Sunday. At first, she wasn't really sure why she thought it was relevant. Nothing more than a tug from deep down. She shrugged it off and headed to the bathroom.

Sitting on the toilet and emptying her bladder, the realization struck her.

And made her cry.

Sheila stood at the top of the stairs, listening. She could hear the rustling whisper of paper being wrapped. He must be done, or at least taking a break from the chainsaw. She didn't want to be in such a cramped space with the ruckus of the chainsaw rattling off the walls around her. It would make her head feel like it was going to pop.

Carefully, she descended the wooden staircase hoping not to slip and fall. The planks groaned under her feet on her way down. She stepped onto the concrete. Greg was by the table he'd made out of a door. Meat and blood covered the top. He had black trash bags around him filled with the scraps he wouldn't use.

He tore off a generous piece of tape and taped the butcher's paper on the bottom as if wrapping a present. Turning to add it to the pile next to him, he spotted her.

"Hon?"

She smiled. "Good morning."

His eyes looked heavy with exhaustion, yet still alert. "Morning?"

"Yeah."

"Wow. I've been down here all night..."

"*All* night."

"Damn." He let his rubber-gloved hands drop onto the table. He looked at her. "How are you?"

"Not so good."

He nodded. "I wouldn't expect you to be dandy."

You have no idea.

"How's the booger butt?" he asked.

"Sleeping still."

"Good. He needs his rest. The wounds?"

"His eye has almost completely grown back."

Greg smiled. "Amazing, isn't it?"

She nodded. "Thank God too. I thought we might have

lost him."

"I don't even want to think about that," he said. Stepping away from the curtain, Greg peeled the gloves off his hands. He tossed them onto the discarded bits. He went over to her and wrapped his arms around her. She didn't hug him back, so he pulled away. "What's wrong?"

"This. All of this. Again."

"It's part of the job."

"What *job?*"

"Parenting."

Sheila heaved a sigh. "And what do we do now? Call your new identity buddy?"

Greg shook his head. "Not this time."

Sheila nearly gasped. "What?"

"I want to stay."

"Even after..." She thrust her chin toward the body parts, indicating the Parkers.

"Maybe not stay in this house. We can use all the crazy disappearances as a reason to relocate."

"I don't know if I could stay here anyway. Looking next door, seeing the empty house and...knowing..." Her lip started to quiver. Her chest felt tight.

"I know, honey. And we won't. Not for long."

"Why do you want to stay?"

"I like this town. And, we have real shot at a life here, I think. With all this meat, Gabe will have plenty to eat...and I'll be drawing again, making us some real money again..."

"I can start making some new jewelry."

"There you go." He smiled. "There's another positive. So, do you want to stay?"

"Just not in this house."

"Right. Maybe we'll move somewhere a bit more

secluded."

"No neighbors."

"Right."

"But Greg, where do we draw the line?"

"We don't draw a line. You're making it sound like we're giving him just enough rope to hang himself with. We just need to keep pouring as much good into him as we can and hope it sticks. Right now, he's going through changes. I think he's getting interested in girls, but after what Jenny did to him, he's terrified of them."

"Maybe it's best that he is."

Greg nodded. "Maybe it is."

"I just want to do the right things for Gabe."

"So do I. And I think in the long run, we are. Remember, we did anything we could to have a baby, and with Dr. Conner's help, it happened. Gabe was given to us like a blessing from God, we have him and it is our responsibility to do whatever it takes to keep him safe. I'm not saying that it's easy...but we have to do it."

"I'm pregnant, Greg."

Greg sucked in a breath as if he'd been slugged in the stomach. His arms dropped down by his sides, limp, slightly swaying. He looked like a haggard druggie, dazed on some mind-altering drug that had turned his brain to mush.

Sheila nodded. She knew once he'd heard the news, he would return to reality. Whenever he got time to himself, he liked to escape to a world of denial that only existed in his mind—places with happy endings. And that world that Greg liked to pretend they were a part of didn't exist. It never had and never would. Usually, she just listened and nodded, pretending to be enlightened as she offered suggestions until Greg talked himself out of the farfetched fantasies he'd been dreaming about. She didn't do this to be mean or spiteful. It was pity, which in some ways could have been worse, she supposed. But she didn't have the patience to play along this morning. Greg needed to know what she'd realized earlier.

They couldn't stay here. No matter what.

Greg dropped down to his knees, winded, his eyes wide and darting. "Are you sure?"

"I'm over a week late. I've been on a schedule every four weeks since after Gabe was born. So, yeah, I'm sure."

"Damn…it…"

Sheila stared down at Greg. He looked so pitiful on his knees like that. A defeated man who'd just had the last of his fight sucked right out of him. She knew how he felt. This had happened to her years ago. She got down in front of Greg. Leaning forward, she rested her forehead against his. He put an arm over her shoulder, then the other. She did the same to him, welcoming his embrace this time.

They held each other for a long time.

Then they started to cry.

ABOUT THE AUTHOR

Kristopher Rufty lives in North Carolina with his three children and pets. He's written numerous books, including *Hell Departed, Anathema, Jagger, The Lurkers, The Skin Show, Pillowface,* and many more. When he's not writing, he's spending time with his kids, or obsessing over gardening and growing food.

His online presence has dwindled, but he can still be found on Facebook and Twitter.

Made in the USA
Coppell, TX
16 August 2022